BATTLEMASTER

BATTLEMASTER

VICTOR OF TUCSON ✝ BOOK 5

PLUM PARROT

Podium

BATTLEMASTER

1

FAINHALLOW

For the first time as he passed through a world portal, Victor didn't feel alone; the whole way through, he felt Valla clutching his hand. He couldn't see her, couldn't even see himself, really, but he could feel her warm, tight grip, and it kept his mind from spiraling away with his doubts, hopes, and fears. As a circle of light rapidly approached out of the void, growing larger with each heartbeat, he stared at it, trying to see through. Despite his efforts, he could only get an impression of hard stone and bright blue.

As the circle grew to the size of a window and then to a doorway and, in the blink of an eye, passed around them, Victor and Valla stumbled out onto a hard, dusty white marble dais. The air was crisp, almost cold, a sharp departure from Coloss's sweltering heat. The breeze smelled fresh and rich, and Victor was put at ease by the pale blue sky and high fluffy clouds. As he let his gaze drift down from the heavens, he came to realize that he and Valla were standing high among mountaintops and, not far away, a walled town or enormous keep sat against the mountainside, colorful pennants flapping in the wind from its many gabled towers.

"Fainhallow," Valla said. Victor looked down at her and saw her gazing at the walled keep. She gave his hand a final squeeze and then let go, walking down the stone steps of the dais toward an enormous, arching span of stone that crossed the chasm between their mountaintop and the one on which the keep and its outbuildings sat.

"Fainhallow?" Victor asked, following her down the steps.

"The academy. It's not too far from Persi Gables as the crow flies. It might take us a week to hike down out of the mountains, though."

"Yeah? I feel like people have mentioned this place before, but I don't remember what about."

"It's a well-respected school for studying the arts of magic, from spell-crafting to alchemy. I'd say it's basically a boarding school for rich brats whose families have too much money and not enough patience."

Victor looked up at the gray-white stone walls and the high towers with their flapping pennants, and his mind started drifting toward old movies, VR experiences, and games he'd played revolving around magical schools. "Shit, I haven't thought about games in a long time," he muttered. At Valla's arched eyebrow, he added, "Lots of stories about magical schools from my world. So, like, are there kids here, or it's more for adults?"

"Young adults, generally, though some noble families view their young as exceedingly special and might send them here as adolescents. Rellia wasn't fond of the place; she favored real-world experience and conflict." As she spoke, Valla began to climb a second set of steps toward the stone archway, and Victor followed. Up close, the archway was even larger than it had first seemed—if he walked toward the middle of it, he doubted he'd be able to see over the edges, which was just fine by him.

"You think they can help us get down to Persi Gables faster?"

"I'm certain of it. If we can't use one of the portals, we can at least wait for their next supply ship." She looked Victor in the eye and clarified, "Airship."

"Ah!" He nodded, walking beside her onto the span, wondering how such a long stretch of curved stone had been put into place—it had to be half a mile long. "I suppose some earth elemental caster built this bridge?"

"Probably." Valla nodded. She gave him another look and then asked, "You haven't finished mastering Tes's spell for resizing yourself, have you?"

"Uh, between running from the Warlord, killing Karnice, and stepping into the portal that brought us here?"

"I meant before that! I couldn't remember how far you'd gotten with it."

"I'm close, but no." Victor paused, considering, then asked, "Why? You think they're going to react badly to my size in there?" He knew he was verging on giant-sized even without using his Titanic Aspect spell. Judging by how he towered over Valla, Victor figured he was probably more than eight feet tall.

"No, not necessarily, but you'll have to duck through many doorways." As they strolled along the bridge, Victor working hard to match Valla's much shorter strides, he saw her look down at herself, then over at Victor, and she added, "We'll be respected here. If not for my family name, then for our power. Victor, we were strong fish who spent some time in the ocean, and now we're back in our little pond. Our armor, our weapons alone, are likely without peer in this world."

"I'm glad I learned to hold in my aura."

"As am I!" Valla chuckled. "You just gained two levels, yes? I imagine your control is even greater. I'll wager you'll master Tes's spell next time you really work at it."

"Yeah, well, you're pushing Tier Six. Not many people that rank on Fanwath, are there?"

"No, I don't believe there are." Valla stood very straight as she rested her hand on Midnight's pommel. Victor reflexively reached down to let his palm brush Lifedrinker's haft. Smiling, feeling good about their accomplishments, he looked up and noted two chainmail-clad guards holding long metal pikes standing outside the gates ahead. "Victor," Valla said, "perhaps relax your hold on your aura just a bit. Let them have a taste, but don't crush them with it."

Victor frowned. "You think intimidation is the way to start? I'd rather try being friendly first."

"Well—" Valla, too, frowned, but she relented. "I'll follow your lead in the conversation, then."

They were still a hundred yards or so from the far end of the stone bridge, so Victor's mind had time to wander again, and he asked, "Do you think Tes is okay? She was going to give me a means to contact her but never got around to it."

"She has your blood. She knows what world we've come to; if she wants to meet or speak with us, she'll find a way. As far as her being okay . . . I hope so. I think so; if she couldn't beat the Warlord or get him to stand down, I'm sure she'd be able to escape."

"Yeah, I agree." Victor remembered how Tes had given Valla and Barn potions that would turn them into smoke so they could escape danger. If she could whip something like that up, there was no way she wouldn't have her own mechanisms to escape danger. The thought, at least, was comforting, and Victor found his lips curling into a smile as he pictured Tes and imagined how she was probably sipping one of her potent alcohols, wondering what trouble Victor was getting into. "Speaking of trouble . . ." he muttered as he saw the big furry Vodkin guardsman stepping forward, his pike leveled toward the two of them as they approached.

"Halt! This is a place of learning and study, and we want no trouble!"

"Calm . . ." Valla started to say, but Victor rested a big hand on her shoulder.

"You said I could lead the conversation," he said, interrupting her. Valla smiled crookedly, then gestured toward the guard as if in invitation.

"Hello, good sir!" Victor said jovially. "We don't intend any trouble."

The Vodkin's bristling fur settled a bit. His stern expression softened, making his big moist black eyes more cute than intimidating, especially as his whiskers twitched and wriggled beneath his button nose. Victor had known a few Vodkin reasonably well, and he knew they could get angry and were quite tough, but they certainly had a disadvantage when it came to intimidation. "Please declare yourselves; what's your business in Fainhallow?"

"Well, we're just passing through, really. We traveled here through a world portal and need to get down to Persi Gables. We can pay for assistance . . ."

"I'm Valla ap'Yensha, and this is Victor, War Leader of my clan. You needn't fear us, for my lady, Rellia ap'Yensha, is a Fainhallow alumnus and donor." Valla held up her family signet ring, one Victor had only seen her display twice before, and, at her words, the guard immediately lifted his pike, striking the butt into the cobbles and saluting.

"Welcome to Fainhallow, ma'am and sir! I am Guardsman Barnt, and I've heard of you, m'lady! I served in the Legion for a good many years."

"Ah, well met then, Guardsman Barnt. May we pass?"

"O'course! Stand aside, Klym. Let these two pass!"

Victor followed Valla past Barnt and the much smaller blue-skinned Klym, and when they stepped through the gatehouse, he muttered, "I thought you were going to let me . . ."

"I'm sorry, Victor, but I'm eager to get home." Valla offered him a smile, and he couldn't find the energy to be upset with her.

"War Leader, huh?"

"I thought it explained you the most easily. I could have gone on about your homeworld or your various feats and accomplishments. I thought of calling you the Champion of Coloss, considering you bested Karnice."

Victor sputtered, unsure how to react, finally settling on a snort of laughter. He opened his mouth to reply but found his mind drifting away from the conversation as he took in the courtyard beyond the gate; he'd been gone from Fanwath long enough that the various peoples seemed odd to him again—slight, blue Ardeni; lithe Ghelli with their dragonfly wings; tall, proud, red-skinned Shadeni; and here and there, glimpses of rarer species—floating, alien Onaghi; severe, gray, black-eyed Ilyathi; tiny, painted Bogoli; and even a goat-like Cadwalli.

The square was crowded, and everyone seemed cheerful, festive even. Victor towered over everyone, and though he and Valla were dressed in fine, beautiful armor, he felt they were very out of place wearing it with weapons on display, especially Victor with his glowering helm. Still, he'd been ambushed once too often lately for him to want to remove it, and he didn't mind that people gave the pair of them a wide berth.

They passed through the market and followed the road, really the only proper street inside the walls that Victor could see, and soon they were approaching the central building, which had to be Fainhallow's main, original structure. "It's strange to be back," Valla said.

"You've been here?"

"Oh, yes—not to study, but to see off cousins and pick them up for holidays. Rellia often sent me to see how the 'softer' members of our family were living. I'm sure it was meant to teach me some sort of deeper lesson, but all it really did was make me resentful."

"I can see how that might happen." Victor chuckled, gazing around at the manicured lawns and tall brick and stone buildings constructed in a gothic style, complete with stained glass windows and gargoyles. Clusters of what had to be students walked here and there, some in gray robes while others were in blue or maroon. As Victor and Valla approached the big open hallway leading into the main building, students hurried out of their way, some stopping to gape openly.

"You're making your usual impression." Valla chuckled.

Victor shrugged, admiring the inside of the building as they climbed the steps. He saw great wooden beams, many-colored sprays of light coming from the stained glass windows, and high chandeliers, large enough to require wrist-sized chains to hold them aloft. The space was bright, cavernous, and full of intriguing art, from tapestries to portraits, but before he could take the time to really look at them, a loud, commanding voice coming from somewhere around his knees got him to look down.

"Pardon me! I didn't know we were expecting dignitaries today!" A white-painted Bogoli, no more than three feet tall, wearing silky black robes, stood looking up at them with blue, crystal-like eyes.

"Hello," Valla said. "We weren't planning this visit; a world portal we traversed opened onto your platform across the chasm."

"Ah! Well, I'm Professor Yunsha. I can help you, or"—she glanced search-ingly up at Victor, a strange expression in her eyes—"was there someone else you sought to speak with?"

"No," Valla said. "We just need guidance on the fastest way down to Persi Gables. Do you have any active portals?"

Yunsha held a thumb to her chin, thinking. After a moment, she scowled and waved away a pair of Ghelli wearing blue robes, "Get to class, you two! Haven't you been mixed up with enough excitement lately, Adaida?"

"Apologies, Professor," the auburn-haired, pale young woman said, duck-ing her head. Victor thought she was very beautiful, but something about her looked strange; her skin was wan, and her eyes seemed almost haunted, despite their bright amber color. She stared up at Victor, her expression hard to read, but he swore he saw something like puzzled recognition there. The other woman, slightly taller with blonde hair, grabbed hold of Adaida's elbow and pulled her away, deeper into the building, glancing over her shoulder with a sharp scowl at Yunsha.

"As I was saying, the only portal open at the moment is the one to the new human colony. I could send missives to some of the noble families in Persi Gables to ask if they'd be willing to open . . ."

"What colony?" Victor interrupted, his voice rumbling in an uninten-tional growl.

"Oh, the humans. They're new to Fanwath. One of them is a student here—quite gifted. She's off investigating some trouble down by Persi Gables. In any case, she and some others of her kind have set up a portal here that leads back to their settlement."

"Humans?" Victor repeated. Valla had gone quiet, her eyes narrowed, turning to look at Victor with an expression he couldn't read.

"That's what I said. Are you familiar with them? I believe they've had some small dealings with Gelica and Persi Gables and some frontier towns, of course."

"How did they get here?" Victor was struggling to process the informa-tion, struggling to make sense of the strange little woman's words.

"Oh, goodness! Are we to stand in this hallway all day while I fill you in on these matters? Is it so important to you?" Her frown softened as she took in Victor's expression and glanced over his figure, from his armor to his axe, to his enormous size. "I apologize, sir." She turned back to Valla. "I'd invite you to sit in my office so we could speak more comfortably, but your friend would struggle with the furniture. Perhaps we could walk about the grounds? There's a lovely fountain with a spacious bench not far away."

"That sounds nice, Professor, and yes, this matter is quite important to my friend here."

"Very well," she said, striding around Victor and Valla and leading the way down the steps. "Follow me, and we'll talk away from these crowds."

Victor had to move slowly to keep from walking over or past the little woman, but he suffered through it, waiting for news about something he'd never thought to hear; humans were on Fanwath? The little Bogoli lady led them down a side path between two more big stone buildings, and then they walked out over a manicured lawn toward a wrought iron gate that opened into a garden. Few students were around, at least at that time of day, and Yunsha began to speak again as they walked among the flowering shrubs.

"Humans came to Fanwath through the blackness of space from a world called Earth. They traveled on ships of technology. I'm not sure exactly when they first settled down in the frontier, but it must be nearly two years ago by now. One of them, Olivia Bennet, is a student here, and—"

"Say that again?" Victor squatted down so he could look the woman in her gem-like eyes, and his voice was thick and intense.

She shrank back from him but repeated, "Olivia Bennet is a student . . ."

"Is this a fucking joke?" Victor stood up and shoved his fists against his head, staring at the sky, his eyes suddenly filled with water.

"What is it, Victor?" Valla asked.

"Bennet. It was my mom's last name. Before she married my dad."

"Are you saying . . ." Yunsha backed up, her eyes wide and her mouth twisting in a strange expression between shock and embarrassment. "I'm sorry, sir, but are you a human?"

Victor snorted and turned, wanting to walk away, wanting to find a quiet place to think before he lost his temper and did something stupid. Was he human? The question hurt more than it should, but only because it was something he'd been wondering, too. Meanwhile, his mind was racing, trying to connect some dots he couldn't quite see. Bennet was his mom's last name, but he couldn't think of any cousins or aunts named Olivia. Could he? He traced his thoughts over the people in his memory, over his mom's sisters, her brother, and his wife, all of their kids, but he couldn't find anyone named Olivia.

He felt a gentle hand grasp his wrist, and he stopped walking and looked down at Valla. Suddenly his temper and his desire to retreat seemed stupid. This was a friend who cared about him and wanted to help. And before him was a chance to get some more answers. He nodded, forcing a smile, and turned back toward Yunsha, who still stood where he'd left her in front of a lovely peach-colored flower bush. He walked back to her.

"Yes, Yunsha," he said, again squatting to look at her more directly. "I'm a human, but I have a strong titanic bloodline. Can you tell me about Olivia? About the humans? They came here through space? I don't get it—only a few astronauts were going into space when I left Earth. Some private companies were starting to build some kind of giant ship in orbit . . . I can't remember what it was called. I didn't pay attention; it was supposed to take decades."

"How long have you been away, sir?" Yunsha was clearly uncomfortable having a giant man squatting before her, but she must have seen he wasn't angry, only desperately interested, so she bravely smiled as he answered.

"I'm not sure. Eight months? A year? More? I've spent a lot of time traveling, fighting, and being a captive, so it's all a blur. I think it was summertime when I first arrived, though. I was summoned by an asshole down in Persi Gables . . . He had some material!" Victor looked at Valla. "Could he have summoned me with something from Olivia Bennet?"

"Quite possibly!" Yunsha said, answering for Valla. "You say your mother shared Olivia's surname?"

"Yeah, but like I said, I don't know an Olivia . . . and there weren't space-ships full of humans flying around the galaxy . . ." He stood up and grasped his head again, then he looked at Valla, his eyes widened in panic, and his voice rose in pained confusion. "Jesus, Valla, am I from the past?"

2

CONTRACTS AND CONCLUSIONS

From the past?" Valla frowned, but Victor could see in her eyes that she was starting to connect the dots. "You mean, the humans here could be from your world but from a different time? Or, more accurately, you're from a different time?"

"Could that happen?" he asked, glancing from Valla's narrowed eyes down to Professor Yunsha.

"I . . ." Yunsha gently tapped her white-painted chin. "You were summoned?" Victor nodded, and she continued, "I'm not an expert on summoning magic, but using Energy to breach great distances could be tuned to also stretch through time. I've read texts from more advanced worlds where such things occurred—civilizations on the brink of disaster reaching back through time to pull forth a great hero. I was studying temporal paradoxes at the time, and it was a case study. If I recall, the author was of the opinion that a new timeline was created at the moment of the summoning . . ."

"I can't concentrate on a lesson right now," Victor growled. He stood and began to pace again. He wanted to rub at his hair, so he yanked off his helm and stored it away. "Valla, can you remember exactly what Rellia's investigator said about the material used to summon me?"

"Let me see," Valla said, bringing forth one of her notebooks. "I have the messages and notes from Rellia here." She spent a few moments flipping through the pages and then said, "Aha! Originally, we simply knew that you were summoned using material from a 'particularly gifted student at

Fainhallow.' It was later, though, when we questioned Boaegh's cabal member that we learned he was first hired by Lord ap'Gravin."

"Ap'Gravin?" Yunsha's voice rose in disbelief or surprise; Victor wasn't sure which.

"That's right. Do you know him? He's quite influential in this part of the Empire." Valla turned to look more directly at Yunsha, awaiting an answer.

"Lord ap'Gravin, no. It's his son that I'm quite familiar with—Professor ap'Gravin."

At Yunsha's words, Victor felt a surge of heat in his Core, felt his pathways begin to fill with rage-attuned Energy and his control over his aura slipped as he whirled to face the diminutive woman with a growl. "One of your fucking professors is responsible for yanking me from my world?"

Yunsha blanched. She stumbled back a few steps, and a shimmering, egg-shaped shell of crystalline Energy formed around her, not entirely transparent, but clear enough for Victor to see her blazing gem-like eyes and her lips moving as she spoke. "Contain yourself, sir! I don't wish to raise an alarm, but if you intend violence, you'll find that we at Fainhallow are not easy victims!"

Victor growled, slowly reaching for Lifedrinker's haft, but he felt Valla move to stand next to him, and he took several deep breaths, trying to think of the right way to proceed. Attacking this little woman and all of Fainhallow by proxy didn't seem wise or warranted. "I'm not looking to fight a bunch of teachers and students, but I need to see this ap'Gravin guy."

"I can understand why, but I must speak to the director and the Heads of Class. We must proceed delicately, for if ap'Gravin is guilty of what you imply, he will likely attempt to flee or prepare a defense for your accusations. Will you trust me enough to give me one night to seek counsel from those more knowledgeable than myself?"

"I think that's fair, Victor." Valla reached to grasp his wrist, the one resting on Lifedrinker's haft.

"It sounds fair, but how do I know this woman isn't ap'Gravin's friend or accomplice?"

"Easily," she said, and suddenly the crystalline Energy shell fell away in a shower of glittering motes, and she produced a book and a quill. "I'll write a binding contract. If I warn the professor or his lackeys, I'll suffer Energy death. That's how much my word is worth. In return, I ask that you agree to avoid violence in this academy."

"For how long?" Victor lifted his hand from Lifedrinker and folded his massive arms over his chest.

"Indefinitely . . ."

"No. I'll agree to remain peaceful for two days. If I don't get some answers before that time is up, then I'm going to take matters into my own hands."

"Victor . . ." Valla started to say, but Yunsha interrupted her.

"Very well. I think that's reasonable. We'll put a two-day limit on this contract." She nodded and began rapidly scribbling out some runes and words on a blank page of her notebook, shimmery Energy flashing with each quill stroke. Victor worked to cool himself down as she wrote, pushing his rage-attuned Energy back into his Core and laboriously gathering up his aura and pulling it tight. He saw a crease between Yunsha's eyes where she'd been scowling slowly relax, but her makeup was indented from the intense expression.

"Thank you," Valla sighed, giving his wrist another squeeze.

"There we are," Yunsha said, ripping the page from her notebook. "I've already bonded with the contract. It only needs you to do the same."

"This is a System-binding contract?" Valla asked, reaching to take the page.

"It is. Feel free to examine it for duplicity. I was transparent in my wording."

Valla scrutinized the page, then said, "Victor, it says that you won't initiate any hostilities within the walls of Fainhallow until this time, two days hence. Yunsha has agreed to seek counsel about ap'Gravin and to bring you answers without alerting him in the same amount of time."

"Here." Victor held out a hand, and Valla passed him the contract. He looked it over and saw many magical runes that meant nothing to him mixed in with clear, easy-to-read words. What he could read was precisely what Valla had said. He nodded and trickled some Energy into the paper.

*****Alert! You are entering into a binding contract with Professor Yunsha of Fainhallow. Should either of you fail to uphold your agreement, you will suffer Energy atrophy that will lead to your slow decline and death. Do you wish to continue? Yes/No*****

He studied the wording of Yunsha's contract again, trying to see any duplicity, but she'd specifically said he wouldn't "initiate" any violence, she'd given the contract a two-day limit, and she'd bound herself to it. He shrugged and selected the yes option. The page flared brightly for a moment with the same silvery Energy Yunsha had used to inscribe it.

"Would you like to hold it, or shall I?" she asked.

"Let's have Valla hold it." Victor passed the contract to his friend, and she smiled, tucking it away in a dimensional container.

"Thank you for your patience and for agreeing to the binding contract, Victor. Would you two like to stay in the academy, or would you prefer the inn down by the square? It's a nice facility with many suites—most visiting families get rooms there when they come to Fainhallow."

Victor looked around the garden, over the hedges at the big gray buildings with their fancy gothic architecture, and he thought about all the students wandering around. He liked the place fine, but he didn't really feel like having magical nerds ogling him while he hung around trying to figure out the mystery of his origins. He cleared his throat and said, "We'll get a room down in the market. By the way, when's the next airship to Persi Gables?"

"That's a good question, and I'm sorry, but I don't have the answer. If you ask at the inn, I'm sure the innkeeper will be able to find out if any supply ships are inbound or leaving soon. Now, would you mind if we walked back toward the main road? I'd like to start trying to get to the bottom of this little mystery." Yunsha gestured toward the path leading to the central academy.

"All right," Victor said, taking the lead. He heard Valla and Yunsha speaking quietly behind him but tuned them out. He was irritated that he'd come upon this barrier with regard to finding answers about himself, but on the other hand, he was also glad that he'd managed to control himself and had a substantial lead. Even if this Professor ap'Gravin didn't give him the answers he wanted, he knew how to find his father, and Victor wasn't afraid to break some noble heads if he had to. He'd feel a lot better about that than rampaging through a school.

He paused at the garden gates while a group of young women, all wearing gray robes, hurried past, giving him alarmed glances and tittering as they scurried down the path as though they'd just witnessed something startling and crazy. He sighed heavily, looking down at his glittering wyrm-scale shirt, at his fine boots and pants, all clean, unscuffed, and whole. His armor had repaired itself so rapidly after he'd yanked Karnice's spear out that he didn't think he'd ever really noticed the hole.

Were the students startled because he was an unusual sight or because he was a monstrosity of a man? He frowned, reached up, scratched the stubble on his chin, and continued walking. "I'm going to finish that damn spell tonight," he muttered, taking long strides down the path, listening as Yunsha and Valla's conversation faded even further.

Victor was still trying to wrap his mind around the idea that, possibly, a distant relative of his had been at this school, was still a student there, and that someone had taken some material from her to summon him. What was it?

Blood? Hair? He shook his head, aware that he was thinking around the main problem with what he'd learned—the humans had come from a civilization more advanced than his. Did he even want to meet them? If he were honest, he really didn't give a damn about them, except maybe this Olivia person.

"Olivia . . ." Victor frowned as, once again, he tried to run the name through his memory of cousins, aunts—anyone. He shook his head as he came up with no answers again. Then, as he stepped off the garden path and onto the main road, his mind wandered to his *abuela*, and he had to lean over, his hands on his knees, as a thought occurred to him: if he was from the past, then his *abuela* was surely long dead and buried. She'd been old in Victor's time . . .

"Victor?" Valla asked, resting a hand on his shoulder and looking into his eyes. In his position, leaning over, they were almost on a level, eye to eye.

"My *abuela*," he said, his words thick with emotion, and reached up to rub at his eyes. Valla stepped toward him and wrapped her arms around his big neck, pulling his chin toward her shoulder. She gently stroked the back of his head, brushing her hand over his thick black hair again and again.

He was aware of the scene he was causing, a giant weeping man being consoled at the edge of the busy street, but he didn't give a shit. All the time he'd been lost, fighting for his life, then later, exploring worlds and fighting in arenas, he'd held a glimmer of hope in the back of his mind that he might see his grandma again. "Hush, Victor, it's okay. We don't know anything yet."

"I can feel it, Valla. I think I'm right. My *abuelita* . . ." His words choked off as his throat grew thick again.

"Come," she said, still stroking his head. Dimly he was aware that Yunsha was standing to the side, a frown of concern on her face, but he ignored her. Valla kept speaking. "If you were summoned from the past, why not your gran? It's possible! Think about it!"

"I . . ." Victor sniffed, then straightened; his back was getting a kink in it from leaning over so long. He rubbed his forearm over his nose. "I guess that's something to think about." He looked around, his eyes a little bleary, and saw many students begin moving, talking in hushed voices as they scurried this way or that.

"You should head down to the square and get a room, sir," Yunsha said. "Word will be all over the academy soon about your . . . presence, and it's best if people simply don't know who you are."

"Yeah." Victor sniffed again, then he held out his hand, immeasurably comforted and relieved when Valla took it, and they began to walk away from the academy proper toward the merchant square. "Thanks, Valla."

"You're welcome. You aren't alone, you know. Many people in this world care about you. Now that you're back, you could try visiting with your Old Mother and Thayla. I mean with your spirit magic."

"Hey," Victor said, his mood suddenly lifting, "that's a damn good idea! Thanks."

She gave his hand a squeeze and replied, "Of course. There are more, too. Lam, her little lieutenant—what was her name . . . Edeya? I met with her a few times before I came out to the plains to find you."

"Yeah, that's right." Victor nodded and spoke with more conviction. "Let's go to Persi Gables as soon as possible, all right? I don't want to go to the human colony, wherever it is. Not yet. We've got work to do, and I feel like . . . I don't know; it will be too much of a distraction. How long have we got until we're supposed to start marching?"

"A matter of weeks. Less than a month. Rellia's last missive to me sounded strained; she grows worried we won't return in time."

"She doesn't have to worry. We'll make it, and then we'll kick some ass in the Untamed Marches. First, we need to talk to this asshole professor, though."

Valla laughed and said, "There's the old Victor." They'd rounded the corner and entered the market square again. Colorful stands and carts crowded the area, leaving a narrow roadway for vehicles and people to traverse, and Valla called out to a woman operating a table covered with wax products from soap to candles and asked, "Excuse me, would you mind pointing us toward the inn?"

"Oh, surely," the white-haired, matronly Ardeni said. "You and your large friend will find it across the square. See that tall stone-and-mortar building with the high gabled roof? The one with the green banner out front? It's the inn. Tell Innkeeper Ranel that Yallie ap'Hira sent you. He'll make sure you get a good room."

"Thank you, Madam ap'Hira," Valla said, ducking her head, then she tugged on Victor's hand and pulled him through the market square, deftly avoiding the crowds, and soon they approached the indicated building. Up close, Victor could see the green banner flapping in the mountain air more clearly; it was embroidered with a golden-scaled serpent but no words. He followed Valla up the steps and, ducking deeply, stepped under the lintel.

The inn's common area was spacious, with many wooden picnic-style tables and a cold stone hearth. At that time of day, only a few patrons sat on stools or at tables, and Valla walked straight up to the long wooden bar. A burly black-haired Shadeni leaned forward, elbows on the bar, and let out a low whistle, his big, ruby-red eyes wide. "Welcome! I'm afraid I've no beds to fit you, sir."

"Just some blankets and pillows then," Victor grunted, having thought about this problem in advance.

"Of course, of course. Will you both be needing a room?"

"Yes. Just one. My friend is weary of being stared at, and we're both tired from our journey. Here." Valla tossed a small sack of beads on the counter. "Please show us to our room and bring us up a generous portion of your dinner menu."

"Yes, ma'am! I've a room just at the top of the stairs; follow me." He snatched up Valla's purse, then hurried out from around the bar and started for the stairway at the far side of the room. Valla followed, still clutching Victor's hand, and he couldn't help the warm feeling in his heart and the smile that touched his lips when he thought about how she was trying to take care of him. Had he made that big of a scene back at the academy? He supposed he had.

The inn had a high ceiling, and Victor could stand straight as he made his way to the stairs, though he had to carefully avoid a hanging light fixture halfway. He had to duck at the top of the stairs and in the short hallway, too, but when he stooped through the door to their room, he found the ceiling was high enough to allow him to stand, if barely. The room was simple, though spacious and neat, with a large bed covered in fresh, pale-yellow linens and a trunk against the wall under the window. Other than that, it was empty, which was fine with Victor—more room for him to camp out on the floor.

"Bathroom?" Valla asked as the innkeeper held open the door.

"Just down the hall betwixt this room and the next. There's another across the hall if it's occupied." He stood back, craning his neck to observe Victor as he walked into the room. "I, uh, I'll make sure one of my serving lads brings up a lot of food, and I've got a girl doing laundry as we speak; she'll bring you a few blankets and pillows."

"Good." Valla nodded. "Thank you, sir. We'll be fine for now." She hovered until the innkeeper nodded and began to back out. "I'll let you know should we need anything more."

Victor heard the door click shut, then turned and said, "I guess I really need to finish learning that spell. There aren't giants in this world, and I'm sick of standing out. Can you imagine if I cast my Titanic Aspect spell?" He chuckled.

"You're all right, Victor. If you learn and use it, that would be fine, but if you don't, it's fine, too. You have power that few in this world could imagine. People will accommodate you when they learn about you."

"Yeah," Victor sighed, sitting down, folding his legs under himself. "I guess that's true, but I'd like the option anyway." He pulled out his notes—pages and pages of copied spell patterns and Tes's original—and said, "I'm going to get started. Thanks for everything today, Valla. I mean"—he looked up and met her eyes as she walked away from the door and stood before him—"I'm so damn glad you were with me when I learned that shit today."

"I'm glad too, Victor." She folded her legs and sat before him, a few inches past his mess of papers. "Do you mind if I sit with you?"

"Hell no." Victor sniffed, still feeling emotional. "Before you feel you need to say it, I know what you're thinking—I'm diving into this spell as an excuse to avoid thinking about the other humans and my *abuela*. I know I'm avoiding it. I have to right now, okay?"

"Okay." Valla nodded and stared into his eyes, and for the millionth time, Victor stared at them and thought about how damn pretty they were.

"All right, here goes." He forced a smile, tore his gaze away from those shimmering, depthless teal pools, and started reviewing his notes about Tes's spell.

3

ELDER MAGIC

Not long after he'd begun working with Tes's pattern, Victor was dimly aware that someone had come to the door and delivered some blankets and pillows. Valla took them and stacked them on the foot of her bed, then busied herself with some small tasks Victor had seen her perform a hundred times. She polished her boots, went through her spare clothing, checking for stains or tears—a sign of fading enchantments—and oiled Midnight's blade and scabbard. He'd asked her before why she did it, knowing full well that Midnight would never rust, and she'd just shrugged and said it was habit.

He didn't pay too much attention to her, though—the spell was enough to keep every bit of his brain occupied. Before they'd left Zaafor, Victor had managed to copy each part of it perfectly, but never more than half all at once. He'd gained some stats since then, thanks to Karnice, and as Tes loved to say, practice and persistence made perfect. He wished she could be there if he finished; he'd love to see her reaction, and if he were honest, he loved impressing her.

He'd made it through the first half of another written copy of the spell pattern when a knock sounded, and Valla answered the door again. Victor's nose told him what this disturbance was about; he smelled fresh bread, something savory like stew, and the unmistakable aroma of baked apples. When he looked up from his work, he saw Valla holding the door open while a young Ardeni man wearing a white apron carried in a tray heaped with food. Hot on his heels, a boy and a girl, both bearing a strong resemblance to the man, grunted and heaved as they pulled a narrow table through the doorway.

"Pardon us! We don't often have folks choosing to dine in their rooms, but I keep telling the old man he needs to put some tables in 'em. Anyway, this one'll be all right for ya, I'd wager. Set it there, twins, and then go get them stools. Hustle, now!" He chuckled as the two youngsters hurried, cheeks huffing in exertion as they set the table near the corner of the room behind Victor and hurried back through the door.

"That's nice of you. Thanks for accommodating us," Valla said, moving closer to the door.

"Nah, 'tis a pleasure. It's a slow season for us—school's in full swing, so there aren't many parents visiting."

Victor cleared his throat and turned further so he could look the man in his bright coppery eyes, "Speaking of visiting, do you know if any airships are coming soon? We're trying to get passage to Persi Gables soon."

"Not off the top o' me head, but I can ask around. How about if I have an answer for you by tomorrow?"

"That would be perfect." A clatter in the hallway, forestalling any further comment from Valla, announced the twins' return, and soon they were dragging two short cushioned stools into the room. Victor chuckled at their efforts, then thought about himself sitting on one of those stools, and his smile widened further. His knees would be up to his chin.

"Appreciate your efforts, youngsters. Come here before you go." He beckoned the little ones close. As they approached, they ducked their heads, hiding behind their coppery curls, and Victor fished around in his storage rings for something he could give them, something better than a few beads. Suddenly he remembered the rings in his pocket, the ones he'd taken from Karnice, and he scooped them out, holding them in the palm of his hand. "Just a minute, you two. I'm looking for something."

Victor picked up the first ring and sent forth a trickle of Energy, bonding with it. Nothing happened, and he chuckled, lifting it to see why Karnice might have been wearing a non-magical ring. It was a band of silvery metal but heavy and richly lustrous. "Platinum, I think," he muttered, turning it around, admiring the nicely etched designs—it was a thick band, and all along it were alternating etchings of towers and fangs. Nothing was on the inner band. Victor liked it, but he didn't like Karnice and didn't want a platinum ring on his finger to remind him of the asshole.

He flicked the ring to the little boy and said, "I got that from a great warrior in another world. It's not magical, but it's a rich metal; maybe you can get it enchanted someday."

"Oh!" the little boy said, snatching it out of the air. "Really?"

"That's too fine, sir," the man in the apron said, starting to step forward.

"Nonsense," Victor growled, perhaps louder than he intended. "It's nothing. Now, for you." Victor winked at the little girl, and she giggled, further ducking her head. "Just a minute . . ." Victor tried to bond with the other ring, and sure enough, he became aware of a vast dimensional space. He sighed heavily as he began to sift through it, but his initial irritation at the tedium soon gave way to excitement; Karnice had a lot of nice things!

"Ah," he said, flicking his consciousness through a corner stacked high with Energy beads of all sorts, stored carefully in labeled bags—beads attuned with water Energy, beads attuned with fire Energy, beads with multiple attunements; it went on and on.

"What is it?" Valla asked, watching his face.

"Karnice was an organized guy. Like, borderline crazy organized. Hang on . . ." Victor skipped past the mass of beads, through boxes of gems and precious metals, then he skimmed through dozens and dozens of weapons, from knives to axes to bows, and then, taking up half the space in the dimensional container, quite literally hundreds of spears. "Sir, is your daughter planning to train with any sort of weapon?"

"Well, I . . . My wife's a guardswoman, but she used to be a huntress out near Tarn's Crossing. You wouldn't have heard of it—'tis a frontier town. She wants to send Beela out there to train with her grandfather. Isn't that right, Bee?"

"That's right, Da! I'm going to be a huntress." She grinned at Victor, and her sharp little teeth glinted in the glow lamps, her eyes narrowing fiercely.

"A Huntress? I've got just the thing." Victor ran his mind through the ring again, over all the spears, looking for one that wasn't nine feet long and didn't weigh a thousand pounds. He settled on one made from a silvery wood, graceful and slender with a leaf-shaped, brassy blade. He produced it, holding it before himself, and said, "Here's a fine spear to get her started. I'll let you take it, sir, and pass it on when the time is right."

"Are you . . . are you serious, m'lord?"

"Very serious. I have plenty, don't worry." Suddenly Victor thought about Tes and how she'd passed up treasure after treasure on the monster hunt. She probably looked at those things the way Victor did these extra weapons. These weren't even Karnice's favorites—he'd taken his two best spears after the battle and doubted he'd ever use them. "This is the smallest one I could find among my things, but I think it's just right."

"Take it, Bee," the man said, his voice hushed, and the little girl stepped forward and slowly reached out with a tiny blue hand. She grasped the silvery spear shaft, and her eyes widened with wonder.

"It's full of Energy, Da!"

"Bond with it. Do you know how?" Victor pressed.

"I do!" She nodded solemnly, and then, after a couple of heartbeats, the spear flared with golden light, and she laughed. She lifted the spear, easily two and half times as tall as she, and walked backward toward her father. "It's light as a feather, Kip!" she said to her brother, who was watching her with wonder in his eyes. Suddenly Victor felt as if he'd given the boy the short end of the bargain, and he began to fish through his ring again.

"What will you be when you grow up, Kip?"

"Sir, you spoil them! Already you've given the lad a king's ransom!"

"It's true, sir," Kip said, holding up the ring. "I'm so happy with this gift. Thank you."

Victor frowned for a second, then nodded. "Yeah, my pleasure. Seeing some happy kids makes me feel better. Trust me; I got more in the giving than you did in the receiving. Use them well."

"Many thanks, lord," the man said, grasping his kids by the shoulders and pulling them toward the door. He looked at Valla and said, "Lady." Then he stepped into the hallway, pulled his kids through, and closed the door.

"Ha! It was like he was retreating from battle." Victor chuckled.

"You just gave his two children more wealth than he likely has squirreled away from all his time in this job." Valla snorted and walked over to the table, sitting on one of the stools and inspecting the food.

"If that's true, it's just sad. There are probably two hundred spears in this ring, and that was one of the least impressive ones."

"Come get some food. And, yes, it's sad, but it's not something you should cry over. He has a happy life, working in this inn. His wife has a nice job, and they have happy children. He's chosen this safe, stable existence in exchange for not finding treasures and gaining power. He's probably out there trying to think of a way to talk his daughter out of using that spear, but you've lit a fire in those children's hearts; they're going to remember the visit from the strange giant for the rest of their lives."

"Heh." Victor stood and, leery of the close ceiling, hunched over and walked to the table where he sat on the floor again, forgoing the little stool the children had brought him. "Well, I wasn't lying—I enjoyed it. Shit, man, I enjoyed it so much; I feel like going out to the square and giving stuff to all the little kids. Call me Santa."

"Hmm?" Valla asked, dishing two bowls full of rich, meaty stew.

"Nothing. I'm just punch-drunk from staring at the spell and all the other stuff we've been through lately." He took the bowl Valla passed him and leaned back against the wall, holding it before himself as he spooned a big bite into his mouth. "That's good stuff." It was peppery and thick with the rendered fat of the meat, and he wolfed it down, enjoying the vegetables as much as the meat. He swallowed his fourth or fifth bite and said, "What about you?"

"Hmm?" Valla asked again, taking a pull from a frosty glass of ale.

"Well, I'm not the only person with feelings around here. How are you holding up when you're not worried about me falling apart?"

"I'm . . . good, Victor. Truly! I hate how we left things in Coloss, but it felt wonderful to beat that bitch, and I did it easily. The run through town, your fight with Karnice—they're a blur. We've only been here half a day, and I'm wondering what to report to Rellia in the book. You should think about that, too—what you're going to say to Lam, I mean. Most of all, I'm just happy for the things we learned, for my time with Tes, and for our friendship." As she finished speaking, Valla nodded and took another drink of ale.

"That was a long speech for you, Valla!" He laughed as her cheeks darkened and reached for the glass of ale she'd poured him. "Nice! It's icy. I was getting tired of wine, but it seemed like everyone liked it more in Coloss."

"We had some good mead and a few ales . . ."

"Yeah, I know, I know."

Valla continued eating, so Victor followed suit, leaving her alone while they devoured the food. Between the two of them, not a scrap was left over, not even any of the butter in the little crock nestled beneath the loaf of fresh bread, and definitely not a crumb of the apple crisp they found for dessert. With a full stomach and a warm feeling in his chest, Victor pushed himself away from the little table, scooted himself back over to his spell pattern, and got back to work.

"How many times have you written the whole thing now?"

"Twice, but I've done each section a lot more than that."

"Why don't you just try casting it, then? Are you afraid it will go wrong if you make a mistake? Usually, a spell won't finish forming if it's off."

"I don't know . . . I guess it's because that's how Gorz taught me my first few patterns; practice writing it out till you get it perfect and then try forming it in your pathways."

"But your will is so high, you probably can form the spell with Energy lines more easily than you can draw it!"

Victor thought about her words, and he shook his head in wonderment. Was he really that dumb? Writing the spell used his intelligence and dexterity, but forming it with Energy in his pathways used his intelligence and will. His dexterity wasn't even a fifth of his will. "Uh," he said, dropping his pen. "I think you're right. Shit!" He laughed, then sat back on his elbows, blowing out a deep breath, trying to relax.

"Anyway, I *hope* you're right. This might take me a few minutes." He gestured to the pages and pages of spell notes arrayed before him. "As you can see, the pattern is rather lengthy. Please don't let anyone interrupt me."

"Wait!" Valla said. "Cast your orb!"

"Holy . . . " Victor slapped himself on the head. "Why didn't . . . My mind's a mess right now. Thanks, Valla." He quickly formed the pattern for Globe of Insight, and as the inspiration-attuned Energy bathed the room in its bright, revealing glow, he laughed and cast Inspiring Presence as well. "Might as well go all out!"

"I was wondering why I hadn't felt that yet." Valla nodded approvingly, letting out a soft sigh as she reclined, apparently intent on observing him.

"I'm serious, though," he said, shifting a little, strangely unnerved by her staring at him. "This could take a while. Like hours."

"I'm just relaxing, Victor. If I get bored, I'll do some cultivating or something, don't worry."

"Speaking of that—how's it coming with your affinity? I know Tes taught you a new cultivation method that could increase your—"

"It's coming along well! I've made some gains but still have much work to do. It's wonderful to know it's possible, though."

"Are you going to share your knowledge with people here?" Victor sat back, suddenly eager to distract himself from the task at hand. The room was warm, the sounds from the tavern growing louder as the evening lengthened, and he could hear music coming from the square outside their window. Why was he in such a hurry to get back to work . . .

Valla seemed to sense what he was thinking, though, and, as any good friend might, she helped to steer him back on course. "Let's talk about me and my cultivation later. Am I really distracting you? I could leave."

"No, no. It's fine. You're right." Victor waved his hands in surrender, then sat up and tried to refocus. He closed his eyes and turned to his Core, observing his three roiling, dense pools of Energy. He stared at them for a long time, using their shifting, pulsing light to center himself, then let his perception expand until he could observe his pathways and his tightly constrained aura, held in place by a nearly subconscious effort of will. He took deep breaths for several minutes, focusing on how the air entered his body, expanded his lungs, and slowly flowed out as he exhaled.

When he felt calm, centered, and ready, Victor turned his gaze to his most expansive pathway, just outside his Core leading upward toward his heart and head. It was there that he began painstakingly building the pattern for Tes's spell. He'd memorized most of it, but this part, the initial base, was firm in his memory, and he managed to put it together in just a handful of minutes. He built it by pulling forth a fat ribbon of inspiration-attuned Energy, one that he had to strip into a hundred tiny threads, all meant to be woven into the strange, multidimensional pattern he'd learned.

As he'd hoped, his will was far more nimble with the Energy in his pathways than his hand was with any sort of writing instrument. He pulled and stretched the Energy threads, weaving, bending, curling, and winding them into the pattern, and when he'd finished the first section, he knew it was right, could feel it resonate in his very being. Encouraged, Victor began the next section, carefully clamping his will around his progress as he occasionally opened his eyes to glance at his notes.

As he'd predicted, this went on for hours, and he was so focused on the task that he completely lost track of Valla, forgot about his nervousness, and lost himself in the process. Each time he reached a milestone in the pattern, he could feel it deep in his bones. When he was on the last stretch, the final, complicated weave at the end of the pattern, he could feel the spell's potential reverberating in his pathways, ready to launch into something far beyond any magic he'd ever cast.

As he began to draw the final threads together, the culminating flourish on a wild, surging masterpiece of design, Victor began to fear his pathway was too narrow; already, the pattern strained against the sides of it, forcing him to realize, for the first time, the exact shape and extent of those Energy-carrying tunnels. Would it burst him apart when it was finished and he released the spell's pent-up designs?

The disturbing thought only furthered his determination, and Victor buckled down, pulling those dozens of branches toward the spell's climax, checking his notes a final time before he began to tie them all off. A strange grin twisted his lips as an absurd thought ran through his mind, some old quote one of his coaches had been fond of—something about how if a person didn't risk going too far, they'd never know how far they could go.

With a final surge of his will, he wrapped the last loose threads together, completing the pattern, and then, unable to contain the bucking, thrashing spell, he let it go and felt it surge with life, bursting into a work of magic almost too wild to manage or grasp onto as it poured through his pathways, spread into his body, and began to *change* him.

The spell was hungry, pulling at his Core, draining his inspiration-attuned Energy. Victor, desperate not to lose all of it or let the magic starve out in its infancy, began pushing some of his rage-attuned Energy into it, feeding it with that hot, potent brew. The spell surged anew, spreading through his body, wrapping around each of his trillions of cells, engulfing them and constricting them, following the intent Victor had built into the spell's weave—to make himself smaller.

In seconds, his rage-attuned Energy was drawn down to less than half, and Victor, not wanting to be left with nothing but fear-attuned Energy in his Core, tapered down the flow and pushed that dark, purple-black pool toward the pattern. He opened the floodgates again, allowing the magic to feed from his third affinity. Victor could feel the spell working, felt it altering him, not just in size, but in density, the potent Energy sinking into his titan-enhanced cells, and he knew, had he been a simple human, he would have torn himself to shreds.

He was enhanced, though, far from his roots back on Earth. His body was a hundred or thousand times more durable, his bones and flesh solid and dense, capable of absorbing far more Energy than a simple mortal's. To compare Victor's physical form to a natural human's would be like comparing a thin sheet of tin foil to a brick of gold. And so, the spell did its work, pulled his Energy until his third affinity was nearly drained, and then Victor realized he could stop it anytime—the more he fed it, the further it would do its job, but it could be "done" whenever he decided.

Rather than dump more Energy into it, he tapered off the flow until, like his first two affinities, only a tiny thread attached the spell, woven through his every cell, to his Core, maintaining it and keeping it active. When he felt the magic settle and cease its alterations, he smiled. He still felt very much like himself and was quite at peace. His Core equalized, and he saw his three orbs of Energy gradually swell until they each pulsed with light, less than half their original size—the spell was hungry and seemed to require a lot of Energy to maintain.

When Victor opened his eyes, ready to observe his handiwork, a System message took up his attention:

Congratulations! You have earned a new spell: Alter Self, Basic.

Alter Self, Basic: You have mastered the magic necessary to change an aspect of yourself, reducing your physical size and mass. This spell will last as long as you supply it with Energy, though it will reduce your maximum Energy pool so long as it is in effect. Due to the spell's reduction of your Core's potential, you'll find that your other abilities and spells are similarly reduced in efficacy. Energy Cost: Variable, 5000 minimum. Cooldown: Long.

Congratulations! You have gained a new feat: Elder Magic

Elder Magic: You've gained an understanding of spell weaving beyond those designed and granted by the System. Your ability to grasp and manipulate the threads of Energy in yourself and the world around you is enhanced. Beware the freedom this ability affords—great harm walks hand in hand with great potential.

"Nice!" Victor said and was momentarily confused by a certain lack of timbre in his voice.

"It worked!" Valla said, and Victor looked up at her. She was no longer sitting on the bed but standing before him, and he quickly stood, hoping to use her size as a measurement for how much he'd changed. He felt a bit woozy for a second, his vision darkening at the edges. When he recovered, he looked down at Valla and smiled. He was still taller than she, but nothing like before. He held a hand up and touched the ceiling—where before the top of his head had brushed the planks, he now felt the gap between the top of his head and the wood and estimated he'd shaved something like a foot and a half off his height.

"You're around the size you were when we first met, I think," Valla said, exposing her sharp teeth in a grin as she clapped him on the shoulder.

Victor quickly glanced at his status sheet, looking to see how his attributes and Energy had changed:

Energy Affinity:	3.1, Fear 9.4, Rage 9.1, Inspiration 7.4	Energy:	9274/9274 (4274/4274)
Strength:	202 (93)	Vitality:	302 (153)
Dexterity:	82 (38)	Agility:	105 (48)
Intelligence:	74 (34)	Will:	455 (209)

"Holy shit! It worked, but my attributes are all diminished. It seems proportionate to the amount of Energy being sapped from my Core. *Mierda!* Can you imagine Tes's stats when she's not shrunk down to our size?"

"It would depend on her true size, I suppose . . ." Valla frowned, contemplating.

Victor laughed, suddenly feeling a wave of relief and pride—he'd done something incredible, worked some magic beyond what the System usually granted, and managed to solve a problem that had been gnawing at the back of his mind for months. "Thank you, Tes!" he said, pumping his fist, unable to stop smiling. Suddenly he saw something strange in the air around him, a dozen little bright motes of light, sparkling like iridescent pearls, shimmering with a rainbow sheen.

"Are those Energy motes?" Valla asked, taking a step back. "I've never seen them look that way . . . They're growing!"

She was right—the tiny pearls grew to baseball-sized bubbles of Energy, their weird, colorful sheen pulsing and throbbing, reminding Victor very much of soap bubbles in sunlight. They shimmered and bobbed and gradually floated toward him, and he stood still until they each sank into him, soaking through his clothes and flesh and then exploding into his pathways. The surge of Energy poleaxed him just as much as when he'd helped to kill the wyrm in the wastes. Those pearly bubbles were far more potent than the golden or purple motes he'd experienced before.

When his paroxysms of euphoria faded, and Victor found himself standing, dazed and flushed, before Valla, he had another message from the System waiting for his attention:

*****Congratulations! You have achieved level 49 Titanic Herald and gained 12 strength, 22 vitality, 12 dexterity, 12 agility, 12 intelligence, and 12 will.*****

4

A NIGHT AT THE TAVERN

"Holy shit," Victor muttered, swiping away the System message. "I gained two levels for learning that spell."

"You gained two . . ." Valla sighed and then, shaking her head ruefully, laughed. "You're charmed, Victor. I've never heard of anyone moving through Tier Four as fast as you have. Of course, I've never seen Energy motes like those before, either."

"Well, I'm not complaining." He winked at Valla, then stretched left and right, twisting his torso as though he had a kink. "I feel great; how couldn't I after that Energy boost? But I was sitting around on the floor too much today."

"Huh. I know people who don't use furniture at all; they sit on the ground for meals, sleep on mats . . ."

"Yeah, yeah." Victor chuckled. "I'm just not used to it, all right?"

"Well, you'll fit in the bed now . . ."

"Oh! I should get us a room with two or maybe a second room, huh?"

"Nonsense! It's a big bed, and I'm sure we know each other well enough not to worry about propriety by now."

"Right. Propriety . . ." Victor looked down at himself, at his clothes, all of which had shrunk to fit him, then he bent to pick up Lifedrinker in her harness. He slung the straps over his shoulders, as usual, and they constricted to fit him nicely. Lifedrinker still hung beneath his right arm well enough, though her handle was a good deal closer to scraping the ground. "It's not like I'm small now, but you didn't shrink at all, did you, beautiful?"

"I like you better when you're full of might and rage. You seem meek now!"

"I seem meek?" Victor asked, outraged.

"Your aura is smaller, lighter! I know you did this to yourself, or I'd be thirsting for the villain's blood!"

Victor was torn between amusement and embarrassment at Lifedrinker's admonishment. He glanced at Valla, and she looked at him with that strange, skeptical expression people took on when he spoke to his axe, offering no help at all. He gently rubbed Lifedrinker's shiny metal head and said, "I'm fine, *chica*. I can end this spell anytime I want, and then all the Energy I'm tying up to change myself will flood back into me."

"Did you learn this magic for deception? At times it is wise to keep your enemies ignorant of the length of your fangs. In that case, I approve."

"Thank you." Victor chuckled, then looked at Valla and shrugged. "I'm not tired, are you? Wanna go down to the common room and have a drink?"

"I'd like that." Valla nodded, picking up Midnight and wrapping her belt around her waist. She was wearing her typical uniform-style clothes, having taken off her armor earlier in the day when Victor first began to study his spell. He, too, had removed his wyrm-scale vest and didn't think he'd need it to enjoy a drink or three. He fingered the fine fabric of his gray shirt and decided it was adequate.

"Right. After you," he said, pulling the door wide and holding it for Valla. She mock curtsied and stepped out, and Victor had to smile—he liked this side of Valla. She'd loosened up with him, and he was seeing it more and more. They made their way down the stairs to the common room, and Victor quickly snagged them an open table near the window. It wasn't difficult; more than half the tables were vacant.

He fished his little watch out of his pocket, wondering if it would be accurate in Fainhallow—did they have time zones on Fanwath? If they did, would the magic of the watch compensate? In any case, the little device told him it was just after nine at night. Even so, outside the window, in the market square, lights were bright, people were still about, and he even heard music playing. "It's like a party out there."

"I imagine students keep the small number of businesses quite busy in the evenings."

"How many students go to Fainhallow?"

"I've no idea, but it must be hundreds. We saw that many just in passing."

"Right." Victor looked up as the man who'd brought them their food earlier, the father of the two children Victor had spoiled, approached their table. He wore a quizzical expression and was openly staring at Victor.

"Excuse me . . ."

"Yeah, it's me, not my smaller brother. I used a spell to make myself more comfortable in your establishment."

"Amazing, sir!" He ducked his head, then turned to Valla. "Welcome to the Gilded Serpent's tavern and common area. Would you like to order some food?"

"Just drinks," Valla said. "We rather enjoyed that frosty ale you served us earlier. We'll start with a couple of those."

"Right away!" he said, hurrying to the bar.

Victor leaned back in his seat and enjoyed the sounds and smells of the tavern. More than the pleasant aromas of well-cooked foods, and the distant hum of music, he appreciated the sounds of jovial conversation and laughter. People here were happy; they didn't worry about wars, dungeons, wyrms, or invasions. They did their jobs or studies and then unwound at the end of the day with people they cared about. He could see the appeal in that. Still, he felt he'd get bored after a while. No, he'd tasted a little too much glory and seen what true power looked like; there was no way he'd be willing to give up those pursuits for a quiet life such as these folk lived.

"I think you have an admirer," Valla said, startling him from his reflections. "Huh?"

"The girl Yunsha chased away in the academy—the pretty auburn-haired Ghelli. See? By the bar?"

Victor followed Valla's gaze to the bar and, sure enough, past a table where a pair of Bogoli argued good-naturedly, he saw her. The pale, dragonfly-winged girl with the silky blue robes leaned against the bar, holding a small glass of liquor and staring directly at him. When their eyes met, she apparently took it for an invitation and began to work her way through the common room toward him and Valla. "Huh. Guess she's coming over."

"Presumptuous," Valla said. Victor glanced at her and saw her sitting up straighter, her face falling into the severe and deadpan expression she'd worn all the time when he'd first met her.

"Excuse me," the lithe Ghelli said. Her hands were clasped before her, and Victor saw that she was nervously wringing them, waiting for their reaction.

"Uh, yes?" Victor answered. Valla simply sat, stoic and unresponsive.

"Are you, um, forgive me, but are you a human?" With a visible effort, the young woman unclasped her hands and reached up to brush a thick curtain of beautiful hair back away from her face over her left shoulder.

"He is, Ghelli. Is there something amiss?" Valla asked before Victor could respond.

"I'm sorry. Sorry to intrude. I just, well, I'm close with one of your people, a woman from your colony; she studies here, and I was hoping you had word from her. Do you know her? Olivia Bennet?"

"It's not my colony," Victor replied, an unintended growl in his voice. The woman flinched and started to back up a step, so he quickly altered his tone, trying to sound friendly. "Sit down, though. I'd like to hear more about Olivia."

"Oh, thank you," the Ghelli said, carefully pulling back the chair on that side of the table, placing herself between Valla and Victor. She avoided looking directly at Valla the whole while. "My name's Adaida."

"Adaida, huh? Nice to meet you. I'm Victor, and this is Valla."

"Captain Valla." Before Victor could analyze his friend's insistence on her title, the barkeep returned with two very frosty mugs of amber-colored ale.

"I didn't know you had a friend joining you. Would you like something more to drink, miss? I see you left your brandy at the bar . . ."

"Oh, um, no, thank you." Adaida continued to fiddle with her thick hair, clearly nervous, perhaps because of Valla's stony-faced silence, perhaps because humans frightened her—Victor had no idea.

"Let me know if you change your mind. I'll be round to check on your drinks." He turned to leave, but Victor stopped him.

"Hey. Hold up a sec—what's your name?"

"Oh, of course, of course. I'm Harl, lord." He ducked his head and then hurried away, once again moving as though retreating from a battle.

"Huh. People are skittish around here," Victor said, turning to Adaida. "Hey." He thumped his palm on the table and said, "Relax, would you? We're nice people, aren't we, Valla?"

"We are," Valla said, though her face didn't offer any proof to her words.

"I'm sorry. I'll try; I honestly haven't been myself lately. I . . . I used to be more confident." Adaida moved her hands to the tabletop, and Victor was struck by how thin she was. Her fingers were very slender and pale.

"Have you been ill?" he asked, trying to soften his voice.

"More a sickness of the heart or mind, perhaps. It's why I came to you, hoping to hear word of Olivia; we didn't part on the best of terms." She bit at her lower lip, nervously glancing between Victor and Valla.

"Oh? Well, I don't have any news of her, but I might see her soon. We're heading toward Persi Gables, and I have a few questions for her. You want me to pass on a message?"

"Truly?"

"Yeah, sure. I mean, I'm not promising anything. We might miss her, but I definitely want to talk to her." Victor shrugged and took a long pull of his ale, enjoying the cold, crisp drink as it tickled his throat on the way to his stomach. "Damn, that's good. Drink up, Valla! You sure you don't want one, Adaida?"

"Can . . . can I ask you something? Weren't you a lot bigger earlier today? I'm sure I'm not losing my mind, but . . ."

"Yeah, yeah. I was. I learned a pretty cool spell that lets me appear a bit smaller than usual. Makes things like sitting at tables a lot easier." Victor nodded approvingly as Valla drank from her mug, though he was a little annoyed that she hadn't joined the conversation at all.

"I thought you looked human, but I didn't know they could be so large. There's something more, though, something about your eyes or the expressions you make—I swear you remind me of Olivia. I've met a few other humans, and none gave me that impression."

Finally, Valla broke her silence. "That's interesting. Still, you remind me of a few Ghelli I've met. I doubt it means anything." Victor closed his mouth, rethinking what he was going to say. Valla was probably right—probably best to keep his possible relation to this Olivia Bennet person to himself for now. What if this Ghelli went to the academy and started blabbing his secrets? What if ap'Gravin found out and ran away before Victor could confront him?

"Right. Of course, it's nothing." Adaida nodded.

"Well?" Valla asked.

"Well?" Adaida echoed, her voice small, her tone rising nervously.

"Do you have a message for this Olivia person, should we encounter her?"

"Oh! I do! I, um, I learned how to enchant a Far Scribe page. Will you pass it on to her? I've already written a note for her at the top. I'm hoping she'll reply to it."

"Hey! That's pretty cool," Victor said, nodding, then drained the rest of his pint.

"Yes, we will," Valla said, her stony expression softening slightly.

"Oh, thank you! She was depressed when she returned to the academy after our last break. I wasn't as understanding as I should have been, and I said some things I regret. It's been keeping me up at night for weeks. My heart's just sick . . ." She trailed off, her pale cheeks reddening with embarrassment. "Anyway, here's the page." She produced a tightly rolled piece of cream-colored parchment wrapped delicately with a lavender ribbon. Before

Victor could reach for it, Valla snatched it and made it disappear into one of her rings.

"I'll be sure to give it to her if we cross paths. I'm sorry for your heartache, young lady." This time, Valla's face really did soften, and she offered the girl a gentle smile.

"Thank you," Adaida said, sniffing, then she pushed her chair away from the table and, with a deep breath and a forced straightening of her shoulders, she stood up and nodded to Victor. "It was nice to meet you, Victor." She turned to Valla and said, "Captain Valla." Then she was winding her way through the tables toward the door.

"That was weird," Victor said, meaning more than Adaida's request. He squinted at Valla and said, "You're always so stern with people you don't know."

"Not always . . ."

"Well, definitely with that poor girl. She was just lovesick, I think." Victor held up his empty mug, hoping to catch someone's attention.

"Yes, I finally realized that. I was afraid she was snooping—a spy or something else. Should I read her note to Olivia?"

"No!" Victor wasn't sure why he was so adamant, but he shook his head and repeated, "No. How would you feel? I mean, I know I'm probably no older than that girl, but she seemed so innocent. So naive. She's clearly led a sheltered life. She reminded me of the girls at my old school."

"It's easy to forget you're so young." Valla nodded. "You don't look it. Your face is hard and weathered. Your eyes reflect what you've seen; no one looking into them would see a child. Even now, in your . . . reduced state."

"Ha! My reduced state!" Victor laughed, not just in amusement at Valla's words but in pleasure as he saw Harl approaching with not two but four mugs of ale. "You're a wise man, Harl."

"Well, I saw how fast that first one went, sir." He grinned, bowed, and quickly backed away, leaving the four frosty pints on the table.

"Come on, Valla. Keep up," Victor said, picking up a glass and draining half of it. Valla narrowed her eyes, took a deep breath, then, shaking her head, finished off her first glass. "Now we need to talk about something important. I'm going to ask Khul Bach and maybe Old Mother some advice, but I'll hear your take first."

"Oh? Am I to be held in the same esteem as those great ones?" Valla grinned, her earlier stony expression long gone. She licked at her ale-dampened lips, and Victor felt a familiar, often ignored, warmth in his chest as he observed her.

"Yeah, 'course you are. So, I've got three powerful treasures . . . things I need to use, and I'm trying to decide if I should just bite the bullet and use them all now. I've got that racial advancement, the epic one I bought from the warlord, and I've got two . . . potent hearts."

"Two hearts? I thought you burned one for your ancestors!"

"Tes gave me another from the night brute prince. She gave it to me right before your duel, almost as if she knew something would go wrong."

"Oh?"

"Yeah. What are your thoughts?" Victor had been speaking in a low tone, hunched close to Valla, and he glanced around the common room, noting that everyone was busily conversing, laughing, and living their own lives. Fainhallow was a different place from Coloss, but he still sort of wished he could block out other people from hearing him the way Tes used to do.

"I don't know. What rank is your racial advancement up to?"

"Advanced two."

"Do you think an epic item is meant to be used when you are in the epic tier? Would it be a waste to use before then?"

"No idea, but that's a good question for Khul Bach, I bet."

"As for the hearts, what did Tes say?"

"When she gave me the night brute prince's heart, she said to hold onto it until I had 'gained more strength,' but I have no idea how much. She also said to eat the wyrm heart first."

"Well . . . are you feeling pressured to eat them?"

"I guess so. It's mostly because of the weird blood I got back in that dungeon when I was Tier Two. I sat on it for months and could have really benefited from it a few times. If I'd had that feat when I fought Rellia . . ." he stopped speaking and frowned. He supposed Valla was the wrong person to talk about the what-ifs of fighting Rellia.

"I understand. Don't worry," she said, reaching over the table to grasp the top of his hand. Her fingers were warm and soft, and Victor felt an electric tingle run through his skin. He wanted to react, to turn his hand and grasp her fingers back, but he also didn't want to do something stupid or scare her off, so he sat there and just enjoyed the feeling, nodding his head.

"Yeah," he said, his brain slow to form the words he was looking for. "Anyway, I don't want to wait forever to claim some strength that might help me." He paused, licked his lips, and added, "Or the people I care about."

"So," Valla said, slowly pulling her hand back, "she said to wait until you were stronger. You've gained four levels since then, but she also said to use the wyrm heart first. Why not go ahead with that one and then go from there?"

"I like your logic, Valla. I'll run it by Khul Bach and maybe Oynalla if I'm not too drunk for a Spirit Walk tonight." He chuckled and drained his second pint.

"Excuse me," Harl said, surprising Victor; he hadn't heard or noticed the barkeep walking up to the table. "You were wondering about airships, sir?"

"Yes!" Victor said, noisily slamming his empty mug onto the table. Was the ale hitting him that hard? It didn't seem that it should be, not on Fanwath. He frowned as his muddled thoughts tried to make sense of it, then it clicked—he'd severely reduced his overall attributes and potency with his magical alterations. "Sorry about the noise; I'll slow down on the ale." He offered Harl a sheepish smile and then turned to include Valla in it. She chuckled and shrugged, sipping from her glass.

"No worries at all, sir. I wanted to tell you that I was just speaking with Master Gan-dak over there"—he gestured toward a table filled with black-robed academy personnel in the far corner—"and he said that a ship is due tomorrow from Gelica, supposed to be dropping off a load of vellum and mistvine planks for the students to practice with."

"Oh?" Valla said. "Thank you for the information, Harl, and before he has a chance to say it, please just call him Victor. He loathes having people spoil him with honorifics."

"I loathe . . ." Victor repeated, trying to figure out if Valla was messing with him.

"Of course, of course." Harl clasped his hands and sketched a funny little half bow. "Very good, very good." He nodded happily and turned to walk back to the bar.

"Damn," Victor said, choosing to ignore Valla's comment. "Tomorrow's a bit early. I was hoping to stick around to mess with that ap'Gravin dude."

"Victor. Oh silly, innocent Victor. We have the means to hire dozens of airships or buy several outright. We could have the captain of this ship wait six months, never mind a few days." Valla's smile widened as she moved on to her third ale.

"Huh." Victor nodded. "You know what? If you keep outdrinking me, I'm going to cancel this spell and cast Berserk to boot, and then we'll see who can handle the most ale."

5

COUNSEL

Victor woke the following morning feeling very rested and relaxed. He stretched, unwinding the soft white sheet from his torso; he'd somehow gotten quite tangled in the night. He glanced to his right, saw the empty bed, and wondered where Valla had gone. "Probably breakfast," he sighed, arching his back in another stretch.

When he realized he was sleeping in nothing but his underwear, a brief panic rushed through his mind as he scrabbled at the blurry memories of the night before. He laughed at himself as he remembered getting drunk, stumbling upstairs with his friend, and then stripping down and collapsing into the bed. "Nothing to worry about." Talking aloud reminded him of Life-drinker, and he jerked his head to the side, a wave of relief washing over him as he saw her leaning against the wall next to the bed.

He sat up, swinging his feet to the floor, and yawned again. He was tempted to follow Valla down to the common room, assuming that's where she was, but he decided it was an excellent time to get some conversations in with some other people. He found his pants on the floor—clean, thanks to their enchantments—and pulled them on, along with the loose, comfortable button-up gray shirt he'd been wearing. That done, he went into the hallway and walked down to the bathroom to wash up.

When he returned to the room, Victor locked the door and sat on the floor at the foot of the bed. He turned his wrist to better see the pink gem set in his bracer, then activated it, sending Energy into the stone. As always, the ancestor shard pulled a torrent of Energy from his Core, and Victor felt his surroundings displaced by the weird, grayscale realm that existed in the crystal. Sharp angles changing the gray to white or darker gray were the only features of the strange place. Other than the hulking, brooding giant that sat before him, Victor revised.

"Welcome, scion. It's been long, but I see you've progressed in your hunt for power."

"Hello, Khul Bach." Victor smiled, noting that his "self" in this strange plane was not reduced by the spell he'd confined himself with back in the normal, physical plane. It felt good to be himself, and he wondered if he'd grow to enjoy being a giant of a man more and more the longer he constrained himself with Alter Self. "Did you notice we left Zaafor?"

"We did? No, I had no sensation of the change."

"Well, we're on Fanwath now—the Warlord tried to pull some kind of stunt on Valla and me. Even Tes was surprised by him, I think. We had to run, but I'm more determined than ever to go back there someday."

"As you should be, scion. A titan does not flee from his destiny."

"Right. Speaking of destiny, I came to you for some advice. You remember how I told you about my ancestors' kind of strange habit—you know, eating the hearts of their foes?"

"I do."

"Well, I have a couple of potent hearts I'm supposed to eat, but I'm not sure I'm ready yet. I also have something called an 'epic racial boost.' Should I use that before my race is epic?"

"Why do you hesitate to consume the hearts?"

"It's something Tes said. When she gave me one of the hearts, a night brute prince's heart, she told me to wait until I was 'stronger' to eat it. Since then, I've gained four levels, but I don't know if that's all she meant."

"Your ability comes from your bloodline, yes?" When Victor nodded, he continued, "I would use that epic racial boost now. To answer your earlier question, it won't hurt to use it before you have reached the epic tier; you'll gain a great deal from any sort of treasure of a tier that's your equal or higher. It's lower-tiered treasures that would be wasted on you."

"And the hearts?"

"Once your bloodline has advanced, you may well feel powerful enough to take on the heart Tes warned you about, but why not start with the other?"

"Valla said something similar."

"So, the small blue friend you told me about is still with you?"

"Yes . . ."

"Good. Gather your allies. Learn from them, form bonds, and lean on one another—you'll need fellowship to achieve greatness." Khul Bach nodded to himself, then shifted and asked, "Well? How go the other tasks I set you on? Has your axe skill reached the epic level? Have you made strides with your Sovereign Will?"

"I've been using Sovereign Will almost all the time, really only dropping it when I sleep. It's still only advanced, though. As for my axe skill, I've practiced a lot, and Karnice, before I killed him, thought it was near epic, which was a surprise to me. I thought I'd be working for years on that, considering what Polo Vosh told me about his own advancement."

"We each face a journey unique to our own experiences and talents. Is this Polo Vosh a powerful warrior?"

"He's one of the strongest in this world," Victor said, then scratched his chin and shrugged. "I mean, I think he is. Really, I've never met anyone from the capital, and I got the impression that's where all the oldest, strongest people live."

"Very well. If Vosh has more axe skill than you, seek him out and practice with him. It's the best way to advance. What are your plans? Do you not have lands to conquer here? Put Vosh in your army!"

"I'll, uh, try. When I get to Persi Gables, I'll ask Rellia about him. Well, shit, I guess I could send a message to her or Lam right now. If nothing else, I could pay Polo to travel and practice with me."

"Yes, leverage your connections and wealth. You're learning, young warrior." Khul Bach clapped his big hands, rubbing them together as if to signal the end of the conversation, and said, "You have your tasks. Be about them! Each minute you should be striving to better yourself."

"Okay." Victor sighed and shrugged. He didn't like being dismissed so quickly, but what did he expect? Khul Bach wasn't his buddy; he didn't want to sit around talking about feelings or what Victor had for dinner. He supposed that if something were getting in the way of his advancement, Khul Bach might take an interest. "Talk to you soon, maybe after I eat all these things, 'cause I'm close to Level Fifty, and I might want some advice about my class selection."

"Good! Until then!" Khul Bach nodded firmly, and Victor severed the connection between his Energy and the stone, bringing the real world back into focus, banishing the ancestor fragment's odd, sharply angled, gray-white expanse.

"Kinda weird he was rushing me out of there. What's he do with his time, anyway? You'd think he'd want me to hang around as much as possible." Victor didn't know why he was speaking aloud; Lifedrinker still leaned against the wall near the bed, and there was still no sign of Valla. He stood up, summoned his helmet and armor from his ring, and put them on. Then he picked up Lifedrinker and, holding her crossways over his knees, sat down and cast Manifest Spirit, using inspiration-attuned Energy.

His ghostly pack of coyotes shimmered into existence, yipping and growling softly, pacing in a circle around him. "Hello, *amigos*," Victor said. "Keep an eye out for me, will you? I'm going on a Spirit Walk. Let's see if the Old Mother is as clever as always and waits for me."

As the coyotes continued to pace or sit around him, Victor cast Spirit Walk, and suddenly he was sitting on the bare rocks of the mountains, high above the sprawling plains of the spirit realm. As always, it was twilight there, and the glittering jewels of silvery stars filled the sky, giving him pause as he stood up and turned to look at the strange, shadowy peaks that piled one behind another for as far as he could see to the west.

Victor knew the plains he could see to the east weren't the same ones that led to Oynalla. No, he instinctively knew that he'd need to go north and find another great grassland before he could travel to his friends. "Not far for a spirit, though," he said, breaking into a run, racing down a rocky slope between the mountains, his mind and heart focused on Oynalla.

The mountains blurred past, and occasionally Victor saw bright spirits out there in the shadowy heights, but they avoided him, perhaps sensing his might. He could feel it himself, the torch of his spirit as it blazed in the starry light of the spirit plane. He was without peer, at least in this part of the plane.

As usual, his journey to Oynalla was quick; soon, the mountains fell away to hills, then he was tearing through grasslands, and before he could grow weary of the joyful freedom of his speedy travel, he found himself in the grove where Oynalla had first taken him. Shadowy canopies hung above him, obscuring the stars. A babbling brook rippled through the center of the hollow, silvery and beautiful, and there, sitting in the grass beside the sandy bank, was the beautiful young version of Oynalla.

"I've waited for you, warrior. It felt long to me, but was it? I think not too long."

"Oynalla? Old Mother?" Victor asked, approaching her with no small amount of trepidation. Something was different; something was off about her, but he couldn't quite place his finger on it.

"Ha!" she cackled, and though her voice was youthful, the tone was the same as he'd heard a hundred times while living with Tellen's clan. "You look confused and troubled. Be not, mighty one. I'm proud of you, Victor. I wondered if you'd return and, if you did, if you'd be the same. I see your spirit is still bright—powerful, but bright. It will give me comfort to know you are still here when I move on."

"Move on?"

"Is it such a surprise? They didn't call me Old Mother because I was young and vital!"

Victor hurried forward to crouch before the beautiful, youthful woman. She wore a fringed, beaded vest over leather pants, and she clutched something in her hands, something he'd never seen Oynalla touch in the physical world—a shimmering short bow. "What's going on? Is Thayla coming?"

"She's busy, brave one. She has many new responsibilities, but she told me to tell you she'd look for you during the three nights following every new moon. Surely you can find her then?"

"Sure, I can, but why don't you just bring her?"

"I can see you know the answer, though your mind fights valiantly to hide from it. Come, Victor; you can see the change in me, can you not? I'm not tethered to the physical plane any longer. I waited for you, but after we speak, I'll be off, moving to my next adventure."

"You died," Victor said flatly, falling back to sit on his rump, something like a lump of lead forming in his gut. "Did someone kill you?"

"No, foolish boy," Oynalla's spirit said, reaching out to rest one of her shimmering, luminescent hands on his knee. "I was old, old long before I ever met you. Before you ask, no, I didn't need you to try to rescue me with some racial advancement boon or another. I chose to live my natural years when I was young. Many a night did I spend in this realm speaking to old spirits, learning of their ways and where they were going. I determined back then, nearly two hundred years ago, that I'd also like to explore these pathways."

"But the clan . . ."

"If I tell you something, a secret I've held here"—she touched her chest—"for a hundred years, will you keep it?" Victor nodded, and she continued, gently thumping his knee. "I was weary of my life in the clan! I didn't want to eat some mystical fruit, grow young again, and then have to break all of their hearts by saying I wanted to leave.

"Instead, I determined to explore these realms, journey past the spirit plane, and see what was next for me. It was an easy escape without breaking any hearts. There are those in the clan who might have sacrificed everything to try to make me young again, but they all knew better than to offer it. My 'Spirit Guides' said it was my time!" She cackled, and Victor had to chuckle with her. What a crazy old woman!

"So, you're leaving." The lump in his belly was gone, but a hollowness remained.

"This is fine, Victor. You're going to be fine, and when you think of me, try to imagine me like this—young, beautiful, full of energy and excitement! I'm going somewhere new for the first time in a very long time. Won't you wish me a good journey? Will you not bless my steps with well wishes?"

"I'll do better than that, Oynalla," Victor said, his voice growing thick with emotion. "When I honor my ancestors and send Energy their way, I'll count you among them. I don't know how it will work, but I know it will. Take my offerings, and use them to make yourself great in your next life. Will you promise me?"

Oynalla's eyes narrowed, and her lips twisted as she wrestled with his words. Finally, she nodded and said, "Shrewd one, aren't you, warrior? You'll keep a hook in me, but I'll gain a benefit. Well, then. Should your spell work and connect you to me with gifts of Energy, then I'll seek to return the favor. Should I grow powerful, 'great' as you put it, I will send you aid when I can."

"It's a deal," Victor said, something like relief rushing through him; he was losing Oynalla in this world, but he'd still have a connection—he was confident his spell would work, though he really didn't know why; he might think of Oynalla as a surrogate grandmother, but she wasn't really related to him. Did it not matter? No, it didn't matter, he decided. His intent was enough. "I'm going to miss you, Old Mother."

"Young Mother now," she cackled, then stood up and smashed him into a hug, pulling his head into her belly and stroking his hair with her small, shimmering hands. "Such a big man you've become! Your spirit is so bright; you'll see a hundred thousand more sights than old Oynalla ever saw. I'm proud of you! Don't forget about Thayla and Deyni! Visit them in this realm and, if possible, in the physical world. Promise me."

"I promise!" Victor said, breathing in the scent of spices, campfires, and herbs that clung to the spirit. Tears burst into his eyes when he realized it would be the last time he ever smelled that particular combination of scents. "Do you have to go now? Couldn't you linger for a while?"

"Don't ask that of me! I don't want to become one of these sad old spirits that loiter here, watching the living, waiting for a way to interact. I want to see what's next, Victor!"

"I understand," he sniffed. He reached up, wrapping his arms around the little woman, squeezing her tight until she grunted and laughed.

"You can't keep me here that way either!"

"I know, I know. I have my own adventures to get back to."

"Yes, you do. I know great things await you and great challenges, too, warrior. Be careful. Use this"—she gently tapped his forehead—"as much as you use that thirsty axe of yours. Promise me!"

"I promise!" he said for the second time. Then Oynalla pushed against his shoulders, worming her way out of his grasp. She hefted her glittering, translucent bow and offered him a quick wave.

"Wish me luck now, warrior."

"Good luck, Old . . . Oynalla. Good luck, good hunting, and may you find what you seek." He stood up and waved as she turned and started jogging away, following the little babbling stream, and Victor felt the hollowness return with a vengeance when he wondered if that was the last he'd ever see of her. He sighed, his heart heavy, and looked around Oynalla's special place. He memorized every detail, from the stream to the trees to the little shrubs and the soft grass. One thing was certain; he'd ensure this place was visited regularly, and if Thayla and Deyni didn't know their way here, he'd show them.

After taking one more long look around the vale, he bent to drink deeply of the brook, then stood and ended his Spirit Walk. When he opened his eyes, Victor saw his coyotes, shimmering and bright, sitting around him. Beyond them, sitting on one of the little stools the youngsters had brought in the day before, was Valla. To his immense surprise, she was petting one of his coyotes sitting near her feet.

"Welcome back," she said, not looking up.

"Hey," Victor said, and some of the emptiness in his heart must have seeped into the word because Valla looked up sharply, and her reddish-purple lips turned down in a frown.

"What's wrong?"

"Bet you're getting tired of hearing about my problems. It's nothing to worry about; Oynalla has died and moved on. I'm sad, but it was what she wanted." As he spoke, his coyotes grew agitated and paced, their whining intensifying. "Hush!" he said, chuckling and shaking his head. "Okay, pups, time to go. Do some hunting in the spirit plane, hmm? Catch a spirit rabbit."

As his companions disappeared in clouds of glimmering mist, Valla stood and walked over to him. Once again, he found himself embraced from a sitting position. Valla, though, knelt and rested her chin on his shoulder, hugging him tight. "I'm sorry, Victor. I know you enjoyed speaking to her, and I know she was more to you than just a mentor. It's a lot you've been through lately . . ." Victor thought she might have kept talking, maybe mentioned how he'd realized his *abuela* might be long dead, too, but he didn't give her a chance.

He stood up, careful not to bump her, then when he was on his feet, he gently hugged her back and said, "I'm all right. Really. I'm sad, sure, but how many people get to speak to their loved one's spirit before it departs? She's off doing something she's dreamed about for longer than I've been alive. I can't begrudge her."

"If you want to talk . . ." Valla pressed, pushing away from him, still holding his shoulders at arm's length and looking up into his eyes.

"Maybe, but not right now. We've got a lot to do in this world before we move on, Valla, and I think it's time we get a start on things. I'm going to take that epic racial boost now. Will you watch over me?"

"I will, but when you say 'before we move on,' can you elaborate a little?"

"Yeah. You're starting to scratch at greatness the same as I am. Are you content? Will you be content to live in the Untamed Marches after we tame them with Rellia and her clan? Me? I want to see more worlds. I want to see more wonders, and I want to go back and beat the shit out of the Warlord in Coloss someday."

"I'd like to see Tes's home," Valla said softly.

"There you have it then. We've got a lot to do." Victor chuckled, reaching into his ring and pulling out the heavy silver flask that contained the boost he'd purchased in Coloss.

6

YOLOTLI

"Before you drink that," Valla said, touching her fingers to the silver flask as though to keep him from immediately chugging it down, "let's talk about what you want me to do while you're out. We don't have the Warlord's cultivation chamber here—you could be out for hours or days."

"Ah, shit. You're right." Victor sighed and stretched his neck, suddenly feeling a lot of tension in the back of his skull. "Should I put it off?"

"Not necessarily. I can go speak to the airship captain, pay him to wait and take us to Persi Gables when you're ready. As for ap'Gravin, do you trust me to speak to Yunsha on your behalf should she come round before you wake?"

"Yeah, of course. You know what I'm trying to find out—what did he take from the human student here? What does he know about the summoning spell? Why was his father paying Boaegh to do the summoning? All that stuff. If I'm not awake by the time Yunsha comes, when I do wake up, the contract will be expired. Maybe remind her and the other academy authorities that if they don't think he deserves punishment, I might decide otherwise. Shit, now that I think about it, maybe it's best if I'm not there at first; I can already feel my blood getting hot."

"Understood." Valla nodded and pulled her hand back. "I'm going to write a message to Rellia. I'll let her know we're here and that we should soon be in Persi Gables. I'll also ask her to get eyes on Lord ap'Gravin, in case you want to follow up with the father."

"That's a good idea." Victor took a deep, steadying breath. He hadn't been lying—his Core was roiling, and some of his rage-attuned Energy was seeping into his pathways. He firmly pushed it back, clamped down the storm at his center, and forced a smile. "Thanks, Valla."

"You're welcome. I'll keep people away from here until you're done."

"Perfect. I think I'll write a message to Lam before I drink this." Victor held up the heavy flask and then turned toward the center of the room and sat down on the floor.

"That's probably a good idea. I'm sure she's worried, and I doubt Rellia relays every message I send her way. While I was down having breakfast, I heard some merchants speaking about the airship—it had already been sighted. I'm sure it's arrived by now. In any case, I'll be back to check on you soon." Valla turned to the door and quickly stepped out.

Victor had been digging through his ring for his Far Scribe book and belatedly offered her a wave, but she was gone. Lifedrinker was still at his side, and he rested a hand on her haft. "She wasn't upset about anything, was she? Seemed like she left in a hurry."

"*I know not. I care not. Will we battle again soon?*" Lifedrinker's sharp, smoky voice filled his mind, and Victor couldn't help smiling at her savage disregard for anything so mundane as a person's feelings.

"Probably, beautiful, probably." Shaking his head, he released her handle and pulled out a pen, one that he'd gotten from Thayla. "Seems like a lifetime ago," he muttered, then opened a blank page in the Far Scribe book.

Lam,

Before you read further, be certain that no one you don't fully trust reads this message.

I hope you're doing well. I haven't written to you much, and I hope you haven't been too worried. I know Rellia's been hearing from Valla, so you must know that we aren't dead. Hopefully, you've been fine, keeping yourself busy with your various industries and helping to raise the army. You'll be glad to hear that Valla and I are back in Fanwath. We're up in some mountains near a magical school called Fainhallow. We should be in Persi Gables soon, though—Valla's off trying to hire an airship as I write this.

I've learned a lot since we last spoke in person. I mean a LOT. One thing I've learned, though, is that nothing beats having a good teacher, and I really enjoyed my time with Polo Vosh. Do you think he'd want to come on the expedition with us? Would you mind offering him an invitation? I need to work on my axe skill, and the most I ever learned about the axe was when I practiced with him. Tell him I'll be happy to pay—whatever his going rate is, I'll double it.

I could probably write for a hundred pages about all that we've seen and accomplished in the last couple of months, but I'm not a writer, and I'm sure you'll hear plenty about it through Valla and of course from my mouth when we next speak. Let's just say that we fought some incredible monsters, I battled my way through another arena, and we have a lot of knowledge to share—things that will make whatever society we try to build in the Untamed Marches that much stronger.

A thought occurred to me, though, and I think we should start to take precautions: some of the powerful people we met on Zaafor (the world we traveled to) seemed surprised by the lack of knowledge on Fanwath. The System Stones provide for travel to other System worlds, and there should have been travelers to and from this world to other, more advanced worlds. There should be more known here by now. I'm worried that the old powers in the Empire are hoarding knowledge and that they won't be pleased with what Valla and I have brought back.

What route are we planning to take to the Untamed Marches? Will we pass through the heart of the Empire or skirt it? It might be wise to consider a circuitous route, one that will be more difficult to predict, one where we might avoid, more easily, ambushes or other trouble. I know you and Rellia are working hard to build a strong force, but will it be enough if the Empire moves against us, even if they do it in secret?

These thoughts have been heavy in my mind as I learn more and more about the deficiencies in Valla's training and knowledge—she's Rellia's favored scion, yet she's been misled for much of her life. If that's happening to her, then how far out of the inner circle is Rellia? How far removed are the nobles in Persi Gables and Gelica from the center of the Empire, the older cities? I guess the point of my rambling here is that we should be prepared for problems coming from places other than the Untamed Marches.

Please think about these matters, and we'll speak more when I return; hopefully, in a few days.

—Victor

Victor sighed heavily as he closed the book. Those thoughts had been tickling the back of his mind for a long while now, and it felt good to put them on paper, but they also worried him. Could he trust Lam? She'd helped him many times in the past, and she was "new" nobility, so he didn't think there was any chance she was in league with the old powers of the Empire. No, she was making a grab for power; if anyone had something to fear from the established nobility, it was her. He was confident she was the right person to hear his concerns.

With a final nod, as though he were assuring himself he'd done the right thing, Victor put the book away and lifted the heavy, silvery flask. "Well," he said, twisting the red wax–sealed stopper, "here's hoping you don't knock me out for a week or two." In truth, he wouldn't be all that upset if it did—it would only mean he'd made some tremendous advancements. As he pulled the waxy, spongy stopper free, his nose was assailed by a robust citric tang. Not wanting to waste any potency, he lifted it to his mouth and began to drink.

As soon as the syrupy fluid touched his tongue, his tastebuds exploded with flavor so sickly sweet and rich that he almost gagged, almost spat out the precious liquid. With a determined effort, he stopped breathing so as to lessen the impact and choked it down, swallow after swallow of something that tasted like orange juice laden with every sweetener known to humanity. As the last drop fell into his mouth and he drank it, his mouth exploding with saliva and his stomach roiling, Victor dropped the canister and fell back, staring at the ceiling as his legs and arms splayed out.

With a visceral snap, he felt the spell he'd cast to constrain his person come apart. He grunted as the Energy he'd packed into it flooded back into his Core, and the floorboards creaked and groaned as his true mass suddenly reasserted itself. It felt good, really, like having an immensely heavy blanket he'd gotten used to suddenly pulled off his body. If it weren't for the roiling in his gut, he might have smiled, but all he managed was a piteous groan.

Victor closed his eyes and tried to focus on his Core, trying to see inward so he could take his attention away from the discomfort in his physical body as the potent elixir began to bubble and surge in his stomach, growing hotter and hotter by the second. Victor focused on his three globes of attuned Energy, watching how his rage smoldered, his inspiration softly pulsed, and his fear glowered and lurked. As his mind began to calm, he felt the discomfort in his belly fade away, and a warm, gentle wave spread outward through his chest and out into his extremities.

He opened his eyes, or thought he did, but Victor was still engulfed in blackness, and if he could have controlled his face, he might have smiled—he knew he was going on a trip when stars began to blur past, nebulae and galaxies swirling away in his passage. Unlike before, though, he didn't find himself immediately sucked down into a vision; instead, his strange journey through the universe halted, and he remained bodiless, floating in a rainbow-tinted cloud.

Pulsing colors and bubbles shimmered and flowed around him, and Victor tried to shift his perspective, but he was without agency, simply a presence in that weird, brightly colored expanse. Since he couldn't look any other way, he studied what was in front of him, trying to see a clue as to what was happening. Still, nothing changed other than the weird shifting color streaks and the even weirder bubbles of color that seemed to float up in front of him, only to pass away beyond his field of view.

He tried to utter a curse or a question, but nothing came out of his mouth. Unable to do anything else, his mind began to wander. Whatever was happening would happen, and he'd either wake up or not—he wouldn't mentally flail about, worrying. His mind drifted to other concerns, such as what he'd do when he got to Persi Gables. He wanted to meet Olivia and hoped she'd still be around, but that was a minor thing, which he supposed was strange. Shouldn't he be more focused on learning about this mysterious human relative?

No matter how he looked at it, though, he couldn't get too worked up about the idea of meeting her. He'd spent too much time focusing on, worrying about, and planning for what Rellia needed. Namely, he was stressed about having to lead an army. He'd never led a group bigger than two into any kind of battle, so how was he supposed to manage thousands? He hoped there would be a lot of delegating and plenty of guidance, but then he also hoped he'd learned enough not to let people shove him around; he didn't want to be a figurehead or a puppet.

As his thoughts drifted that way, Victor noticed a change in his surroundings—the colors began to swirl, and he was pulled into a tightly spiraling funnel toward a distant, bright light. He started moving slowly, but his speed seemed to compound exponentially, and suddenly the bright light shone into his eyes, and he felt the heat of a sweltering, steamy summer day on his face.

Yolotli shaded her eyes from the sun, looking down the long grassy slope at the little people gathered and waiting for her. Olmecs, they called themselves, and long had they worked to earn an audience. They knelt in the grass, heads down, the blood of their offerings pooled in the glade below, the pyre of their victims burning beside it, the smoke giving the pale blue sky a yellow-brown haze. She supposed she should be honored by their obsequious sacrifice, but it wasn't something she relished, unlike her more war-hungry kin.

She progressed down the slope, and when she was ten long strides from the first of the little folk, their garments bedecked with bird feathers and their macuahuitls in the grass before them, she paused and waited. Which of their people was their leader? Ichtaca had approached her, but Yolotli didn't see her there. "Well?" she asked, growing impatient. "You learn well from your encounters with us—I see sturdy macuahuitls and deep respect. Who will speak for you that I might resist the urge to smear your juices into the grass with the soles of my feet?"

"Mighty Yolotli!" one of the Olmecs cried, lifting his feather-bedecked head. "We have heard tales of your kindness toward our kind, your desire to speak rather than kill! Please hear us now!"

"Are you yet dead? No? Then speak, and tell me your name, insolent one!" Yolotli was toying with the man; she had no desire to squish the little thing, but it didn't hurt to keep these people respectful lest they utter a rude word in the presence of her more violent brothers and sisters.

"Praise you, Yolotli! I am Toltecatl, the leader of these people! We've slain a thousand of our foes there in honor of you and your people!" He gestured down the slope into the vale where the pyre smoldered.

"And what do you seek, Toltecatl? You've learned the art of the macuahuitl. You bear the feathers of serpents and birds. You've gained respect and humility. What more will you learn from the Quinametzin?"

"We seek your leadership, great Yolotli! We are beset by strange people and beings. They destroy our temples, destroy our cities, and vanish our people! We cannot stand before them, but surely you can! Surely one such as you can take the battle to them and vanquish them from our lands. Surely you don't want them to sully the fields here around your jungles and mountains! Thus far, every battle we've fought has been lost! I am the seventh ruler of my people in as many years, and our numbers dwindle, thousands lost every season!"

Yolotli frowned. Had another people come to their shores? Had it not been enough that her kin had smashed the great scaled serpents? Was it not enough that they'd driven the strange winged men with their metal armor back over the seas? "Since your kind learned to respect my people, we've had no quarrel, but why should I crush this enemy of yours? Tell me about them."

"They have tails like monkeys but scales rather than fur! They bear horns and have eyes that blaze like embers in the dark! They are tall and strong, flinging my people about with their clawed hands. They are savage and cruel, eating the flesh of our women and babes while they yet live! As we kill one, four more spring from chasms in the earth, great fiery pits that blaze with strange magic and reveal weird worlds beyond their flickering flames. They speak in clicks and hisses, words that make no sense to our ears, and refuse any sort of parlay. We seek your aid, great Yolotli; only the Quinametzin can crush these devils!"

"Devils? An apt designation. Again, I ask, why would we help you? Did your people not attack us once, thinking we were too few to stand against your verminous numbers?"

"A lesson we learned much from, Mighty One!" Toltecatl fell to his face in the grass, his hands in the air, and wailed, "Please! Please help us! Even now, a band of the devils approaches one of our cities!"

"A band? Do they not send an army?"

"They don't need an army, so savage are they! For every devil, we lose a hundred fierce Olmec warriors!"

"And who were these?" Yolotli gestured to the blood and the pyre beyond it.

"Invaders from the north! We captured them as an offering to your glory!"

"If you truly wished to honor me, why not bring me one of these devils you so fear?"

"Great Yolotli! Every battle we fight with the devils brings us great loss! Any offering of their kind would be pitiful. Surely this great sacrifice is a better honor!"

"How many warriors have you here? I do not wish to count your tiny bodies."

"Before you are one hundred warriors! The greatest of my people!"

"Very well. I will take you and this one hundred, and we will meet this band of devils. Stand up, small ones."

"Oh!" Toltecatl's voice wavered, and Yolotli heard the gasps of his people, his "greatest" warriors. "But, great Yolotli, we are not a match for the devils. Surely you should get more of your kin and crush them! Send them back to the realm from which they crawled."

Yolotli might have been patient for her kind, she may even have had a bit of a warm spot in her heart for these little people, but this chieftain was beginning to wear on her nerves. She took two steps forward and snatched him up, gripping one of his scrawny arms and lifting him so she could look into his war-painted face. "You will never grow strong if you do not fight for yourselves. I will guide and help you, but if you wish to throw these devils out of your lands, you will bleed in the battles to come."

"Yes," he whined, grimacing as the tendons in his shoulder strained. Yolotli dropped him and then turned to the kneeling Olmecs. She unleashed her aura, shaping it to grant boons to these little folk, wrapping it around them, giving them courage and strength. At the same time, she let it ripple out around the clearing, relieved to let it hang heavy in the air around her. Any enemy that came near would feel it and beware.

The Olmecs howled in delight and fervor, standing up and grasping their macuahuitls, lifting them into the air. They began to chant some rhyme about killing and ravaging their enemies, and Yolotli smiled; they were like children, but they had an enthusiasm that warmed her heart. "Are you pleased, children? Do you feel my might, my bravery? I share it with you that we might smite your foes and drive them from these lands. Remember this great honor, and always respect my people—few are as kind and would just as soon squash as help you."

Victor's eyes snapped open, and he felt extremely disoriented momentarily as he stared at the wooden planks above his head. He licked his lips, dry as sandpaper, and coughed, trying to circulate some saliva around in his mouth. He saw System messages waiting for his attention, but his eyes felt blurry.

"That wasn't so bad," Valla said from somewhere to his right. He blinked several times as she continued, "You were only out for three days, though I've never seen someone so still; I barely could tell you were breathing."

"I," Victor croaked. He licked his lips and swallowed again. Finally feeling some moisture on his tongue, he tried again. "I saw a different ancestor."

7

INTERROGATION

Well, you've grown again," Valla observed, watching Victor struggle to a sitting position. She must have been right; he seemed to be taking up more space on the floor than he remembered.

"Great," he grunted. "Anything else different?"

"Well . . . your skin is more lustrous, your hair has a sheen I've never seen before, and, well, you have a sharper look to you—like you're all bones and muscles. It's quite nice, really, if I'm being honest. Your eyes, too; they're like luminous pots of honey." Valla looked down quickly, and Victor chuckled.

"What are you, a poet? Anyway, thanks; I'm glad I'm not monstrous, at least."

"I didn't say that—" Valla choked off her words, laughing as Victor shot her a glance, eyes narrowed.

"Gimme a sec," Victor said, focusing on the System messages:

*****Congratulations! Your spell, Inspiring Presence, has morphed to: Inspiration of the Quinametzin.*****

*****Inspiration of the Quinametzin, Epic. Prerequisites: A direct and profound connection to the Quinametzin bloodline. Affinity: Inspiration. You infuse your being with the power of inspiration and the fierce presence of the Quinametzin titans. Nearby allies will be granted a portion of your potency. Energy Cost: Minimum 750, scalable. Cooldown: Long.*****

"Huh, that's pretty badass," Victor muttered softly, pleased with the message. He pulled up his status sheet, wanting to see exactly how much his race had advanced:

Name:	**Victor Sandoval**
Race:	**Human (Quinametzin Bloodline): Advanced 7**
Class:	**Titanic Herald: Legendary**
Level:	**49**
Core:	**Spirit Class: Advanced 2**

"I gained five ranks to my bloodline," he announced. Then as Valla's eyebrows rose, he said, "Tell me what this feels like to you," and cast his new spell.

"Ancestors!" Valla said, standing up from the bed and arching her back. "That's amazing! I feel like we could take on anything!" Her eyes went distant momentarily, and then she said, "Victor, my strength and vitality each improved quite a lot! Nearly ten percent!"

He nodded and said, "It's my old Inspiring Presence spell—somehow, my advancement in my bloodline jumped it straight to epic and gave it some new effects for my allies."

"What a boon! This will be very helpful on the field of battle, no?"

"Yeah . . ." Victor's mind drifted to the scene he'd witnessed of Yolotli and the humans begging her for help. He wondered how their battle had gone, sort of wishing he'd seen it play out.

"Speaking of allies," Valla said, bringing him back to reality as she sat down. "I had a long meeting with Yunsha and the headmaster of the academy, Jaxin-dak. They're holding Professor ap'Gravin in a cell, waiting for you to question him. He hasn't been cooperative."

"Oh? They don't have some magic they can use to get him to talk?"

"They do, but Jaxin-dak feels their authority is lacking, and ap'Gravin has powerful resistances. Apparently, he's something of a mind mage—a lesser affinity and licensed by the Empire—and Jaxin thinks he's locked away his secrets. Ap'Gravin is demanding to have his father alerted to the charges against him. The academy leadership is dragging their feet, but they feel the word has probably gotten out. Our window to speak with the man without interference is quickly closing."

"And they're cool with me slapping the guy around?"

"No, no," Valla chuckled, "not exactly. The contract you signed is gone, but when they told me they were willing to let you speak to him, they suggested that intimidation without actual harm to the man was all they would stomach."

"Mm-hmm." Victor nodded. He closed his eyes then cast Alter Self, feeding the spell enough Energy to reduce himself to the size of a large, but not absurdly so, human. When he finished, he lithely hopped to his feet—his improved body had undergone the transformation more efficiently, using less Energy, but it still had taken nearly half of his reserves. "Stand in front of me," he said, using Valla as a guide to ensure he'd gotten the spell right. When he saw the top of her head came to just beneath his chin, he nodded. "Right. Well, how'd it go with the airship?"

"It's moored to the academy wall, waiting for our departure. The captain, ap'Veral, was happy for a few days of paid rest."

"You're awesome, Valla." Victor grinned at her, then dug around in his ring for his armor and helmet, donning them as she watched.

"You plan to speak to the professor right away?"

"Yep." He adjusted his wyrm-scale vest, made sure it hung just over his dragonsteel belt, and then he grunted, lifting the weighty Kethian Juggernaut helm to his head, sighing with relief as it magically transferred its mass to him.

"Intimidating, but not so much as revealing your true nature."

"All things in time, Valla." Victor bent to pick up Lifedrinker, slipping his arms through her harness. "Right. Let's deal with this asshole. Then we can take off, hmm? Nothing else keeping us here is there?"

"You're so sure you'll get what you need from him in one meeting?"

"One way or another," Victor growled, striding to the door, pulling it open, and making his way down to the common room.

As he stepped into the room, noting the bright windows—he had no idea what time it was, but apparently it was daytime—and the busy tables, he paused as Harl called out from the bar, "Lord Victor! I'm so pleased to see you up and about. We were all hoping for your speedy recovery."

"Oh?" Victor asked, taking a step closer to the apron-wearing man.

"Yes! Captain Valla told us of your lingering injury; I can't imagine how you kept from showing your pain the other night, though I figure the ale helped, eh?" He winked and chuckled, setting down his bar rag, and then added, "Can I get you something to eat?"

"Not at the moment, Harl. I have an appointment." Victor nodded, his helmet's angular eyeholes doing nothing to make the gesture appear friendly, and then strode out of the inn. When he and Valla were progressing across the square, he asked, "What kind of injury did you tell him I had?"

"I said you had a wyrm's stinger in your gut, and it was slowly working its way free."

"What the fuck, Valla?" Victor's voice rose in outraged disbelief.

"What? I wanted to give him something to gossip about—these people have hardly heard of a wyrm, let alone seen one." She slapped him on the shoulder and added, "Besides, I wanted to give them a good reason to keep away from your room; I told them you were delirious from the pain and venom."

Victor shook his head, lost for words, and continued his speedy progress toward the academy. "Where do we find this ap'Gravin guy?"

"We're supposed to ask at the administration offices for an escort, and then they'll take us to his holding cell."

"Uh-huh." Victor looked up the street to the yawning, open doors of the academy's central hall. Students were out in large numbers, and he wondered if they were on their way to classes. He glanced at the sun, saw it was high overhead, and revised his guess; it was lunchtime. "Do you know where that is? The admin offices?"

"Yes, that's where I met with Jaxin-dak." Valla moved past him, and Victor followed behind. He and Valla still garnered a lot of strange looks from the students, but Victor figured it had more to do with their armor, weapons, and general lack of any resemblance to people who belonged in an academy than his size, which was nice.

"So, the contract's gone, right? I'm not going to kill myself if I start a fight?"

"Correct, but please don't," Valla replied, glancing over her shoulder and offering him a pained smile. "I'd rather not have all of Fainhallow and their alumni out for blood."

"I don't plan to, but I want to keep my options open."

As they climbed the steps to the entrance hall, Valla asked, "Have you thought about what you're going to say? Do you want me to do anything?"

"I'm going to go with my gut. As for you, I'd appreciate it if you would keep people from interrupting me while I'm in with the professor." Victor had some ideas but didn't feel like talking about them while he walked. He'd try good old-fashioned anger and intimidation; if that didn't work, he had some plans involving Project Spirit.

"I'll try . . ." Valla said, though her tone didn't elicit confidence. "It's just that I have a feeling they'll want a representative in there with you."

"We'll see." Victor twisted his mouth into a frown and felt some rage, always quick to respond to his thoughts, seeping into his pathways. He followed Valla through side passageways and up one flight of stairs, and then they walked into a wood-paneled room with a receptionist's desk and two doors leading off to the left and right. Comfortable-looking chairs and couches lined the walls, intermixed with bookcases and a stand where a steaming pot of tea and several pastries sat waiting on a tray.

Valla approached the petite older Ardeni woman sitting at the desk and cleared her throat. "Excuse me, I'm Valla ap'Yensha, and this is my companion, Victor. We were told to request access to Professor ap'Gravin here."

"Oh?" The woman sat back, closing the book she'd been reading. "I see, I see," she said, taking in Valla and Victor glowering behind her. "Excuse me while I check with Professor Oylla-dak."

"Not Jaxin-dak?" Victor growled, wondering if they were about to be shoved off onto some lesser bureaucrat of the academy.

"Oh no, I'm sorry to say the headmaster has had to leave on business. He's gone to the academy in Tharcray for a tournament."

"A tournament?" Valla asked, then shook her head and quickly added, "It's unimportant. Please check with whoever's in charge."

"Yes, yes," she muttered, standing up with a groan and stretching. "I've been sitting too long!" She walked to the door on the left and added, "Please take a seat. I'm sure she'll be with you as soon as possible."

Valla turned and walked over to the tray of pastries, snatching one with pink frosting, and Victor continued to scowl, pacing back and forth over the rust-colored rug that ran down the center of the large room. "Not hungry?" Valla asked, taking a bite. "It's a little stale but good." Victor grunted, and she shrugged, taking another bite and sitting down. "I do hope you're not planning to bring this building down around our ears, Victor. You seem to be working yourself up to something . . ."

"I'm not planning to do anything crazy, but I've got a real impatient feeling in my gut, and I don't know why. God, I hope it's not my damn bloodline. I wonder if I'm starting to think like a Quinametzin."

"Do you think that spell you learned from Tes to reduce yourself is limiting that effect at all? I wonder if you'd be smashing through walls if you were your normal self." She licked at some frosting on her thumb, and Victor stared at her, his eyes going wide as she spoke.

"Are you serious, Valla? Are you trying to stress me out? I'm not going to lose control of myself, regardless of how big I am. You know my will stat!" While he spoke, he realized what she was doing, trying to make him think about his emotions and talk himself through them. He might be impatient and cranky, but he was still Victor; he was in control. "You're clever, you know that?"

"Thank you," she said, taking another bite and smiling impishly. Just then, the door through which the receptionist had gone opened, and she reappeared, followed closely by an imposing Shadeni woman. She was tall, close to Victor's current height, with enormous, folded red wings and eyes that reminded him of a starry night sky—depthless pools of black, teeming with bright white motes.

"Valla, Victor, may I introduce Professor Oylla-dak?"

The woman stepped forward and smiled broadly, revealing long, pointed canines. She was beautiful, with a long, slender nose, high cheekbones, and full lips, but Victor found himself viewing her as an authority figure almost immediately and didn't feel the slightest urge to flirt. "Just Oylla is fine. Welcome. I'm to show you to that scoundrel, ap'Gravin, hmm?" When Victor nodded and opened his mouth to reply, she continued speaking, forestalling his words. "No, no. No need to explain—Jaxin-dak left me with thorough instructions. Very well. Follow me, please."

Valla hopped to her feet and hurried to Victor's side as he followed the professor out of the room and down the hallway. She continued to speak as they walked. "He's not far away. We have a detention cell or two for stronger Energy users here at the academy, meant to keep them from harming themselves or others while we work out disciplinary actions. Usually, they're occupied by intractable students, but ap'Gravin isn't the first professor to wait for justice in one of them."

She rounded a corner, descended a short flight of stairs, and stopped in a round, plaster-walled room lit by orange Energy lamps. Three gray metal doors were evenly spaced on the curved wall, and she pointed to the one on the left. "He's within. I'll need to accompany you for your questioning."

"I don't think that's a good idea," Victor grunted, walking toward the door.

"Pardon me?"

"Listen," Victor said, turning to her, looking into those weird, star-filled eyes, "I'm likely to get a little angry, and my aura might start to leak, and it will be uncomfortable in there. I don't intend to hurt the man, but he's not going to enjoy my company unless he's very forthcoming with the answers I'm seeking."

"Hmm," Oylla said, folding her arms and staring right back at him. "Nevertheless, I'll accompany you."

Victor frowned, finding it necessary to push his rage back down into his Core, but then he shrugged and said, "If you want to leave, don't feel bad."

Then he turned and walked to the door, staring at it while he waited for Oylla to unlock it.

To her credit, Oylla didn't respond or argue. She walked to the door and held something shiny against the handle, and when it clicked, she pulled it open and gestured for Victor to precede her into the room beyond. Victor peered through, saw a man lying on the only furnishing within—a simple cot, low to the ground—and stepped through. The man was an Ardeni with uncharacteristic long black hair, a hawkish nose, and bright green eyes. His face was dotted with dark stubble, and he looked a bit bedraggled. Victor was taking in his dark black robes and noticed a gleaming red metal collar on his neck.

"You collared him?"

"Well, his abilities are a bit much for the student wards in the cell to manage," Oylla said, stepping into the room after Victor.

"What's this?" The man's voice was sharp, slightly nasal, and thoroughly outraged as he sat up, his lanky frame hidden by the folds of his robes.

"Ap'Gravin, this is Victor. He's a human who was done great harm by a man in your father's employ." As ap'Gravin absorbed her words, a deep frown etching a furrow between his eyes, Oylla turned to Victor and said, "I'll be right here, behind you, but I'll leave the interview to you now."

"Thanks—" Victor started to say, but ap'Gravin's outburst interrupted him.

"What have I to do with my father's henchmen? What have I to do with some brutish human? This is preposterous, and when I have my day before the council, I'll see you, Jaxin-dak, and that fool Yunsha stripped of your honors and titles and sent packing!"

"That's enough," Victor growled, putting some rage into his voice, letting slip the leash on his aura just a bit. Ap'Gravin backed up, scooting toward the wall against which his cot rested, and his face lost some of its color, fading to a paler shade of blue. Victor rested a hand on Lifedrinker's shiny metal and stepped closer to the professor, and he spoke from his belly when he asked, "What did you take from Olivia Bennet? What did you steal to give to your father and Boaegh so they could summon me?"

"What?" Ap'Gravin jerked his gaze from Victor to Oylla, and he wailed, "What's the meaning of this? Such a preposterous accusation! Is this why I'm being held here? My father will have all of your heads!"

Victor reached into his Core and pulled out a thick river of fear-attuned Energy, letting it flood into his pathways, then he fully released his hold on his aura. His eyes, usually bright and golden, filled with darkness, and a flickering purple-black halo limned his shoulders and helmeted head as he let his aura pour forth. What's more, he cast Project Spirit, and a dark surge of fear-attuned Energy rolled out of his chest, bathing the professor in its clinging, midnight waves.

He heard a gasp from behind him, but his eyes were focused on ap'Gravin as he cried out and tried to press himself through the wall's stone. His eyes were haunted, and his mouth hung open in abject terror. "Answer my question, *pendejo*! What did you take from Olivia Bennet?"

Amazingly, the man still struggled against him, even collared as he was. Victor could see him fighting against the pressure of his spell and the struggle of his will as he pushed against the waves of dark Energy, and then the professor forced out a strained reply, "I. Took. Nothing!"

Victor felt his fury surge. He was furious at this man for resisting him, but he was also angry at himself for a seed of doubt that began to nibble at the corner of his mind. He knew it was this guy who'd taken the sample from Olivia; he knew he must have an idea what his father had been up to, why Boaegh had summoned him through the universe to this world and dropped Victor into one hellacious experience after another. How was he resisting him? What tier was he, anyway? "Enough," he growled and ended his Alter Self spell.

Suddenly a great wave of Energy rushed back into his Core, and every cell in his body, freed from a self-imposed prison, surged with power and density. His body erupted with growth, his hulking shoulders and neck pressed against the ceiling as he stooped over to avoid smashing his head through the stone. He loomed over the professor, cringing on his cot. He felt his true aura fall like an avalanche around him, eliciting another yelp from Oylla-dak and bringing a wail of despair from the ghost-white face of ap'Gravin.

Victor wasn't finished, though; he reached out a hand, grabbed hold of ap'Gravin's robe, and turned, glowering at Oylla-dak. He growled, "I need more space." Then he dragged the limp, wailing professor through the door into the larger room beyond. The ceiling was much higher there, accommodating the stairs that led up to the next level, and Victor set ap'Gravin down, standing to his full height.

Valla stood near the stairs, clearly bothered by his aura but managing it much more easily than ap'Gravin. After all, she'd been exposed to it many, many times. She stood there, one hand on Midnight's hilt, and raised an eyebrow at him, glancing at Oylla, who had followed him out of the holding cell. "What are you going to do?" her arched eyebrow asked.

Oylla, a grimace on her face, voiced a similar question, strain evident in her voice. "What are you doing? You can't take him anywhere! Don't harm him!"

"I'm not taking him anywhere. As to harm, it's entirely up to him," Victor growled, and then he cast Iron Berserk.

8

COUNTERBALANCE

Victor expanded, as he was wont to do, and ap'Gravin fell away from him, collapsing onto his rump, scrabbling toward the wall between the door to his cell and the next, closed one. Victor was thankful for his Iron Berserk upgrade, specifically his ability to keep his rage simmering in the background, because, truth be told, he was angry enough as it was. Something was wrong with his approach, his bullheaded charge for the answer to his burning question.

Ap'Gravin had been prepared, somehow resisting Victor, because if Victor were any judge of a person, he'd say the man was plenty frightened. He either didn't know the answer, or he was hiding it. Victor chose to believe the latter. That left him with a choice. De-escalate, start over, and try to work his way to the answer in a roundabout way, or, more to his liking, escalate things further. If simple fear wasn't enough to crack the man, then perhaps a taste of Quinametzin-inspired madness would do the trick.

"Good," he growled, voice deep, grating and cracking off the walls of the circular stone room. "Grovel there. Sit and watch what I do with my foes." Victor glanced over his left shoulder to see Oylla watching him, small now, at least next to his hulking form. She had a strange, purple-red shimmer in her eyes, perhaps shielding herself from his aura now that she'd recovered from her earlier surprise. When their eyes met, he gave her a brief nod, trying to reassure her, then he reached into his storage ring and pulled out the night brute prince's heart.

Grinning madly at ap'Gravin, looking into his wide, haunted eyes, he lifted the heart from its container and tore into it, ripping a huge bloody chunk away, chomping it, and swallowing it noisily. Victor had thought about this—briefly, sure, but he had thought about it. He didn't know what would happen when he ate this heart, but he figured it would be impressive, and the night brutes had been fear-attuned creatures; maybe the spectacle caused by eating the prince's heart would help convince ap'Gravin to take his questions more seriously.

Tes might not approve, or, Victor thought, swallowing another bloody chunk, she probably would. She'd probably laugh and give him that eager look she always had when she watched him doing something stupid, brave, insane, or brilliant. He almost forgot what he was doing, thinking about Tes like that; he started to picture her eyes and her smile, and hear her voice in his ears. He began to wonder about his slowly growing feelings for Valla and if they were really something he should pursue—hadn't he determined some-day to be worthy of pursuing Tes?

"What in the name of the Old Father's bones is this madman doing?" ap'Gravin cried, pushing away from Victor, who was hunched in front of him, dripping great gobs of night brute blood onto the stones as he chomped and chewed the dark, steaming heart, kept fresh and hot in Tes's magical jar.

"He's a Quinametzin titan, and you've driven him to this madness. Pray the heart sates his hunger," Valla said, and Victor could hear the amusement in her voice.

Victor took his third bite, chewed it, and tried to refocus on what he was doing. He squatted lower, holding the dripping, bloody organ before him, his great form hanging over ap'Gravin as he chewed. With each bite, he grunted and growled, letting the juices sluice off his chin to form a puddle that ran between his feet toward ap'Gravin's robes. His grin widened and grew more savage as he saw the man try to melt back into the stone wall.

Something was happening in his gut. It was starting to roil, and Victor felt strange, tingling lances shooting out into his torso, but nothing painful, nothing that might cause him to look away from the haunted professor's eyes. He was more than halfway through the enormous heart now, but his hunger had barely abated—something about eating hearts when he was in his titan form kept him ravenous.

"What's happening to him?" Oylla asked from the side, perhaps echoing ap'Gravin's unspoken question because he nodded frantically at her words. "He's exuding shadows . . ."

"Guard yourself," Valla said, and this time her voice wasn't amused; Victor could hear her moving away up the steps. As he took another bite, perhaps the penultimate one, he was dimly aware that Oylla had stepped sideways into ap'Gravin's cell and had pulled the door halfway closed. Ap'Gravin, for his part, began to wail, writhing this way and that but going nowhere. How could he? Victor's giant form hung above him, madly grinning as the blood pooled on the stones and dark shadows began flowing from his flesh.

As Victor lifted the last morsel of the prince's heart to his mouth, chomped it with his mighty teeth, and swallowed it down, he thought he was losing consciousness for a moment because his vision grew darker on the edges. When he glanced around, tearing his eyes from the whimpering, cowering ap'Gravin, he saw the room was filling with tangible, wispy, clinging shadows that poured from his flesh. The effect reminded him of a smoke bomb; they were streaming thickly out of him, filling the area with their dark influence.

"Huh," he grunted, lifting a hand to watch the dark ribbons wisp away from his skin, obscuring the man before him. Victor didn't worry about that; the last he'd seen, just a moment ago, ap'Gravin had been muttering some repetitive phrase, his eyes squeezed shut and his entire body trembling in a paroxysm of terror-fueled spiritual fervor. The wisps of dark, clinging Energy began to pack the space, what was left of it, anyway, after considering Victor's fifteen-foot bulk. He sat down, falling out of his squatting position, and kicked his legs out to either side of where he'd last seen ap'Gravin—no sense letting the worm wriggle away.

Perhaps it was his berserk state, perhaps it was his increasingly Quinametzin mindset, but Victor wasn't particularly worried about what was happening, not yet. He'd anticipated the heart having a profound effect; he'd banked on it, in fact, expecting not only to improve himself but to disturb the subject of his interrogation. Still, it was weird how quiet everything had become, how thick and heavy the darkness around him was. He reached out a hand to swipe at it, and that's when he realized he couldn't really feel his body anymore. Was he unconscious?

Oylla-dak stepped back from the stairwell, away from the hulking giant and the strange, clinging shadows erupting from his form. She'd felt his aura, felt the weight of his power, and she wasn't sure she should try to intervene, at least not yet. She wasn't entirely sure she could stand against him, and even if she could, there would surely be collateral damage if things came to blows.

No, Valla ap'Yensha was from a reputable clan, and Jaxin-dak had instructed her to be lenient with the human's request. She'd wait and see what happened here.

Something about how the giant had looked at her, nodding slightly, had instilled her with some confidence; he wasn't disregarding her admonishment about harming ap'Gravin. Whatever he was doing with the gruesome display of eating that monstrous heart and erupting with clinging shadows had something to do with the interrogation; he was setting a stage, trying to break the professor down. Oylla got the impression that Victor had been surprised when ap'Gravin had resisted his initial questioning but also that he was far from discouraged.

She reached through the partially closed door, feeling the wispy shadows beginning to compound on each other, filling the space. They clung to her like greasy, slick silk, sliding against her flesh as she pulled back, sending shivers through her skin and reminding her of when she was a child, fearful of things in the dark.

What sort of Energy was this? Was this giant a Mind Caster? No, this was different. It felt primal, emotional even. A Spirit Caster, then. Yes, it made sense—when he'd grown to the size of a giant, she'd felt the heat of rage in his aura, felt as though it would be wise to vacate the area, a deep urge in the pit of her being to get away from him. Could she stop him if he went mad? If she hit him unawares with her most potent abyssal Energy blast, perhaps.

"Perhaps," she repeated softly, pulling her hand back as the stairwell filled with dark Energy. It continued to compound on itself, rapidly multiplying as the thick shadows piled up. She couldn't see the giant or ap'Gravin any longer, and not wanting herself to be engulfed, she pulled the door shut. "What do I do now?" she asked, looking around the cell that had previously held the disgraced professor.

Victor felt something happening at his Core. At first, he felt a surging, pulsing sensation that seemed similar to cultivating, similar to how it had felt when the Energy from other enemy hearts had replenished him. Something was different, though, and unable to see anything outside his eyes, he turned his vision inward. He could see the dark Energy in his pathways, flowing through them to his Core, but then he saw the problem he'd created for himself—the dark Energy was only feeding one aspect of his Core, his darkly throbbing and pulsing fear-attuned orb.

"Shit," he muttered, or thought he did, but he couldn't hear himself. He tried to reach out with his will, tried to pull some of that Energy away from the fear-attuned orb and shove it into the smoldering red sphere of his rage. It moved with his will but slid off his rage-attuned orb, quickly flowing back to his fear affinity. "Shit," he repeated and tried again, this time trying to steer some of the Energy into his inspiration orb. Just as before, it moved in response to his will but simply passed around the white-gold orb, flowing directly back into the now surging globe of fear-attuned Energy.

Panic began to enter his mind, even stubborn as it was with the effects of Berserk and his bloodline. He'd hardly begun to process the dark Energy in the air around him, and his fear-attuned orb was rapidly swelling, becoming more prominent and denser than his other two affinities. Oynalla's words came back to him, her many warnings about never letting his fear affinity outweigh the others. Suddenly, Tes's admonition about waiting until he was stronger before using the heart struck home; she'd meant his Core.

He tried to push the Energy out of his pathways, forgoing the boost it was trying to offer him, but it was impossible; the shadows might have manifested outside of him, but the heart was in his belly. No matter how he pushed and strained against it, it just slipped around, finding another opening and surging to his Core. His will was prodigious, though; he tried to form barriers at all his pathways, blocking the Energy from his Core. He held it for a while but then began to suffer bone-deep pain as though his very being was coming undone.

Fearing the worst, that he'd literally burst from the pressure, he eased his resistance and watched as the dark Energy streamed into his Core, further swelling his rapidly expanding fear affinity. It grew so much that its outer edge approached his other two orbs. If Victor had to guess, he'd say it was nearly double their density. "*Pinche* fucker," he groaned, "that heart was strong!"

What would happen to him if his fear affinity so badly outweighed the others? Oynalla had thought it would spell disaster for his mentality. Would it change his personality? Would he become ruled by fear or his desire to spread it? He thought back to when he'd first cast his Aspect of Terror spell and how he'd nearly gone wild, terrorizing the countryside, starting with Valla. No, he couldn't let that happen; he wouldn't become a Fear Caster.

If his other two affinities wouldn't absorb this dark Energy, then he'd have to think of another way, and only one thing came to mind. When he'd built his inspiration orb and his fear orb, he'd done it with Energy taken from his other affinities. First, he'd made his inspiration-attuned orb with the remnants of the shattering of his original rage-attuned Core. Then, he'd broken the attunement of some of his Energy from his inspiration and rage orbs and created his fear affinity. Hadn't Thunderbite said he had other affinities lurking within his spirit? Was it time to find another?

It was the only thing he could think of, so while he continued to think and speculate, Victor began to pull Energy from his three orbs. For every one part of rage and inspiration, he drew four parts of fear, and he began to wind them into a fourth ball, forming it in opposition to his fear orb. The Energy from the heart continued to flow into his fear-attuned orb, but he was draining it faster than it could grow. He pulled those threads of Energy down, wound them together, and with the considerable pressure of his will, he began to press and grind them, smashing them into each other, breaking their affinities.

Victor didn't have Thunderbite to tell him when to stop, to tell him when he'd taken exactly enough to create an orb that was a fourth of his total Energy, so he had to eyeball it. He watched the muddy orb he was forming start to pulse and lose its color, becoming a slowly growing globe of gray, unattuned Energy. Still, it was smaller than the other three, and the fear-attuned orb was too large, so he continued pulling threads into the gray sphere, squeezing and pressing them until they took on that same gray hue.

He'd been at it for what seemed a very long time when the Energy from the prince's heart finally tapered off and ceased to feed his fear orb. Sighing with relief, Victor measured his new orb against the other three, and when it seemed they were in balance, he stopped pulling Energy from his three affinities. He stared at that new gray globe and wondered what he was supposed to do now. He didn't have Thunderbite's wisdom. He couldn't even speak to Valla; he was oblivious to the world around him.

It seemed to him that his rage and fear were a more potent force on his mind than his inspiration. To him, his fear affinity was a negative influence, and his rage was sometimes negative and sometimes positive. He enjoyed his inspiration more than the other two and wished his affinity with it was stronger. He wished it could counteract those other two more easily. Wouldn't it be nice if he had another affinity he found to be positive, another affinity to act as a balance to his fear? What if he couldn't find an affinity at all? Would this Energy be lost? Would he ever wake from this weird state?

Victor tried to remember how Thunderbite had led him to his fear. He remembered answering questions about his actions, about his motivations, but it was all sort of a blur to him. He shook his head and decided to try another approach—he wanted something like inspiration, and he remembered how he'd found that. He'd been in one of the lowest points of his life, lost, discouraged, deep in Greatbone Mine, and left for dead by some thugs. He'd let his mind wander and thought of Lam, streaming in, wings glittering, and smashing the shit out of some monsters, saving Victor and inspiring him to act beyond what he'd felt was his quitting point.

"That felt good," he said or tried to; again, no sound of his voice came to his ears. What else felt good in his life? His mind immediately went to Thayla and Deyni, how he loved how he'd helped them, how it felt good that he'd done the right thing for once. This led him to other thoughts like that. He remembered killing Jikrak and saving Tellen—how he'd rampaged all night long, celebrating his victory. That brought to mind the arena battles he'd been in, how it felt to hear the crowd's adulation, and how he loved to put on a display, despite his protestations. Even when he was angry at the people, at their bloodlust, he loved to hear them cheer, to feel the energy rolling off them.

Perhaps because that feeling of joy in victory was something that had been with him since he was just a kid, first learning to wrestle, Victor focused on it, on those moments of glory. He grasped the common thread among those brief, joyful triumphs in his life and tried to push that feeling into that slowly pulsing, flat gray orb of Energy at his Core. Almost as quickly as he remembered his fear affinity forming, the gray sphere flared with a sparkling golden luster, starting at the very center and then warmly populating the whole mass.

Victor sighed with relief as he saw and felt his new affinity; it might not be wholly good like inspiration, but it was certainly more positive, at least in his mind, than fear. He'd done it, kept his fear from growing out of control, and formed a new affinity all on his own. He smiled at that warmly sparkling golden Energy, a stark counterpoint to his glowering, purple-black fear affinity—glory.

Victor opened his eyes and wasn't surprised to see the shadows had gone and that he was once again able to see and act. Whatever state the prince's heart had put him in was gone now that he'd dealt with its Energy. He found he was no longer berserk but was still seated in front of ap'Gravin, a leg on either side of him. The man had pulled his knees to his chest and buried his face in them, his dark robes completely obscuring his form. Victor decided to ignore him for a moment. Instead, he focused on the System messages that had appeared in his vision:

Congratulations! You have gained a new feat: Born of Terror.

Born of Terror: You have a strong affinity for fear and have consumed the heart of one born of its dark cousin, terror. Your will attribute will be doubly effective when dealing with fear, terror, or their related affinities.

Congratulations! You have improved your Core and gained a new affinity: Glory.

Congratulations! You have achieved level 50 Titanic Herald and gained 6 strength, 11 vitality, 6 dexterity, 6 agility, 6 intelligence, and 6 will.

Level 50 Class refinement is available. Class refinement is permanent. Human Energy cultivators will next be offered a Class refinement selection at level 60. To view your options and make your selection, access the menu through your status page.

"Well, shit," Victor said, pleased beyond his greatest expectations. Ap'Gravin looked up at him, his eyes bloodshot, streaks of moisture at their corners and on his cheeks. Victor grinned at him but held off speaking just yet. He wanted to look at the numbers:

Name:	Victor Sandoval			
Race:	Human (Quinametzin Bloodline): Advanced 7			
Class:	Titanic Herald: Legendary			
Level:	50			
Core:	Spirit Class: Advanced 5			
Energy Affinity:	3.1, Fear 9.4, Rage 9.1, Glory 8.6, Inspiration 7.4		Energy:	11823/11823
Strength:	220	Vitality:	335 (369)	
Dexterity:	100	Agility:	123	
Intelligence:	92	Will:	473	

"Not bad," he said, chuckling.

"You're a madman," Ap'Gravin said, his voice cracking and quavering.

Victor rubbed at his chin and glanced to the left, where Oylla-dak had pulled the cell door open. He could hear Valla returning down the stairs, her boots scuffing gently against the stone. He turned back to ap'Gravin and said, "Not really. Anyway, tell me something, Professor. Are you ready to talk?"

9

DEPARTURE

W hat was the point of that display?" ap'Gravin muttered, perhaps trying to cling to some semblance of his earlier bluster.

Victor grinned, shifting to a more comfortable sitting position, pushing Lifedrinker's handle back and to the side; she'd been pressing into the stone floor now that Victor wasn't titan sized. "Oh, I just wanted to give you a taste of what you're facing here. I wanted you to understand that I'm not leaving you alone until I get what I want from you, and if the other professors here don't want me to harm you on their property, I'll take you away, and nothing in this world will stop me."

Ap'Gravin stared at him, his eyes hollow, his blue flesh wan. He looked over to Oylla, who still lingered by the door to his cell, and asked, "You'll stand by and let this animal threaten me?"

"There's no love lost between you and me." Her voice was flinty, not an ounce of sympathy in it, then she shrugged and added, "If this man takes you too quickly for me to follow or too forcefully for me to stop, I won't lose sleep. I'll make my report and be done with it."

"I might be down, woman, but I'm not out. I will come back from this, and you know with my father's resources, I'll make you pay for that insolence."

Victor leaned forward and rested one of his large, strong hands on ap'Gravin's shoulder. "I don't think making threats is going to serve you well. You should hunt for a new tone to use."

Ap'Gravin shook his head slowly in defeat and said, "Oylla. Remove the spell script from the back of my neck. A bit of fire is all it will take. Not enough to injure me!"

"Oh? What is it, a mind trap? Have you locked away the memories Victor wants you to share?"

"That's right, wench," he growled, leaning forward as Oylla brushed aside his hair, revealing the flesh of his neck. Victor couldn't see what she was doing from his position, but a moment later, a wisp of pink smoke drifted into the air, and ap'Gravin cursed—a word the System didn't translate—and glared at her. "You did that on purpose."

"Did I?" She smiled and leaned a shoulder against the wall, looking at something behind Victor and smiling. Victor followed her gaze and saw Valla standing there with her arms folded, a rather wicked grin of her own revealing sharp teeth.

"Well?" he asked, turning back to the still cowering, haunted-looking man.

"Bah! It's nothing—a trifling transgression. To be honest, I'm not sure why I locked this memory away. I took a bit of blood from the infirmary, a sample the nurse kept after that upstart was cracked in the head by a stone. I gathered many such from many promising students. My father was doing research into bloodlines with the help of some off-world mage. A complete waste of time, if I recall correctly; he abandoned the project and cut ties with the charlatan."

"Nurse Tyliste helped you?"

"What? No. She was unaware. What does it matter? This is nothing! Why, it's practically my right as a senior professor!"

"I don't think so," Victor growled.

"You'd be correct, Victor." Oylla moved away from the wall and produced, seemingly out of thin air, a pen and a length of parchment. She held them out to the bedraggled ap'Gravin and said, "Professor, I think I'll need you to write a statement and list the names of every student whose privacy and security you violated."

"I think not!" He pointedly looked away from the proffered writing utensils and focused his eyes somewhere near the base of the stairs to Victor's right.

"So, what sort of summoning spell was your father doing with Boaegh? So far, you've told me very little I hadn't figured out for myself."

"Exactly as I said! Summoning relations of gifted students. I don't know the details of the summoning rituals; I was never a part of them. I handed my father the samples on visits home, and that was that."

"That was that?" Victor pressed. "A *senior* professor at an esteemed magical school finds out his father is doing a ritual to summon people from around the universe to 'research bloodlines' and doesn't get at all curious?" Victor held up his fingers in quotation marks as he spoke, though it seemed the gesture only served to confuse the professor. The sarcastic tone wasn't lost on the man, though; he shifted uncomfortably.

"Fine, if you must know, the charlatan insisted he knew a way to steal bloodlines and, failing that, to siphon potency from powerful Energy users. It was laughable, though. Those few he attempted to summon from this world resisted his efforts, and most of those summoned from off-world were so pitiful in their development that they were utterly useless. My father sent the slithering fool packing after a few months." Ap'Gravin's voice cracked, and he licked his lips, clearly suffering from a dry mouth. He'd recovered a bit from the ordeal Victor had put him through, but he was obviously still shaken.

"The spell, though, tell me about it. Could it have pulled the victims from the past?" He leaned closer but eased his attempts to intimidate; it seemed ap'Gravin was ready to talk.

"An intriguing question." Ap'Gravin sighed and sat up a bit straighter, leaning back into the stone wall. He glanced at Oylla, at the parchment in her hand that she'd let fall to her thigh, and sighed again, more dramatically. "Oh, old lady's bones! I'll tell you what I know, but it isn't much. My father hired a dozen Energy users to work with that snake. The only prerequisites to their hiring were a strong will, a large Energy pool, and a willingness to sign a binding contract, one that wouldn't allow them to speak about his work. I only know that much because my father bragged to me about how easy it was to bend people to his bidding with a bit of treasure."

"Go on." Victor's voice was calm, but his steady gaze and stony countenance made him appear implacable.

"So, he had more than two dozen of these pocket casters, essentially living Energy stones. Boaegh's summon spell could have been potent indeed, given the right ritual space, which, for the record, I never saw. Still, my father did talk about it; he'd spent a fortune on rare materials, one of which was a primal fire conduit. So, to answer your question, I'd say with that sort of ritualized effort involved, breaching time as well as space would have been possible."

"Is that true, Oylla?" Valla asked from behind Victor.

"I'm not an expert on summoning rituals, but it sounds plausible. I don't understand how summoning through time would work, however. What's to stop me from summoning an earlier version of myself, thereby making it impossible for her to experience my life and, in the end, summon herself? Isn't that a paradox?" Oylla lifted one hand to tap the pen against her chin, her eyes staring distantly into space.

"You are ignorant." Ap'Gravin snorted.

"Go on," Victor growled, some of his earlier irritation entering his voice.

"When you alter a timeline in such a way, it creates another. In this time-line, Oylla, you weren't summoned. In your hypothetical example, the earlier Oylla would cease to exist in her timeline, removed as though mysteriously murdered or lost. Life would go on without her, just as it would if you died now—in a matter of a few weeks, the school would hire a new professor, and all of your simpering, fawning students would forget you as they went on with their lives."

"Lovely as always, Professor." Oylla frowned, shook her head, and added, "Still, he is more expert in these matters than I. I suppose it makes sense with what I know of multiple universes. I do recall reading about timelines and their many branches in one obscure text or another."

Victor stood up, shaking his head. He didn't feel as if he'd gained much at all from ap'Gravin. A bunch of maybes and possibilities. He looked at the still cowering man and said, "Well, it looks like I'll never know exactly what happened unless maybe this guy's father was present for the summoning. Maybe he has the details of the spell, or he knows the names of some of the *pendejos* that helped Boaegh." He turned to Valla and added, "Unless we killed them all when we dealt with ap'Horrin. Anyway, the father's easy enough to find, huh? Pretty famous noble around Persi Gables?"

"My father? He owns much of that city and Gelica. Approach him at your peril." Ap'Gravin managed to sound proud, disgraced though he was.

"You can put him back in his cell. You want me to?" Victor leaned forward as if to grab the professor by the robes, but the man squirmed to the side and, on his hands and knees, scurried into his cell. Oylla smirked and closed the door behind him.

"I'm sorry you went to all that trouble." She gestured at the pool of drying blood near Victor's feet and the room in general as if to indicate the shadows that had once filled it. "For very little gain. At least I heard his confession about stealing students' blood; he'll be disgraced, and many powerful families will demand justice. Endangering students in such a way will be a black mark on his family's name for decades."

"Oh, I didn't gain much from him, but I gained plenty from my . . . theatrics. It's hard to explain, so I won't. Let's just say I'm sorry you had to see that; I know it was disgusting." Victor pulled a towel from one of his storage rings and worked on scrubbing his chin; he could feel the drying blood beginning to itch uncomfortably.

"I've seen worse. Tell me, Victor, how do you manipulate your size the way you do? Weren't you my height when you first came to my office?"

"He was," Valla said, stepping closer. "It's an uncanny ability of his, though not one that can be taught. Sorry, Oylla."

Victor offered Valla a quick smile; he wasn't sure why she felt the need to speak for him—he knew better than to share Tes's magic—but he didn't mind. He concentrated for a moment, then cast the spell in question, feeding it the same amount of Energy as he had back in the inn. A moment later, he was no longer looking down at the professor but stood eye-to-eye with her. "That should keep me from banging my head on the lintels, eh?"

"If only just." Oylla chuckled.

"Listen," Victor said, "I appreciate you standing by and helping me to bluff that guy when I threatened to take him out of here."

"He's always been a bit of a thorn in my side. I was happy to play along. I'm glad to hear it *was* just a bluff, by the way."

"Yeah, of course." Victor shrugged and reached an arm around Valla's shoulders. "I wouldn't want to cause that kind of trouble for Valla and her family."

"That's good to hear . . ." Valla patted his wrist and smiled up at him.

"Things worked out well enough," Oylla said, speaking almost simultaneously with Valla. She lowered her volume and trailed off a bit when she realized she was interrupting. Valla just shrugged and nodded to her, then the professor added, "Will there be anything else? I'm sure Jaxin-dak will send a report to the ap'Yensha household along with all the other alumni with news of ap'Gravin's confession and subsequent punishment once the board metes it out."

"What if he locks his memories away again and denies everything you say?" Victor asked.

"Little chance of that with the collar he's wearing. He'd struggle to create a light, let alone practice advanced mind magic."

"All right, then. Let's go, Valla. I don't know if I'll ever learn more about how I was summoned, but I suppose we can ask the professor's father if we ever find the time. Right now, we have an army we're supposed to meet."

"An army?" Oylla looked intrigued.

"Victor's leading a conquest of the Untamed Marches with my household."

"Truly? That'll be the first expansion attempt in a very long time. More than my lifetime, for certain." She turned back to Victor, her eyes narrowing with renewed interest. "Do you have a large force?"

"Well, Lady Rellia and Captain Lam have been gathering troops for months now. I think they were hoping to gather some two thousand, but I don't have the latest numbers." Victor looked down at Valla, wondering if she'd provide more details.

"Oh! Wait a moment," Oylla said before Valla could chime in. "Rellia ap'Yensha, Persi Gables . . . Now it's falling into place!" She tapped her temple. "There's been an army growing there all spring! Some of the students were talking about it when they came for the new term, thousands of tents out in the grasslands beyond the city's walls."

"That's right. Victor's being modest, as well." Valla shifted out from under his arm and gave his shoulder a friendly slap. "Rellia has raised nearly a full legion—six thousand men and women ready to push into the Marches for glory."

"Glory," Victor said, smiling at the coincidence of her phrasing.

"Something funny?" Valla raised an eyebrow, taking another step back.

"I'll tell you later. Anyway—" Victor turned to the tall, sparkling-eyed Shadeni and held out a hand. "Thanks, Oylla-dak. I appreciate your patience with me."

"I won't say I wasn't worried, on the verge of acting, honestly, when you filled the room with those cloying black shadows, but still"—she reached forward to grasp his hand, her grip surprisingly strong—"it was nice to meet you. Good luck with your conquest; I'm sure we'll be hearing more about you and your escapades."

Victor nodded, smiling, more relaxed than he thought he should be. He hadn't really learned much from the disgraced professor, but he felt more at ease, more accomplished. As he turned to the stairs, gesturing for Valla to precede him, he wondered if his good mood had more to do with what he'd accomplished with his Core than anything involving ap'Gravin. As he followed Valla up, he turned his vision inward, admiring the four pulsing, throbbing spheres of his attunements—smoldering crimson rage, gleaming white-gold inspiration, glowering purple-black fear, and glittering golden glory. Victor was pleased with what he saw.

Valla quickly guided them to the main central hallway of the academy, and Victor moved to walk beside her as they turned toward the bright, sunlit exit. "I leveled when I ate that heart. I also gained three ranks in my Core and unlocked a new affinity." He laughed when Valla rewarded him with the expected outrage.

"Seriously?" she cried, her voice rising with disbelief. "How does someone so reckless always come out on top?"

"In my defense, it was a close thing—that heart wanted to boost my fear affinity way past my others. I almost lost myself to it, but then I had the idea to use the extra Energy to create a fourth affinity."

"How is that in your defense?"

"Well, I mean, it wasn't just luck; I had to scramble to avoid some pretty hefty consequences for my reckless behavior. You see?"

"I see. So. You're Level Fifty. Before you tell me about that, tell me about your new affinity." Valla quickened her steps, moving around some slow, gossiping students, their ribboned, curly-haired heads pressed together as they whispered.

"Well," Victor replied, hurrying after her, "that's what I was grinning about back there. It's glory. My new affinity is glory."

"Glory? That's an affinity?" Valla frowned but nodded as she thought it over. "I suppose it's not much stranger than inspiration. In stories, Spirit Casters always have affinities like hate, fear, and love. One story I remember had a king of the Urghat whose affinity was greed, and he drove his people to wild, terrible acts of war in pursuit of riches."

"Glad I didn't find an affinity like that . . ." Victor narrowed his eyes, remembering his hurried thoughts as he'd struggled to find his new affinity. He'd followed his emotions and hadn't really had a say in the matter when the gray, unattuned orb began to fill with glory. What would he have done if it had started to fill with something like hate or greed?

Valla interrupted his dreary what-ifs, asking, "Well? What about your level? Fifty is quite a milestone!"

"I haven't looked yet! Been busy talking to you, that creepy professor, and that not-so-creepy Oylla-dak."

"She was something else, wasn't she? I've never seen a Shadeni with eyes like that. Is it a bloodline, do you think?"

"Maybe." Victor shrugged.

"Okay, so . . ." Valla almost stepped on a little girl rolling a bright red wooden ball over the cobbles. "Oh, dear!" She scooped the little Ghelli up and carried her to the sidewalk with her ball. "I almost stepped on you, sweetie. Be careful! What if I had been a roladii?"

"You don't look like a roladii," the girl replied sweetly, brushing a wave of curly hair out of her eyes to inspect Valla more carefully.

"Cheeky." Valla laughed, holding out her ball. "Take this and be more careful!"

Victor watched the interaction with a stupid grin, happy to see something so innocent play out. "Better than talking about war, I guess. Shit," he said as they started walking again, "that reminds me! Rellia really raised that many troops?"

"She and Lam. People are hungry for adventure and conquest. The Empire has stagnated for too long, the power locked up by too few. If we don't go soon, Rellia fears our little army will be the seed of a true insurrection."

"You called it a 'legion.' Is that a technical term? I mean, 'cause you call the Empire's army 'the Legion,' too."

"The Ridonne Empire keeps a standing army of six thousand troops at the capital. That's the main Legion, with a capital L. Of course, there are six other equally sized forces loyal to the Empire stationed in strategic locations. When people say 'Legion,' they're talking about any of those armies."

"So, a legion is six thousand soldiers?"

"That's right. Each legion has ten cohorts led by a captain, and each cohort has six divisions led by lieutenants. Smaller units within each division are called squads, and those are headed by sergeants. I'm sure Rellia and Lam have been busy trying to organize the troops in such a fashion."

"That's so weird." Victor scratched his head. "The System is translating some of those military offices and terms in a confusing manner to me; some of the words, like captain, sound like modern terms, I mean from my world, and then others, like legion and cohort, are straight out of ancient history."

"Yes." Valla nodded, guiding him past the busy square and toward the gatehouse where the main road intersected the wall. "That's how it works. The System is trying to best fit the meaning of the word I'm using with the word in your vocabulary. I'm not surprised they don't match your world's military terms; I mean altogether."

He heard her words, but a new sight grabbed his attention as they rounded the corner. "Ah! So that's the airship!" Victor shaded his eyes and looked over a rooftop. He could just see the corner of the wall surrounding the academy grounds and a ship hanging in the air tethered by a series of long, thick cables to the crenellated tower. It looked pretty large, but the perspective of looking up from some distance away made it hard to judge. Still, he thought he saw figures moving on the deck, which gave the impression of a vessel similar in size to pirate ships he'd seen in movies and games.

It was shaped like a wooden galley, with high fore and aft decks and portholes along the sides, but the resemblance ended there. The sails were more like wings—huge silvery spans held taut by wooden beams jutting out from either side of the hull. Big circular metallic rings lined the keel and emitted yellow, pulsing light. Were those what kept the craft aloft?

"Yes! There it is," Valla replied, "the *Wind Dancer*. Are you sure you want to get going right away? Shouldn't you explore your options for refining your class?"

"I'll do it on the ship. How long will it take to get to Persi Gables?"

"Only two days on the airship, assuming nothing goes wrong." Valla pointed to a stone stairway leading up to the top of the wall next to the gate. "We can get up to the rampart there."

"Right. Let's get aboard, and then I'll check out my refinement options. You aren't interested in that, right? I'll just lock myself in my cabin and . . ." Valla turned and punched him hard in the shoulder, and Victor laughed. "Hey!"

"You better tell me about your refinements!"

"I was joking! Sheesh!" He winced, hamming it up, rubbing his shoulder as though she'd hurt him, and Valla chuckled, shaking her head. Together they mounted the steps and made their way over the ramparts toward the ship, and Victor was glad to be moving to the next phase of his adventure; he'd had enough of Fainhallow.

10

ABOARD THE *WIND DANCER*

Victor stood on the prow of the *Wind Dancer* and watched the mountain slopes drift by beneath the ship. They'd just cast off a few minutes ago, but the academy was already lost to sight, having slipped from view as the ship traversed the mountain passes. The weather was good, and according to Captain ap'Veral, it was easier to keep the vessel down among the peaks so long as they didn't need to avoid storms. Victor turned away from the railing and walked over the springy, polished decking to the hatch leading down to the crew compartments. He and Valla had each been assigned a small room.

"Where are you going?" Valla called, hurrying over. She'd been speaking with the first mate, a hairy, goat-horned Cadwalli named Grez.

"Down to my room; time to look at my upgrade options." Victor grinned at her outraged face and pressed on, "I was going to tell you before I selected something."

"Oh, I would hope so! Come, let's see what's in store for you." She ducked past him, through the narrow doorway, and down the short flight of steps to the cramped hallway below. Victor followed, very grateful for the spell Tes had taught him. If he'd had to traverse the ship's narrow, low-ceilinged passageways at his full height, he might just have found his room and stayed there for the entire voyage. Valla stopped before his door and waited for him to catch up and open it.

"Come on, then," he said, stepping into the room. It was small but very nicely appointed. A narrow bed lined one wall, a small writing desk and chair sat near the door, and built-in cabinets and shelving lined the walls. The shelves were all protected by a brass bar that could be lowered to access the contents; it was meant to keep things from falling out during rough weather. Currently, the shelves were lined with books and curios that Victor hadn't had a chance to examine; presumably they were there to give the space more of a lived-in look, or perhaps they had been left by a former occupant.

He stepped over to the bed, neatly made with a gray blanket and two fluffy white pillows, and sat on the edge. Valla sat in the desk chair after closing the door behind her. "I'll be patient. Take your time and read through them," she said, folding one long, uniformed leg over the other.

"All right." Victor nodded, then he went to his status menu and selected the option for class refinement:

*****Class refinement option 1: Titanic Champion, Legendary. Prerequisites: 1. The strong presence of a titanic bloodline originating from an Elder race. 2. A Spirit Core with affinities for Glory and one or more of Inspiration, Bravery, Honor, or Loyalty. A paragon of your people, you thrive on achieving the impossible. You stand ready to take up the fight when others flee the battlefield. Class attributes: strength, vitality, will, agility, dexterity, intelligence.*****

"Oh, shit!" Victor said, grinning broadly at Valla after reading his first option. "I got a really cool-sounding option!"

"I'm not surprised." Valla chuckled. "Another legendary class?"

"Yeah. Titanic Champion, and it requires my new affinity. It doesn't give unbound attributes, but the ones it does give are listed in a different order than my current class. Attributes listed first are usually given more points, right?"

"That's right." Valla nodded.

"Right. Well, let me read the next one." Victor moved to the next option and studied it:

*****Class refinement option 2: Quinametzin Foe Slayer, Legendary. Prerequisites: 1. Sufficiently advanced Quinametzin bloodline. 2. Epic-level Berserk or Berserk-like ability. 3. Epic-level strength or vitality. You have unlocked the secrets of one of your primogenitor's classes. Accepting this new Class will grant you abilities based upon those buried deep in the history of your blood. Class attributes: strength, vitality.*****

"Uh. Well, it's not going to be an easy decision, I guess." He frowned and scratched absently at the stubble on his cheek while he read through the description again.

"Well? What is it?" Valla pressed.

"I thought you were going to be patient."

"I was, but then you told me about your first option, so now I'm too curious to relax!" She leaned forward, and Victor smiled, enjoying this bit of leverage he had over her.

"Well, it's not that great. I don't want to tell you something embarrassing. I mean, you didn't talk to me when you went through your Tier Five refinement . . ."

"Victor! I've been Tier Five since you met me!" She leaned forward and punched him in the knee, and her knuckles delivered a surprisingly painful crunch.

"Easy!" he said, laughing. "All right, all right. It's a Quinametzin Foe Slayer. I guess it's based on my bloodline; the System message seems to indicate that it figured out the class based on my progress with unlocking my, uh, inner Quinametzin. It only grants strength and vitality on level-ups, so you can kinda guess what sort of class it is."

"I could guess that from the name—Foe Slayer. The description doesn't contain warnings like that Rager class you were offered last time?"

"Nope."

"I suppose it would be nice to learn more of your Quinametzin ancestry, to gain some of their abilities beyond what you know, but the champion class sounds better to me." Valla shrugged and held her palms up on her knees as though showing she had nothing more to offer.

"Well, yeah. Let me see what else there is." Victor advanced the System screen and read the following page:

*****Class refinement option 3: Quinametzin Spirit Channeler, Legendary. Prerequisites: 1. Sufficiently advanced Quinametzin bloodline. 2. Sufficiently advanced Spirit Core. 3. Epic-level will. You have unlocked the secrets of one of your primogenitor's classes. Accepting this new Class will grant you abilities based upon those buried deep in the history of your blood. Class attributes: will, intelligence.*****

Victor described the third class and asked, "Do you think I'm getting these Quinametzin options because I took the Titanic Herald Class last time?"

"It would make sense. Didn't the description of that one say something about bringing your ancient bloodline to light or some such?"

"Yeah. Again, not an easy decision, but based on the class attributes, I think it would be a pretty big change from what I've been doing. I wish the

System would tell me more about the damn classes rather than that vague, 'You have unlocked the secrets, blah blah.' Like, what secrets? You know?"

"Yes, it's frustrating . . ." Valla's eyes opened wide, and she twisted a little ring on her pinky. "Wait! Tes gave me books from Coloss about class advancements! Let me see if I can find anything."

"I doubt there'll be anything about Quinametzin," Victor said, frowning, but Valla was already flipping through a thick book, so he just looked at his next option:

*****Class refinement option 4: Battlemaster, Epic. Prerequisites: 1. Sufficiently advanced bloodline. 2. Sufficiently advanced weapon skills. 3. Sufficiently advanced attributes. 4. A Core with appropriate affinities. 5. A history with and love for combat. In your life, you've known strife well. Not only have you survived the many conflicts in your path, but you've thrived on them. A Battlemaster seeks to become a paragon of conflict, an aficionado of destruction and survival. Class attributes: strength, vitality, agility, dexterity, will, intelligence.*****

"What the hell?" Victor frowned, rereading the option. Valla looked up from the book and raised an eyebrow, so he continued, "My fourth option was only epic. It sounds really plain, but it has a lot of prerequisites—Battlemaster."

"So, you were offered three legendary classes and then an epic one?" Valla drummed her nails on the book, then said, "That is very unusual. I've only ever heard of options increasing in rarity on the System's menu."

"So, maybe it's more rare." Victor frowned and shook his head. "No, it can't be. I'm the only Quinametzin alive, right? Maybe it's more exclusive? Has harder-to-meet prerequisites? I don't know."

"Maybe. Let me see here. That might be easier to find." Valla reopened the book, and Victor checked to see if there were any other class options:

*****Class refinement option 5: No Refinement. You are pleased with the path on which you find yourself and choose to continue until your next refinement option.*****

"That was the last one."

"Mm-hmm. Just a minute. Oh, Victor! Battlemaster is in this book!" Valla grew quiet, and her eyes rapidly tracked the text she was reading, so Victor tried to be patient. He leaned back on the bed and stared at the ceiling, thinking about his options. If he had to choose at that moment, he felt he'd lean toward the first one, the Titanic Champion Class. "Victor, the Battlemaster Class is almost never offered and highly sought after. It seems the Vesh often strived to get that offering. The hardest part is the final prerequisite; the

System isn't fair or methodical about whom it awards the 'history with and love for combat' prerequisite to."

"Huh?"

"There are countless anecdotes about warriors, gladiators, and duelists trying to gain this class. Very few see it offered early on—before Tier Ten—and usually, by the time they do see it, they've started down a road they don't want to change. One man, a great arena champion named Lobsos, claimed to have a record of more than ten thousand personal combats on his way to Tier Ten but never was offered the Battlemaster Class."

"So, what's so great about it?"

"Two things. Apparently, people with the Battlemaster Class are often awarded skills and abilities that outperform those of other epic-level classes. More, though, it's a prerequisite for some legendary classes that are highly coveted on Zaafor. Let's see. Huh." She frowned. "You'd think those skills and abilities would be listed, but it starts to get vague again. Here's an anecdote about a Battlemaster who could 'project his blade, sweeping the battlefield of chaff,' whatever that means. Another anecdote of a Battlemaster who was nearly impossible to harm. He left Zaafor in search of greater challenges."

"Okay, does it list what the classes it opens up are?"

"They're only hinted at. It seems the Battlemasters who advanced were a bit tight-lipped. Victor! The Warlord was a Battlemaster!"

"Seriously?"

"Yes! At Tier Seven. He never told anyone what class refinements he took after that."

"Huh." Victor frowned and groaned. He still lay on his back, his legs hanging off the bed. He rubbed his eyes with the backs of his hands and sighed. "Why isn't any decision ever easy? When I read my first option, I was like, this is it! Now I have no idea what to do. Do you think it would be wise to step down from a legendary class to take an epic class in the hopes of some hinted-at, super rare refinements?"

"I don't know. What about your mentor?" Valla gestured toward the bracer on Victor's wrist.

"Yeah. I was going to ask him, but I kind of wanted a better idea of what I was going to do first. Khul Bach is a little . . . judgmental." He chuckled and shook his head ruefully. He reached for the pink gem on his bracer and said, "I'll be right back. I'm not sure you'll even notice I'm gone." Before Valla could reply, he channeled Energy into the gem, and the world around him changed.

The color bled from everything, and then the walls, furnishings, and even Valla faded to nothing. In that weird plane of white and gray light and strange, sharp angles and reflections, he saw Khul Bach seated before him, as always, his eyes open and expectant. "You come to me much improved, young titan! You've grown in power. I sense a new complexity in the Energy you sent into the crystal. A new affinity?"

"That's right," Victor said. "I uncovered an affinity for glory. Are you familiar with it? I haven't done any experimenting yet."

"Glory! Cousin to pride and the light side of shadowy lust. It's a good affinity, especially for one set on fighting his way to greatness. Congratulations, Victor."

"Thank you. I also reached Level Fifty and have a difficult decision to make."

"Ah! Tell me, then, lad. What are your options?"

Victor pulled up his class refinement menu again and read through the various options. Khul Bach nodded along, making little sounds of interest and even a few exclamations like, "Oh!" a few times. Still, it wasn't until Victor read his final option that Khul Bach began to get agitated, clearly eager to say something. When Victor finished reading it, he nodded and said, "That's the one."

"But it's only epic." Victor's lips quirked into a small smile at his words—imagine saying "only" epic!

"Yes, but it leads to one of the best legendary classes known to my people."

"Do you know what it is? 'Cause the book Valla got in Coloss only hints about it."

"Of course I do. The leader of the Degh during my youth, Brodarak, was a Battlemaster. He joined the Ancestor Stone shortly after I did, and I learned of his refinement. What's more, you met one who was a Battlemaster, did you not? The upstart mutant, the king of the Vesh, Warlord Thoargh."

"Yeah. Valla said the book listed him as one of the few who'd gotten the Battlemaster Class. He never told anyone what his refinement was, though."

"Ha! Yes, he did! Why, I called him by his refinement just seconds ago."

Victor looked at Khul Bach blankly for a moment, but he wasn't stupid; he connected the dots and said softly, "Warlord? That was his class refinement?"

"Yes. He may well have ensured that he was the only one after he broke the Degh."

"Is it that good? You really think I should take this Battlemaster Class?"

"Indeed. I believe it will make your conquest of Zaafor that much easier."

"Do you think the, uh, Warlord kept that refinement, or do you think he changed it after ten levels and just made people keep calling him that?"

"I have no idea about the answer to that one. It may be that the class is so good that it's worth keeping over other options, or it may be that it led him to better and better refinements. Regardless, your choice is clear. Follow an assured path to greatness, or gamble with one of your other offerings. You're young and still relatively low tier, though. If you take Battlemaster now, you will have further chances to refine it into something else. Perhaps Warlord, perhaps something better. You know what I recommend." Khul Bach folded his arms and settled back, his shoulders slumping slightly to indicate that he was done with the matter.

"All right. Thanks, Coach. I'll speak with you again soon."

"Coach, hmm? Let's not get too flippant, young titan. Very well. Continue your good work."

Victor smiled, pleased at the praise, then he severed the connection between his Energy and the crystal, and the world snapped back into being, replacing the white, angular expanse of Khul Bach's crystal plane. As he refocused on his room in the airship, he heard the tail end of Valla's words: " . . . just wait for you here."

"I'm back!" He laughed, sitting up on the side of the bed again.

"So fast? Wasn't he available?"

"He was! We spoke for several minutes. Time in the crystal is weird. Anyway, he gave me some advice. It was kinda weird, to be honest. Last time he made me listen to all his reasoning, then he led me to the decision I wanted to make. This time he basically just told me what to do."

"Which was?"

"He thinks I should take the Battlemaster refinement. He said his old leader or ruler, or whatever, had that class. He also told me what the Warlord's refinement was." Victor grinned, wondering how best to tease Valla about what he'd learned.

"Truly? He knew the Warlord?"

"He knew of him. Still, you're going to feel silly when you learn what the refinement is . . ."

"Warlord!" Valla clapped her hands together as she connected Victor's ham-handed clues.

"Really? You got it that easily? I just had to say you'd feel silly?"

"It was obvious after that." Valla nodded. "Well? What will you do?"

"Honestly? I want to resist all the advice. I want to make my own choice and go with one of the Quinametzin classes or the first one, the Titanic

Champion. I mean, they all sound better than Battlemaster to me, and I hate being told what to do." Valla nodded, but her eyes narrowed, and Victor could tell she was about to give him some advice, so he beat her to it. "Look, I said I want to do that. I didn't say I was going to. That book says the Battlemaster Class is rare and coveted, Khul Bach told me to take it, and that might be enough, but really the thing that clinches it for me is that the System presented it last, even though it's an epic option and my others were all legendary."

"I couldn't have said it better." Valla nodded. "It might feel like a step back, going from a legendary class to an epic one, but I think it will pay off. I think you're making a wise decision. A mature one."

"Oh, brother." Victor chuckled. "You trying to get me to change my mind?" Valla's eyes widened, and he laughed. "Just kidding. Well? Should I do it now?"

"Yes, unless you want to ask the sailors for advice."

"Tempting, but nah." Victor opened his menu again and scrolled through the options until he saw Battlemaster and selected it.

Congratulations! You have refined your Class: Battlemaster.

Congratulations! You have earned a Class spell: Energy Charge, Basic.

Energy Charge, Basic: Use the Energy in your Core to shield and propel you in a straight line at terrific speed for a short distance. Those in your path will be knocked aside and suffer damage. Energy Cost: 1000. Cooldown: Short.

Congratulations! You have earned a Class feat: Battlefield Awareness.

Battlefield Awareness: You have an uncanny knack for knowing where you are needed on the battlefield. You can sense when a line is about to break or where people suffer the most. You can also gauge, at a glance, the relative strength of one group of soldiers versus another.

11

A DETOUR

Victor stared at the ceiling of his cabin, watching the shifting light coming in through his porthole as it flickered over the wooden planks. The ship was moving quickly, and the clouds outside made the light and shadows dance in hypnotic patterns. They were more than halfway to their destination, still passing through intermittent mountain ranges but rapidly approaching the Beliss Peaks, where the ship would break free and, supposedly, fly over Lake Beliss and make a final approach to Persi Gables. Victor had seen enough of Lake Beliss to know that it wasn't something a ship, even an airship, would cross in a matter of minutes. No, if he were to guess, he'd say the lake was similar to the Great Lakes back on Earth, more an inland sea by conventional terms.

While the ship progressed through the sky, Victor was relaxing, wasting time, and waiting for dinner; the captain had invited him and Valla to his table on this, their last night aboard. Victor had gone to his cabin a little after noon with plans to cultivate Energy or study his spell patterns—he'd had the idea of trying to improve or combine some of his existing spells now that he knew a lot more about spell patterns in general, and now that he had the elder magic feat.

As soon as he'd entered the cabin, though, and reclined on the bed, he'd had a hard time focusing on anything productive. His mind kept wandering to Old Mother and wondering how long she'd waited for him on the spirit plane. He thought about Thayla and Deyni, sort of wishing he could drop everything and visit them, but knowing full well that he couldn't afford to disappear for a week or more, not when a legion of soldiers awaited him. Those thoughts spurred a whole rabbit hole of others—would he be taken seriously by the soldiers? Would he know what to do? How would he manage while fighting on a battlefield?

It seemed he'd made a good choice with Battlemaster as his new class; his new feat seemed tailor-made for his near future. "Maybe a lot more than near future," he amended softly, thinking about going to war with the Vesh on Zaafor. It seemed battles, wars, and armies would feature prominently in his future. Thinking of his future made him think of Tes, which made him think of Valla, and more stress began to build in his chest, banishing any hope of a productive afternoon. Growling, Victor sat up and pulled his Far Scribe book from his storage ring, hoping Lam had written back to him with some news that would distract him.

He wasn't surprised to find a letter from her; she'd probably been desperate for news and had written to him immediately. Thinking that, he felt a little bad for waiting until now to check. With a scowling brow, he began reading, noting right away that the message was in Lam's flowery hand, not Edeya's neat print:

Victor,

It's wonderful to hear from you. I'm pleased to know you've made so much progress while you were away. I never doubted that you'd return, for the record. Despite Rellia's reluctance to share her captain's missives with me, she did so, even if it took far too much prodding and poor Edeya wearing a rut between our two villas. Speaking of Edeya, she's done an excellent job clerking for me, and she's stepping into an administrative role for the legion.

You've heard, I'm sure, that our recruitment is progressing beyond our wildest hopes. We've gathered more than six thousand troops, many of whom are veterans and fortune-seekers, not just desperate Tier Ones and Twos. We have plenty of those, but I'd say our average level is better than many of the Empire's armies. This brings me to your concerns.

You're wise to voice them to me, first of all, and I'd like to suggest you keep them between us. I'm not sure who we can trust. I want to trust Rellia, but I fear she's been playing the game for far too long. If she sees a way to make gains for herself or her family in our betrayal, I wouldn't be shocked. I'll leave it at that as far as she's concerned; I have no evidence that she's being disloyal or dishonest, but I have a general level of distrust when it comes to the nobility.

Secondly, I'd like you to know that we're planning an unorthodox approach to the Marches. We'll avoid significant population centers, avoid well-traveled roadways, and yes, this will slow our progress, but it will make ambushes difficult. Rellia has two airships, one she owns and the other she's hired, that will scout for us. Nearly twenty percent of the army is mounted, and we've been working on mobility drills for months now. An ambush will be difficult, but should it happen, I think anyone without up-to-the-minute intelligence on our force will be surprised by its strength.

As to your request for a sparring partner, I have good news: Polo Vosh is already with the army. He and many of my old friends are taking on leadership positions with the force. He's eager to see what you've learned and to spar with you, by the way—I shared your request, and he was enthusiastic.

Please keep correspondence between us in this Far Scribe book and keep others from viewing it; never leave it lying around. I feel foolish and a bit embarrassed to write such obvious words of advice, but I fear it's my nature; I cannot abide an unchecked box. Stay well, travel safely, and keep your guard up; there are, as you have guessed, many snakes in this Empire, and few of them wish for our endeavor to be successful.

In great anticipation,
Captain Lam

Victor smiled, imagining Polo Vosh shouting orders to some undisciplined recruits. He was glad that Lam's thinking regarding risks from the Empire or other nobility matched up with his own. He still had hopes of meeting with Olivia Bennet while in Persi Gables, but as far as he was concerned, the sooner the army got moving, the better. He wanted to get on with this chapter in his life, fulfill his obligations to Rellia and the others, and be done with it. There was a big universe to explore, and he wouldn't make the gains he needed here, not on Fanwath.

He thought about that, about the "gains" he needed, and he chuckled. His mind kept going back to Tes, but he knew that would probably fade. Could he really keep a crush alive for ten, fifty, or a hundred years? "Well, what if I meet her again before then? Maybe she'll want to check in on me." Victor sighed again and frowned. He knew it wasn't healthy, especially when it made him push away perfectly wonderful people like Valla. "I haven't really pushed her away, though, have I?" Once again, his mind descended into turmoil—guilt mixing with desire, mixing with doubt.

After he'd chased his thoughts about relationships out of his mind, a more pertinent thought occurred to him, and he pulled a pen from his ring and began to write in the book:

Lam,

Message received. Don't worry, I only trust one person within a hundred miles of me, and that's Valla. I know, I know, she's loyal to Rellia, but we've been through a lot. Trust me, she's good. That's not what I'm writing about, though; I need you to find someone for me. It turns out other humans are on Fanwath, and one of them might be related to me and might have something to do with my summoning. I'd like to speak to her, and I believe she's in Persi Gables. She left Fainhallow by airship about a month ago and, according to the school's administrators, is still in the city. Would you locate her, please? I'd like to get the army moving ASAP, but I'd like to speak to her first. Her name is Olivia Bennet.

Thanks,
Victor

Victor slapped the book closed, put it away, and surged to his feet, suddenly feeling stifled, irritated, and too cooped up. He grabbed Lifedrinker and exited his room, moving to Valla's door. He knocked on it and called, "You in there?"

"Mm-hmm," Valla's voice replied. A few seconds later, he heard the door's lock click, and then she pulled it open. He stared at her—sleepy eyes, unkempt, glossy pale-green hair, white shirt hugging her slender form, tucked into her usual sleek uniform pants. She looked into his eyes, blinking and stifling a yawn, and said, "Something wrong?"

"What?" Victor realized he was holding Lifedrinker, unharnessed, and chuckled. "Nah. I just want to get my mind off a lot of . . . things. How'd you like to spar a bit up on deck?"

"Now?"

"Did I interrupt something important?" Victor grinned crookedly.

"I was napping! This ship lulls me so nicely, and the little bed is so cozy. What time is it?"

"I don't know. A few hours past noon. We've got time before dinner if that's what you're wondering about."

Valla stopped trying to fight it and yawned hugely, covering her mouth with one hand and squinting at him the whole while. When she was done, she nodded and said, "Fine. I'll meet you on deck." Then she closed the door.

Victor turned, walked to the end of the hallway, and bounded up the steps to the hatchway. Once outside, he found his guess was probably about right; the sun was moving toward the western horizon, but the shadows among the mountains were long and deep, and it felt later than it was. He looked about the deck, found it too crowded with sailors, ropes, and gear, and moved toward the aft section, up a few steps to the deck there. Plenty of open space greeted him, and Victor smiled, proceeding to stretch and limber up.

A few minutes later, Valla joined him, still dressed the same but walking, nimble and graceful as ever, with Midnight's naked blade resting on her shoulder. "So, some physical exertion is needed, hmm?" She glanced around the aft deck, watching an Ardeni sailor carrying a coiled rope down midship.

"Yeah. My mind was driving me crazy. I can't stop thinking about things."

"Nervous about the army? Or Rellia?" Valla gave him a sly smile as though she'd uncovered some sort of secret.

"Rellia? Nah. I'll let you handle her."

"Handle?" She frowned, then sighed. "Not exactly what I meant."

"Well, I am nervous about the army." Victor leaned forward on Lifedrinker's haft, her shiny metallic head resting on the wooden deck. "I love to fight. I'm good at it, too, but I have no idea what to do when it comes to leading soldiers."

"You'll catch on. Listen to Lam, listen to me, and we'll help you sound like you know what you're doing."

"Right. Sorry, sometimes I forget your title isn't just, you know, a title."

"That I actually earned it?" She winked at him, and Victor was trying to think of something clever to say, but then he saw her eyes tracking something behind him.

"What?" he asked, turning to look into the darkening blue sky. He saw a few distant dots hugging the eastern mountain slopes, flying in a sort of V pattern. "Birds?"

"Maybe, but don't they seem too large?"

Just then, a sailor's voice cried out from the watch castle on the foredeck, "Wings! Wings to stern, Captain!" His voice was strained with something like panic, which prompted Victor to stare harder at the flying dots, trying to see what the worry was.

"I wish I had some binoculars or something," he muttered, but then he saw Valla out of the corner of his eye, holding a brass tube to her eye. "Shit, you have a telescope?"

"Sure. It's not as powerful as some, but I can see . . ." She trailed off as she seemed to have zeroed in on the object of everyone's interest. "Strigaii with riders!"

"Strigaii?"

"Here," Valla said, handing him her scope.

Victor held the narrow end to his eye and felt a tickle of Energy in the device as it expanded his vision, zooming in on the five dots. He had to steady the brass tube, carefully moving it back toward the dots as it magnified his view. When it steadied, he saw what Valla had been talking about. Apparently, strigaii were giant lizards with wings and beaks and resembled nothing more than scaled chickens with enormous black wings.

Only one of them was in his view, but he saw a rider on its back, a man wearing glittering, pale-blue scaled armor. Atop his red-fleshed head, two enormous black horns rose from his forehead and curved backward, tapering to fine points. His face was set in a grimace of determination, and Victor could see his eyes glowing with sparkling, golden Energy. "Who's that asshole?"

"Good question. Tamed strigaii aren't cheap. I've only ever seen one before, and it was when I was in the Legion. One of the Emperor's principes flew one over our formation, performing an inspection."

"So, five? Chasing our ship? Can't be good, can it?"

"I wouldn't think so, but perhaps it's a coincidence. Perhaps they're merely traveling toward Persi Gables as well . . ."

As she spoke, amid the clamor of shouts and activity behind them, the watchman in the miniature wooden tower at the front of the ship cried out, his voice cutting through the rest of the noise, "Fire incoming!"

Victor pulled the tube from his eye, and, in his much broader view, he saw a dot of bright white-yellow light hanging in the sky behind them. "What the fuck?" Valla offered no explanation, and he continued to watch as the dot of bright light grew slowly larger. Suddenly the airship banked, and Victor stumbled into Valla, the two of them slamming against the waist-high wooden railing. Victor looked over his shoulder, heard shouts from the captain and crew, and realized they were trying to dodge the slowly approaching ball of fire.

"That's not going to work." Valla grunted, straightening and moving out from between Victor and the railing. "It's tracking us."

"Shit," Victor breathed, watching as, sure enough, the—much larger— ball of bright, roiling Energy shifted in the air and continued to pursue the ship. "It's going to hit us," he growled, reaching into his Core and severing the bindings on his form. Valla gasped in surprise as he suddenly increased in size, and the planks beneath his feet groaned and creaked as his mass suddenly intensified. "Stay by me," he said, moving between Valla and the incoming fireball.

"We should get below . . ."

"And be trapped? As this ship crashes? Look!" Victor pointed behind them, and Valla followed his gaze.

"More . . ." she breathed, noticing what Victor had seen as his titanic bloodline was unleashed and his vision improved: three more balls of fire were surging through the air toward the ship, tracking it.

"I'm guessing this little transport ship isn't designed to withstand attacks like that." He looked back at the scurrying crew and listened to the panicked, rapid orders of the first mate and captain. He turned back to the incoming fireball and guessed they had about twenty seconds before impact.

"Likely not," Valla said, shifting so that Victor was between her and the incoming projectile. Victor nodded, then began to step backward, one hand holding Lifedrinker, the other reaching back and holding onto Valla's shoulder, ensuring she walked with him. They'd just descended the aft deck's stairs and lost visual of the rapidly expanding ball of fire when the ship shuddered and surged. The helmsman was trying a last-minute dodge, driving the vessel straight upward. Victor squatted, his axe-wielding hand going to the steps to steady himself, and he felt Valla grab onto his belt.

The maneuver was for naught; with a deafening roar and concussion that flung the ship upward further, the fireball impacted the keel and sent splinters, embers, and smoking, smoldering projectiles through the air, darkening the skies on both sides of the ship. Crew members screamed and ran about, some were flung overside, and the captain bellowed and roared commands that were ignored—the airship was going down, and more missiles were incoming.

Victor had seen enough. He stood up, cast Iron Berserk, and as his size doubled and furious power filled his pathways, he grabbed Valla up, hugging her to his chest as he did back in Coloss when they had fled the Warlord. In two strides, he moved to the starboard side of the ship and scanned the mountainside below, growing closer as the vessel lost altitude. Victor watched the slopes and turned to look over his shoulder, trying to time the next fireball impact.

"Victor, what are you doing?" Valla asked, but she didn't struggle in his grasp.

"We can't stay here," he grunted. When he thought he couldn't wait anymore, he bunched his legs and leapt toward a stand of tall, greenish-blue trees below. Laterally, he only had to move fifty yards or so, so he didn't jump as hard as he could. Still, the decking cracked and exploded as he hurled himself over the railing, soaring through the air, trying to aim between two massive trees. With his Titanic Leap ability, he wasn't worried about harming himself as he landed, but he worried about Valla. He tucked her close, wrapping both arms around her, Lifedrinker still gripped tightly in his fist.

To her credit, Valla didn't scream, but he felt her press her face into his chest, and he didn't blame her—they were probably dropping five hundred yards toward the tree-covered slope, and it would have been terrifying if he weren't the size of a Quinametzin and filled with furious rage-attuned Energy. When he landed, the ground shuddered, nearby trees shook, dropping ten thousand blue-green needles to the ground, and Valla would have been yanked from his arms by the momentum if his arms weren't like enormous steel cables, holding her tight to his chest.

Still, Valla groaned and cried out, and he knew the impact hadn't been easy on her. Gently, Victor set her down, and she wobbled then fell to her butt on the loamy mountain slope, shaking her head dazedly. "Ancestors," she groaned. Victor didn't speak, but he turned and scanned the sky, waiting to see if any of their pursuers followed them. He was thinking about climbing a tree when Valla said, "Victor, put on your armor." He turned to see her doing just that, and he nodded.

"Good idea," he grunted, then he produced his wyrm-scale vest and shrugged into it, chuckling as it grew to accommodate him; he'd last worn it as a much smaller man. Once he'd sealed up the front of the vest, he pulled out his Kethian Juggernaut helm and put it onto his head. Thus girded for war, he hefted Lifedrinker and growled, "Come on, you fuckers. Come and look for me."

12

GUILTY PARTIES

A distant rumble sounded off to his right, muffled by the trees, and Valla said, "The ship went down."

"Yeah. Shit!" Victor grimaced and ground the knuckles of his left hand into the tree's rough bark, squeezing out sticky sap and sending crumbles to the soft, needle-covered ground at his feet. "I should have done something to help them!"

"You acted quickly. What could you have done? Leap into the air and try to block all the fireballs? I'm the one who should have stayed! I should have waited for the riders to get closer and struck them with lightning!"

"Nah," Victor said, his thoughts clarifying as he heard Valla's self-recrimination. "They weren't coming into range until all their little flaming missiles hit. They knew what they were doing."

"No, they didn't, not if they were sent for you. Did they really think a crashed airship would stop you?"

Victor grunted in response, scanning between the trees, trying to see any sign that the strigaii riders had landed and were searching for him. They must have seen him leap free; he wasn't exactly small. A flicker of movement downslope caught his attention, and he held up his hand for silence, staring at the spot. His eyes were good, amazing really, if you compared them to how he remembered his vision back on Earth. The flash of movement must have been half a mile distant, glimpsed between trees and underbrush, but he'd seen it, and as he stared, he caught another sighting of something bright, glinting in fading sunlight.

He pointed toward what he'd seen, and Valla nodded, shifting behind a tree, Midnight held ready in her two hands. Victor motioned to the right, then pointed to himself. When Valla nodded, he pointed to the left and then at her. She didn't wait for further instruction, slipping away through the trees, silent as a ghost as she glided down the hillside. Victor altered his Sovereign Will boost from strength and vitality to agility and dexterity and, surprisingly quiet for a giant, began to work his way through the trees to the right, downslope, trying to flank whomever he'd seen.

He held Lifedrinker ready in his hands and kept his rage-attuned Energy at bay in his pathways, ready to surge and explode into violence. Anyone seeing his face would have felt a near-irresistible urge to turn and move quickly in the opposite direction. His brows were heavy with fury, his mouth twisted in a grimace that promised violence. As he skulked through the trees, Victor channeled some fear-attuned Energy and cast Manifest Spirit, summoning a pack of silent, menacing purple-black coyotes. With a thought, Victor sent them out in a wider net, looking for his foes.

He'd covered half the ground toward the spot of color he'd seen and was moving between two massive blue-green needle-clad trees when, in a haze of white heat, a ball of flames erupted from the undergrowth not twenty yards ahead of him. Victor roared and stepped into the fiery missile, swinging Lifedrinker at it as though he meant to hit a baseball into the stands. The projectile of flame was larger than it appeared, and though he smashed the axe directly into its center, it exploded into a conflagration that stripped the area around Victor of life, blistering plants, blackening bark, and doing a fantastic job of stoking Victor's fury.

The impact with the fireball had awoken Lifedrinker, and her glowing, molten-metal fury came to the surface, rippling the air around her with waves of heat. Victor jumped, more forward than up, lifting Lifedrinker's smoldering, white-hot axe blade over his head in a two-handed grip. His armor was untouched by the flames, though his pants were singed and his arms and face reddened by the exposure.

He streaked through the air, trailing smoke, the forest behind him ablaze, and when he crashed through the shrubs, his knee impacted a tall Shadeni wearing heavy red robes, smashing him to the ground. Victor could feel bones snapping and guts bursting as his enormous titan-sized form bore down on the man. Still, he stood, fluid and graceful with his heightened agility, and brought Lifedrinker down, severing the man's head from his shoulders.

Victor lifted his face toward the reddening sky and roared, his great lungs bellowing his fury. The sound echoed and reverberated among the trees and distantly off the far side of the valley. Suddenly, the forest around him was filled with howls and yips as his hunting companions responded, unable to resist the urge to sing with him. Victor's soot-stained lips pulled back in a feral grin, exposing bright white teeth, and he charged into the trees, scanning for any sign of his next enemy.

His coyotes found someone before he did, and Victor could feel their excitement and hear the success in their howls and yips, so he turned sharply to the right, sprinting toward them. Somehow, he knew where they were, the knowledge coming from somewhere deeper than his bones. When he burst through a thin stand of saplings, sending twigs and leaves flying and slender trunks snapping and whipping in his passage, he found three of his coyotes growling and circling an Ardeni man, one different from any other Victor had met.

The man was tall and slender, wearing form-fitting, gleaming silvery armor—some kind of metal that looked impossibly fine and light; could it really provide protection? Victor's mind only had a moment to contemplate before he noticed the man's catlike ears, oversized angular eyes, long black claws, and swishing blue-furred tail. He was so startled and drew so many amusing connections to jokes Thayla and Valla had made about growing tails that he almost lost hold of his rage. A demented chuckle escaped his throat before he got a grip on himself, and, in that brief moment, the blue-skinned and furred man, striking like a viper, dispatched one of his coyotes with a long curved knife.

Victor surged forward, filling the gap left by his vanquished companion, stepping through the black mist the poor coyote left behind and whipping Lifedrinker in a sideways cleave, aiming to separate the man's top half from the bottom. He was slippery, though, graceful in a way that even Valla would struggle to replicate. As Lifedrinker smoked through the air, the Ardeni slipped under her arc, came up close to Victor, and brought that wicked blade around as though he meant to cut Victor's kidney out.

Victor was no slouch, no novice of the axe. When Lifedrinker didn't make contact, he quickly recovered, and as his opponent came close, really only standing about as high as Victor's waist, he released his grip on the haft with his left and reached down to grasp the slender man's shoulder. The Ardeni's blade skittered and scraped against his wyrm-scale vest, and his eyes went wide with surprise. Had his wicked stab never been defeated before? Victor wasn't surprised; he could feel the Energy in the man's movements—he'd conducted a powerful attack.

Still, the blade didn't penetrate his armor, and now Victor had ahold of him. "Game over," he growled, then bore down with all his might, squeezing the slender shoulder until he felt bones grinding against each other. He lifted the struggling cat-Ardeni from the ground and, choking up his grip on Lifedrinker with his right hand, hacked the blade sideways, burying her gleaming edge deep between his enemy's ribs. The man gasped and clawed at Victor's arm, dragging those long claws along his flesh, raising welts but nothing more.

"No," he moaned, his voice full of disbelief as the light faded from his eyes. "No! How?"

Victor released his shoulder, dropped him to the ground, and pressed him to the soil with Lifedrinker's handle, watching his face. "Who are you?" he growled, giving the axe a bit of a twist.

"Oof!" the man grunted, blood spattering out of his sharp-fanged grimace. From the corner of his eye, Victor saw the man's long-clawed hand twitch, and a bright red, swirling bulb of liquid appeared in it. Seeing the potion and not knowing where his other enemies were, Victor decided to seek his answers elsewhere. He pushed down with all his weight, driving Lifedrinker's edge deep into the man's chest cavity, and then he gave her a savage twist. Wet cracks sounded as the Ardeni's ribs spread apart, and gouts of dark blood watered the forest floor.

Victor pulled Lifedrinker free, her blade gleaming with inner molten fury. He smiled at her and growled, "You didn't have trouble with that armor, did you?"

"Let us hunt! There are more foes about!"

"Right," he grunted, whistling and gesturing for his coyotes to take up the chase. He'd been so focused on finding the source of movement and color he'd seen earlier, so caught up in his two quick skirmishes, that he hadn't spared Valla a second thought. Now, though, he began to worry a bit. If there were five attackers, and he'd dealt with only two, Valla could be in trouble. "Valla!" he called, turning in the direction she should be coming from if she'd been able to flank this foe with him.

Victor didn't see a sign of her, and as he thought about it, he didn't see any sign of the winged mounts the two men he'd killed should have left behind. Frowning, he began to jog across the slope, slipping between trees, looking and listening for any sign of his friend. He'd run for about thirty seconds when he felt something from one of his companions—a target and a hint of something like recognition. "Valla!" Victor elongated his stride, leaping over undergrowth and fallen logs, the ground trembling with the impacts of his enormous boots. When he burst into a clearing, he found Valla standing over the dead, bloodied corpse of an Ardeni man. Facing her was the huge Shadeni, the one with the enormous black horns Victor had seen flying toward the airship.

Valla circled him, her form blurred by gusting breezes and tiny electrical charges, sliding over the ground quick as thought, clearly confounding the big Shadeni, who wore a round black metal shield and gripped a thick, fiery, cleaver-like sword. His pale blue armor rippled in the sunlight, though Victor could see a tear under his right ribcage where, presumably, Valla had given him a taste of Midnight. He glanced at the corpse, saw many bloody rips in the man's white leather armor, and almost pitied the fools for trying Valla this way.

Valla saw him standing at the edge of the clearing, but the Shadeni failed to notice him. Victor started forward, and Valla gave him a quick nod, so he focused on the blue-armored figure and tried out his new Energy Charge. Perhaps because he was already channeling so much of it, or perhaps because it came so naturally to him, Victor cast the spell with rage-attuned Energy and howled with mad battle lust as his vision blurred, and he flew, trailing a cloud of red smoldering Energy motes that hung in the air behind him.

With a bone-crunching impact into the Shadeni's shielded side, Victor found himself standing where his target had been and saw the horned figure flipping, head over heels, to crash into the bole of a mighty tree. The impact resounded through the clearing, and leaves and dead branches cascaded down, knocked loose by the concussion. Victor marveled at the spell's effect—sure, he was much larger than the Shadeni, and hitting him at speed should be devastating, but Victor had barely felt the collision.

The Shadeni groaned and writhed on the ground where he'd fallen, some of his limbs badly twisted and bent; Victor had given him some new joints. "Ancestors," he moaned, "receive me. Take me to your host."

In a blur of motion, Valla moved to stand over the large man, her sword at his throat, but she didn't kill him. She looked at Victor, an eyebrow raised.

"Not yet," he grunted, stomping to stand over his broken foe.

The Shadeni looked up at him, pain writ plainly on his face. His eyes, earlier blazing with golden Energy, were dim now, but his lips pulled back in a sneer as he gasped, "Kill me then, beast. Finish what you've started." His left arm was twisted and broken beyond movement, but the Shadeni's right hand began to twitch, the fingers waggling in the air, and Victor wondered what he was trying to do. Cast a spell? Summon a healing potion? Insult him? Rather than wait to find out, he brought Lifedrinker down and severed the appendage.

"Ah!" the broken man wailed as dark, thick blood pumped from his wrist into the loam.

"Where's the fifth?" Victor growled.

"Eat my balls, scum!" The insult was so out of left field, nothing like anything anyone had said to him since coming to this world, that Victor barked a short laugh.

"Eat your balls? Holy shit. Valla, is that something people say in this world?"

The horned man looked at Valla and, spitting loose a fragment of broken tooth, said, "So, you are Valla. Ancestors damn you both!"

"Who sent you?" Valla asked, pressing Midnight's edge against the man's flesh. He was clearly a sturdy fellow, powerful for this world, or he'd have died from the accumulated injuries to his person. Victor noted how his wrist had already ceased bleeding and that, if he watched carefully, it seemed his limbs were slowly straightening; he had some regenerative powers.

"My question first," Victor growled, resting one enormous foot atop the man's twisted knee. He didn't press on it, but the threat was clear.

"Wait, wait," the man gasped, lifting his stump toward Victor's foot as though he could somehow halt the impending pain. "The fifth? So, you've met the four of us here in these woods, not just poor Ulvish and me? Well, forget the fifth. She'll have fled after sensing our demise."

"Where was she?" Victor asked, allowing the smallest fraction of his bulk to rest upon the swollen, broken joint.

"Old Father's twisted cock! Please stop! She was with the strigaii, downslope, just beyond the trees."

Valla looked at Victor, met his eyes, and he said, "Now her question."

"Why? You'll kill me anyway. Why destroy my honor before I go?"

"Your honor, worm?" Valla sneered. "Was it honorable to send a dozen merchant sailors to their doom?"

"I had my orders."

"Ah." Valla nodded. "The Legion, then."

"You traitorous whore . . ." His words were cut off, replaced by a wail of agony, as Victor, growling, pressed down on his knee.

"Watch your tongue. Answer her questions." As he spoke, though, Victor felt an alert from his remaining coyotes; they'd found something. "My companions found her." He turned in the direction he felt them, straining his ears.

"Wait!" the man gasped. "Let her live, and I'll answer your questions. She had no part in the attack."

"Well." Victor nodded, lifting his foot. "That's a start. So, tell Valla your name and the name of your friend, and I'll try to keep my companions from killing her."

"She's not my friend; she's my wife. I'm Chokodo-dak, and my wife is Reesha-dak. I'm a princeps of the Empire, and you've made great enemies today."

"Oh, that's a little stupid, don't you think? I mean, we must already have had those enemies because you started this shit." Victor looked at Valla and asked, "Do you recognize the name?"

Her face had lost all expression, and she was staring at the man, peering into his flickering, golden-lit eyes, and she said, "Aye, Victor. I do. This doesn't bode well for the expedition."

"Ha!" Chokodo spat, blood sluicing down his chin. "Your expedition, or do you mean your rebellion? Do you think the Empire so blind, so deaf?"

"You have any way to bind this asshole?"

"We could hood and tie him. Even a powerful Energy user would struggle to cause trouble for you or me with such restraints. If we bring him to Rellia, she'll have the means to hobble his Energy use."

Chokodo slumped at her words, defeat plain on his face. "Could you not spare me an elixir to speed my recovery? I'll not struggle further. I am beaten."

"Take his rings, stow his weapons, and tie him up, and I'll go fetch his wife." Victor looked at the bloodied man for a long moment, thinking about the sailors, probably dead, and spat to the side. "No healing for him. He's mending fast enough."

"Understood," Valla said, picking up the man's severed hand and peeling the rings from the fingers. She glanced at Victor, still standing there, reluctant to leave, and added, "Go. He's in hand."

Victor grunted and turned, bounding through the forest toward his coyotes, instinctually aware that they had someone cornered. He only had to cover about a mile before he broke free of the trees onto a long grassy slope that led down toward a river that cut through the center of the valley. He saw, staked not far away, the five strigaii, their wings folded back and their beaks low to the ground. Victor narrowed his eyes to see what they were doing and saw bones and hunks of meat; they were eating. Just past them, back to a tall tree as though she'd tried to flee upslope, was a Shadeni woman grasping a golden rod, using it to fend off the tentative lunges of his companions.

Victor strode toward her and, with a thought, called his coyotes away, urging them to back off and expand their circle around her. As they obeyed his command and the woman looked up to see the furious, armor-clad giant stomping toward her, a great smoldering axe in his hands, she blanched and looked around, perhaps seeking an avenue of escape. Her gaze settled on the strigaii, and Victor knew she was thinking about trying to run through two of his companions, past him, and onto the back of one of the beasts. He cleared his throat, reached into his Core, and severed the flow of rage that was feeding his Iron Berserk spell.

As his size diminished, Victor lifted Lifedrinker to his shoulder, holding her haft with one hand, and then he called, "You don't look like a fighter. I don't know your role in all of this, but you'll fare better if you don't try to run."

The woman, Reesha-dak, lifted her rod, and a shimmering, blue, egg-shaped barrier flickered into being around her. She said, "I can defend myself, sirrah!" Her voice trembled, and she held the scepter sideways in front of her lacy black blouse.

Seeing the scepter and her fancy shirt, Victor studied her for a moment, taking in the many rings, bracelets, and necklaces. He was no expert, but he'd seen plenty of gems since leaving Earth and recognized some valuable, perfectly cut stones among her jewelry. Her hair was pulled tight to her scalp, back in a perfectly coiffed bun, and atop her head was a delicate golden tiara bedecked with sparkling rubies. A gauzy black veil hung from the edge of her crown, covering her face and held firm by softly glowing purple gems at its bottom fringe. Victor could just see the purple-red hue of her eyes through the dense gauze.

She had to be wearing more wealth than he'd ever seen on display, even considering Rellia or the noble Vesh in Coloss. "What's your story, Princess?" he asked, sighing. "Why'd that dipshit, uh, what was his name? Choco? Why'd he bring you along to attack my airship?"

"How dare you? You aren't fit to speak Chokodo-dak's name, let alone question his actions!"

Victor chuckled, moving closer, now just a few feet away. He could feel the Energy she'd expended to create her shield and knew he could smash that little barrier with barely a thought. Still, he paused in front of her and said,

"Your companions are dead. Your husband is in chains. You'll both answer for your crimes today. Don't make me embarrass you further."

"Crimes? Chokodo serves the Empire! He acts on the Emperor's explicit orders!"

Victor growled, feeling his rage surging, wanting out of his Core. In a compromise, he released his hold on his aura, letting it spread out around him, and Reesha fell backward, sliding down the trunk of the tree, tears springing into her eyes as the scepter rolled out of her hand. Victor leaned forward and said, his voice thick with righteous indignation for in his mind, he was innocent of blame—he hadn't started this shit—"I'll let Rellia sort out what you're guilty of; as for the Emperor, maybe that asshole needs to answer for his crimes, too."

13

❧

FIRESIDE

Victor stared at his prisoners, sitting in the grass a dozen feet away from their tethered mounts. He and Valla had stripped the pair, Chokodo and Reesha, of their jewelry and weapons, secured their hands behind their backs, hobbled their ankles with a short length of rope so they couldn't run, and blindfolded their eyes with dark strips of cloth Victor had torn from an old cloak. Valla felt confident neither of them would be able to effect an escape, but Victor still felt nervous about them; he knew if it were him, some ropes and blindfolds would never hold. "How long did she say?" he asked for the third time.

"Sometime tonight. Make a big fire, and they'll have no problem finding us in this valley."

"And you don't think these two will have help coming?"

"Chokodo says no. He says he and his men acted without sanction; they were meant only to observe us and report back. We'll see." She shrugged as if there was nothing more to be done.

"Not what his wife told me . . ."

"Yes, well, it's quite possible he hadn't been entirely forthright with his wife, don't you think?" Valla smirked and tapped a long, black-polished nail on the pommel of her sword.

"I guess. Well, we need to watch them closely. How about you keep your eyes on them, and I'll go collect the bodies and build a fire." He glanced at the shadowy form lying in the grass, the man Valla had killed. She'd brought the body back in a storage ring, leading the badly injured Chokodo to see if Victor needed help. By then, he'd already bound Reesha and was thinking about going to fetch her.

"Right. I suppose we can't leave them where they fell, not with potential information or wealth in their containers. Rellia will be able to identify them, even if Chokodo or his wife don't want to share."

"Whistle if something happens. I'll be listening," Victor said, turning to jog upslope into the woods. He had a good sense of direction, far better than it had ever been in his old life, though he'd never tested it the way he did on Fanwath. Twenty minutes later, with no alarms from Valla, he'd tossed the other two bodies next to the first. Valla had built a small fire near the prisoners and was watching them as the shadows of night lengthened, the sister moons mostly obscured by clouds. She saw him and nodded, offering a short wave before returning her gaze to Reesha and Chokodo.

Victor stooped to the dead bodies, pulling rings off fingers, checking necks and wrists for other jewelry. He tucked anything that seemed as if it might be a dimensional container into the little sack where he'd stowed Chokodo and Reesha's jewelry, then he put the rest, including their weapons, into one of his own rings. He'd just finished and was taking a last look at the weird cat-Ardeni when Valla called to him. Victor walked over the grass toward her, and halfway there, he called out, "What's the deal with the cat-looking guy? The Ardeni."

"A Feeradi? Truly?" Valla looked surprised.

"They killed Evwin?" Reesha said, her voice hoarse from screaming and crying earlier.

"I told you I killed them. What would you have done? Fall to your knees and let them kill you?" Victor growled, tired of the woman acting like he was the bad guy in the situation.

"Yes," Chokodo said, his voice sullen and weary, "he was a Feeradi. His bloodline rank was approaching the epic tier. What a loss."

"It's an uncommon bloodline, Victor, but that doesn't excuse vile behavior. He was a criminal of the worst kind, hiding behind his social rank to commit atrocities." Though Valla addressed Victor, it was clear she was speaking to Reesha.

"He," Reesha croaked, struggling to speak with her sore throat—whatever healing abilities Chokodo had, she didn't share them, "he was serving the Empire!"

"Killing a bunch of sailors is serving the Empire?" Valla spat. "Your husband has already come clean, Reesha. He and his lackeys weren't sanctioned in this attack."

"He's saying what you want to hear! What he *can* say!" she cried, her words fading to a rough whisper.

"Hush, dear. Hush. I've heard of Rellia ap'Yensha. She's known as a fair woman; let her hear our tale."

Valla snorted, but Victor turned and stomped toward the trees. He'd heard enough. He needed to get a bigger fire burning to guide Rellia's airship to them. At first, he'd tried to talk Valla into riding the strigaii to Persi Gables, but she'd refused; apparently, the beasts were finicky, hard to master, and very loyal to a given rider. She said Rellia's people would need to spend months retraining them. Luckily for them, Valla had been writing a lot more often to Rellia, so her copy of the Far Scribe book was constantly monitored. When they'd reported the attack on their airship, Rellia had redirected her scout ship from practice maneuvers to pick them up. "Here's hoping she's not overly optimistic about them finding us."

Victor hefted Lifedrinker, remembering how, in a Viking movie he'd watched, one of the warriors had lectured his son about using his war axe as a tool. "You don't mind, do you, *chica?*"

"A tree will not harm me, love."

Victor grinned, enjoying her use of the endearment more than he probably should have. He lifted her high and brought her down on a tall, slender tree with white bark. The bole was probably only eight inches in diameter, but Victor laughed with pleasure as Lifedrinker ripped through it in one swing. The tree toppled downslope, and Victor cut another just like it for good measure. An hour of honest exercise followed as he chopped the trunks and branches into yard-long segments and piled them together in the big meadow.

Nearby, he constructed the bonfire, stacking the logs loosely in a square that tapered together with each layer. All told, he figured he'd used about half a tree's worth of lumber to build it. "Valla," he called, "you have a spell to light this up?"

"Yes. Come watch these two."

Victor switched places with Valla, but he put the slope to his back so he could observe the prisoners and Valla at once, and he grinned happily as she ignited the wood. It wasn't dry and would have been difficult to light with conventional means, but a bit of Energy apparently solved that. As Valla walked back, she said, "I'll teach you that. It's funny the gaps in your knowledge. Simple things every child is taught, you don't know, but how to battle an ancient wyrm? That's something you can do."

"Yeah, well, trial by fire, I guess."

"So, it's true. You were off-world?"

"Did I give it away?" Valla asked, her tone taunting. "No ancient wyrms on Fanwath, are there? So, tell us, Chokodo, who at Fainhallow alerted you to our presence? Why did you seek to slay Victor? Why not get some of this out in the open before Rellia has to have her mind mage dig it out of you?" Chokodo frowned beneath his black blindfold but didn't speak, and Valla shrugged.

"You think it was someone at the academy?" Victor ran his mind through all the people he'd spoken to in the little town around the school.

"It had to be; where else did we go?"

"Well, I mean, we both sent messages in the books." Victor jerked his thumb toward the north. "Could be a leak in that direction."

Valla frowned and plucked at some grass. "I think not. Rellia only has two people watching the book, and they're well trusted. She and Lam both have too much to lose to let information like that slip out."

"I hope you're right." Victor stretched and sat down on the grass. He was feeling quite good; not long after he'd disarmed Reesha, he'd received a decent influx of Energy for his victories, and though he didn't level again, he still felt energized and fresh. "If you're tired, take a nap. I'll watch these two." Victor eyed Chokodo for a reaction to those words, but the man still sat, slumped, defeat written in his demeanor. He didn't trust him, though, and Victor didn't intend to give him an inch of freedom, not until he was much more thoroughly bound.

"No. I'm not tired at all."

"Listen," Reesha said, her voice a whisper, "would you please allow me to wear my veil? It's unseemly to have my face thus exposed."

"No, lady," Valla said. "Your veil has enchantments, and it's bonded to you. Those gems felt quite potent. Would you like me to wrap more cloth over your face rather than just your eyes?"

"No, no." Reesha sighed, her voice cracking with emotion as she looked down.

"What's the deal with that? The veil? I've never seen anyone in Persi Gables or Gelica wearing one."

"She's in line to be one of the Emperor's wives." Valla shrugged as if her sentence made perfect sense.

"Come again? I thought Chokodo was her husband." Neither of the prisoners spoke, but Valla seemed happy to fill him in.

"Only in name. His relationship with her is more like a big brother or guardian. The Emperor has dozens of such women similarly bound to him."

"*Chingado*," Victor said, his voice rising with disbelief. "People just stand for that? Him claiming women?"

"It's not just him, and it's not just women." Valla tugged some blue-green grass blades and tossed them toward her little fire. Then she looked over her shoulder toward the bonfire, illuminating the clearing for a hundred yards in every direction, perhaps weighing her words, perhaps lost in memories the discussion had pulled to the surface.

"It's really only in Tharcray," Chokodo added. "Those with the Ridonne bloodline, the rulers of the Empire."

"Like you?" Victor asked.

"I'm a princeps, true, but no Ridonne blood runs in my veins. My authority is granted at the whim of the imperial family." He paused, and everyone was quiet for a little while, and then the blindfolded man said, "You're strong, Victor, stronger than we were led to believe, but you'll pay for what you've done here. The Ridonne will hunt you, and they're a force to behold."

"*Pfft*," Valla scoffed, turning away from the distant bonfire. "No one's even seen the Emperor in my lifetime. The Ridonne are just as puffed up and soft as you. Victor will crush any that come after him."

"Uh, not to mention, all I 'did here today' was keep you assholes from killing me and Valla."

"You're *wrong!*" Chokodo said, facing Valla, though he couldn't see her. "You might not have experience with them, but there are those of the Ridonne who could bat me aside and pull the flesh from my bones with two waves of their hand. I might be 'puffed up,' but believe me, there's a reason the Ridonne rule Fanwath."

"We'll see," Valla sighed, sitting back on her elbows, her eyes drifting up over the prisoners and the tethered strigaii behind them, looking into the night sky. "It's good to see familiar stars again."

Again, silence fell, allowing the crackling of the campfire and the distant roar of the bonfire to fill the night air, and Victor began to relax, thinking about Tharcray, wondering if it could possibly stack up to Coloss. He'd heard the name Ridonne plenty of times and had known it was the name of the Empire, but he hadn't known it was a Shadeni bloodline. Could they really be all that tough, though? He'd already speculated that the Empire was hoarding knowledge and hoarding access to more advanced worlds. Was it such a stretch to think the people in the capital, especially the ruling party, all members of some potent bloodline, wouldn't be stronger than the average Energy user?

When Victor thought about brutal fights in his life, the one that stood out the most was his duel with Rellia. He'd come close to dying plenty of times, sure, but she'd really schooled him. If she was weak compared to the Ridonne, then he supposed it was worth being cautious, especially if they were acting against him and the expedition.

"My wrists ache," Reesha whispered, her throat apparently too raw for more than that.

"This is harsh treatment for one such as her," Chokodo said, and Victor gave him a long look. The man's limbs were all straight; each of his many fractures had healed. He wore a simple white shirt over a heavily muscled chest, for Valla had stripped him of his pretty blue armor. Still, he looked strong and dangerous. Victor didn't reply but stood and moved around behind the man. He was a huge Shadeni, to be sure, probably close to seven feet tall, but next to Victor, he wasn't very imposing, especially bound on the ground as he was.

"Lean forward," Victor said, bending at the waist and pressing Chokodo between the shoulder blades. He saw his wrists were still bound and that the man still sported a stump for a left hand. "Can't regenerate your hand, huh?" Victor didn't doubt Chokodo could pull his wrist free from his bindings, what with no hand attached to anchor the ropes. He hadn't done so, though; had he truly given up all resistance?

"No, sirrah, I cannot."

"Use respect when you address him!" Valla growled, her voice thick with venom.

"No, sir," Chokodo amended, frowning.

Victor simply grunted and stepped past him to Reesha, and, using a sharp knife he'd picked up from one dead enemy or another, he cut the bindings on her wrists. "Oh," she sighed softly, pulling her hands before herself and rubbing at the dark spots on her soft, pale red wrists. Victor reached down and took hold of her upper arm, pulling her effortlessly to her feet. "No! Please! Don't hurt me!" she croaked, trying to yell despite her lack of a voice.

"Don't take her!" Chokodo wailed.

"Relax," Victor said. "I'm just moving her over by Valla, so she can't get herself in trouble trying to help you or something." He gently pulled the woman's arm, guided her around the fire next to Valla, and said, "Sit here." As she collapsed, clumsy with her eyes covered and a length of rope holding her feet close to each other, Victor pointed to the bonfire and said, "Be right back." Valla nodded, and he walked over to his pile of logs.

While he tossed half a dozen big logs onto the fire, he thought about the System and how it seemed to breed corruption. People who grabbed power were rewarded, perpetuating their positions of strength and incentivizing them to keep what they'd earned. Never satisfied, the System seemed to encourage people to continue their climb, always seeking the next advancement. He let his mind drift back to home, to Earth, and he almost laughed at himself, at his own naivety.

"It doesn't take a System for people to want power." At least with the System, with Energy, he figured people with good intentions could grow powerful. Back home, it didn't always feel that way. He knew that was a cynical take, and he also knew he'd been a dumb kid, too worried about sports and girls to really know much about how things worked, but he couldn't help the feeling that things *could* be better with Energy. He wondered if every world would be like Zaafor and Fanwath with a corrupt ruling class. Maybe some of them were more egalitarian; maybe some had systems in place to share treasures and Energy.

"How would that work, though?" Victor frowned, staring into the bonfire. How would he feel if he went and cleared a dungeon, doing all the work, only to have to share his trophies with the people back home who'd been too lazy or scared to go with him? "Yeah, that would suck," he sighed. His mind started to wander away from the topic, mainly because he felt he had a lot to learn, and there were probably people who'd done a lot of thinking on the subject already—something to study on the road with the army, perhaps.

A soft breeze blew in from the northern end of the valley and lifted embers and sparks up into the black night sky. Victor watched them swirling, wondering about the future, wondering if the Empire would move against his legion openly or if some of the Ridonne would come to challenge him. He hoped not, not yet; he wanted to get done with the conquest of the Marches, get some defenses established, and bring in the people loyal to ap'Yensha and maybe some others.

"What others?" Victor asked the night, watching the smoke rise from the fire, and his mind drifted to people he'd met, people he wouldn't mind seeing settle in lands he conquered. What about the Naghelli? They didn't have a home, and they were supposedly fierce fighters. Maybe he should reach out. Hadn't Vellia told him to? Hadn't she given him a necklace for just that purpose? He let his inner eye drift through his dimensional containers, and there he saw it, the silver necklace with the big ruby gem.

Perhaps on a whim, perhaps listening to his instinct, or perhaps being foolish, Victor took the necklace from his ring, held the gem tightly in his fist, and thought about Vellia. Nothing happened at first, but after a few moments, the jewel throbbed in his hand, and he felt her. She was far away, a distant presence off to the north and east, but he remembered her words; she'd know he was holding the gem, know he was looking for her, and she—they—would answer his call. "Good." He nodded. "Maybe they'd like to earn a new home."

He almost put the necklace back in the dimensional container but paused. What if she couldn't feel it in there? The chain was too short to wear around his neck, so he slipped it into one of the pouches tied to his belt, protected by the wyrm-scale vest. "Who else?" he mused, turning back to look at Valla and her two prisoners. They sat as before, though it looked as if Valla was speaking to Reesha, and Chokodo was slumped forward, perhaps asleep.

"Tellen?" Victor asked the night, though he knew he meant Thayla, knew he really wanted to see Deyni. "Wouldn't they like lands to hunt in outside of the Empire? Wouldn't they like their own hunting grounds where they wouldn't have to worry about brigands or imperial patrols?" He turned to the sky, searching for Gallia, the little moon. He saw her edge peeking out behind a cloud and reckoned she was nearly full. "That means Thayla will be looking for me on the spirit plane soon," Victor said to Lifedrinker, grasping her handle and resting her cool metal on his forehead. "Remind me, will you? I'd like to talk to her and try to convince her to come with us."

"More fleshy women for you to lust after." The axe sounded irritated, her voice sharper than usual, and Victor bit back an automatic denial. Instead, he thought about what she'd said, taking her seriously.

"Is that what you really think? You know me better than anyone, Lifedrinker. We've been through hell together, and I've never lied to you. You've seen me at my lowest, my worst. Tell me the truth. Is that really what I'm after?"

"No, love. Can I not tease thee? You gather those who are lost like yourself. You gather those about whom you care. I see you and your spirit, and I carry not an ounce of regret for my bond with you. Do what you will, but remember, I am here. I am always here. You are never alone so long as you have me at your side."

"Thank you, beautiful. Thank you." He clutched her handle warmly and then walked back to Valla's little campfire and their prisoners, willing Rellia's scout ship to hurry; he had work to do, plans to make, and people to lead.

14

THE ENCAMPMENT

Victor once again stood on the prow of an airship, this one piloted by Rellia's people and equipped for war. He'd noticed the magical ballistae, two on each side of the ship, as soon as it set down to retrieve him, Valla, and their prisoners and captured mounts. When they'd climbed aboard, they'd been greeted by the ship's captain, a stodgy, old-looking Cadwalli who'd apologized for taking a bit longer than expected—they'd spied the wreck of the previous airship and done a sweep for survivors. The crew had found several mangled corpses but also signs that several survivors might have escaped on foot, traveling toward Persi Gables.

Victor had wanted to seek them out, but Valla had insisted that the countryside was gentle, they'd had hours of a head start, and the airship would have a hard time spotting them in the thick forests approaching Lake Beliss. The captain had sealed matters, agreeing with Valla and insisting that Lady Rellia wanted them brought to safety as soon as possible; they didn't know what other threats might be imminent where Victor and Valla were concerned. The crew was friendly, though too deferential, and hardly spoke to either of them after that initial discussion. In fact, it felt as though they were terrified of the two of them.

He thought back to when he'd first met Valla, back when he'd gone to visit Rellia after their duel in the arena. He remembered how she'd hardly spoken, using clipped phrases. He smiled at the memory, thinking about how she'd been even more perfectly coiffed back then, standing straight as a wooden board. He supposed she had a reputation not just as Rellia's adopted daughter, but as a captain in the Legion. Victor leaned forward against the railing, gripping it in his large, strong hands, and smiled, thinking about how Rellia and Lam would react to the changes in him and Valla.

He was his natural size, something over eight feet tall, and he figured he'd keep it that way until he had to go inside a structure again. Why not tower over some people, larger than life? "Especially when we first arrive," he grunted, squeezing the railing until the wood creaked. He had half a mind to cast his Titanic Aspect spell; let them see whom they'd recruited to lead this expedition—a living, breathing Quinametzin. It was a thought, but he ultimately shook his head, deciding against it. He didn't need to impress Rellia or Lam more than he already had.

Victor turned to look over his shoulder and saw Valla standing not far away, speaking to an Ardeni in a crisp sailor's uniform, one with some special insignias on the shoulders. "Hey," he called, getting her attention.

She clasped the man's shoulder, said something, then walked over to Victor. "Hey."

"So, where's the ship taking us? Rellia's estate? Some airship dock in Persi Gables?"

"I'd prefer it if we went to the estate, but apparently, Rellia sent orders that the ship is to drop us off at the legion's encampment. Lam and Rellia are both there, overseeing some final logistical matters."

"Oh, really?" Suddenly Victor wasn't feeling quite so cocksure; was he ready to be seen by the soldiers he was meant to lead?

"Yes. News of the attack on our airship has escalated things."

"Right, right." Victor nodded. "Makes sense. How long do we have?"

"Minutes. We'll be done passing over Lake Beliss shortly, though too far south to see Persi Gables, and then it's just a short journey over the bordering woods to the plains where the army is encamped."

"Damn. All right." Victor stood up straight, releasing the railing. He'd been watching the passage of the lake, the moons' reflections flickering oddly over its choppy waters. The ship was low, far lower than Victor imagined airplanes flew, and the view, coupled with the rushing winds, had kept him engaged for an hour or more. "Should I change?"

"No, your armor and helmet are impressive. As you can see, I'm wearing my armor." Valla reached up to her neck, touching the choker Victor had given her, and he realized she'd kept the top part of her hauberk open so it didn't cover the sparkling, pale blue crystals.

He smiled and said, "You look great. Are you nervous?"

"Only about seeing Rellia."

"Right. Yeah, I know there's a lot between you two, or I'd try to offer some advice. As it is, I have no idea what to say except that she'd be an idiot not to be proud of you." His words pulled a smile out of her, and she looked down briefly.

"Thank you. I hope Rellia sees it that way. I hope she doesn't send me off on meaningless tasks to keep me in my place."

Victor frowned. He knew she wasn't used to receiving much praise, so he added, "Seriously. You've accomplished so much! You're on your way to being one of the most personally powerful people in the world. You captured one of the Emperor's principes. You're returning with wealth far beyond what anyone could have reasonably hoped for. Meaningless tasks? As far as I'm concerned, you will be right by my side for this entire expedition. I'll insist on it."

"You'd do that?" Valla smiled, resting a hand on Midnight's pommel.

"Are you kidding me? I need someone with me I can trust no matter what. You and, like, three other people are the only ones in this world who fit that bill, and you're the only one strong enough. Do you understand? You're invaluable to me."

"I—" Valla stepped forward, dropped her hands to her sides, and straightened up. Victor wasn't a military guy, but to him, it looked as though she was standing at attention. She cleared her throat and spoke firmly and quickly, her words chasing each other out of her mouth. "Thank you, Victor! I won't let you down."

Victor wanted to crack a joke, to try to lighten the tension in the air, but he knew she was being serious. He saw this meant something to her, so he met her gaze and nodded, then simply said, "Thank you, Valla. I know you won't." He turned back to the ship's prow and said, "Come on, let's see if we can see the army when we approach."

"It's dark, so you'll see their fires."

"Well," Victor said and pointed to the horizon, "it *was* dark, but the sun's coming up." Sure enough, the sky, dark and gloomy directly overhead, was ever-so-slightly paler where the sky met the ground in the distance. He glanced over his shoulder, saw that the sister moons were nearly obscured by the opposite horizon, and guessed the sun would be up in minutes.

"Now that's going to set the augurs talking—the commander of the army arriving as the new day dawns, unshaken from an imperial assassination attempt!"

"Ha!" Victor snorted, surprised at Valla's creativity.

"You laugh, but I promise you; Rellia will spread the tale. She's very image conscious."

"Sometimes I can't tell if you love her or loathe her." It had been a long while since he'd seen Rellia in person; he remembered her being beautiful, far younger than he'd imagined, and far more pleasant. He wondered how much had been an act to get him to sign on to this expedition. "God, I was so naive. I can't believe how much has changed since I fought her."

"Perhaps a bit green." Valla paused and nodded. "But your instincts were good. Rellia was sincere in her dealings with you. I know her well, and I'm sure of it. She wants a better start, a better, less corrupt place for our family and allies to prosper. I truly believe it, Victor."

"I hope you're right." They stood on the prow, watching the water speed by for several minutes, then it gave way to a shadowy forest, the air warming noticeably as they left the lake behind. Victor glanced up and said, "Wow." He pointed to the horizon again. "Look at those colors!"

As the sun began to brighten the distant horizon, the clouds hanging in the air had taken on brilliant shades of yellow and orange, deepening to pink and red. As Victor took it in and Valla leaned forward, also taken with the sight, he watched as the slowly emerging sun began to illuminate the dark green-blue landscape—expansive grass plains for as far as his eye could see in any direction. He was watching the ground lighten when Valla grabbed his arm and pointed. He followed her finger to see hundreds of tiny motes of light in the grassy plain.

"Campfires. It's the army."

As the sailors began to yell to each other, tightening or loosening ropes, preparing the ship to land, Victor watched as the shadowy shapes of tents came into view, hundreds of them. No, he amended, thousands. A great corral had been staked out near the encampment, and Victor saw thousands of animals within, mostly roladii, but a few other creatures, including great, elephant-sized birds. He searched his memory for what they were called and uttered, "Bundii."

"Aye. To pull the bigger wagons," Valla said, pointing toward a row of dozens of massive wagons lined up inside the earthen bulwark surrounding the entire encampment. The whole place looked like a town under construction to Victor as they drew closer. He even noticed wooden watchtowers around the perimeter and a large, permanent-looking wooden fortification at the camp's center. "The ship will tether there, at the perimeter. See? They've built a docking structure. No, two of them."

Victor saw what she meant; two stage-like structures on stilts stood about fifty yards from each other and about twice as far from the earthen bulwark, and the ship was rapidly descending toward the one on the left. "Impressive for a camp."

"This is sloppy, actually. I suppose some leniency can be expected, considering they've been using this as a recruitment camp for the last ten months. Still, we'll have sharper camps on the road, or I'll personally be handing out discipline." Valla spoke plainly, as if she was reciting well-known facts, and Victor had to give her a double take.

"You putting on your legion captain persona?"

"Yes! I want this to be a successful endeavor, and that means discipline. I'll be the mean old gran if I have to." As she finished speaking, Victor chuckled. He wasn't familiar with the idiom about a mean old gran, but he got the idea; he could imagine his *abuela* whipping some sloppy soldiers into shape just fine. A surge of sad nostalgia rose from the pit of his stomach as he thought about his grandma, but rather than banish the thought, he embraced it. If she were truly gone, then he'd cherish every memory that came to him of her. He shook his head, reminding himself that he wasn't sure about anything yet.

"Ah, they've sighted us. See the parade coming toward the landing platform?"

Victor followed her gaze and saw what she meant. A column of tiny soldiers was marching down the central boulevard through the encampment. They'd probably arrive as the ship's sailors were finishing with their mooring lines. "Well? Shall we?" He reached down as if to take her hand, but she shook her head.

"Let's not give the soldiers and sailors more to talk about than they need. You're the commander of this army, Victor. Rellia might see you as a figurehead, but you're not. You'll soon show them as much. I don't want to be seen as a . . . a lady friend of yours."

"Oh," Victor said, nodding and pulling his hand back. He was trying to be cool but felt as though he'd just been rejected by a prom date. "Right. Sorry, Valla. I wasn't trying to imply anything . . ."

"I know you weren't! I'm sorry, too, but we both need to be respected by the troops, especially if you expect me to act as tribune."

"Tribune?"

"Yes, Victor!" Valla's exasperation had slipped its leash, but she quickly recovered and added, more calmly, "And you are Legate Victor Sandoval."

"I thought I was a commander."

"A commander is a general term, and it is accurate, but with regard to a legion, such as the one encamped around this airship, the leader is called a legate. Mark my words, Rellia and Lam will attempt to label themselves as co-legates. You should insist they are tribunes."

"*Pinche mierda*," Victor growled. "Why doesn't the System translate all this shit consistently? Why don't I hear modern terms for everything?"

"I don't know. Perhaps it's because we, on Fanwath, place a lot of weight on tradition when it comes to the Empire and the Legion. The System may be trying to help you recognize that we use different terms rather than generic possibilities like 'commander.' We can talk about this more when we're alone, but right now, the ship is nearly down, and we're about to be surrounded by important people. Are you okay?"

"Yeah, yeah. I'm fine. It's just messing with my head that we've got legates and tribunes but also captains and lieutenants. Forget it. I'm sure it'll all fall into place up here after a few conversations." Victor gave his forehead a good knock with his knuckles.

"Good. Let's stand by the gangway. I'd prefer to meet Rellia on solid ground than here on the ship." She waited for Victor to walk before her, keeping pace with him but always a stride behind. Victor didn't doubt that she was following some protocol she had learned in the Legion. The sailors moved out of his way, and as the ship bucked and pulled, slowly winched into place by the attendants on the landing platform, he stood before the gangway, waiting for it to drop.

It took a bit longer than Valla had predicted, and by the time the big wooden gate lowered, becoming a bridge, Victor saw that Rellia already stood on the platform, a dozen others, some of whom Victor recognized, flanking her. Right away, their uniforms caught his eye. Everyone on the platform wore them, similar in design to the ones Valla was always sporting, though with starkly different colors. Where Valla's pants were usually white, everyone on the platform wore slim-fitting black pants. Above their pants and shiny boots, they wore red, high-collared shirts and over the top black military-style jackets with gold brocade. They looked very fancy, very sharp.

Rellia stood at the center, her jacket adorned with ribbons and medals. Next to her was Lam, tall, slender, shimmering wings creating spectacle enough, but she too wore the uniform, and her jacket was nearly as heavy with metal as Rellia's. Slightly behind Lam was Polo Vosh, looking huge as ever, his fuzzy head and shoulders above even Lam, but he'd done a hell of a job cleaning up, and someone had stitched a uniform that fit his thick body. Victor saw Edeya next to Polo, looking much as he'd left her, though if Victor were pressed, he might admit she'd gained a few pounds in muscle.

The rest of the people were new to him, though some of their faces might have been vaguely familiar; staff or hangers-on of Lam and Rellia. He started down the gangway, Valla shadowing him. When he stopped before Rellia, she craned her neck, looking up to meet his eyes, and performed an interesting salute, standing straight, clicking her heels together, and pounding her fist into her chest over her heart. As soon as her fist thumped home, everyone else on the platform mimicked the action.

Victor didn't want to look like an idiot trying to copy the salute, so he smiled at the quiet crowd, pressed his fists into his hips, elbows akimbo, and said, his voice deep and booming, "Thank you. It's great to see you all."

"Welcome home, Victor. Valla." Rellia stepped forward and held out a hand. Victor reached down and enveloped her slender blue hand with his, and, like before, he felt the electricity of her touch. Something about her was charged, full of force. Once, he might have thought it a sexual thing, but he'd grown a bit, and he thought it was simply her powerful personality, an effect of her aura, or some combination of the two. She was a born leader.

Victor nodded, and Valla said, reverting to her old, clipped speech, "Thank you. Ma'am."

"Victor! You've grown again!" Lam said, chuckling and stepping up beside Rellia. Victor let go of Rellia's hand and reached toward Lam, only to have her step closer and try to pull him into a hug. Her face pressed into his chest, and he awkwardly gripped the backs of her shoulders, careful not to touch her wings; he had no idea how sensitive or fragile they were. "It's good to see you so well." Her words were quiet and muffled by her embrace, but they still brought a smile to Victor. Nevertheless, he wasn't used to affection from Lam, so he gently pushed her back, a tickle in the back of his mind warning him—was she trying to earn some favor by this public display, if not with him, then with the army?

"I have grown. Yeah." He shrugged. "It's my bloodline. Hey, Edeya! Hey, Polo!" Edeya beamed hugely as he said her name, snapping him another salute, and Polo nodded, a toothy grin spreading his furry cheeks.

"Victor," Rellia said as Lam stepped back beside her, "I know you must be tired, but might we have a word?"

"He is weary, Lady Rellia." Valla stepped forward, and Victor felt something like pride in his chest, seeing her looming over Rellia in her wyrm-scale armor, her hand on Midnight's pommel. "We just fought off an assassination squad and missed a night of sleep."

"Even so," Rellia said, glancing over her shoulder. Victor followed her gaze over the platform's edge and saw that an enormous, hushed crowd was beginning to gather around the tethered airship. "This is the first time the soldiers have seen their legate. Do you think you might have a word for them?"

"Oh, Ancestors!" Valla hissed. "What sort of ambush is this? He's not prepared a speech! I thought we'd have days or weeks before you brought us before the army."

"That's hardly my fault," Rellia said, her voice low but hissing. "You should have prepared him for this!"

Lam stepped forward and opened her mouth, but Victor held up a hand and said, "Hold on. You want me to address this army? Right now?" He tried to keep his face neutral, his voice low, but his first instinct was to balk, to refuse; Victor Sandoval might like to fight, but he didn't do public speeches.

"You don't have to," Valla said, angling herself so she stood between Rellia and Victor, facing them both.

"It would be a huge morale boost if you did," Lam managed to interject.

Victor frowned, recognizing the churning, dark thing in his chest—fear. His strongest affinity was, once again, reminding him that it was often the root of his decisions. "Where?" he growled, trying to cover his nervousness with a bit of anger.

"Here. You're on the platform; the soldiers are gathering, curious."

"And you conveniently made no orders to the contrary." Valla sighed.

"My, but you're crabby, daughter. We'll need to have some words, hmm?"

"Indeed we will, ma'am."

"Now?" Victor asked, still fighting a battle of his own, trying to decide if acting in spite of his fear was just as bad as acting because of it. If he refused, he'd be giving in, but now that he knew he was afraid, was the solution to react to his fear and do the opposite? What would Old Mother tell him? He felt she'd say something rather unhelpful, something about not letting his fear rule him.

"In a few minutes. Let the troops continue to gather."

"I'm loud but not sure I'm loud enough for six thousand people to hear me."

"I have something for that," Lam said, holding out her hand, in which a golden chain appeared. Dangling from the chain was a circular black stone inlaid with gold-etched runes. It was large, with thick links, and Victor knew she hadn't had the device made for herself. Victor took it from her, frowning.

"What's this?"

"It will amplify your voice for a time, something between ten and fifteen minutes. After that, it will need a day or so to recharge."

"Come, Victor," Rellia said, her voice soft but entreating. "Just a few words. Rile them up. Tell them we'll be victorious. Nothing special; they're already excited to follow you. Rumors of your exploits have traveled from fire to fire, especially how you bested me in the arena."

"That's the least of his accomplishments," Valla said, surprising Victor. Had she grown so loyal to him?

Rellia scowled at Valla, but Victor forestalled further bickering by lifting the chain over his helmeted head. Once it was around his neck, he ran a hand over his chest, opening his wyrm-scale vest and tucking the stone medallion within. Before he sealed his armor, he asked, "Do I have to bond with it?"

"Aye." Lam nodded.

Victor did so, and he felt the chain shorten a bit so it hung in the middle of his chest, then he closed up his armor. He looked at Polo and then Edeya, trying to see what they might think, figuring they might have a more neutral opinion about things. Polo looked ready to fight, as usual, his moist black eyes not giving away any emotion, and Edeya, well, she looked ready to charge into hell at his command. "*Jesucristo*," Victor muttered and received nothing but puzzled expressions in response.

Victor stepped between Lam and Rellia, startling them with the abrupt move, forcing them to move aside hurriedly. He lumbered up to the railing of the landing platform to look out over the tents and the rapidly assembling mass of men and women. Soldiers, he reminded himself. These were people signing on to fight to the death, to follow him into unknown lands to face enemies there and along the way. Did they not deserve to know who they were following? Did they not deserve to decide if he was worthy of leading them?

"Just send a bit of Energy into the necklace to activate it," Lam said from behind him.

Victor didn't respond but reached up, unsnapped Lifedrinker's harness, and lifted the great silvery axe, holding her before him with both hands. "At least I have you, *chica*; I always have you. No matter the battle I face, even in this one, a battle with my mind, you bring me comfort."

Always, the axe replied, and Victor grinned savagely.

"He still speaks to the axe, I see . . ." Lam said, perhaps trying to be funny with Edeya or Valla, but her words choked off as Victor reached into his Core, cast Titanic Aspect, and released his aura.

15

INCITING THE TROOPS

Victor's intention hadn't been to impose his aura on his friends and allies nearby, but he felt stronger, more powerful, and more capable when he wasn't working to hold it back. With it released, coursing out of him, he felt as if he'd just set down a sack of cement he'd been hauling around on his shoulder. Sure, he could carry it, but things were much more comfortable when he didn't have to. Still, he flinched a little when he heard the gasps behind and around him, and he hoped he hadn't driven anyone to their knees. He glanced over his shoulder, saw Rellia helping another woman to steady herself, and quickly looked forward again. Now wasn't the time to start feeling guilty for being powerful.

With that in mind, hoping to bolster his friends to alleviate his worry about them, he cast Inspiration of the Quinametzin. White-gold Energy poured through his pathways, seeping out through his very flesh, limning him in a pleasant, soft light that seemed to pulse through the air around him in a great circle, encompassing not just the platform he stood upon but the ground around him for dozens of yards in every direction.

Victor instantly felt the relief of those standing nearby, felt them shift and sigh, and knew that his spell was more than mitigating the effects of his aura, at least for those he considered allies. More than that, Victor felt the inspiration—stronger, deeper, and more profound than ever before; this spell was like a floodlight next to the lightbulb of his old Inspiring Presence. His back straightened, he widened his stance, and he reached up to touch the chain around his neck, channeling a bit of Energy to activate it.

Standing tall as he was, nearly fifteen feet of corded muscles wrapped in gleaming wyrm-scale armor, high above the ground on the airship platform, he was easy to see for the gathering troops. Their initial trickle had become a rush, and now they crowded closer. Victor could see sergeants, lieutenants, and even captains near the front, holding them back, keeping them from going wild as they witnessed Victor's gigantic, softly glowing form.

He didn't know exactly how well the necklace would work to project his voice, so he started by clearing his throat. The sound echoed over the encampment, sounding more a growl than anything else, and some of the clamor from below settled as the soldiers realized he was preparing to speak. Victor didn't even know how to address them all; was "soldiers" the right word? What was he going to say? His mind darted from idea to idea, and he began to feel a real sense of panic; did he look a fool?

Still, the inspiration coursing through him wouldn't let him falter for long. He grunted, cleared his throat again, squared his shoulders, and remembered that these people had come to fight for him; he wasn't trying to sell something. Why would they judge his words harshly? He stared at a section of soldiers who were more unruly than the others, pushing at the widespread arms of several sergeants and a captain. He faced them and said, "Settle down, soldiers. I have words for you." Again, the necklace did its work, pushing his voice out over the encampment, and stillness fell upon the assembled mass.

"Good," he heard Rellia breathe. Perhaps she'd been afraid he'd fail to find his voice.

"Soldiers!" Victor began, his mind racing toward the things he wanted to say. "I know you've come to fight under my"—he glanced to his left and right—"*our* banner. You know what's ahead of you: a long, possibly harsh journey. An unknown foe in the Marches, unknown enemies between here and there. Just last night, a new enemy showed me his face when his agents tried to kill me and Tribune Valla." He jerked his thumb toward Valla, then paused. What was he doing? He looked out over the sea of faces at the soldiers, some in armor, some in uniforms, some half dressed as though they'd just woken up. They were quiet. This didn't feel like it was what he should be saying.

Victor glanced down at Rellia, and she nodded, motioning for him to keep going, so he turned back to the soldiers and said, "It's not important; like any enemy that faces us, they were beaten." That got a little reaction out of them, some half-hearted cheering, clapping, and maybe a bit of laughter.

Were they laughing at him? No. Victor shook his head; that didn't make sense. Still, things didn't feel right. He felt as though he should be pumping them up, not lamely describing what he wanted to do.

"I'm not sure what you all have heard about me. Yeah, yeah, the big fight in the arena . . ." He trailed off as that got a bit more of a reaction, some soldiers cheering, others hooting, a lot more talking. "Things have changed since then—a lot. I've been to another world. I've fought giants and great wyrms. I've learned a great deal, and I'm going to use what I've learned to push you to victory!" Victor's voice gradually grew into a shout, and he lifted Lifedrinker as he finished speaking. Many of the soldiers clapped and stamped their feet. Quite a few cheered, but in Victor's mind, it was lame. These were soldiers. There were more than six thousand of them out there. Their response should be thunderous.

He decided to change tactics; it was time to talk them up. To get them fired up as he might do to his wrestling team before a match, just on a larger scale. What should he say, though? He stared out over that mass of colorful people, trying to gather his words. Would he be honest? Would he warn them of the troubles to come? He shook his head; he didn't need to. "I'm so goddamn proud when I look out over this encampment!" he bellowed. The soldiers stared at him, quieter than he'd expected, perhaps wondering at the sudden praise. Victor pressed on, "Look at you! Ready to take on the whole fucking world!"

Still, the soldiers were silent, some with open mouths, unsure. Had Victor gone too far? He laughed. Again, he lifted Lifedrinker high with one of his massive arms. "I know, I know. You want to conquer the Untamed Marches. You want to claim land for your loved ones, your people. Still, look at you!" he shouted. "Look!" He gestured left and right with his axe, and finally, the soldiers did as he asked; they looked around.

"Those are your brothers and sisters! Ready to seal their bond with you in *blood*!" He screamed the last word, and when it felt as if the soldiers weren't catching his mood, weren't feeling his enthusiasm, were in fact starting to look a little disturbed, Victor decided he'd had enough. He built the pattern for Berserk in his pathways, and just as he'd done to learn Inspiring Presence and Heroic Heart, Aspect of Terror and Inevitable Huntsman, he cast the spell with a massive torrent of glory-attuned Energy.

Glory infused his being. It was an Energy unlike any he'd ever felt, hot like rage but good like inspiration. It crackled through his pathways, igniting him with enthusiasm, purpose, and zeal for facing any sort of adversity, but particularly for fighting—for conquering. He didn't feel that he was losing himself; in fact, he felt more in control than ever. Still, he felt so incredible, so full of potential and power and the verve for life, that he lifted his head and roared. He was so busy savoring the sensation that he hadn't noticed what was happening around him.

A System message appeared in his vision, and when he lowered his head from his thunderous outburst, he quickly read it before dismissing it:

Congratulations! You have learned the spell: Banner of the Champion, Basic.

Banner of the Champion, Basic. Prerequisite: Affinity, Glory. Channeling the lust for Glory that lives in your heart, you manifest that aspect of your spirit in the form of a banner that hangs in the air behind you, bestowing a fraction of your potency and desire to those allies of yours who look upon it. Conversely, enemies who see your banner will suffer a malus that will reduce their will and build dread in their hearts. Energy Cost: Minimum 100, scalable. Cooldown: Long.

Victor looked behind and up, and there it was, hanging in the air behind him, blazing with brilliant, sparkling golden Energy—an enormous banner. It was rectangular, two yards wide by three or four high, with a pale, creamy background on which a golden sun blazed, nearly as bright as the one in the sky. From the bottom of that blazing sun, rivulets of blood ran down the pale background to drip from the banner's bottom edge, each drop exploding like a little red starburst behind Victor's back.

Victor roared again when he saw it, driven nearly into a frenzy by the inspiration and glory in his pathways. He lifted Lifedrinker into the air, and this time her silvery head exploded into glorious molten fury, black smoke billowing into the air from her hot, razor-edged blade. The soldiers, staring at Victor, mouths open, eyes wide and transfixed by the immense blazing banner behind him, finally started to feel what he was experiencing; they cheered. They lifted their weapons and screamed. Victor, feeling what he'd been waiting for, the adulation of a crowd, bunched his knees and launched himself off the platform, heedless of the damage he caused with his explosive movement.

He landed squarely on the ground just before the center of the assembled soldiers, and, as those closest to him stumbled and fell from the concussion, he lifted Lifedrinker again and bellowed, "We are going to destroy any force that confronts us!"

Again, the soldiers cheered, their titanic leader ablaze with golden and white Energy, an enormous standard hanging in the air behind him, filling them with the lust for glory, striding among them, roaring and shouting his praise. "You're the best damn soldiers on the planet! We'll smash our way through the Untamed Marches! No one will stop us!" He went on and on, exhorting them to scream and roar and howl. "Let me hear you!" he thundered, pumping his blazing axe toward the sky.

"Ancestors!" Rellia gasped as she helped Chev-dak to his feet. Everyone on the platform was staggered, struggling to stand without stepping on the shattered planks left in the wake of Victor's leap. Everyone seemed to be all right, uninjured. In fact, they seemed better than all right, and Rellia could relate. She felt good, incredible even; the effect of that man's Energy and his huge blazing banner were undeniable. She wanted to draw her rapier, to leap from the stands and follow him. She wanted to crush her—their—enemies and see them driven before her. She wanted to hear the praise of her people and see the adulation in their eyes as they witnessed her victories.

"Where's he gone," Lam asked, then she launched into the air, her wings humming as they carried her aloft.

Lam's little assistant, Edeya, cried, "He's among the troops! Look how he towers over them like a giant! Roots! My heart felt like it was squeezing out of my chest when his aura fell on us. Thank the Great Tree he cast his inspiration on us! Can we follow him?" Her voice was thrilled, excited, desperate. Was the man's pull so strong?

"A titan, not a giant," Valla said, stepping around Polo Vosh to stand near the cracked, bent railing. Rellia frowned at her daughter's back but moved between two of her attendants, urging them to step away from the broken center of the platform, and when she got to the edge, she looked out at a scene that seemed cut from myth.

The soldiers surged and moved in great waves around Victor's gigantic figure, buzzing with excitement, cheering, screaming, howling, and falling to their knees in ecstatic, frenzied pandemonium. Victor's deep voice rumbled above the din, shouting encouragement, roaring, and bellowing his praise. "What have we unleashed," Rellia asked, her eyes wide, her jaw falling slack. Despite her words, she too wanted to get out there, to follow Victor. If he wanted them to march into battle right that moment, she'd be ready to join him.

"A titan," Valla said again.

"You've seen this?" Polo asked, his deep voice rumbling, trembling with, if Rellia were any judge, excitement.

"Um, similar. Not that banner, though; that's new." Was that pride in her daughter's voice? As if she could read her mind, Valla turned to Rellia and said, "Was this what you were hoping for?" Now she sounded smug, as though she'd seen Rellia make a mistake. Had she? Rellia frowned but didn't respond. She watched the titan-sized man out there among the troops, striding around, the soldiers moving like water in a tide pool, surging and ebbing around his progress. If she were honest with herself, this was a less-than-ideal development, at least for her.

She'd hoped that, by springing the speech on Victor, he'd recognize his inexperience and see that he needed people like Rellia, and their partnership would be solidified. This, though, was beyond anything she could have imagined. These soldiers were going to be fanatical in their loyalty. Victor would feel more secure in his role, and she'd be further sidelined. She began to worry that she would lose control of this entire expedition.

Valla had turned back toward Victor, so Rellia stepped closer to her and said, softly, just for her ears, "Are you angry with me, daughter?"

Valla frowned and glanced at her. She'd become more beautiful, more powerful. It was apparent from the way she carried herself to the feeling of her aura, more pronounced now that Victor's was farther away. What's more, the girl had let her hair grow and was wearing that, arguably quite impressive, armor rather than her uniform. Rellia had tried for years to get her to stop dressing like a legionnaire! Now that she wanted her to dress the part, she'd decided to gird herself like a warrior? "Aren't you pleased that he announced you as a tribune?"

"Certainly, I'm pleased. Are you?" Valla's frown curled into a smile, though Rellia wondered if she saw a touch of cruelty in those eyes. "As for whether I'm angry with you, the answer is no, Mother. We have much to discuss, however."

Rellia's frown deepened, easier for her now that Victor's banner grew more and more distant. For the first time, she worried that she'd made a mistake sending Valla to shadow Victor. What had she experienced in such a short time to change her so much? Just a few months ago, she'd never have taken such an insolent tone. Where had the doting daughter gone? The one who'd clung to her like a barnacle on a sea ship when Rellia had lost her foot, so protective . . .

"Mother, he seems to be winding down. Is the command structure there, inside the central palisade?"

Rellia jerked her eyes up, looking out at the distant, glowing figure, still towering high, still waving around that smoking axe. *Great Mother, that axe!*

Rellia shivered, remembering its bite. "Yes, Valla. Tell me, though, why do you think he'll stop anytime soon?"

"Look more closely. The soft white light, his inspiration Energy, is gone. If he's pulled it back or ended that spell, likely he'll end the others soon as well."

"Those are spells, then? Not his bloodline?" Polo asked, joining the conversation.

"A combination," Valla replied, shrugging. "He's a potent package. His bloodline alone is devastating, but combine that with his powerful Spirit Core and his affinities . . . I pity our foes."

"Aye," Polo grumbled, "he's grown much since we last sparred. I don't know how he thinks I'll be useful to him."

"He's not always titan-sized. He still has much to learn about the axe." Valla offered Polo a smile, and Rellia felt her heart stir with a bit of pride. She was a good girl at heart. Perhaps it was good that she was feeling her independence and becoming more of an individual.

"Very well. Come," Rellia said, moving to the wooden stairs, careful to step around the shattered boards at the center of the platform. "We'll walk to the palisade gate and wait for him." She was pleased that her foot, artificed by a cousin in Tharcray, provided enough feedback to help her navigate without a stumble.

"He's got them so damn riled up," ap'Jinna groused. "It's inspiring, sure, but look!" He gestured left and right as he came down the steps. "Half the tents are trampled. I'm going to call a captain's meeting. Is that all right, Lady Rellia? We'll need to instill some discipline and get this camp organized."

"Don't ask me. Your tribune is right there." Rellia pointed to Valla.

"Really, Mother? I thought you'd have assumed the role of legate by now."

"No, not yet. Lam and I wait to speak with Victor about our placement in the ranks."

"And yet Captain ap'Jinna just asked you for permission . . ."

"Oh, Daughter! Must everything be difficult with you? Yes, Virt! Gather the captains. See to it." Rellia dismissed the man, waving her hand at his sputtered apologies. Then she began to stride purposefully toward the palisade gate, irritated by this whole affair; nothing had gone to plan. Where was Lam? She scanned the skies and finally looked back toward Victor, distant now, toward the back of the encampment, and she saw her wings pouring motes of Energy as she streaked around over his head, circling him and his banner.

"I'm not trying to be difficult, Mother, but I must keep a critical eye on everything, including you and the other nobles and everyone who will vie for Victor's loyalty. He depends on me."

Rellia's budding irritation at Lam slipped from her mind as she turned to her daughter. "What do you mean, depends on you?"

"He's named me his tribune primus."

"Oho? You, who've never led more than a cohort? I had others in mind for that role. Lam herself mentioned an interest."

"Regardless. Victor has chosen."

Rellia looked around, saw that her retainers and the other officers who'd been on the platform were following a respectful distance behind, and allowed some affection into her voice as she said, "I'm proud of you, Valla."

Finally, Valla's expression softened a little, and she glanced quickly toward Rellia, meeting her eyes. Rellia felt something melt in her heart, a spot where she held memories of the little girl she'd taken in all those years ago. Valla had such beautiful eyes, a color right in the middle of green and blue, big and angular, angry like a storm at sea when they wanted to be or gentle, like placid waters on a soft, sandy beach when the moment was right. As their gazes locked, the girl—the woman—on whom she'd pinned the future of her household said, "I missed you, Mother."

Rellia felt moisture spring into her eyes, and she quickly looked away, walking stiff-backed toward the fort in the center of the encampment. Things hadn't gone perfectly, but they hadn't gone badly. Her daughter was home, and she was closer than ever to the titanic champion still railing away out there among the troops. Rellia may not have gained an edge over Victor with her little speech ploy, but she'd strengthened the morale of her army, and word would travel. Her enemies would feel something they might not have felt for a very long time, perhaps never in their lives—doubt.

16

COMMAND COUNCIL

Victor walked, surrounded by cheering, excited troops, toward the command structure. He was no longer the size of a titan, and his banner had faded away some time ago, disappearing in sparkling motes of golden Energy; he'd nearly drained his Core dry of glory and inspiration, and he didn't think rage or fear would serve his needs at the moment, so he'd let his spells drop and shouldered Lifedrinker, slowly making his way back to the center of the encampment. That said, he still felt as though he towered over everyone around, even Lam, who'd landed to walk beside him.

The soldiers around him were abuzz, noisy and eager, talking about the campaign, commenting on Victor's display, and speculating about when the order to march would come down. Even with their excitement and noise, he heard Lam clearly enough as she spoke up. "That was impressive, Victor. You've gained much strength since I saw you in the arena with Rellia."

"Thank you," Victor said, slowing his pace slightly so he could more easily return Lifedrinker to her harness.

"She's fully Heart Silver now, I see. What about the fire? How'd she learn that trick?"

Victor appreciated Lam referring to Lifedrinker as a person. "She drank the life out of an ancient wyrm, one with magma for blood. Well, not really magma, but it felt like it." Victor kept his eyes forward, his long legs easily devouring the distance. In minutes they'd be walking up to the central palisade, and he'd have more than Lam throwing questions at him.

"Did I do something to upset you, Victor?"

Her words startled him, and Victor slowed down, giving her more of his attention, meeting her emerald eyes. At the concern on her face, his steps faltered, and he stopped, turning to look at her squarely. "What do you mean?"

"You were, oh, I don't know, cold toward me earlier. When we met on the airship platform."

"Uh . . ." Victor felt heat rising in the back of his neck, his old awkwardness returning so forcefully that he could almost forget that he'd just whipped six thousand soldiers into a frenzy, could almost forget that hundreds of soldiers were still following him and the captain, were in fact forming a big circle around them, though standing a respectful distance away as they spoke. "God, Lam. No, I'm not mad at you! I'm just an awkward fucking guy when it comes to women I happen to idolize. It caught me off guard when you hugged me, and yeah, I had some paranoid thoughts, but really, I think I was just surprised that you'd done it. We're good, okay?"

Lam smiled, and Victor noticed a scar above the right corner of her mouth that formed a kind of extra dimple when she did it. She nodded and reached her wiry, tattooed right arm toward him, holding her hand out. Victor took it, wrapping his long, powerful fingers around hers, surprised at their length and how she could grip his enormous palm. "I'm glad we're good, Victor." She released his hand and nodded. "Come now, let's get to the command fort. I've got a million questions for you, and so do the others, I'm sure. Let's start with that banner of yours—it's amazing. It'll be invaluable on the battlefield. How often can you create it?"

"Probably anytime I need to. It has a similar cooldown and Energy cost to my basic Berserk spell. We can talk about that and other things later, but first, Lam, tell me about your tattoos. I don't see many Ghelli with marks like that." In his mind, Victor thought he was being clever, changing the topic, and turning the focus back on Lam. Later, on reflection, he might think it was clumsy and might have sent the wrong signals to the captain, but she handled it well, nodding and holding up her left arm.

"Largely, they're from my time in the Legion. From my time in Urwa ap'Challa's cohort and later, after I was given my captaincy, from my cohort. Most of them are commemorations of deployments and battles. See, like this one." She pointed to a scene depicted on the inside of her arm. It pictured a pile of skulls on a field littered with broken spears. In the background, a crooked stone tower stood before a mist-covered moon. "This is from my time with Urwa's cohort. The battle of Rook Tower—not a pleasant memory.

At this battle, our entire legion was wiped out, and the supporting legion lost half its troops rescuing survivors like me."

"Shit," Victor sighed, shaking his head. "Sorry for bringing it up."

"It's not your fault I carry my memories on my flesh. It's not your fault one of the Emperor's cousins went mad, created an army of golems, and tried to usurp the throne."

"Seriously?" Victor slowed again, not wanting to arrive at the palisade before finishing the topic with Lam. "Was he a Ridonne?"

"Oh, yes. A golemancer with a full-fledged Ridonne bloodline. I never laid eyes on him, but it was enough to see his creations. I'll tell you about them sometime over some very strong alcohol." Lam gestured ahead. "We're here. Thanks for your interest, Victor."

"Yeah, of course." Victor stepped up to the wooden gateway where Valla, Rellia, Edeya, Polo, and four others, all Ardeni whom he didn't recognize, waited.

Lam stepped ahead of him, taking a position by Rellia's side and speaking into her ear, though not so quietly that Victor couldn't hear, "Our troops are ready to follow him into the abyss."

"Victor!" Edeya said, blushing and glancing quickly at Rellia and Lam, but unable to contain herself. "Those spells! Your aura! It was amazing. I'm so excited to be a part of this expedition with you!"

"At ease, Lieutenant," Rellia sighed.

"Lieutenant? Nice one, Edeya." Victor chuckled, holding out a fist nearly the size of the young Ghelli's head. Edeya smiled at him but didn't move to bump his knuckles, so Victor pulled it back with a sigh; Valla would have understood. At the thought, he looked at Valla, saw the wry grin on her face, saw how she stood close to Rellia, and wondered how things had gone with her mother while he'd been out rallying the troops.

"Victor, we have much to discuss. Would you like to join us in the map room?" Rellia asked, her voice terse, probably trying to head off any further small talk.

"Yeah, all right. Valla?"

"Right here," Valla said, moving away from Rellia to stand at his side. Victor smiled at her. His intent had been to ask if she was coming along, but he liked how she was demonstrating her loyalty to him.

"This way." Rellia turned and walked through the gateway, Lam close behind. Everyone else waited for Victor and Valla to pass through before following. The inside of the little palisade was much as Victor had imagined.

A rough rampart lined the wall, stables for the officer's mounts were on the right, a practice yard was on the left, and directly in front of the gate was a two-story wooden structure, rough but sturdy looking.

Seeing the stables brought Thistle to Victor's mind, and he said, "Hey, I don't suppose anyone got our mounts from that inn in Persi Gables, did they?"

Valla looked at him with amused eyes and said, "Some of us were in much closer contact with our Far Scribe books. I believe our mounts are at Rellia's estate."

Rellia glanced over her shoulder, offered Victor a nod, and said, "I'll have them brought over unless you two are planning a trip into the city?"

"It depends," Victor replied. "Have you or Lam"—he spoke up so Lam would recognize he was including her—"managed to get any information about Olivia Bennet?"

Rellia held up her hand to forestall Lam's response and said, "We have information. Let's speak after we've handled some legion formalities and have a smaller group of ears." With that, she walked up the steps and inside. Everyone followed her through a spacious, if rough, entry hall, then left, through a wide pair of double doors, and into a well-lit room featuring a huge table with a map at its center. It wasn't as nice as the map in Rellia's home back in Gelica, but it was plenty detailed to Victor's eye.

"We're roughing it a bit out here, but after the incident on your airship, we felt it wise to be with the troops. We have two airships, now that you're back, scouting the area for any signs of aggression," Lam said as the group filed in.

Rellia stood before the map table, and Victor remembered the last time he'd seen her doing so; she'd been missing a foot. His gaze fell to her shiny black boots, and when she caught him looking, he offered her a slight shrug. She cleared her throat and said, "Edeya and Darro, sit to the side and take notes, please." Edeya, her little wings pulling close under Rellia's scrutiny, hurried to the side of the room where a row of straight-backed wooden chairs lined the wall and sat down. One of the Ardeni Victor didn't know joined her, a young man with bright red hair and eyes, wearing an unadorned uniform, much like Edeya's.

"Can we start with introductions?" Victor asked, pulling one of the large wooden doors closed. Valla closed the other one, nudging Polo to move farther into the room so he didn't block the doorway. "I'll start." He turned to face everyone, those he knew and those he didn't. "I'm Victor Sandoval. You all can call me Victor, but if we're in front of the troops, be sure to use the appropriate title, which, I'm learning, is legate. Yes?"

"That's right, Victor." Lam nodded her approval, but she looked to Rellia to introduce herself next. It seemed to Victor that Lam had taken on a subordinate role with Rellia, and he felt a little relieved to see it; he didn't want to be caught in the middle of power struggles between those two.

"Oh, all of us, Victor?" Rellia frowned as he continued to stare at her. "Well, you all know me, but I'm Rellia ap'Yensha."

"And your role with the army?" Victor pressed.

Rellia's eyes narrowed, and she nodded to him, his heavy-handed game made clear. "I'm the noble sponsor of this legion, and, as for rank, I thought we could discuss that. I have several ideas."

"Good, good." Victor looked at Lam, raising one eyebrow.

"Lam of the Blue Deep, newly minted Lady of Gelica, Captain of the Imperial Legion, and hopeful tribune of this fine fighting force." She snapped a perfect salute, her fist and heels striking in unison, and stared directly into Victor's eyes.

"I'm Valla ap'Yensha, Victor's Tribune Primus." Valla spoke quickly, stepping away from Victor's side so she could face them all, filling the brief silence after Lam's salute. Victor hadn't heard the term "tribune primus" before but could infer what it meant and didn't disapprove. He'd told Valla back on the airship that he wanted her close, that he was relying upon her above all others. Looking back, her show of formality made more sense now. He nodded, face solemn, but that didn't forestall an objection from one of the older men in the room.

"Excuse me, but is that true?" the Ardeni asked, his piercing yellow eyes looking up at Victor.

"It is. Introduce yourself before we speak further." Victor turned the full focus of his glower on the man.

The white-haired, medal- and ribbon-bedecked fellow swallowed noisily and cleared his throat. "I am Borrius ap'Gandro, former Legate of the Imperial Legion and a close friend of the ap'Yensha clan."

"Ah," Victor said, nodding. Now he saw why Borrius might be annoyed at Valla's high rank. He dug deep for what he hoped were the right words, trying to imagine how Tes might smooth things over. "Thank you for bringing your experience to this army, Borrius. As you must know, however, some qualities are less tangible than experience. Some qualities that a legate must heavily value—good judgment, bravery, loyalty, strong character, intelligence, grit, brilliance under pressure; I could go on, all day really, about the fine qualities Tribune Primus Valla has shown me over the last few months, but I think I've made my point. I'm not saying you aren't similarly endowed with fine qualities, sir, but at this late hour, I must consider what I know, not what I hope."

"As you say, Legate," Borrius said, snapping a salute, his face stony. "May I ask what rank you'll bestow upon me?"

"Tribune, of course."

"Thank you, sir."

"Ahem," Polo said. "Well, I'm Polo Vosh, and I've been filling the role of captain, commander of the seventh cohort."

Victor held out his hand for Polo to grasp, and as the two large men gripped each other, Victor grinned and said, "Captain it is, but let's not forget your other duty—sparring with your legate."

"Aye, sir, I've a trick or two with the axe I haven't yet shared."

Victor turned to the only man left to speak, a tall, well-muscled man wearing just a handful of medals on his uniform. He had a severe, hawkish expression with bright silver eyes that, as was the norm for Ardeni, matched his hair. Like Victor and Valla, he wore a weapon openly, a short, broad-bladed sword that hung from his belt in a gold and black scabbard. He was the only other person in the room with a weapon on display. Even Polo Vosh kept his axe in a dimensional container, so Victor wondered if this last member of their little group might have a conscious weapon.

"I am Ordus ap'Yensha, Rellia's youngest, most handsome uncle."

"Ugh," Rellia said, then looked mortified that the sound had escaped her lips.

"Ordus?" Victor frowned, rubbing his chin. "I don't think Rellia mentioned you to me. What capacity do you hope to fill in the army?"

"He's been acting as captain of the newly formed tenth cohort," Rellia supplied.

"Just so." Ordus smiled, offering a rather sloppy salute, his fist thumping his chest long before his heels haphazardly clicked.

"Right. Good to meet you, Ordus." Victor looked at Rellia and asked, "Shouldn't there be eight other captains here?"

"Exactly right." Rellia nodded. "I'm sorry, but Ordus, you and Polo should head outside; ap'Jinna is gathering the captains to see to restoring some order to the camp in the wake of our legate's . . . enthusiasm."

"Of course," Ordus said, showing off a dazzling sharp-toothed smile and sketching a half bow.

Polo snapped a much cleaner salute and turned to leave, but Victor called after him, "Polo, meet me in a few hours outside, huh? I need to work out some tension."

"Will do, Victor." With that, he and Ordus slipped out the door, closing it behind them.

Victor looked at Edeya, then over to the other young officer, and asked, "Do we need him? I'd like to speak frankly about a few things, Rellia."

"Darro is one of mine. He's fine, Victor."

"If you're sure. Um, not to be overly blunt or to offend anyone, but are we good?" He gestured around the room, "To speak openly, I mean."

"As the only other person here with whom you're unfamiliar," Borrius said, "I can only assume you're concerned about my loyalty. Yes?" When Victor didn't reply, he pressed on. "Fear not. I stand with Rellia on all matters, even those concerning the fools in Tharcray who sent assassins your way."

"I trust Borrius," Rellia said.

"He's clean," Lam added. "I spent a pretty penny vetting him and a few others."

"You what?" Borrius's voice rose an octave with outrage.

"Relax," Rellia said. "I encouraged her. It's for the best, Borrius; my word alone wouldn't suffice for Lam and Victor to feel comfortable speaking their minds otherwise."

"Right. Well, let's get down to the meat, then," Victor said, voicing something that had been on his mind ever since Chokodo-dak told him who he was. "Is the Empire going to attack us?"

Several people spoke at once, Lam, Borrius, and Valla, but Rellia held up her hand in the din, and Victor focused on her as she said, "None of us know, but we should have a better idea soon. My people are interrogating Chokodo and that imperial consort as we speak. I can tell you this much, though—don't believe anything that man told you. Principes aren't known for being honest, and anything he said would likely have been engineered to avoid having the Ridonne pull the bones from his still-living body."

"So, no intelligence to share?" Valla asked.

"Not yet. Let's save it for our next meeting. Victor, might we talk about my placement in the ranks? It will be important as we deal with the troops, the nobility, our enemies, etcetera. I had hoped to operate as a co-legate with you."

Victor frowned at Rellia's swift co-opting of the meeting, at her redirection of the discussion away from what he felt was the only truly important topic. Still, he indulged her, saying, "Rellia started this whole endeavor; the Writ of Conquest belongs to her family, and I wouldn't be here if not for her. I'm open to her idea, but what do you all say?"

"It seems fair." Borrius nodded to Rellia, and Victor mentally noted that he was likely a member of the campaign as a dependable vote for Rellia.

"I," Lam started to say, but then shook her head and started again. "Rellia has staked her entire future, and that of the family members she cares about, on this campaign. I've also poured a fortune into it, but only a fraction of what she's done. I won't object."

"Thank you, Lam." Rellia smiled at her almost sweetly, and Victor found himself suddenly mentally rearranging certain ideas he'd taken for granted. He'd thought Lam was mostly out for herself, that she didn't really like Rellia, and that she'd work to undermine the noble at every turn. It seemed either she'd come to trust and like Rellia, or she was playing a more subtle game than he'd anticipated.

"Valla?" Victor prodded.

"Me? Well, I'm biased, as you know. Rellia, being my mother, has my loyalty and support, but as your tribune primus, I must always act in your best interest. I believe it's important for the troops to have a clear line of command. Should you and Rellia ever disagree, what would they do? Would it result in military strife? No, just as there is a tribune primus, there must be a legate primus. Victor should take the top role, for without him, Rellia's family standing would have been diminished to the point that she couldn't have possibly mustered these troops. In any case, it's clear the troops would favor him."

Victor nodded. The idea sounded good to him; it gave Rellia legitimacy with the troops but kept things clean in terms of rank. "What do you say, Rellia? I'm happy to say, here, in front of all and for the record"—he nodded to Edeya and Darro—"that I don't intend to make any major decisions without discussing matters with you and Lam. I understand I lack experience in some . . . arenas."

"Interesting choice of words." Rellia nodded, her lips quirking into a half smile. "My daughter is wise. It's to be expected, considering she sat at my knee and listened to councils much like this for a large part of her childhood. I will accept the role of subordinate legate with regard to military matters. On matters of diplomacy and budget, I must insist on an equal role. Can we draw up a contract to reflect those terms?"

"Yeah." Victor nodded. "I'm not sure how this usually works, but just so we're clear, I'm not signing any contracts that require me to bind my Energy to it. I did that at Fainhallow for a short minute, and I wouldn't say I liked it. It feels too much like enslavement. I won't have any of you do it either. Not for this army."

"Well, Victor." Rellia shook her head with a baffled, rather condescending smile and said, "How else do you plan to guard against treason? Usually, everyone in the command structure signs Energy-bound oaths of fealty to the legion."

"Yeah, and who writes the contracts? Who keeps them? Who would be the responsible party? Me? 'Cause I'm at the top? I don't want people enslaved by magic to my cause!"

"You didn't say any of this at Fainhallow," Valla interjected.

"I've had time to think about it since then. It felt too much like when the mines owned me. I don't like the idea of people's free will being taken away!"

"Victor." This time it was Lam trying to get past his stubbornness. "We can phrase the contract in such a way that no freedoms are lost, other than those that might lead to our defeat. Something simple like, 'Before you may act in a way that you believe would be detrimental to the legion, you must resign your post.' That way, we'd at least have a bit of warning when a person was disgruntled or not intent on helping us secure our victory."

"So, what? We'd just imprison or kill anyone who resigns their post?"

"No! That could also be a part of the contract on the legion's side; we have to allow people to walk away from their post unharmed." Rellia seemed earnest, seemed as if she wanted to find a compromise.

Victor sighed and held up his hands. "I'm not trying to be unreasonable. I hear you. Let me think about it, all right? I'd like to think our cause is worthy of loyalty, that we are worthy of loyalty. I know that's naive, but when I preach a certain philosophy, I feel I should practice it."

"It's not naive," Valla said. "It's admirable." Victor looked at her, then at Lam and Rellia, and as he saw the concern and willingness to listen in their expressions, he sighed and nodded.

"We can find a compromise. Thank you for working with me. Now, let's talk about when you want to march."

17

✦

OLIVIA

Victor sighed and stretched, arching his back, listening to the bedframe creak its protestations. Though it groaned, the bed was comfortable. He wished he could say the same about the room—too small, too noisy, and too full of light. Through the thin wooden walls he could hear sergeants or lieutenants barking orders. He could hear troops marching in time, chanting their strange marching rhymes. He could smell food cooking, bacon grease for sure, and something like bread, but sweeter. Someone was making biscuits, maybe. Despite the noise and sun streaming into his eyes, Victor felt damn good. He was relaxed, mind at ease, more ready for what the future held than he could remember in a long while.

His meeting with Rellia and the senior staff had lasted a few hours the day before. They'd discussed the marching route, going over likely ambush sites and possible alternatives. He'd learned quite a lot about army logistics, a topic much different than he'd anticipated when considering the ubiquitous nature of dimensional storage containers. When Victor had asked about the need for any wagons at all, he'd been informed that the wagons themselves were dimensional containers, each holding a vastly greater amount than a simple ring could contain. Among the twenty-five wagons serving the legion, Rellia and her people had stashed enough food and camp equipment to last the army, at its current size, more than two years.

Additionally, to ensure against the possible loss or destruction of the wagons, each captain carried enough food for his or her cohort to last a month in an emergency-access-only dimensional pouch. Beyond supplies, Victor had learned that the airships had limited range and required constant recharging, so their specialized crew ate a significant portion of Rellia's budget, quite a lot more than Victor had anticipated. He'd suggested getting a squad together of flight-capable Ghelli but had been swiftly schooled about how rare true flyers like Lam were. In their legion, only four were capable of covering more than a couple of miles at a time. Even Lam insisted she'd be exhausted if she had to scout for more than an hour or two now and then.

Not to put too much of a damper on things, Rellia had oozed praise to him and Valla about the captured strigaii, insisting that, thanks to those rare mounts, they'd be able to retire the hired-on airship after a month or so. Victor could recognize a bone being thrown to appease his ego, so he'd just nodded and smiled, biding his time, holding his tongue as he took in the information, learning as much as he could because he was determined not to be a figurehead or a simple brute on the battlefield; he wanted to learn to truly lead these soldiers. The summative point of the command council was that Rellia and Lam wanted to march soon, tentatively scheduling their departure for dawn in three days.

Later in the afternoon, Victor had met with the captains, thanked them for their hard work, and put a face to their names. He didn't doubt he'd need some reminding, but Valla seemed eager to help with that aspect of his job. After that meeting, he'd sparred for hours with Polo Vosh, and, exhausted from a couple of hard days, Victor had gone to sleep early. "And now I get to go meet Olivia, my long-lost relative." A chuckle escaped him as he sat up. In truth, he didn't think much would come of the meeting. What could Olivia tell him? He supposed she might be able to shed some light on how they were related, at least.

Victor dressed, opting to wear his armor but leaving his helmet in his storage ring. The helmet was great, and it didn't feel too cumbersome to wear, considering it was a gigantically heavy hunk of metal, but his head felt a lot better without it. His thinking was that he'd be able to put it on if a fight looked likely, and if he got surprised, his Quinametzin bloodline was working to make his skull pretty damn hard anyway. He slung Lifedrinker in her harness, and after a visit to the rough but private bathroom, he made his way down the rickety wooden steps to the fort's entrance hall.

He wasn't surprised to see Valla standing near the door, waiting for him. "Morning," he called.

She frowned at him and said, "You're small again."

"Small?" Victor's voice rose with indignation. "I don't think so!"

"I mean, you aren't your usual size, which means you're binding your potential. We're about to ride into a city where assassins may lurk."

"Yeah, I get it. I just wanted to fit in my bed. Is that a crime?" Victor reached into his Core and severed the connection to his spell, suddenly surging upward, more than a foot taller and a hundred pounds heavier. "Better?"

"Your helmet?"

"*Pinche* . . . I'll put it on when we get close to town." Victor paused in front of her, noting her critical expression, and decided to give her a little trouble of her own. "Hey, I have a job for you, Primus."

"Oh? What's that, Sir Legate?"

"Remember when we arrived in Persi Gables, and I went to deal with that pit boss, Yund?"

"Yes, and you sent the indentured fighters to the army when you liberated them."

"Good memory. Anyway, I was asking around yesterday, and I guess the leader of that group, Sarl, was made a lieutenant. I want you to pick one of the captains for him to replace."

"What?"

"Yeah. Pick one of the captains, preferably not Polo or Ordus, and give him their post. Well, I don't care about Ordus, but he's your uncle, so . . ."

"What do I tell the captain I'm cutting loose?"

"Isn't that something you can handle, dear Primus?"

"Can you tell me why I'm doing this?" Valla hadn't really shown any emotion about the request, but she didn't look happy.

"Trust is number one, Valla. That's why I have you as my right-hand . . . woman. I trust Sarl, so I'd like him to be in charge of one of the cohorts."

Valla nodded, idly tugging at one of her strands of bright, teal-colored hair. Victor kept wondering if she would cut it and put it back into its tight, formal military style, but he knew better than to make a remark. "I can do that. I'll arrange for the promotion and the handover when we return from Persi Gables. Will that be all right?"

"Yeah, perfect."

"Shall I strip the unlucky captain of his or her rank, or shall I allow them to retain their captaincy while acting as a lieutenant?"

"That's fine." At Valla's nod, he walked through the open doors, squinting at the bright sun and breathing deeply of the fresh air. "How are we traveling?"

"We'll take Rellia's coach to her residence where, hopefully, Olivia Bennet will meet us, and then we'll get Uvu and Thistle."

"Oh? She didn't confirm?"

"Rellia's agent delivered your request, and she seemed open to the meeting, but nothing is certain." As she spoke, the two walked out the palisade gates to find Rellia's sleek black coach waiting, drawn by two vidanii, quite a bit smaller than Victor remembered Thistle being. He gave the coach a second glance and frowned.

"Really, Valla? You couldn't wait until we got out of the coach on the other end to bug me about my size?"

Olivia finished her tea and motioned for Innkeeper Zel to approach her table. As the rather silly, rather sweet, older Vodkin came near, pushing his spectacles up on his white-furred nose, she placed five of her quad-attuned Energy beads on the table and said, "It's been wonderful staying here the last few weeks. It's about time I got back to work, though; the notes from my professors grow increasingly irate."

"Ah, so you weren't here on academy business?"

"Well, I told you I was, and it was true at first, but that was settled after just a few days—an overzealous death mage trying to work out a portal to a plane best left disconnected from ours. My mentor expected me to return to the academy, and the older student, the one responsible for our 'mission,' wasn't too pleased to leave me here." Olivia chuckled, remembering Relip's face when she'd said she wasn't going with him back to Fainhallow. She shrugged and added, "I needed some time, and I've had it, so now I think it's best I get back to work."

"Just so, miss, just so. Well, we've certainly enjoyed your company, and you've been the best-paying client I've had in some time. If you need me to vouch for how hard you've been studying, just say so! I've seen you with your nose in those books sitting here all evening, every evening."

"Thank you so much, Mr. Gorse, but I'll be all right. I've had some leniency granted due to some . . . circumstances last year. Still, I hope to return soon. I hope you'll pass my compliments on to your wife; I haven't been this well-fed in a long, long while." Olivia stood and brushed a few crumbs from the front of her splendid magical robes, currently colored a soft, pale sky-blue. She reached up, adjusting the Crown of Nightmarch, wondering, as she often did, if it was too much. It didn't matter; she'd promised Alyss, dear Professor ap'Rall, that she'd wear it and that she'd ignore her self-doubt. It was a promise she meant to keep, the least she could do for her lovely, lost friend.

"Farewell, Miss Olivia!" Mr. Gorse called from the inn's doorway as she strode up the cobbled avenue, and Olivia raised one hand to wave, allowing a bit of Energy into her pathways so it was limned with blue flames.

"Right! Now, let's go see this mysterious Victor fellow. How'd another human get here, I wonder? Something to do with the fae?" The streets and sidewalks were quiet; it was the end of the week, and few people did much in Persi Gables, she'd come to learn, in the morning hours on weekends. As usual, she marveled at the people she did see and, of course, their animals. She was always on the verge of asking little kids or friendly-looking adults about their pets—questions like, "What would be a good companion for a person living in the academy who travels frequently?" or, "Is that cute little bunny-looking thing as friendly as it seems?"

She saw a Shadeni coaxing a large draft animal, an elephant-sized bird, out of an alley, and she admired his long, thick horns, wondering why Oylla-dak didn't have such. Then again, Oylla had those star-filled eyes, and Olivia had yet to broach the subject of them with the woman. "Must be something to do with a bloodline. Perhaps I could bring it up in relation to Morgan. I could say he wanted to know more about bloodlines in general . . ."

"Did you say something, miss?" an older man sweeping the walk she'd just trodden across asked.

"Sorry, good sir! I'm someone who tends to talk to herself. Nothing to worry about!"

"Right. Good day to you." He nodded his white-haired head, lifted the pipe he'd been smoking back to his lips, and returned to sweeping, not sparing her another glance.

Olivia resumed walking and chatting aloud. "I'll bring it up next time we're having a friendly meeting. I do want to study bloodlines, and it makes a perfect segue into asking for more access to the closed libraries." Olivia sighed and pressed her lips together, realizing she was getting carried away with her self-talk. She'd been doing it more and more, ever since coming to Persi Gables and spending so much time alone, away from her friends and Adaida. Sadness loomed darkly behind her eyes as she continued following the messenger's directions to the ap'Yensha estate.

She'd not heard of Rellia ap'Yensha, which she supposed was a good thing. The only nobles she'd come to know anything about all seemed quite villainous. Lord ap'Gravin was the prime example, and she still had half a mind to pay him a visit. Morgan had insisted that he was handling the matter, and she had plenty on her plate, or at least it had seemed that way when they'd parted ways. Was he back yet? Surely there must be some news by now.

A surge of guilt blossomed in her stomach as she thought about the colony, the council, and all the people there who relied on her or, at least, would rely on her while Morgan was gone; shouldn't she have been helping somehow? Wasn't it selfish of her to hide out in an inn for weeks on end? "And now another wrinkle," she sighed, stepping up to the guardhouse outside the ap'Yensha estate.

"May I help you, miss?" the liveried young Ardeni asked.

"I'm Olivia Bennet. Here to meet Valla ap'Yensha and a fellow named Victor."

"Right, right. I have a note right here. Please walk to the estate." He gestured to the left of his little guard station, up a lovely path lined with flowering shrubs and the occasional well-trimmed fruit tree. "Just follow this cobbled path, and someone will be waiting for you."

"Thank you." Olivia lifted her robes slightly in a curtsy, something she'd picked up from Adaida and Shani back when they'd been closer. "Oh, God. You act like you've been estranged for years; it's only been a month or so!" Shaking her head at herself again, she walked up the path, oblivious to the guard's slack-jawed expression. She hardly noted the beautiful, blooming flowers, the scents hanging in the air, and the nearly perfect spring weather. Her mind had, once again, found something darker to focus upon.

The guards at the front door ignored her, but a young woman in a plain gray dress and a white apron guided her through a few nicely appointed rooms and hallways until they came to a set of glass-paneled French-style doors. "The lady and her guest are within," the soft-spoken young woman said, wringing her pale blue hands and hurrying away.

"Oh," Olivia said, walking up to the doors. "I'll just let myself in, then, I suppose." She turned the handle, but before she pulled on the door, she saw the man she was supposed to meet through the glass. It had to be him. At first, she thought he was sitting in a child's seat, so thoroughly did his frame dwarf it. That illusion was shattered, though, when she saw the fully grown Ardeni woman sitting beside him, her body easily encompassed in an identical chair. Victor, for this must be him, was an enormous man.

Still, Olivia didn't pull the door open. She stared at him, some strange sense of *déjà vu* or recognition puzzling her mind. He was clearly human, but unlike any human she'd ever seen. Even if she compared him to Morgan,

Olivia didn't think she'd ever seen anyone pull the gravity out of a room as Victor was doing. She couldn't stop looking at him, couldn't stop trying to figure him out.

His size was the first thing that caught her attention, but it was hardly the only thing. He had thick black hair, cut short as you might imagine a military man would do. His eyes gleamed from under his dark, heavy brows like amber, honey-filled wells. The bones of his cheeks and jawline were sharp as though he were chiseled from granite, and everything about him simply screamed power, vibrant, rich, and ready to spring forth. Olivia had half a mind to activate some of her defensive spells or to take on an elemental form. She settled on pouring a bit of Energy into the shielding runes she'd tattooed onto her body. Finally, exerting her not-insignificant will, she forced herself to pull open the door and step through.

Victor heard the door latch jiggle, but Valla was in the middle of a sentence, so he didn't look up right away. " . . . and, yes, I think it makes perfect sense that you're wary about the contracts. I feel Lam's proposal of a relatively benign one is a good compromise, though, don't you?"

"Yeah, I guess," Victor sighed and turned to the door. The glass reflected the sun from the open balcony doors; they were in one of Rellia's seldom-used sitting rooms, and it was a nice place for their little interlude. They had a pleasant view of a blooming orchard outside the wide open double doors. That said, the glare made it hard to see through the interior door, though he thought he saw a figure standing there. "Is that her?" he asked softly.

"Perhaps it's the maid. You frightened her, you know—" Valla stopped speaking abruptly as the door opened, and a woman stepped through. Victor felt a lot of strange, conflicting emotions when he laid eyes on Olivia Bennet. Firstly, he was stunned by her beauty. She was tall and thin, with long black hair gleaming like spun onyx in the sunlight. She had pale, almost porcelain skin, and fiery, pale-blue eyes met his from beneath her dark brows. Those crystal-clear irises literally looked as if they had flames dancing behind them.

Victor caught himself admiring her attire—multilayered robes that hugged her figure yet created a flowing silhouette, intricate jewelry, shiny, clearly magical boots, and on her head a black crown that exuded a power of its own. Victor saw that crown and couldn't help a little nagging tug of jealousy at the center of his being.

If you took away Olivia's exotic features and fantastic clothing, what really stunned Victor into an awkward silence was that she looked very much like photos he'd seen of his mother when she'd been young. He stared at her for a long while, dimly aware of Valla standing to shake the woman's hand. He heard Olivia say something to him, but all he could do was mentally erase the obvious racial enhancements Olivia had gone through and try to compare her to his mom; everything else was just background noise.

". . . all right?" Olivia asked, and Victor shook his head, cleared his throat, and stood up, towering over the two women.

"Sorry," he grunted, then held out a hand. "Good to meet you. I'm Victor."

"Good grief!" she said, looking him up and down. "Were you a football star back home?"

"Ah! Right! So, they told you I'm from Earth, huh?" He gestured to the seat across from his and added, "Sit, please. They brought us some tea and little cookies. They're not bad."

Olivia looked at the tray on the table between all the chairs and daintily bent to pick up one of the cookies. "I do love a sweet." Then she sat down. Victor and Valla followed suit.

"So, yeah, I'm from Earth, but if my suspicions are right, my Earth is a little different from yours."

"Go on. How'd you get here? Have you heard about us? The arkship? *Pilgrim-9* was our designation. I'm sure you studied our mission, about when we left orbit, yes?"

"Nah, that's the thing—when I left Earth, there weren't any arkships. I think they might have been conceived, started even, but I was a kid; I was worried about community college and my girlfriend. I hardly ever watched the news. What year was it when you left?"

"Well, we left orbit in 2074. Add a couple of hundred years to that, though, if you're wondering what year I think it is on Earth now . . ."

"*Pinche* fuck!" Victor sighed, sitting back and rubbing his hands through his short, stiff hair.

"Did I say something wrong?"

"Well, when I got summoned here, it was 2031. And, no, I haven't been kicking around here for a couple hundred years. I've been on Fanwath for more like two."

"How . . ." Olivia frowned, and Victor saw the flames dancing in her eyes start to move a little faster, and then she looked at him more directly and asked, "Why did you want to meet with me, specifically? Was it just my proximity, or was there something more?"

Valla shifted, and Victor glanced at her. Her face was impassive, but he wondered what she was thinking. Was he making a mistake laying all this out for Olivia? He didn't know her at all, other than that she might be related to him. She certainly didn't seem like a normal human, spacefaring or not. Still, Victor wasn't one to beat around the bush, and he wanted to get on with his life. "They didn't tell you anything, huh?"

"No. Lady ap'Yensha's messenger said another human, not from our settlement, was in Persi Gables and wanted to meet with me."

"Well, I got summoned to this world by a real asshole wizard and the noble he was working for. A guy named ap'Gravin."

"Ap'Gravin!" This time Victor was sure of it; Olivia's eyes began to blaze with blue fire, and, more than that, her shoulders, head, and crown came to life with flickering white-blue flames. "The professor or his father?"

"Well, both were involved. You see, in order to summon me, he needed something from someone related to me, someone attending Fainhallow."

Olivia surprisingly cooled noticeably at Victor's words, her flames faded away, and her hands, previously clenching the arms of her chair in a death grip, relaxed. "In that case, it's high time I paid the fool a visit. Are you familiar with First Landing? The human settlement in the western frontier of the Empire?"

"No." Victor looked at Valla, and she, too, shook her head in the negative.

"Well, not to bury the lede, I mean about us being related, but Lord ap'Gravin has given us plenty of trouble. As I said, I think it's time we, I mean we at First Landing, did something about him. But, Victor! Tell me! How are we related? I swear I see something . . . a hint of familiarity in your eyes, maybe?"

"I was hoping you could tell me. When were you born? Who are your parents?" Victor leaned forward; for the first time, he felt some excitement about this encounter. He liked something about her, especially when she got mad.

"I was born in 2046; my parents were Cindy and Thomas Bennet."

"Thomas! Holy shit!" Victor looked at Valla, met her wide eyes, and said, "My cousin. My mom's nephew."

"So, your mother was my grandfather's sister? Victor, I . . . I remember something about one of Grandpa Bennet's sisters dying in a car crash. It's a distant memory, something said at a family dinner. We, well, my parents didn't live near their cousins—my dad took a job at a tech startup in Boston when I was very small. I don't remember any mention of a missing cousin . . ."

Victor sighed and sat back, many thoughts and feelings crashing through his mind. "That makes sense. Your family didn't want shit to do with me."

"Is that true?" Olivia looked shocked, hurt, and embarrassed. Victor felt bad for dumping his old hard feelings on her.

"Yeah, as far as I know. Unless my dad's family was lying. I don't know why they would." He shrugged. "It's not your fault." It felt good to have an answer, to know more about what had happened. It also felt terrible to think that everyone he'd known back on Earth was dead—dead for hundreds of years. "Why'd that asshole have to summon me from the past?" He groaned, driving a thumb into his pounding temple, trying to massage the pain out. "*Abuela.*"

"I'm, uh, it's unsettling, isn't it? To think no one you know is alive back home." Olivia frowned and reached out a hand, gently resting it on Victor's knee. "I know that feeling, Victor. Often, I think about my parents, friends, and colleagues back on Earth rather than sleeping, pushing away the final thought that they're all dead until the last possible second. Sometimes it's with tears soaking my pillow that I find rest."

"Why, though?" he repeated. "Why not one of your relatives who's alive?" Victor groaned, rubbed his head again, and while Olivia looked at Valla, perhaps wondering what to say, Victor shook his head and said, "I'll never know. The wizard who cast the spell is dead. Ap'Gravin's just the money behind the operation. Still, if he's fucking with the humans, maybe we should kill him before we march." That got a reaction from Valla; she opened her mouth to say something, but Olivia beat her to it.

"You're . . . marching somewhere?" Olivia lifted one eyebrow, then said, "Maybe we should tell each other what we've been up to in this new world, hmm?"

18

LESH

So, you have a full-on town going, huh? Thousands of humans?" Victor had spent a good hour giving Olivia a very rough overview of his adventures and foibles on Fanwath and a few short sentences summarizing his time on Zaafor. After he'd explained the Writ of Conquest and his plans with the Untamed Marches, Olivia had shared quite a lot with him about First Landing, the human colony, and some of the hurdles they'd overcome.

"Thousands of humans, thousands of other species who have taken on citizenship, and, if my theories and hopes bear fruit, we may have another hundred thousand fertilized embryos in orbit. I'm of the opinion that the System teleported us down here but left the *Pilgrim-9* alone. Theoretically, it would have achieved orbit with the autopilot program."

"So, you all are building a ship to go up there?"

"Not exactly, but I have some theories about Morgan's void attunement. He's the one I told you about, my friend with an advanced bloodline. He can create portals, as I explained, and he has some feats that give him resistance to the void; in fact, he gains bonuses . . ." She paused and frowned, shaking her head as if irritated with herself. "I'm getting lost on a silly tangent; it's all theory right now. What's important to me is that you seem to believe the Ridonne Empire is corrupt."

"Yeah, I'd say it's pretty damn definite by now. Wouldn't you say, Valla?"

"It seems we're placing our trust in your discretion, Olivia Bennet," Valla said, frowning at Victor.

"I'll be discreet." Olivia nodded, looking steadily into Valla's eyes as though she wanted her to see into her, to recognize that she wasn't being duplicitous.

"I won't speak openly about my family's stance on the Empire, but I will say that I don't disagree with what Victor just said. He and I recently survived an assassination attempt, and it's rather evident that the Empire has designs against us. Victor's role with the army my mother has raised is crucial in our attempt to circumvent the corruption that grows unchecked in the nobility." Valla paused, looked around the little room as if confirming they were alone, and added, "This conquest will allow us to secure a foothold outside the Empire's control. A place from which to gather our strength and defend. A place where we can burn out corruption before it buries its roots."

"I'm suddenly very worried about Morgan. As I mentioned, he was traveling to Tharcray to attempt to treat with the Empire. It sounds like he was walking into a snake pit." Olivia's face was pensive, her hands clutched together on the lap of her elegant robes.

"They're sneaky assholes," Victor said, attempting to put her at ease, "but they aren't usually the kind who'll stab you in the face. They'll probably give him a lot of agreements, talk a bunch of bullshit, and then, when they think the time's right, they'll move against the colony. I mean, that's the way things have gone with the nobles I've dealt with."

"He's not wrong." Valla sighed, shaking her head, caught between wanting to agree with Victor and not precisely approving of his words. "Why not join the conquest? Bring the humans to the Marches!"

"Shit! Not a bad idea, Olivia. You guys are kind of hanging out on a ledge by yourselves out there . . ."

"It's not that easy." Olivia started to count on her fingers. "We have children, for one. We have people with livelihoods—people who have worked day and night for years now to build up the town, their businesses, their contacts with neighboring settlements." She gave up on counting on her fingers and set her hand on her lap. "If we sent a significant fighting force with you, it would leave those who aren't so inclined rather open to attack. No, I don't think it will work." Before Victor could say anything, she added, "I'll present it to the council, along with your warning about the Ridonne. Still, if we do join you, it will more likely be after you've finished your, um, conquest."

"Right. After we've done all the work." Victor made a dismissive sound, almost a *tsk*, that he hadn't done in a long time. He looked away from Olivia and started to stand, ready to dismiss her, to move on with the things he found important.

"That's not fair, Victor," Valla interjected. "You only just told her about this. Do you really expect a whole settlement to drop everything they've been working for and march into war for the possibility of a better place to settle?"

"Nah, I guess not." Victor halted his sudden urge to stand and looked at Olivia's face. He saw how it had fallen in response to his comment and felt a little ashamed. Despite Valla's words, Olivia still looked upset, so he added, "Listen, I'm not holding anything against you. I didn't come here looking for help, and I'm still not. You know what a Far Scribe book is?"

"Yes . . ."

"Let's buy a set, and we can keep in touch. If you run into trouble with the Empire, or if we run into a problem, maybe we can help each other out."

"That's a great idea, Victor!" Olivia said, her face lighting up, and then she opened her mouth and leapt to her feet. "Oh my gosh! I forgot something! Morgan's tower! It has teleportation gateways. We could set up a link between it and your new settlement if, no, *when* your campaign is successful."

"Oh, yeah." Victor nodded, seeing Valla's contemplative look. "Sure, that would be cool."

"Olivia?" Valla said, holding up a hand to forestall Victor's next words.

"Yes?"

"I almost forgot, but we met a friend of yours at Fainhallow."

"Oh, shit! That's right . . ." Victor nodded emphatically.

"A Ghelli woman named Adaida." While she spoke, Valla produced the rolled-up parchment Adaida had given her for Olivia. "She seemed rather distraught, upset about something that happened between you two. She asked if I'd give you this Far Scribe parchment; it jogged my memory when Victor mentioned the Far Scribe book."

Olivia's expression had fallen from eager, excited interest to something that looked a lot like guilt and sadness to Victor. She gingerly reached forward and took the parchment, still wrapped in a lovely lavender ribbon, tied in a big, looping bow with curled ends. She looked at it for a few seconds, and Victor thought he saw moisture in her eyes before she made it disappear and said, "Thank you. Can we go and buy the books now? You've kind of ignited something in me. I feel stressed about the colony and my responsibilities. No, that's not fair." She shook her head, taking a moment to gather her thoughts. "I was feeling that way before I came to this meeting. Still, I'd like to get back to First Landing to check on things, and I'd like to look into Lord ap'Gravin. I promise I'll write to you about what I find."

"You think that's smart?" Victor asked, raising an eyebrow, trying to size her up again.

"Victor, I'm very clever when it comes to spells." She chuckled and shook her head, holding up a hand. "I'm not trying to boast! I just want you to know that I'll dedicate some time to researching what happened with your summoning. It already aligns with my own interests, and, well, I can be very persuasive. If ap'Gravin is hiding anything—records, contacts, *anything*—I'll get it out of him."

"Well, shit, Olivia. That would be pretty awesome. I mean, I guess we're kind of cousins, so it's cool to know that, right? We've got some family in this crazy world." Victor looked at Olivia, wishing he was a little better at reading people, that he could see into them the way Tes could. He decided to be blunt with the concern that was itching the back of his mind. "What level are you?"

"Nearly twenty-six, but, well, again, not to be boastful, but I'm stronger than most Tier Two people. I have a high affinity and some good class synergies." She suddenly looked embarrassed and glanced down, hurriedly adding, "I only said that because you seem like you're feeling like you should be concerned about me. You don't need to be."

Valla snorted and started to say something, but Victor was already speaking. "Nah, I get it. But, as I said, use the book. Keep me posted. If you go after ap'Gravin and I don't hear back from you, I'll have to figure out a way to help. I'd help right now, like, go with you tonight, but the army's leaving soon, and I have responsibilities. Why not wait for your friend, the dude who went to Tharcray, then deal with him together?"

Olivia laughed and slapped Victor's knee. It wasn't much of a reach—Victor's legs jutted out from the chair like an adult sitting on a child's stool. "I like that, Victor. I *will* wait for my friend, and I have a few other friends who wouldn't mind paying that man a visit."

Lesh'ro'zellan stood and stretched, arching his back, twisting the thick muscles of his shoulders until he heard popping sounds. "Ah," he groaned, "that's it." He moved through the stone archway, his entrance to the dwelling, and stood on the black basalt ledge, gazing over his domain. Enormous black and gray peaks stood against the crimson, smoky sky, but none so high as his mountaintop abode.

Lesh had been gone too long. Gaining power was important. Crushing his enemies was a worthy endeavor, but it was just as essential to savor his accomplishments along the way. Standing there, he could look down on all the ledges and caves of his people; even his father's home was beneath him. How excellent it was to see his triumphs laid out before him! How fulfilling to know he'd risen to the peak of his clan and that, in time, he'd be able to vie for the crown in the Blood Circle.

"Are you sore, love?" Yassa'wikterl, his ledge mate, asked, her voice sleepy, almost a purr.

"Aye, Yassa. The campaign was too long! So frequently did I fight that my breath Core never recharged. Last evening, I wanted to savor you, not dwell on my troubles, so I didn't mention it, but one of the Chuglan ogres hit me squarely with a flung boulder. My scales earned their metal, but my bones ache!"

"Gods! Your poor back! I hope it didn't harm your wing beds."

"Hush, love. My wings will come in just fine. Another evolution or two, and I'll be soaring."

"Just so, love, just so." Yassa sighed softly, rolling over in their nest, and Lesh admired her form. Everything about her called to him on a primal level, from her coppery scales to the seductive curve of her hips. From her slender limbs to the gentle bumps of the budding horns along her brow, she reminded him of their promised glory, the majesty of their draconic bloodline.

"We've come so far," he said, and Yassa opened one of her wide eyes, narrowing it as she studied him down the length of her coppery snout. Her iris was a pale greenish-yellow, and as it caught the glow of the light crystal, it shone at him with cunning.

"Admiring me? Admiring how we're closer and closer to leaving our kin behind, leaving this world, and joining true dragons elsewhere?"

Lesh hurried back in from the ledge and fell to his knees, grabbing her by the shoulders and turning her to look him fully in the face. "But we are true dragons! Just because we were born dragonkin doesn't mean we are lesser! All the work we've done, all the work left to do, will make us stronger when we join their numbers. We'll be mighty in here." He thumped his chest. "Much stronger than those mewling dragonlings who are lucky enough to be born pure."

"Your father doesn't see it that way." Was she taunting him? Was she trying to incite his wrath? Was she simply trying to help him focus his prodigious drive?

"He's a fool! A small-minded man, worried about this backwater of a world when he should be looking beyond. Why would I listen to him, anyway? His bloodline is barely beyond the basic ranks. He has no horns, while

I have three! He's hardly scaled, but look at me! Look at my metal!" Lesh leapt to his taloned feet, held his thick, half-scaled arms wide, and bared his shiny chest to her. He really was a striking figure; his skin was dark, almost as black as his scales, and the green luster of his eyes radiated the corrosive Energy in his Core.

He liked to think he was close to evolving to the next stage of his bloodline, but in truth, his dark skin gave the impression that he was further scaled than he was. He supposed only about half of his body had those thick metallic scales covering it. Still, it was far more than his father, far more than any other dragonkin in their clan. "There's a reason I'm leading the clan while my father yet breathes." The last was spoken softly, more to himself than to Yassa. He refocused on her and added, "As I said, love, a few more evolutions. Another century or so, and then I'll fight for the crown. When I take control of the World Stone, then it will be our time!"

"Yes, love. Yes!" Yassa pulled back the silken blankets, beckoning for him to crawl back into the nest with him. "Come. Help me to make a strong, healthy brood to support you."

Lesh frowned, though, his lips turning down from his short, toothy snout. Something had appeared in his vision, something he'd only grown accustomed to seeing when he advanced somehow—a message from the gods-cursed System.

*****You have been offered a quest: Travel to the world of Fanwath and slay Victor Sandoval. Reward: One Heart of Evolution. Accept? Yes/No*****

"Elder gods!"

"What is it, Lesh?" Yassa sat up, her slender, coppery tail curling around beneath her.

"The System, gods curse it, has just offered me a quest. Yassa, the reward is a Heart of Evolution—the same as I won from the crag troll king! It pushed me from improved to advanced! Do you remember?"

"How could I forget, love? Tell me, what must you do?"

"Simply slay a man. I'll have to travel off-world, but I'm sure I can gain permission when I explain the quest. I'll need to leave now, though. The trip to Garspire will take nearly a week." He frowned, then added, "Well, I don't see a time limit on the quest . . ."

"Still, best not to tarry." Yassa was on her feet now, naked and wonderful, but she stooped to gather up her skirts, continuing to speak. "What if the System offers the quest to others? Perhaps this man has angered it. You could be competing with hunters from other worlds."

"Gods! You're right, love! What am I without you? I must make haste!" Lesh leapt to his feet and snatched up the handle of his great cudgel, Belagog, the Bone Cracker. The black metallic handle was warm in his hand, flowing between his fingers to allow for a better grip. The weapon was clever and eager to fight, and Lesh always felt a grin pulling his lips back from his long white teeth when he hoisted the two-meter rod of star metal and allowed his eyes to fall on the hundreds of diamond-hard spikes along its length. "We have work to do, blood brother," he said to the cudgel.

Victor sat atop Thistle's back, riding at a steady, easy trot away from Persi Gables. Valla and Uvu kept pace, the big cat occasionally chuffing loudly and groaning, even purring; he was clearly thrilled to see his mistress. Thistle had been well taken care of, fed, brushed, and exercised daily, but Victor couldn't ride him comfortably without reducing his form; the beast was big and strong but not meant to be carrying a half-titan, for that was what Victor had come to consider his natural state.

"You're a good boy, and I missed you, but I might have to send you to live with your sister soon. I won't stand to see someone else take you."

"It's true," Valla said, her tone carefully neutral. "He's a great mount, but you can't ride him into battle. You must be at your full strength when we're in the field."

"Yeah. What am I going to do? Get one of those elephant birds?"

Valla snorted with laughter and said, "You mean a bundii? That would be quite a sight! I've never seen one mounted, but if anyone could do it . . ." Her words were lost in another fit of giggles; she was apparently rather vividly imagining Victor attempting to ride one of the elephant-sized ostriches.

"Well? Seriously! What can I ride?"

"A thunderak, perhaps? Those are the giant—"

"Lizards, yeah, yeah. No thanks. I think I'll take a trip into the spirit plane. I learned a lot when I made Tes's spell in my pathways. I told you a little about the feat I gained, but I think I'm just scratching the surface. What if I used some of the principles that make her spell so potent on one of my other spells, say the one that lets me find and create totems from my spirit? The way I envision it, I think it might allow me to gain more totems; maybe I can find one that I could ride—I saw a mustang in there once."

"A mustang?"

"A kind of horse." Victor chuckled and hurriedly added, "Which is a kind of mount from my world. They're like vidanii, I guess, but without the horns. Maybe prettier, too. I guess horses are known for being clever and spirited, but Thistle's pretty clever, aren't you, boy?" Victor patted the coarse reddish fur of the animal's neck, and he shivered, shaking his head and snorting.

"If you could truly do that, summon a totem you could ride, that would be ideal." Valla tugged on Uvu's reins, pulling him a little closer so she didn't have to shout, and added, "You don't want to try to train a thunderak!"

"Hey," Victor said, changing the subject, "what did you think of Olivia?"

"Your cousin?" Valla grinned at him slyly, and Victor had to wonder for a moment what she was getting at. Was she trying to point out to him that he had some family again? He supposed that was nice. Olivia had seemed like someone he could grow to like—smart, ambitious, pleasant, and he'd enjoyed how she'd spoken in threatening undertones about ap'Gravin. Yeah, he decided, he could grow to like having a cousin like her.

"Well, not a first cousin. But, yeah, I take your point. What did you think of her?"

"She's very talented, according to the professors at Fainhallow. I know, I know, that's not what you're asking me. I liked her. I hope she can produce the results she promised. I hope ap'Gravin won't present her with too much trouble."

"We'll find out," Victor said, shrugging. "We've got Far Scribe books now, so at least she'll be able to update me." He clicked his tongue and twitched his reins, urging Thistle to move a little faster, and as Valla and Uvu surged to keep up, he said, "We're going to be marching in a couple of days! Feels like ages since Rellia first spoke to me about the Untamed Marches. I'm nervous but also pumped as hell. How about you? Are you excited?"

"I am, but also apprehensive. I know you've been in plenty of fights, and you know how ugly combat can be, but it's different on the scale of armies. It's different when those you're responsible for start to die. I hope you're ready for it."

Victor didn't answer her, and his grin faded as a storm brewed behind his eyes. Abstractly, he'd thought about the army clashing with whatever sorts of enemies would be waiting in the Untamed Marches. He'd thought about fighting with ambushers from the Empire, but he hadn't really thought about what it would be like if he, as he tended to do, came out on top, but a bunch of his soldiers died. Right now, the soldiers were mostly faceless to him, a mob of willing fighters, but how would it feel when he stood on the battlefield with them and they started to fall?

Impulsively, he asked Valla, "Who's the best military brain in our legion? Who's going to be coming up with tactics? I know I'm in charge, but who should I be listening to for advice? Other than you, I mean."

"Rellia has a keen mind for strategy, as does Lam, but Borrius is a military genius. Get him away from Rellia to hear him speak frankly, though; his desire to please her can make him agree to stupid things."

"Good advice, Primus. Thank you. Now, try to keep up!" With that, Victor urged Thistle into a gallop, and he howled as the wind began to sing in his ears.

19

FORMALITIES

"Ancestors, Victor!" Thayla cried, leaping up from the soft, springy loam to charge at him, wrapping her luminescent arms around his waist and burying her head in his stomach. "How does a grown man keep growing?"

Victor laughed and gently stroked the back of her head, savoring the feel of her soft hair against his palm. "God, I missed you." He felt emotion welling up, his throat growing thick, all the thoughts he'd been holding back vying to come to the forefront—Old Mother, the loss of hope about returning home, the stress of having so many people expecting so much from him. He squeezed Thayla tight and breathed deeply of the cool, fragrant air in Oynalla's glade. "I thought I'd have to teach you how to find this place. I should have known better."

"Aye, world walker. It was the first place Oynalla showed me."

"World walker?"

"Weren't you visiting other worlds these last months?"

"Yeah, but I don't think that qualifies me. Let me walk on a few more before you start calling me that."

"Fair." Thayla pushed back from him, holding him at arm's length and looking up, trying to see into his eyes. "Your coloring is a little different. More . . . bronze, I guess, and your eyes are lighter. They were always light brown, but now there's yellow in there. Well, more of it."

"You look good," Victor said, reaching for her face, letting his thumb gently trace the line of her jaw.

"I do, hmm? Well, I have much news for you. Will you sit?" She moved back to the spot of soft grass where she'd been when he arrived and plopped down, folding her legs beneath her. Victor followed and lowered himself to the embrace of Oynalla's glade, sighing as he leaned back and his palms sank into the rich turf.

"I have news for you, too."

"Shall I speak first?" At his nod, she continued, "Deyni misses you a great deal, but she's doing very well living with the clan. She's tamed an adristii." At Victor's blank expression, she added, "It's a bird of prey that hunts these plains. The clan is proud of her, and I think she'll have a prominent place among them. She and Starlight are a common sight around the camp, racing hither and yon, Chandri often chasing after, howling about a lesson Deyni's missing."

She chuckled as she spoke, and Victor joined in, picturing Chandri in a teacher's role. "So, she spends a lot of time with her? Chandri, I mean?"

"Much! I know Old Mother awaited you here to bid you goodbye, but did she tell you of my expanded role with the clan?" Thayla's voice was a little hesitant, as though she had news and worried about how Victor would receive it.

"She hinted at it. I take it you've filled in for her, right? You're the new clan, well, not Old Mother, but maybe Mother? Is that how that works?"

She smiled and reached out to grasp Victor's hand in hers, then said, "It's more than that, Victor. Yes, I'm the clan's Spirit Guide; I'm hoping to gain that class when I next refine. It will be many, many years before I deserve that particular honorific, though. No, I'm not the Old Mother, but I'm Tellen's wife. He and I rule the clan together now."

Victor felt her fingers tighten on his palm, and he wondered if she thought he might pull away. Did she think he'd be jealous? Enraged that a woman he'd refused to settle down with had found love elsewhere? He smiled and gently gripped her hand between his thumb and fingers, enjoying the familiar, soft, warm feel of it. "That's wonderful, Thayla. Really. I'm so happy for you . . . and for Tellen! That lucky bastard! So, Deyni and Chala and Chandri—they're sisters now!"

"Yes! Oh, Victor . . . I'm so happy that you're not upset." She leaned toward him, relief evident in her eyes, and Victor chuckled, pulling her close so he could put an arm over her shoulders.

"I love you, Thayla. I know I told you that before, and maybe it put the wrong ideas in your mind, but the kind of love I have for you means I can't help but feel happy when I see you're happy. Understand?"

"I understand, big oaf," she said, sniffing noisily as she pulled his arm tightly to herself, almost hugging it as she leaned into his side.

"Now, I want to talk to you about an opportunity for your people."

"Oh?"

"Yeah. Well, you know about the campaign I'm leading for Rellia, right?"

"Oh no, Victor . . ."

"Hear me out! We've raised a bigger army than we could have hoped for—a full legion. We'll win, Thayla; you have to know that, right? If I have anything to say about things, we're going to claim a lot of land outside the Empire. Wouldn't you like to be a part of that? Aren't you tired of looking over your shoulder? Wouldn't some real freedom mean a lot to the clan? I got to thinking about all the people Rellia and Lam are bringing along with the campaign, lots and lots of really powerful, rich people, not just peasants looking to get lucky. I thought about how so many of them are eager because they know something better is coming to them if we're successful. Well, I want people I care about to get a piece of that, too."

"Freedom always sounds nice, but you can't tell me there aren't risks."

"Sure, there are risks. If the clan followed the legion, though, I'd be sure you were out of the worst of the fighting. Mainly we'd use you for scouting, just the hunters. The kids and noncombat folks can stay with the legion's supply train, well guarded."

"And you get to spend some time with Deyni and Chandri."

"And you!" Victor squeezed her again.

"It's a huge decision, Victor." Her voice was soft, and Victor recognized the tone—she was trying to spare his feelings and let him down easy.

"I know it is. I know you can't say 'yes' right now. You'll need to speak with Tellen and the other clan elders. You'll need to weigh the risks and possible benefits. The good news is that the army is marching east for a long while. We're going to skirt the Blue Deep, which means we'll pass by your spring camp. If you decide to join us, you can do so, and if not, I'll at least get to see everyone again."

"That *is* good news!" She looked up at him and said, "Why so far south? There are roads leading east that go around the Starfall Mountains . . ."

"We don't want our route to be easily predicted. I can explain more when we meet." While he spoke, Victor was watching Thayla's face, looking into her luminescent magenta eyes. Her eyes always told the story of her feelings, and he could see them narrow, and he knew she was connecting some dots.

"You fear trouble before you even get to the Marches?"

"I don't *fear* trouble, but I won't lie and say we don't expect any."

Thayla nodded, and as he looked up from her eyes, he saw that her flesh seemed less corporeal, more translucent. "I'm running out of Energy, Victor. I can't stay here as long as you and Old Mother."

"Well, think about what I said; promise me you will!"

"I will! How long until your army draws near?"

"Two weeks or so, I'd guess. No, maybe closer to three; it took Valla and me about twelve days riding hard."

"Aye. Okay. I'm so glad to see you well."

"Me too, Thayla!" Victor hugged her close, but she felt far less substantial than when he'd first done so. She was fading quickly. "I love you!"

"And I you, oaf!" she tittered, and then she was gone. The only evidence she'd ever been there were wisps of rapidly fading Energy that drifted up into the starlit canopy of Old Mother's glade. Victor sighed and fell back into the soft grass, letting it cradle his weary spirit. He hoped Thayla would truly consider his offer. He hoped she'd try to convince Tellen to join the conquest. He had his doubts, however. She'd seemed quite reserved about the whole thing.

"Maybe she just needs to sleep on it. Let the idea fester in the back of her mind. I wish Deyni had come tonight; I know she'd help me convince her." He sighed and cut the connection to his Spirit Walk spell, and then he found himself sitting on his bed, his five proud, golden, glory-attuned coyotes sitting around it, their eyes glittering and gleaming with the nature of their spirits. "Hey, *amigos.*"

They whined and yipped softly, pacing around his bed, and Victor figured he should send them home; people were probably trying to sleep nearby. "See you soon," he said, and then, as the spell ended, they shimmered and disappeared, leaving pools of glittering golden Energy on the rough floorboards. "That's new," he said, watching the puddles gradually shrink to nothing. "Something to do with the Energy type, maybe?"

Seeing his companions reminded him of what he'd said to Valla; he wanted to try to improve that spell with a twist of elder magic, but his mind was dull, tired, and foggy. He'd only had one good night's sleep in the last several, and he had a busy day ahead. That said, he undressed, leaned Lifedrinker against the wall near his bed, pulled his thin, plain gray blanket up, and went to sleep.

At least, his intention was to go to sleep, but his mind was busy. He still had the ancient wyrm heart to eat, he had to think about what he'd say in the command council the next day, and he had a nagging worry about his newfound cousin; was she biting off more than she could chew? As he pushed those thoughts into a corner, he began to wonder about Vellia and her people. Would the Naghelli answer his call? How would he sell their presence to the army? Weren't they pretty much universally hated? He tried to remember their history and thought it had something to do with when the System had formed Fanwath; did they help the Yovashi or something? "Ugh, goddamn it!"

Victor thumped his fist into his forehead, tossing left to right, twisting himself in his blankets, and trying to think of anything other than his dozens of problems. He let his mind drift to Tes, picturing her eyes, her smile, the way she laughed when he did something clever. Before he knew it, he was floating through clouds, following her as she taunted him, jumping from mountaintop to mountaintop. He always almost caught but never quite reached her. He could hear her giggle, see how her skirts and ribbons trailed behind her, and then the dream shifted, and he was lost to deep slumber.

When Victor woke, it was to an incessant tapping at his door. He was flat on his back, his blanket and pillows nowhere to be found. As the tapping continued, he stared at the roughly-fit planks of the ceiling, listening to the sounds of distant shouts and trying to gather his thoughts. Finally, the tapping registered, and he remembered where he was and grunted, "Just a minute."

"Victor?" Valla's voice said, speaking softly. Was she trying to keep people from gossiping about how he'd overslept? Victor leapt out of bed, flipped up the crude lock, and as Valla quietly came into the room, he pulled some clean clothes out of his storage ring—easy to do since pretty much all his clothes were enchanted to clean themselves.

"Sorry, Valla."

"It's all right. I just wanted to make sure you didn't have anything you wanted to discuss before the ceremony."

"How much time do we have?" he asked, pulling a plain, dark-blue shirt over his head.

"Twenty minutes. Are you going to wear a uniform?"

"Should I?" Victor frowned. "I was going to wear my armor again." He blinked his eyes several times, then took a good look at Valla. She'd opted to wear the new uniform—slim black pants, red shirt, black and gold brocade coat. He saw she'd transferred all of her medals and ribbons from her old Legion uniform.

"For this ceremony, I suggest you wear the uniform. People are going to be swearing fealty to you and the campaign."

"Damn it." Victor started pulling off his shirt, glad he was, at least, wearing some underwear that decently covered him—some silky shorts he'd picked up in Coloss. Valla had seen him like this before, so he didn't feel as though he was doing anything wrong, but when he looked up, she was sitting by the window, pointedly looking outside. As he summoned the uniform he'd been given from his storage ring, he said, "I'm going to be the only officer in there without a chest full of ribbons and shit."

"Your coat will be the only one to bear the rank of Legate Primus." She turned toward him, saw he'd already pulled on his uniform pants, and said, "You could commission some medals for yourself. Ribbons to commemorate your achievements. A wyrm scale ribbon, a token of Coloss ribbon, a Greatbone Mine ribbon, etcetera."

"That wouldn't help me today, and it would look dumb if I suddenly showed up at some point with a bunch of medals and ribbons no one recognized."

"That's partially true, but there are many medals on my chest that require an explanation to most people." She fingered a silvery bar with a blue tassel and said, "Few would know this is meant to recognize that I finished my sword qualifier in under five strokes."

"Sword qualifier?"

"Yes, the Imperial Legion doesn't let anyone use just any weapon; you have to qualify for the weapon you carry."

"Right," Victor said, only half hearing her as he worked to tuck his crimson shirt in without wrinkling the front of it.

"No," Valla said, walking over to him. "You have these pockets up here," she said, demonstrating by pulling one open. They were placed differently than those on other pants he'd owned, up high near the waistline. "Put your fingers in there, and you'll find a hole where you can pull your shirttail back, removing the extra fabric near your beltline."

"Speaking of belts—I need to wear the black one, I'm guessing, and the shiny boots they gave me?"

"Yes. You'll look odd in uniform with random accessories."

"What about Lifedrinker?"

"You didn't look at the dress sling Rellia had made? Take it out."

"Uh . . ." Victor dug around in his ring and pulled out the boots, belt, and a thick, black leather and red silk sash. At least, he'd thought it was a sash, but now he saw that part was stitched with tooled leather and big golden rings.

"This," Valla said. "You wear it crossways over one shoulder, and Lifedrinker will hang on your back. It won't be easy to put her back in there if you have to pull her out, but that'll be the least of your problems. I can help you, or an aide like Edeya can."

"And if I want to sit down?"

"Right, if that comes up, just allow me, or, as I said, Edeya, to help you. This is a formal uniform; you're not meant to fight in it."

Victor shrugged into the black dress jacket, annoyed by the extra level of golden brocade on his compared to Valla's. He'd already tried on the uniform once, bonding with it so it fit perfectly, and Valla had assured him that if he had to expand his size, it would hold up all right. Once he had the coat on, he shrugged into the harness for Lifedrinker, noting that it added quite a bit of flashiness to the front of his uniform, what with its shiny leather, red silk lining, and golden buckles.

"Here," Valla said, picking up Lifedrinker. "Oh! She's heavy!" she grunted. "Does she always vibrate like this?"

"Well," Victor said, watching Valla struggle with the axe, "she's not used to anyone else touching her. It's okay, *reina*; she's just going to help me put you on my back."

"Wow," Valla said, lifting Lifedrinker and slipping her through the golden hoops near the top of Victor's left shoulder. "She calmed right down when you spoke."

"Don't take it personally. At least she didn't melt your hands off." Victor reached up to ensure he could grab the top of the axe, and when his fingers touched her, he felt a surge of amused pleasure. "She liked that one." He chuckled.

"Midnight still hasn't spoken to me."

"Well, keep talking to her. Keep using her. She'll grow." Victor nodded confidently as he spoke, even though his experience with conscious weapons extended precisely as far as what he knew about Lifedrinker. Still, Valla seemed to appreciate it, and she smiled and reached her hand to her sword's pommel.

"You're a sweet, beautiful girl, aren't you, Midnight?"

"Uh, is that what I sound like?" Victor raised an eyebrow speculatively. "Because if that's how I sound, maybe I should . . . Ow!" he cried as Valla viciously punched him in the chest. "Careful, you're going to mess up my uniform."

"If you're done mocking me, we should probably get going."

"I'm done for now." He hurriedly stepped toward the door, flinching away from her as though he expected another blow, but Valla just smiled and followed. "Can I keep my small size on?"

"It's up to you. All the officers will be there; they might feel better swearing fealty if they can feel your full aura."

"How many altogether?" Victor pulled the door open and, as he stepped through, cut the Energy keeping his Shape Self spell going. The floorboards creaked and groaned as his mass instantly increased.

"Rellia, Borrius, Lam, me, ten captains, and sixty lieutenants. The captains will take oaths from the sergeants in a later ceremony, and still later the lieutenants will take oaths from their troops."

"And the words? Rellia didn't have any issue with the final oath?"

"None. At least none she felt she needed to vent to me."

"All right, Primus. Let's get this over with. Time to listen to a bunch of people swear they won't betray me."

"As you say, Legate." Valla winked at him, and they began to march down the steps, her a bit behind him the entire way. Victor's mind wandered while they walked, wondering if he'd ever seen Valla wink before. He might have been concerned about his appearance or forced himself to stand up straight back in his old life, but it wasn't an issue these days. He'd put his body through enough, improved it enough, that his core muscles were probably beyond any Olympian's in history—his back was straight as a board.

He did self-consciously run a hand through his hair, making sure it was still short enough that his lack of a shower or comb hadn't let any strands fall out of place. The bristly feeling against his palm reassured him, and he smiled, dropping his arm as he stepped outside the command fort into the courtyard. He was a little surprised to see the assembled officers standing at attention on the loose, sandy cobbles. Rellia, Borrius, and Lam were arrayed in front, eyes trained on him from the second he stepped through the door. "I thought we were still a little early," he muttered.

20

PLAYING WITH MAGIC

When it came time for Ordus ap'Yensha to take a knee before Victor and place his Energy signature on the oath scroll, Victor felt a twinge of guilt. Why should such a man, someone who'd accomplished so much in his life and who was so much older than Victor, kneel before him? Wasn't half of Victor's power due to luck? He had nothing to do with his bloodline; his ancestors were responsible for that. Was he somehow to credit for his powerful spirit affinities? It didn't seem like it to him; it felt like pure chance. Still, he'd already received oaths from the other commanders and captains, men he respected more or at least knew better than Ordus. Even Polo Vosh had taken a knee before him, and it would be odd to start balking now.

"I swear," Ordus began, his voice oddly tight, emotion heavy in the words, "to endeavor to further the goals of this campaign, to obey the righteous orders of my commanders, and to guard against treachery. I swear that, should my own goals cease to align with those of this campaign, I will resign my post and distance myself from this fine army and anyone who may wish it harm. I make this vow willingly and with a true heart. May the System bleed me of Energy should I break it."

The spoken words weren't necessary; as soon as Ordus sent some of his Energy into the document, he was bound to the contract. The recitation was a ceremony, and Victor was already growing weary of it. He'd had to repeat his part more than a dozen times and had yet to hear the oaths of the lieutenants. Annoyance aside, he sent his Energy into the rolled document and said,

"I receive you into this campaign, Ordus ap'Yensha. I accept your oath and swear to lead this army with victory always in mind. I swear to choose our battles wisely, and when I cannot choose, I will listen to the counsel of my officers and do everything possible to vanquish our foes. If I betray the trust of this army or the campaign it pursues, may the System bleed me of Energy."

Ordus stood, saluted, and smartly turned back to the assembled troops, returning to his position in the row of captains next to Sarl. Valla had given Victor's friend, the disgraced Ghelli noble, command of the ninth cohort. The instant Ordus stopped moving, Edeya called out, "Lieutenant Darro, aide to Legate Rellia ap'Yensha!" Darro marched out of line, straight up to Victor, his youthful face riddled with stress as he shakily took a knee where Ordus had just been. Victor held out the oath scroll, and Darro stretched forth a trembling hand.

The sixty lieutenants took nearly two hours to get through their oaths, and if Victor thought he'd been growing weary when Ordus had kneeled, by the time they were finished he was ready to burst from agitation. It seemed he wasn't the only one, because as the last lieutenant returned to her place in line, Rellia strode forward, turned to the assembled troops, and announced, "Congratulations, officers! You are all dismissed. The next oath ceremony will commence in one hour at each cohort command tent."

The captains and lieutenants cheered, several approaching the stoop of the command fort where Victor stood, vying for the opportunity to clasp his or one of the other commanders' hands. He smiled and shook as many as he could, and when Valla saw him looming over a growing crowd, she stepped up and shouted, "The legate primus has important meetings—time to head out. Come, come, let's go, let's go. Congratulations!"

Most of them heeded her words and quickly began to filter out, but Polo and Sarl lingered. This drew a scowl from Valla, but Victor smiled and clapped Polo on the shoulder. "Thanks for your oath, Captain." He winked down at Sarl and revised, "Captains."

"Thank you for the opportunity!" Sarl nodded. "I'd hoped to ask you a favor before I move off to receive my own oaths."

"Sure, what is it?" Victor asked, still grasping Polo's shoulder. The big Vodkin also looked down at Sarl, his moist, black eyes spelling out his curiosity.

"Well, when your primus here"—he nodded respectfully to Valla—"promoted and reassigned me, my men, the ones from the Wagon Wheel, were left with my old cohort. Can I transfer them to the ninth? I'll send replacements to the second . . ."

"This isn't something the legate should be concerned about, Captain Sarl," Valla interjected. "Speak with Taz-dak, your old captain, and arrange for the troop exchange."

"Ahem." Sarl looked down and straightened his posture, turning to look Valla in the eye, "I tried that, ma'am. Captain Taz-dak wasn't receptive to the request."

"So, you wish to capitalize on your friendship with the legate and go over his head?" Valla scowled.

"Easy, Valla," Victor said. He wanted to tell her to relax and that whatever Sarl wanted was fine with him, but he also didn't want to undermine her. Before she could say more or interpret him wrongly, he added, "Sarl, she's right, however. There are systems in place for how this should work. If Taz-dak is giving you a hard time, it probably means he wants something. Find out what that is, and if you can't manage it, talk to Polo here. He's a great man, and he'll give you good advice. I think it's best if I don't get personally involved."

Polo had stiffened at the mention of his name, but his fuzzy cheeks lifted with a smile as he rumbled, "Aye, Captain Sarl. It's good to meet you properly. I didn't know you were friends with the legate! Let's go talk to that old bastard together, huh? I bet we can sort this out."

"Thank you!" Some of the stress had bled out of Sarl's expression, and he offered Valla and Victor a snappy salute as he turned and walked with Polo toward the palisade. He was tiny next to the bulky Vodkin, but Victor knew that Sarl was built of tough stuff, if not physically, then mentally.

"Thank you for not contradicting me," Valla said as the two captains exited the courtyard.

"Well, you were right. I can't get involved in petty squabbles. I've already intervened plenty on Sarl's behalf. I think if I'm seen bailing him out of every disagreement, it'll just make more problems for him down the road."

"Your solution to that was elegant," Rellia said, startling Victor. She'd approached from behind him, and he saw in Valla's expression that she'd surprised her too.

"Did you use my own bulk to sneak up on us?" Victor asked her, shifting so he could look at both Rellia and Valla while he spoke.

"Not intentionally." She smiled and shook her head, amused. "Still, I heard what you said to that captain, and it was clever. Rather than intervene on his behalf, you gave him a powerful ally. Polo will respect that he's earned your trust and help him with sincerity."

"He's a good man." Victor shrugged. "Polo could do worse than to have him as an ally."

"Mm-hmm, yes. I think the ceremony went very well. The oath is quite a lot less burdensome than the one the Legion uses, but I believe it will suffice. Were you pleased with the compromise?"

"Yes, especially as the contract itself is set to expire in three years or when I decree the campaign is over." Victor held the fancy ribbon-bedecked scroll aloft, then grinned as he sent it into his storage ring.

"That part wasn't unusual." Rellia frowned momentarily, then, exposing her brilliant, sharp white teeth, she curved her lips upward and reached up to smooth back a loose strand of coppery red hair, gleaming in the midday sunlight. "Do you have plans for the evening? I hoped I could get you and Valla to join me for dinner. There's much left to discuss before we march."

Victor looked at Valla, but she offered no assistance, her eyes focused somewhere to the left of Rellia's face. "I wanted to spar with Polo this evening. Right now, I have some work to do with a spell. I know it doesn't sound important, but it might make the difference between me trying to wrestle a giant lizard into submission or having a proper mount."

"I . . ." Rellia's eyes narrowed in confusion. Victor could almost see the wheels turning in her head, but then she gave the tiniest, most sophisticated shrug Victor had ever seen and said, "Let's have a late dinner, then. Say, nine? Surely you can finish your tasks by then."

Seeing she wasn't going to take no for an answer, Victor nodded and said, "I'd like that. Thank you for the invitation."

"My, but you've certainly become smoother with your words than I remember. See you tonight, then, Legate." She looked at Valla, nodded, and said, "Daughter."

Valla said, "Mother," and watched Rellia turn and saunter into the fort. "She's up to something."

"You think so?"

"Nothing terrible. Perhaps she just wants to pester us about the command appointments or marching formations. Mayhap she wants to build up our support for her in the event we have a disagreement within the command council."

"That stuff isn't set yet? Marching formations?" Victor turned and started for the fort before someone else could ambush him with questions or invitations.

Valla followed behind him and replied, "There are many theories on the best way to travel as a legion. Some commanders like a single sturdy column, while others prefer each cohort to march independently, though in a sort of checkerboard pattern, ready to assist each other should combat arise."

"Checkerboard? They have those here?"

"It means alternating tiles of differing patterns . . ." Valla looked at him as if he was daft as they began to climb the stairs.

"Well, in my native language, it also describes a game with a board with a pattern like that."

"I imagine the word I'm thinking and the one you're hearing are different." Valla sighed. "Sometimes I grow weary of the System and the way it has wormed its way into our minds, our language, our customs, our . . ."

"I get it."

"Are you going back to your room?"

"Yeah. Polo's going to be busy for hours with his cohort oaths, so I want to get a start on modifying my totem summoning spell. Hey, speaking of which, did any of those books Tes gave you have, like, information about spell patterns? I mean, I don't know if there's some kind of system for how they work or . . ."

"Yes, of course," Valla said, interrupting him. "Let me just look through this ring she gave me—it has hundreds of books in it." She paused, her eyes sort of glazing over, and then she said, "Ah, here we go. There's a ten-volume series on spellcrafting. Do you want them all?"

"Just for now. I doubt I'll read them all, but it might help with what I have planned. Just holler if you want them back before I'm done messing around."

"That will be fine." Valla nodded and then, one by one, began to summon the texts from her ring, handing the heavy, dense tomes to Victor. He stored them in one of his rings, and when Valla gave him the last one, she said, "Do you mind if I go observe some of the ceremonies? I'm sure Lam and Borrius will be about, walking among the troops. I should make my face seen."

"Yeah. That's a good idea, Valla. I'll be in my room, and if you don't hear from me by the time Polo finishes up, will you grab me?"

"Of course. See you then. Oh, Victor?"

"Yeah?"

"Don't blow us all up with some wild elder magic Energy surge or some such."

Victor widened his eyes and said, "Who, me?" They both laughed and then Valla turned and rapidly descended the stairs. Victor strode over to his room and went inside, locking the door behind him. His quarters were as plain as could be. Spartan, he supposed, was the way to describe them. Rough planks made up the floor, ceiling, and walls, and the only furnishing was the bed. He didn't care; it was a temporary camp structure, and he planned to shop in Persi Gables for something more comfortable on the campaign trail.

He sat on the floor between the door and bed, crossing his legs under him, and then took out a blank notebook. One at a time, he created the patterns for Shape Spirit and Manifest Spirit in his pathways and copied them onto blank pages of his notebook without casting them. That done, he sat back and stared for a while, observing each. After a few minutes, he ripped out the pages and laid them on the floor before him. Side by side, he began to see their similarities and differences. He wasn't sure what he was looking for, though, and after a few more minutes, had to admit that he'd been hoping for some kind of inspiration.

"Inspiration!" He snapped his fingers and cast Globe of Insight and Inspiration of the Quinametzin. In the revealing light of the orb floating over his head, he looked again at the two pages. "That seems familiar," he muttered, tracing part of the Shape Spirit pattern. He picked up his notebook again and conjured the pattern for Spirit Walk into his pathways. After rapidly copying it onto a fresh page, he ripped it out and set it next to the Shape Spirit spell. The Spirit Walk pattern was almost entirely represented by about half the lines of the other spell.

"Of course," he muttered. Shape Spirit forced the caster to go into the spirit plane when they were selecting their totem—half the spell was basically a Spirit Walk. With that in mind, he recopied the Shape Spirit spell, but without that section. He wasn't sure why; it seemed the Spirit Walk was essential, but for some reason, Victor wanted to break the spell down to its basics before he started to tamper with it. In his mind, it was important to understand what he was messing with before he began to modify it.

Looking at the different parts of the spell, the complex patterns, whorls, swirls, interlocking shapes, and almost glyph-like figures, he remembered the books he'd borrowed from Valla and summoned them from his ring. He stacked them beside him and picked up the first in the series, helpfully titled *Hoeghth's Spellcrafting Theory Volume 1*. He thumbed through the delicately thin pages, his eyes bulging out at the dense, tiny script, hoping for some kind of inspiration that would preclude him from actually having to read the entire thing—Victor had never been a fan of textbooks. Still, he'd never minded looking up how to do something he was interested in, either. He and his one-time buddy, Brian, had rebuilt a carburetor on a beat-up old dirt bike one summer after watching a tutorial online. They'd done stuff like that all the time.

He kept thumbing through, reading the headings. The first part of the book was filled with various philosophical theories about Energy. He only skimmed, but it seemed there was a lot of division about where it came from, what it was best used for, and what the System's role was in "modern" spell-craft. After that section, he came to a table of contents and scanned down it until he found a section titled "Common Universal Spell Sigils and Patterns, Their Component Parts, and Compatibility."

When Victor flipped to that section, the very first heading read "Known System Spell Pattern Components—Basic through Advanced." Victor whistled softly as he began to read through them, all categorized by function. Most of them took up less than a quarter of a page, simple designs and sigils that likely would have looked a great deal more complex as part of a larger pattern like the ones Victor had before him. As he scanned through, looking for something familiar, he finally found one that caught his eyes: a complicated whorl that reversed in on itself halfway through, labeled "Intention."

From there, it was a matter of glancing at his patterns, then scanning through the pages and finding matches. Before long, Victor had broken up both of his spells into more than a dozen parts, all labeled with what they were supposed to do. The more he studied them, the more he began to recognize the System's idiosyncrasies with spell design.

When he compared the patterns to the spell Tes had taught him, the only way he could describe their differences was to say it felt like seeing a utilitarian blueprint versus an artist's rendering. He imagined that if you asked the System to design a room, it might look something like the one he was currently sitting in. Whoever first crafted Tes's spell had made a room with a hundred different textures, a thousand features and furnishings, and many levels, windows, and doors.

What it boiled down to, he decided, was a matter of potential. The roots of the System's spells were perfectly functional for what it wanted them to do, whereas a pattern crafted like Tes's spell was rich with potential—filled with hooks and roots for more and more functionality as a caster built upon it. What his Alter Self spell did, modifying each of his cells, reducing the density, reducing the size, and using his own Energy and the potency of those cells to power the transformation, was an order of magnitude more complicated than the two spells before him.

Thinking about the Alter Self spell, he pulled out the last complete copy he'd made before casting it. He chuckled as he unfurled the long scroll of densely packed spell patterns, seeing it next to the elementary totem-summoning spells. He lifted a magical pen and lightly began to circle component parts of the elder magic, and then, with a handful isolated, he tried to find anything like them in the textbook.

He dug around fruitlessly for nearly half an hour and finally decided that if elder magic existed on Zaafor, it wasn't written in this book. Victor wasted another fifteen minutes flipping open the other books in the series, wondering if there were more advanced patterns. He found that there were some examples of epic spells and their parts—but nothing like Tes's spell. Despite his inability to find examples of the elder magic, Victor felt he had a sort of intuitive sense of what many of the parts of Tes's spell did. He wondered if it was due to the many hours he'd spent studying it or if the elder magic feat he'd gained was somehow aiding him.

Setting Tes's spell aside, Victor began to wonder if he couldn't combine the two System spells somehow while still adding additional functionality. Clearly, the System had limited the scope of the spells for a reason; as he'd taken them from basic to improved, he'd gained the ability to summon a second totem. Would he be breaking some kind of unwritten rule if he tried to modify them to allow for a third totem? Should he wait until the System granted them to him?

The main problem with that line of thinking was that Victor was no longer a Spirit Carver, and those spells and their "improved" versions had been granted to him upon leveling in that class. The only way he could see to improve them further was to cast them over and over—how could he do that with the Shape Spirit spell, which only served to allow him to choose his totems? "No, I need to improve these myself."

Staring carefully at the Shape Spirit pattern, he traced every line and whorl, looking for the section that might be what governed or, more accurately, limited his possible totems. "I wish I still had the basic version to compare," he muttered, but he didn't. Regardless of that, he traced the pattern, hoping his intuition, inspiration, or just the component parts he'd labeled from the textbook would jump out at him. He'd gone over the spell a few times, making a notation where the Spirit Walk portion he'd cut out was supposed to be tied in. As he followed a nearby spiraling pattern, he came upon a sort of branch in the main Energy pathway: two loops that led away to the part of the spell he'd cut out.

"That's it. That's where the spell limits me—two paths for two totems." He pulled the other spell, Manifest Spirit, near and looked for a similar "gate" mechanism, and he found it. "Here's where my intention is determined on which totem I want to summon, and then the Energy follows the correct path." He didn't know whom he was speaking to, but it helped him to organize his thoughts, so he continued, "What if I remove that component? Would I be able to summon as many as I want?" Victor frowned. Something seemed off about that. Something felt . . . dangerous.

No, he reasoned, there was a purpose, probably, for why the System put such a hard limit on the spell. Was it to protect the caster? Could he harm himself if he summoned a bunch of totems cut from his own spirit? How would the magic know what to "shape" from his spirit if he didn't do the Spirit Walk first? There were probably untold risks to creating a spirit totem without first solidifying it in his psyche as the first spell was meant to do. "I could put an option in. A determination pathway like the one that's there now, the one that allows me to choose coyotes or a bear."

Victor ripped out a fresh page and began to design a new spell, one that combined the two he currently had. He planned to create a branch at the beginning of the spell; if he wanted a new totem, it would trigger the Spirit Walk component, and if he didn't, it would follow the other branch, allowing him to choose one he'd already found. He removed the limiting gate on the Spirit Walk portion, which would, theoretically, allow him to find as many totems as he wanted.

When he got to the manifestation part of the spell, things began to get more and more complicated. Using his text for guidance and operating on inspiration, instinct, and likely with some knowledge granted by his elder magic feat, he found the two "gateways," which were meant to refer back to the Shape Spirit spell, choosing one of the totems he'd discovered. Again, Victor removed them and instead added a complicated loop that would refer back to his previous Spirit Walks and use his intention to summon the correct totem. He'd basically taken off the training wheels and would have to use his own better judgment not to split his spirit into too many totems.

"And if I can't find a new totem?" Victor frowned. Would he be stuck in limbo forever until he completed the spell? Sighing, he scribbled out a section of the pattern and began to embellish the part of the spell that was meant to guide him to his totem. He could see where it dug into his memories, trying to find options to present. The spell had grown complicated as he'd combined the two originals, and now he was struggling to add the complexity he wanted without ruining parts of the pattern he'd already written.

With a frustrated groan, he looked at the copy of Tes's spell, and an explosion of ideas went off in his mind. "Oh," he said almost immediately, slapping his head. "Of course." He'd yet to try to employ the weird many-dimensional twists in Tes's pattern. "If I do that here," he said, tweaking a branch of his design, "I can build this new section out here . . ." He stopped muttering as his mind began to race with the ideas running through it.

Time bled away as he drew, revised, and drew again. Repeating the process over and over until, as the shadows of the afternoon began to climb up the walls of his room and orange-red light filtered in through his window, he held up a design that was complex, wild, and a hundred times prettier than the System's originals. "Well," he said, wearing a satisfied grin, "at least it *looks* good."

He'd written the spell twice without feeling the need to revise anything, and he felt that it would work; still, he was nervous. He was messing with the building blocks of magic, modifying the System's spells to make something potentially a great deal more powerful. What if he was wrong? What if he *did* blow up the building? What if it was less explosive but just as dangerous and he got himself stuck in the spirit plane or, worse, lobotomized himself with Energy? It wasn't too far-fetched an idea—part of the spell was designed to dig around in his mind, looking for possible totems.

"Nothing ventured, nothing gained," he said and began to construct the new pattern in the wide pathway just outside his Core.

21

DISRUPTOR

Victor, as usual, chose to try out his new spell pattern with inspiration-attuned Energy. He pulled seven threads of it from his Core, keeping them separate but knowing he'd have to weave each of them into the pattern at the right moment. He didn't need to check his written example to get started; the base of the spell was straightforward, and he'd written and studied it enough to begin the weave from memory. It wasn't until he'd constructed nearly the first half of the pattern that he had to look down at his notes and ensure he wasn't making any mistakes.

From then on, he was constantly glancing down, studying a portion of the spell, then closing his eyes to refocus on his pathway where he held the seven strands of Energy in an iron grip with his will. At some point, perhaps twenty minutes into the process, he thought he dimly heard a knock at his door, but he ignored it—he was too close to stop now. Sweat poured down his brow, dripping onto the page in his lap as he tried to finish the last section of the spell.

It wasn't flowing together easily, and he found he was having to force bends and twists into the lines of Energy that weren't on the paper. The truth was, he only *felt* as if the spell he'd written would work; he was guessing at a lot of the pattern's functions, trusting his insight and experience weaving Energies and spells in the past. When it came time to take those written lines and put them into an actual Energy-based pattern, sometimes they simply wouldn't bend the way he'd written them, and he had to adjust on the fly.

Nevertheless, he found ways around the odd blockages, and, in the end, he thought the pattern was better for it.

The biggest obstacles weren't even from the portions of the spell inspired by his elder magic feat and the spell he'd learned from Tes. Those all seemed to work perfectly, and he figured he had the feat itself to thank for that; where study and knowledge failed, the innate ability seemed to compensate. No, the modifications to the original System spells were causing him the most trouble. He bent, twisted, and wove his way to the end, though, and when it finally snapped into focus and pulsed with brilliant white-gold Energy, he grunted with relief and satisfaction.

The spell didn't fire right away, and Victor sat there, looking at the beautiful, complicated pattern in his pathway, wondering if he'd missed something. He froze for several heartbeats, almost afraid to breathe lest he ruin his work, and then he laughed when he realized what was wrong—the spell required intention. He had to think about what he was trying to summon so it could determine if he needed a Spirit Walk or not. Victor concentrated on the concept of a new spirit totem, one that could carry him as a mount. With a flaring pulse of Energy, he felt the spell pull a massive torrent from his Core, and then it ignited in his pathway.

Victor braced himself for the spell to hurl him onto the spirit plane, but as he felt it start to take hold, it seemed to halt jarringly, and then several System messages flashed before his eyes:

*****Warning! The spell being cast incorporates and alters two System-granted spells. If you complete this casting, your System-granted spells will be removed.*****

*****Warning! The spell being cast does not follow System-designed iterations and may be too powerful for you. Proceed at your own risk.*****

*****Warning! Non-System spell pattern detected! You will only receive this warning one time. Do you wish to halt this process? Yes/No *****

"So, the System reached out and paused my spell? Don't like having the control taken out of your hands, do you?" Victor wasn't sure why he spoke his thoughts aloud, wasn't sure why he'd taken on something of a taunting tone, but he certainly didn't think the System was actually listening to him. He rapidly revised that opinion, though, when he felt a blinding pain in his forehead when another message pulsed in his vision, and rather than white text on an opaque grayish background like every other System message he'd ever seen, this one flashed with red text on ominous black, obscuring half his field of view.

***DO YOU WISH TO HALT THE PROCESS? YES/NO ***

Victor growled and mentally smashed the NO option. He saw more System messages flash before his eyes, but as the spell ignited and completed in his pathways, he was ripped away from the physical plane. The transition was abrupt and sudden, and Victor found himself reeling for balance, dropped onto the wide open grassy plain beneath the twilight expanse of stars that always seemed to hang in the sky of the spirit plane. As he made footfall, a pulse of Energy rippled out of him, rolling like a cloud of sparkling, charged smoke, spreading in a great circle with him at its center. It was as though he'd arrived on the wings of an Energy bomb.

Victor stood there, slowly turning, looking out over the plains, wondering if his explosive entrance had done any harm to the realm of spirits or the beings that lived there. He didn't see anything or anyone lingering nearby, but that wasn't very unusual; the spirits of Fanwath had long been skittish around him. With nothing else to do about his strange entrance, and no answers forthcoming, he started walking, no particular destination in mind but a simple desire guiding his thoughts—the need for a mount.

The plains slipped by beneath his boots, and Victor occasionally looked up, always awed by the depth of the star field visible from that realm. He found himself looking for patterns in the stars, recognizing constellations he'd seen before. He wanted to learn more about them, the ones around Fanwath, wanted to know what the people called them. There was so much he wanted to do, and so much he kept pushing aside because of the necessity to keep moving, to try to accomplish one goal or another. Wouldn't it be nice to take a breath? Wouldn't it be good to sit around and study some more spell patterns or learn some military history?

He paused, startled to find that he'd walked down a loose slope of scree and that a long, brush-filled canyon opened before him. "All right," he muttered softly, gathering a deep breath and starting into the canyon, his boots grinding on loose, broken rocks and dry soil. If the temperature weren't cool, like back on the plains, he might have thought he was in Arizona. He didn't see any cacti, but the brush was dry; the cliffs, though bathed in the dim twilight, were ruddy in hue; and not a blade of green—or blue—grass was to be found.

Victor prowled forward, wondering why Lifedrinker wasn't with him. Had the spell specified something about not having a weapon while on the hunt for a totem? The truth was he didn't know; he probably only understood half of the pattern components built into the spell he'd just cast. Still, he pressed forward into the high-walled canyon, and when he rounded a bend, he saw that it ended ahead in a narrow box canyon probably only a few hundred yards in width. Victor paused where he stood, his eyes instantly drawn to the herd of wild horses meandering near the far canyon wall where a stream seeped out of a crevice in the cliffside, pouring into a glimmering, bright blue pool.

Victor's eyes darted over the herd, admiring the horses' proud manes, their fierce eyes, and their flashing hooves as they walked about, eating from a patch of tall grass that grew near the pool, prancing or playing with one another. There must have been nearly fifty horses there, and they were all lovely. Though they were somewhat luminous and ghostly in appearance, much the way anyone was on the spirit plane, he could plainly see their varied colors. Some were a grayish-brown dun, others were bay, and a few were paler, with lots of white hair mixed in with the brown and tan. He saw spotted horses with crazy patterns, and he thought he remembered they were called pintos.

Two of the mustangs caught his attention, though, as they played with one another, rearing on their hind legs and dancing around some of their calmer kin. One was black as midnight, and the other was a deep chestnut red. The red was the biggest horse out there, but the black one was a close match for him and had a clever gleam in his eyes. Victor was just thinking about how to approach them, to size up and assess them better, when he heard some rocks shift behind him. He whirled, hand reaching for an axe that wasn't there, and came face to face with two very strange individuals.

"What's this then? Is it the one, Fox?" the person on the left asked. Her voice was decidedly feminine, soft, and purring. She was probably six feet tall, slender, entirely covered in an orange, brindled fur, and clothed in an outfit that looked very much like what Victor would imagine a swashbuckling pirate would wear, from short, knee-length pants to a blousy white top and a velvety black vest. She had big green eyes, pointy cat ears, and a long, feline tail swishing behind her.

"Is this the source of all the ruckus?" asked the other in a rumbling baritone. His name didn't aptly describe him, for though the first stranger looked like a cat, this man didn't look at all like a fox. He was enormous, someone who would give Victor a run for his money on a pound-for-pound basis, but most of his mass was encompassed by his gigantic belly. He looked human but with limbs too long for his body, and his thick neck was topped with a bulbous bald head. He wore bright green robes, and golden chains hung from his neck in the dozens, covering his chest in their metallic sheen.

"Um . . ." Victor grunted.

"It speaks!" the ginger cat woman announced with a purring chuckle.

"Goodness, but it's young," Fox replied, stepping forward.

"Who the fuck are you guys?" Victor asked, lowering his center of gravity, getting ready for trouble the only way he knew how.

"I smell something old mixed with its young blood." The cat woman stalked to the side, her movements lithe and graceful, soundless and quick. Victor didn't like the idea that she was flanking him, so he took a step back.

"Young indeed, Three. I fear we've come to this meal 'fore the egg's ready to scramble." Fox ambled forward, the stones clicking and sliding beneath his enormous sandaled feat. "What's your name, young disrupter?"

"Disrupter?"

"Doesn't it know what it's done, Fox?" Three, if that was her name, asked, still trying to circle Victor, who continued to backpedal and move to the side, trying to keep both strangers in his view.

"Disrupter, rebel, anarchist, radical, malcontent—surely you get the meaning? The System hasn't abandoned you, has it? You still have your language skill?"

"I'm feeling a bit lost here," Victor growled, the rage in his Core beginning to seep into his pathways.

"It channels Energy, Fox!"

"Yes, Three, I can feel it. Well? Your name?"

"I'm Victor."

"Portentous!" Fox howled, slapping his massive palms together, eliciting a *crack* not unlike thunder that shook through the canyon and agitated the distant mustangs.

"Is it jesting, Fox?"

"No, Three, I believe it speaks true."

"Who are you *payasos*?"

"It thinks *we* jest?" Three had stopped trying to circle Victor. Instead, she crouched low to the ground, her black-clawed, ginger fingers idly scratching patterns in the dirt.

"Perhaps, perhaps. It has a serious disposition. We'll toss this one back into the great ocean, Three. It has much growing to do before we can get a meal out of it."

"Can you please explain what the fu—"

"It speaks with impudence, though!" Three growled in her throaty, weird cat voice.

"A lesson before we go?" Fox raised one bald eyebrow, which lifted his heavy, thick eyelid enough for Victor to see that his eyes smoldered like orange coals deep in the folds of his pudgy eye sockets.

"A lesson! But sweet or harsh? My mother would say harsh, but my father would say sweet. What say you, Fox?"

Victor could feel cold sweat breaking out on his neck and knew very well that he might be in some serious trouble. He wasn't a dummy. He could read between the lines. These people were referring to him as though he were a microwave dinner that hadn't quite finished cooking. It reminded him of how the Warlord in Coloss had behaved, and though he hadn't felt the weight of these individuals' auras, he had a disturbing feeling that they were something altogether worse than the Warlord. He decided to try being less belligerent. "I'm sorry for my confusion, but I'm truly at a loss here. Can I help you with anything?"

"It offers *us* aid, Three!" Fox said, reaching up to rub a wide, meaty hand over the top of his golden-brown dome of a head. "Perhaps a sweet lesson, then?"

"Oh, but Fox! Maybe it would make a good pet! Perhaps we could feed it sweetmeats and tender cuts, make it big and ever so delectable!"

"And if you grow too fond of it? No, Three, we'd better not walk down that road again."

"Oh, bother! You be sweet to it, then!" With that, Three collapsed to her side dramatically, stirring up dust. Then she commenced licking the short fur on the back of her ginger paw.

"Well, young rebel? What have you to say for yourself?" Fox stepped closer, and as the short distance between them disappeared, Victor realized his earlier perception of the man's size was somehow skewed. He felt as if Fox was growing ever larger, looming over him, like Jupiter bearing down on Earth. The stranger must have seen Victor's thoughts written across his face, for he chuckled and said, "Perceptions are funny things, aren't they? Especially in this realm."

"Are you, um . . ." Victor shook his head. "You guys aren't from this part of the spirit plane, are you?"

"Ha! No, Victor," the man said, using his name for the first time. "We felt you. Felt that big shockwave of Energy. You cast elder magic in such a flaunting, noisy way! We thought sure to find something juicier here. Gods, but the System must be cross with you, eh?"

"Cross?"

"Is it daft, Fox?" Three asked, still licking her paw.

"I think just young. Do you remember being young, Three?"

"Not in the least." She sniffed at her furry wrist and then sneezed loudly. "I'm bored! Let's eat it or depart this dull spot."

"Forgive my hungry friend, Victor." His cheeks jiggled as his thick red lips pulled into a broad smile, revealing flat, chisel-like teeth. "Ah, but I'm growing to like that name! In any event, we'll get gone. Be a little more careful using magic like that. Realms like this"—he gestured around the spirit plane—"are bridges to many, many worlds. Tossing out such interesting spells in this place will get you noticed. Good luck with the System!"

"Oh, thanks for the advice . . ."

"True!" Three said, leaping to her feet. She landed so gently that Victor doubted she disturbed a single grain of sand. "You aided it, Fox! I'll take a payment!"

"No . . ." Fox started to say, but it was too late. Quicker than thought, Three snapped out one of her claws and sliced a four-inch gash in Victor's left forearm. Before he could so much as register the attack, she was ten yards away, standing with Fox and sniffing the hooked, razor-sharp nail she'd cut him with.

"So we can find him someday." She grinned, revealing canines that would put a tiger to shame.

"Hey . . ." Victor started, but the duo flickered and shifted toward the horizon, gone before he could finish protesting. "That's just great," he sighed, rubbing at his forearm where the cut had already begun to scab. He thought about what the big man had said about unleashing elder magic in a realm like this. It had to have something to do with the fact that he'd cast the spell for the first time.

A few factors might play into his noisy entrance, he reasoned. The System had warned him about it writing over his other spells, and it had seemed angry and impatient with him. Had it purposefully made his arrival so violent? "It could just be my fault," he muttered. Victor hadn't done anything to try to limit the Energy he was putting into the spell, and he imagined that could be why such a shockwave had followed him into the spirit plane. He'd taken out any governing factors, after all. "I'll have to be more careful, I guess."

The idea that some bloodthirsty cat lady who kept referring to him as an "it" had his blood was a troubling enough thought, but it also sounded like the System wasn't happy with him. "Great," he said again. A soft *chuffing* sounded from behind him, and Victor whirled, once again reaching for a missing axe.

His stressed fighting stance relaxed, though, when he saw the big, dark red bay mustang standing close by, its eyes watching him intently. "¡*Que guapo*!"

Victor held out his hand, forgetting that he'd been rubbing at his cut. The mustang shied at first, dancing back, its big glossy hooves kicking up a little dust. Victor persisted, though, holding his hand out, holding his breath, trying to look relaxed. The mustang snorted and shook its head up and down, causing its dark mane to dance. Victor said, "Come here, *guapo*," taking a slow step forward. The horse snorted again and stepped forward, ducking its head, lifting Victor's hand with its muzzle. Victor laughed, and the horse blew hot breath into his face, sniffing and nickering softly.

"You're a good boy, aren't you?" Victor gently rubbed the velvety fur on the top of his muzzle, reaching up to scratch him between the eyes. The horse watched him, intelligence evident in the big eye he turned toward Victor, and just as Victor was starting to enjoy the attention from his new totem, his spell recognized its success, and the spirit plane faded away.

In a flash of white-gold Energy, Victor found himself back in his room in the command fort, but he wasn't alone. Rearing up before him, the enormous bay mustang pounded its great hooves on the wooden planks, trumpeting its arrival with a loud whinny. "Ah!" Victor laughed, backing up a step. "That's why they probably don't combine the totem-finding spell with the totem-summoning spell!" As he laughed and listened to pounding feet approaching down the hallway, he looked at the pile of System messages that had been waiting for his return.

*****You have discovered a new spell: Wild Totem, Advanced.*****

*****Your new spell renders System-granted spells obsolete. Removing.*****

*****You have lost the spell: Shape Spirit, Improved.*****

*****You have lost the spell: Manifest Spirit, Improved.*****

*****Wild Totem, Advanced: You have begun to master the complicated process of finding and forming fragments of your spirit to use as totems outside the plane of spirits. By carefully formulating your intention prior to casting this spell, you can search your spirit for a totem appropriate to your need. Time spent hunting for your totem will be reflected outside the spirit realm. Totems previously discovered can be summoned instantly. Energy expended will be used to quicken your hunt and/or increase the power of your totem. Energy Cost: Variable.*****

*****Warning! This spell is not a System-designed spell! Use it with caution—there are no safeguards in place. This is the only time you will receive this warning!*****

22

A CARRIAGE RIDE

Whoa!" Victor said, holding up his hands to the stomping mustang. It snorted and bucked, and then, perhaps weary of their heroic efforts, the floorboards gave way, and Victor, his bed, his newly summoned mount, and several hundred pounds of lumber fell through to the bottom level of the command fort. Victor managed a hastily shouted, "Shit!" Then he was too busy rolling free of the shattered flooring and the thrashing horse.

Too late, it occurred to him that he could cancel the spell, sending the horse back to the spirit plane as he often did with his other totems. Too late because the damage was done, and several alarmed junior officers were gathering, gawking at the spectacle. Victor canceled the spell, and, covered with dust, disheveled, and embarrassed, he stood up and looked around. "Well, who let that animal in here?" he yelled, feigning outrage.

"Legate, sir, I don't know how that happened! Where did it go? Was it a monster?" The speaker was Rellia's aide, Darro, and Victor instantly felt sorry for his joke.

"No, no, Darro. I'm kidding. That was my fault. I summoned that animal, but, well, I didn't think it through entirely. Shit." Victor looked at the other gawkers standing around—he'd managed to fall right into the central hall, just a bit past the entrance to the fort where the second-floor stairway sat. "Unless you can help fix this mess, you can move on. Nothing more to see."

"Shall I fetch the engineers?" Darro asked helpfully.

"Yes! Yes, let's get this fixed, I guess. Unless it's too big a hassle; I don't really need a room much longer. We're breaking camp soon."

"I'll find out, sir!" Darro snapped a salute then, like the other onlookers, carefully moved around the wreckage and out of the hall. Victor brushed himself off, then began kicking through the mess, trying to find his notes and the books he'd borrowed from Valla. He wanted to get out of there, embarrassed as he was, but he couldn't leave those behind. He slapped a hand over his shoulder, feeling the empty axe harness, and cursed, scanning for Lifedrinker.

It took him several minutes to find his axe and all the books, by which time Darro had returned with two men wearing legion uniforms. The men were visibly drunk, apparently having started celebrating the oath-swearing ceremony. One of them was an Ardeni with bright green eyes, and he looked at the mess, then at Victor, and paled. He began to stammer, and when Victor frowned at him, he finally managed to choke out some words. "Lord, I swear, we thought this structure perfectly capable of supporting your . . . girth."

"You . . ." Victor tried to see the scene from the other man's perspective, and he couldn't help the laugh that rolled out of him. He slapped a big, heavy hand on the man's shoulder and said, "Listen, my good man, when you're building a structure meant to accommodate me, you need to double your estimates on the required durability." He glanced at the other man, a Cadwalli with one horn that pointed sideways out over his ear, and added, "Is that understood?"

"Yes, sir!" they both said, and they tried to snap salutes, but they were rather sloppy in their inebriated state.

"Can you fix it?"

"Aye, sir!" the first engineer said, emphatically nodding.

"Right. Well, go ahead and enjoy the night. Fix it first thing in the morning."

"Truly?" the Cadwalli asked.

"Yeah. Don't worry." Victor turned, a stupid grin on his face, and walked toward the front of the building. He'd just stepped through a doorway into the entrance hall when Valla came charging up the front steps. He saw the panicked, crazed concern on her face and once again felt guilty. He held up his hands and said, "Relax. Everything's fine."

"I thought we agreed!" she said, standing in the doorway, regaining her composure.

"Agreed?"

"That you wouldn't blow the place up!"

Victor laughed and shook his head ruefully. "I didn't mean to, Valla. It's just my room that's wrecked, in any case. Well, I guess there's a big mess downstairs in the main hall. Anyway, my spell worked! I have some very interesting shit to share with you."

"Interesting shit?" Valla frowned.

"Yes! About spells, the System—oh, and some very creepy, scary people who found me on the spirit plane."

"Oh, Ancestors, Victor! Polo tried to find you earlier. He said you wouldn't answer your door and asked me if we should break it, you know, out of concern. I foolishly told him no, and said you were probably concentrating on something. We should have interrupted you, shouldn't we have?" She stared thunderclouds at him, and Victor wondered how much of her outrage was real and how much was manufactured for effect. He decided to err on the side of it being authentic.

"Hey, it's okay, Valla. Everything worked out. Yeah, I met some scary folks, but they seem like they won't mess with me for a very long time. Well, I hope." He shook his head and moved closer to Valla, reaching toward her as though he'd put a hand on her shoulder, but she stepped back.

"I should have stayed closer."

"Damn it, I'm not a kid. I don't need you to babysit me. Yeah, things got a little crazy, but I accomplished something fucking cool. Will you let me tell you about it?"

"Why not tell us both about it?" Rellia said from behind him, and Victor almost jumped out of his skin.

"Goddamn it, Rellia!" He whirled on her and said, "Stop sneaking up on me!"

She frowned at him, her perfect lips turning downward and her brow drawing together, and said, "I understand you're agitated, but I'm not one to sneak about." Her evident irritation was enough to douse the fire in Victor's belly, and he sighed heavily, looking from Valla to Rellia, then shrugged.

"I guess we might as well have that dinner. I don't think Polo and I are going to spar tonight. Sorry I snapped at you both."

"Understandable." Rellia nodded. "I hear you just fell through the ceiling in the main hall." Before Victor could bluster a response, she added, "Let's take my coach into the city. Lam and Borrius are coming along. I hope that's all right."

"We're not dining here?" Valla asked.

"Heavens no. Our last dinner before we march? Come, you know me better than that. We'll dine at my estate in town." Rellia started down the steps, lithely passing between Victor and Valla. "Darro, let Lam and Borrius know we're leaving." Victor turned just in time to see the aide hurrying up the stairs behind him.

"Well, if we're all riding in your coach, I'm going to reduce my size." Victor followed Rellia, Valla behind him, and began forming the pattern for his Alter Self spell.

"Are you still working on the spells Khul Bach and Tes told you to practice?" Valla asked. He wondered at the sudden change of topic, but he figured it made sense; she was irritated with him and wanted to keep the spotlight focused.

"Yeah, of course. I mean, yes and no. I'm always using Sovereign Will, but I've let up on my Berserk training. I'll get back to it when we're on the march."

"Even though you had that epic breakthrough?"

"Yeah, Tes and Khul Bach think it's worth trying to get it up to legendary. I feel like it'll be years down the road."

"Most likely," Rellia said over her shoulder. "I don't have a single legendary skill or spell, and I've been at this much longer than you."

"Victor's not normal," Valla said, and Victor wasn't sure if he should take it as a compliment or an insult. He shrugged and finished his spell, and both Valla and Rellia stumbled as he channeled torrents of Energy into changing his form. His aura slipped its leash momentarily, and then he snatched it up, smiling around from his new perspective, once again only a very large man, no longer a half-titan.

"Ancestors! I'd almost forgotten that feeling." Rellia paused as though to steady herself, shaking her head gently. She gathered herself quickly, though, and kept walking. A few seconds later, they stood outside the palisade, waiting for Rellia's coach to approach. It was slowly driving down the main boulevard between the army's tents and had nearly reached the gate when Lam, Edeya, Darro, and Borrius arrived.

"Apologies," Lam said, hastily straightening her uniform jacket. "I thought we had a couple of hours yet before leaving."

"My fault," Victor said. "My evening plans got canceled."

"Nobody's at fault. Nobody has suffered. Here we all are, ready to go." Rellia, like the others, still wore her dress uniform and looked very comfortable in the form-fitting blazer and slimming pants. She smiled agreeably at every-one and gestured to her coach. "A pleasant little ride together and then a very nice meal awaits. Let's begin this great endeavor by being positive, shall we? Daughter"—she gestured again to the coach—"after you."

"I think not," Valla said, striding to the coach, opening the door to the flustered protests of the driver, and then reaching in to lower the little hinged step. "After you, dear Mother."

"Oh, Valla." Rellia *tsked* and then climbed into the coach. Lam and Bor-rius didn't quibble about propriety and hurried after her. Victor motioned for Edeya and Darro to precede him, then stepped up to the door.

"You all right?" he asked, looking past Valla toward the darkening horizon. The sun was nearly gone, but the moons looked to be bright that night.

"Fine." Valla shrugged, still holding the door, gesturing for him to get in.

"You're a complicated woman, Valla." Victor tried to smile reassuringly at her but felt it was awkward on his face, so he shrugged and climbed inside. He found that the others had left the central cushion on the far bench open for him, so he crouched low and sort of pivoted, allowing himself to fall into it as Valla climbed in and shut the door behind her. The coach, like most magical conveyances on Fanwath, was enchanted to be larger inside than out, but it was still quite full with the seven of them. Victor scooted toward Rellia on his right, trying to make a bit of room for Valla, and she nodded, seeing it. She'd barely sat down when the coach began to roll.

Victor watched the central fort and then the tents of the encampment fall away and said, "Well, this is nice. Maybe I should have ridden my new mount, though."

"A new mount?" Lam asked, taking the bait.

"Yeah! I was trying to tell Valla about this back at the fort. I managed to alter a couple of my spells, combining them with some . . ." Victor paused. He'd almost mentioned the elder magic, but he worried about opening that can of worms. He'd promised Tes to keep her magic to himself, so how would he explain where he'd learned it? "With some things I learned in Coloss." He looked around the coach and added, "That's the city where Valla and I were the last couple of months."

"Oh, right, right." Lam nodded. Borrius frowned, deepening his already prodigious wrinkles, but he looked intrigued, ready to listen. Victor glanced at Rellia and Valla, saw they were waiting for him to continue, and grinned, enjoying having everyone's attention.

"Well, when I did it, the System gave me a bunch of warnings, said I was creating a non-System spell and I'd lose my originals, blah-blah, then asked me if I wanted to continue or not."

"How much are you glossing over with that 'blah-blah'?" Valla interjected.

"Not hardly at all; I just don't remember the System's exact words. Anyway, when I hesitated and started to get a little mouthy, I think the System yelled at me. Have you guys ever seen a System message with red text?"

"Mine are always green on a translucent, silvery page . . ." Edeya said, then clamped her mouth shut, her cheeks blooming with red roses.

"Mine are always black." Borrius shrugged. "Most everyone sees them differently."

"Well, anyway, I usually see white text, and this time the System sent me a red message, and I felt a terrible pain in my head."

"That's not good!" Valla cried.

"How disturbing," Rellia muttered.

"Are you still in pain?" Lam asked.

Before more of them could speak or throw more questions at him, Victor held up a hand and continued, "Hold on. That's not even the important part. So, anyway, the spell worked, and the System seemed to calm down. My headache didn't last, and I didn't get any more scary messages. At least not right away." He paused, once again enjoying the rapt attention they were all giving him.

"So? What happened?" Lam pressed.

"Right, so the spell I cast was supposed to take me on a Spirit Walk, and it did. I arrived with a literal bang, huge waves of Energy pouring out of me—I didn't put any limits on my new spell, you see, and I didn't hold back the torrent as it came out of my Core. That'll be important in a minute." Victor continued to relate his brief adventure finding the mustangs and with the strange, frightening duo, Fox and Three.

"These beings were that strong? They just took your blood and left before you could even react?" Darro asked, the horror of the idea widening his eyes.

"Yeah, I think so. I'm hoping that threat is so long-term that they'll forget about me, or, hopefully, I'll figure out a way to dissuade or beat them by then."

"Another enemy to add to your list," Valla sighed. "Perhaps Tes will have some advice for you." She looked down as she said that, and Victor couldn't quite read her expression. Was she still annoyed with him?

"Well, anyway," he said, turning back to the group, "the spell worked, and I learned a lot. All in all, I'd say it was a good experience."

"That's good, but the System . . ." Rellia shifted, glancing in irritation toward the front of the coach as it bounced over something in the trail. "What is that driver doing?" She shook her head and then refocused on Victor. "Now we know why your room collapsed—a pity I didn't know it earlier when I gave those engineers a tongue-lashing."

"You didn't!" Valla leaned forward to glare at her mother. "Victor already spoke to them!"

"But I didn't know that! Don't worry, I'll . . ." the coach lurched again, and she and several others were almost thrown out of their seats. "What's happening out there? Kel!" she yelled, reaching to pull angrily on a red tasseled cord that hung from the ceiling. A bell sounded, but the coach didn't slow, still bouncing roughly.

"Something's wrong!" Lam cried, reaching for the door, flipping the catch, and kicking it open. Victor caught a glimpse of tall grass rushing by, and then Lam launched herself out, flying into the air. Valla reached for her sword and leaned toward the door, looking out. Victor wanted to shove her aside and leap out of the coach, imagining all sorts of terrible scenarios, but he held himself still, trying to remain calm. To that end, he cast Inspiration of the Quinametzin, feeling rather self-satisfied as he saw the panic wash out of Darro and Edeya.

Suddenly the coach lurched and began to slow, and Victor heard Lam call out, "The driver is dead!" Those words were all Valla needed; she leapt out of the coach, and Victor was hot on her heels, Lifedrinker clutched in his hands. He'd barely cleared the threshold when he snipped the lines of Energy constraining his form, and when he tumbled into the thick grass of the plains, the ground shook with his impact. He rolled to his feet, scanning the area, wondering who could have killed the driver without alerting anyone in the coach. He was currently boosting his agility and vitality and decided that was best, nimbly leaping to the top of the now motionless coach.

Lam stood on the driver's bench, the reins in her hands, the headless body of the driver slumped by her feet. Valla was stalking around the coach, her sword dark and glittering in the bright moonlight. Beneath him, Victor could hear Rellia and the others getting out of the coach while he looked around, trying to see what had attacked them.

"What's happened?" Borrius asked, his voice more indignant than worried.

"I don't know, sir," Darro replied, and *his* voice quaked with nerves.

"Darro, Edeya, you are charged with protecting Borrius," Rellia said, whipping her wicked rapier through the air, slashing some grass out of her way as she moved toward the front of the coach. She looked up at Lam and Victor and said, "Anything?"

"Nothing . . ." Lam replied, but Victor held up a hand, interrupting her. He'd seen something. Out in the grass, more than a mile away, something was moving toward them. If the grasslands were instead an ocean, he'd call it a wave. It surged through the grass, causing it to bend forward and snap back, but it was subtle at that distance in the dark. Someone might mistake it for the wind, even. But Victor had a feeling in his gut that told him something was coming, either something massive or many, many smaller things.

He pointed and said, "There." He didn't wait for the others to register what he'd seen, didn't wait for whatever it was to get closer. He jumped off the carriage, and before his feet hit the grass-covered turf, he cast Iron Berserk; this time, the ground *really* shook. He heard Lam launch herself into the sky behind him, but he didn't look. He had one idea in mind, and that was to engage whatever enemy had attacked them before it closed on the others, before the lower-tiered Edeya, Darro, and apparently Borrius were caught up in the battle.

He used his Titanic Leap ability and distanced himself from them, launching himself headlong into the oncoming enemy or enemies. As he charged, Victor cut the thread to his inspiration spell; he wanted to use that Energy for something else. He gathered up a vast torrent of it, pulling that white-gold Energy out of his Core, and then he cast Globe of Insight, forming a basketball-sized blazing orb that followed him through the tall grass, laying waste to the shadows, brightly illuminating the plains for a hundred paces on either side of him.

That done, Victor leapt into the air again, and this time as he soared, the wind whistling over his ears, he cast Banner of the Champion. More glorious light erupted behind him as the banner of his primogenitors took shape, hanging in the air above his head. The bloody sun depicted in the ethereal coat of arms blazed with glittering golden light, and it, combined with the Globe of Insight, lit up the night like a fireworks show as Victor hurtled toward the ground.

He saw his foes then, not clearly, but enough to get an idea that they weren't one gigantic monster but rather a host of shadowy, black-clad individuals racing toward him and the others in a tight V-shaped formation. At the point of that charging host, something reflected back the light of Victor's blazing spells. A man, enormous in stature, clad in glittering gold from his feet to the horned helmet atop his head, charged with madness in his eyes. Somehow he locked those wild, insane eyes with Victor's despite the distance between them, and then he screamed—a terrible sound that echoed over the grassy plains, ripping the night like a psychopath's mad howling.

For the first time, Victor became aware that Lam had flown with him out into the plains as she said, with dread in her voice, "Ridonne."

23

TWILIGHT MELEE

So that's one of 'em?" Victor watched the gold-clad man charging toward him, easily ten feet tall but still a child compared to Victor. "Doesn't seem so tough."

"Careful, Victor," Lam said, still hovering above him near his enormous, blazing banner.

"Well, if the Empire is moving against us, this moment was coming sooner or later. Might as well get it over with." Victor set Lifedrinker down and pulled his helmet and wyrm-scale armor from his ring. Rather than waste time taking off his uniform jacket, he simply sent it directly into storage, then he donned his armor. By the time he'd sealed up his vest and lifted Lifedrinker, the enemy force was only half a mile or so distant.

"Something killed our driver. I'll hunt the sky. Be careful." Lam's wings buzzed and sprayed Energy motes as she streaked upward, back toward the coach. Victor watched her briefly, then turned back toward the Ridonne and his soldiers. He began to run straight at the front of that wedge of charging enemies. "C'mon, *chica*, it's time to dance."

"I thirst!"

Victor laughed as he poured red rage-attuned Energy into his pathways and began channeling it into his arms and Lifedrinker. She blazed with furious crimson light, and then, as if in answer to his Energy, her silvery metal ignited, heatwaves rippling off her into the air, black smoke trailing as Victor charged. As he tore over the plains, resisting the urge to leap so that he'd have more control over his trajectory, he began to make out details about the rapidly approaching enemies.

He couldn't count them easily, not clumped and lined up behind each other the way they were, but if he had to guess, Victor would say there were more than a hundred darkly-clad warriors behind their Ridonne leader. They carried gleaming spears, two-handed swords, axes, and mauls, but not a shield was to be seen among them. This was a force of killers, men and women who aimed to overwhelm their targets with a brutal offensive assault. Victor's grin spread further, pulling back from teeth that reflected the moons' luster in anticipation. Blood was about to flow.

The Ridonne towered over his soldiers, but they all ran with grace and unnatural speed, sliding through the grass like wraiths, their passage creating a susurrus that almost sounded like a steady, sustained wind gust. When they were just a hundred paces apart, Victor focused on the golden warrior and his gigantic, gleaming sword, held high over his head and back as though ready to chop forward. With nothing but anticipation and excitement in his heart, Victor roared again and cast Energy Charge. Like an eight-hundred-pound human cannonball, his form ignited with red, furious Energy and streaked through the gap separating them.

The golden warrior cried out, his voice rising in a mad, ululating crescendo, and then he brought his sword down, far too early to hit Victor. Though he was moving almost as quickly as a person's eye could track him, Victor saw the move and felt a surge of excited glee; was the fool so bad at judging when to strike? Then the earth erupted under him, ripping apart, exploding up in a shower of rock, dirt, and grass as the true effects of the Ridonne's blow became apparent. Victor saw the wave of earth coming, saw the ground rupturing from the point of the imperial warrior's strike, but he couldn't waver in his charge. The spell was set, and he was under its impetus; he tore right through that rippling curtain of rock and dirt and smashed into the Ridonne.

The concussion of his impact with the sundered earth and his secondary crash into the Ridonne shook the night, sounding much like a large vehicle slamming into a tree. The golden warrior was far sturdier than Victor expected. He braced himself, just barely lifting his sword in time to keep Victor from trampling it out of his hands. Then Victor, leaning forward, Lifedrinker held high, carrying a thousand pounds of dirt and rock, collided with him. The Ridonne tried to slip him, rolling to the right, but Victor was too large, the concussion too massive, and they both tumbled and tore through the host of smaller warriors, flattening dozens of them and utterly breaking their charge.

"Kill the old man!" the Ridonne screamed, his voice high, shrill, violent, more like a giant raptor than a man. Victor was stunned by his enemy's quick recovery and ability to shout commands after that impact. Victor had tumbled several times and had ended up face down on a pile of injured imperials. He rolled over, grasping a fallen soldier and flinging him away as he surged to his feet. The Ridonne stalked toward him, sword held high, golden Energy shimmering over his entire form like a liquid, crystalline barrier.

He might once have been a Shadeni, but it was clear his Ridonne bloodline had changed him a great deal. He had a hawkish nose, wild, red-blazing eyes, and sprouting from his shoulders and helmet, his forearms and hips were long black horns or spines. Victor didn't know, didn't really care, what the correct term for them was. Moreover, the man didn't wear boots or even have armor below the knees. He had no need; his legs ended in enormous, shiny black hooves upon which he stomped toward Victor, heedless of the downed soldiers he trampled.

"Come on, then!" Victor roared, sidestepping and whipping Lifedrinker in a cleaving hundred-and-eighty-degree arc, savagely maiming several warriors that tried to approach him from the side.

"I said kill the old man!" the Ridonne screamed again, and Victor glanced toward the carriage, nearly a mile away, noting that dozens of the imperial soldiers were almost upon it. He saw Lam's glittering wings looping in a wide circle around the vehicle. He saw something like a miniature light show as Valla channeled a lightning-powered spell. He knew they were formidable, Rellia too, but he worried they'd be overwhelmed.

He grinned at the Ridonne, circling him, swiping Lifedrinker left and right if any of the soldiers drew near. While they faced each other and the Ridonne continued to scream at his soldiers, exhorting them to kill the others and "leave the giant" to him, Victor summoned a massive flood of fear-attuned Energy out of his Core, nearly draining himself of the potent, purple-black power, sending it into another spell. The ground around him erupted in dark shadows, swirling and writhing as they rose up, solidifying into the shapes of five pony-sized, leering, snarling, yipping coyotes.

With a thought, Victor sent them racing over the plains toward the carriage, quickly overtaking most of the soldiers, trampling or snapping at them, spreading fear and panic in their wake. They howled and cried, their weird sounds magnified by their size and the dark Energy that flowed through them. That done, Victor turned his attention back on the Ridonne. Done waiting for him to make a move, he stepped forward, snapping Lifedrinker forward and down, aiming to split him at the crease of his neck and shoulder.

"I've killed larger than you," the man snarled, whipping his huge bastard sword up and to the side, parrying Lifedrinker, and nimbly using the force of Victor's blow to glide sideways over the ground.

Victor wasn't a shit-talker, not during a fight. He just glowered at the smaller man and got to work. He could tell by the way the Ridonne parried and tried to slip his blows that he feared Victor's strength, but the man's speed was a near match for his, and he certainly wasn't a slouch with that sword. They exchanged furious flurries of blows, dodging, parrying, or eating them, each trusting in their armor from time to time. Lifedrinker cleaved great scars in the man's gleaming plate armor, but she never cut through it. Victor didn't hold her responsible—the only blows the man was letting through were glancing. He needed to strike a solid hit.

They fought like that for several minutes that seemed to drag out like eternity as Victor was forced to concentrate on every aspect of the contest, pushed to his limits as he hadn't been in a very long time. Not Polo Vosh, nor Yabbo, nor even Karnice had pressed him that hard. The duel of axe and sword became his reality, his world, and he almost began to enjoy it as the rhythmic contest took on a life of its own.

Lifedrinker sang and screamed as she cut the air, her blazing magma heart growing brighter and brighter. The Ridonne's sword was something special, crafted of brilliant silvery metal; it let Lifedrinker's furious heat roll off, sparks flying like a blacksmith forging steel. All the while they battled, Victor analyzed the man's style and knew he was doing the same. They circled, clashed, circled, and clashed. Victor wondered who would break from the pure combat first. Who would try to end things with a well-timed Energy-based skill or spell?

"So, you're Victor?" the man asked through gritted teeth. Was he tiring? He certainly didn't move like he was. Victor could feel his own Energy levels. His fear was nearly gone but slowly regenerating. His inspiration was more than half full and rising. Even his glory was on the climb, almost recovered from casting his banner. The only pool that gave him concern was his rage, well under half full after several minutes of battling with his Iron Berserk active and constantly channeling the furious Energy into his axe.

When Victor ignored his question, the man hissed strangely and blinked his eyes rapidly, and Victor almost stumbled when he saw the flames in those orbs dim slightly, revealing odd, hourglass-shaped pupils. He clicked his tongue, whipping his sword down in a low cleave that Victor easily avoided. "Do you know me, then?"

Victor grunted, still ignoring the man, and channeled a bit of inspiration-attuned Energy; he cast Energy Charge again, hoping to catch his opponent off guard. He was only a couple of steps away from him, so as the spell ignited around him, limning his form with white-gold light, and he blasted forward, the Ridonne gasped and barely managed to create his shimmering golden shield. He encased himself just in time as Lifedrinker bore down on his shoulder, and Victor slammed into him, sending him flipping backward, head over heels.

"You talk too much," Victor roared, jumping after him, soaring up into the air, and coming down, Lifedrinker's blazing, smoking blade streaking toward the crumpled imperial like a comet. His savage smile widened as he descended, noting the split in the man's golden armor where hot, purple-red blood bubbled forth, brightly illuminated by Victor's banner. The Ridonne was battered, his armor dirt-smeared, long stalks of grass caught between the plates and joints. He was barely up to one knee, using his bastard sword as a crutch, when he saw Victor falling toward him like death incarnate.

"Fool!" he cried, then exploded in a burst of bright golden Energy, tearing over the ground, ripping apart the tall grass, and leaving a trail of fire and smoke as he fled Victor's impact. Victor roared in furious frustration as he crashed into the ground where the man had been, but he didn't linger there. He leapt to his feet and began charging after the fleeing imperial. The trail was easy enough to follow—a trench of blackened, smoldering grass leading farther afield from the carriage.

Once upon a time, Victor might have been unable to consider whether or not he should chase the man. Now, though, after all the work he'd done on Zaafor, after everything he'd endured to improve his Berserk ability, he paused and glanced back at the carriage. He could see Lam's explosive Energy attacks, taking the shape of a giant hammer, smashing down amid the Empire's soldiers. He couldn't make out Rellia or Valla and saw no sign of the others.

He did see and feel his coyotes. He licked his lips as he connected his mind to them and felt their hunger and the pleasure they experienced ripping their foes apart, flinging them left and right, harvesting the terror and fear they drew forth. He felt the call to join his pack, to smash the fools trying to kill his friends, trying to cut the head off his army.

Victor looked out over the grassy plains, trying to track the Ridonne's passage. The smoldering line of his flight ended about a mile away. Was he just running now? Had he teleported? Sprouted wings? Victor had no idea but knew his friends might die if he left them. He turned back to the carriage, and with three running steps, he leapt through the air, crashing to the ground and repeating the process again and again until he was among the rearguard of the imperial soldiers.

These men were probably dangerous, powerful soldiers among their peers, but Victor was stacked with abilities that boosted him beyond his natural, already dominating potency. His banner filled him with vigor, boldness, and a love for battle. His orb granted him a keen insight into the combat taking place around him, showing him where to step, where to swing, and where to move to evade a strike. His Iron Berserk, probably the most potent of his boons, filled him with strength, sped up his movements, and allowed him to shrug off wounds that would have left a lesser man dead or disfigured. What's more, he wore armor that proved impervious to the blows of the imperial soldiers, and Lifedrinker cleaved them apart, heedless of their shadowy chainmail.

All that said, Victor was like a Rottweiler let loose amid a rabbit colony. He cut the soldiers apart, and when they got past his axe and strayed too close to him, he grabbed them by the tops of their heads or their arms and smashed them around like rag dolls. Blood misted the air in his wake, soaking him, splashing onto his banner, and joining the ethereal crimson rivulets that ran down from the edge of the blazing sun. His allies rallied at his approach; in the light of his banner, they grew stronger and bolder, screaming and hacking viciously at the enemies who had earlier harried them.

Victor saw Lam launching herself into the air and descending on her foes, wielding a one-handed, sledge-like warhammer that she somehow expanded into a massive orange Energy weapon that flattened and shocked whole groups of enemy shoulders. As he continued to bathe in his enemies' blood, driving ever closer to the carriage, he finally got eyes on Rellia and Valla, both fighting back-to-back at the carriage door where, he presumed, the two lieutenants and Borrius had taken refuge. All around them, leaping, howling, growling, and furiously biting, were his massive purple-black coyotes.

The bodies of imperials were everywhere. Grievously wounded soldiers wailed and cried, clawing at the blood and gore-soaked grass, trying to escape the insane charnel house that had overtaken the grassy plains around the carriage. Having fought his way to their center, attacking from the rear, Victor paused long enough to bellow a war cry that thundered out of his massive chest. Bloody saliva streamed from his enraged, frenzied face as he screamed, and then the imperials broke. The dozens left who could still run tried to do so, breaking from the melee and charging in every direction away from the carriage.

Victor's coyotes weren't having it; they raced after the runners, snapping them up by the necks, hamstringing them, or simply trampling them in their frenzied need to keep their prey from fleeing. Victor almost joined the chase, but he stomped up to the carriage and bellowed, "Does Borrius live?"

"He does," Rellia said, bending at the waist, pressing a palm against a bubbling, flowing gash above her left hip.

"Are you okay, Mother?" Valla asked, producing a potion and handing it to Rellia.

"Fine, fine," she said, tipping the draught to her lips.

"What of the Ridonne, Victor?" Lam asked, landing atop the carriage.

"He ran. He was a tough bastard, but he bolted as soon as I hurt him."

"There was a Ridonne here?" Rellia asked, and when Victor looked at her again, he was struck by her savage beauty. Her eyes gleamed fiercely in the light of his banner, and her pale blue skin, painted with sprays of her dead enemies' blood, almost matched her copper red hair. He shook his head, trying to get control of the Quinametzin berserker inside him, trying to focus on what people were saying.

" . . . wasn't winged. He had horns all over his body, though, and ran like a charging roladii bull," Lam finished saying as he finally tuned in.

"Damn," Rellia spat. "Without his head, we'll have a hard time convincing the other nobles that the Ridonne tried to assassinate us. Old bones!" She said the last like a curse, and Victor grinned as she continued, "How'd they know to attack my coach?"

"It's not hard to spot, and seeing the shadows still wrapped around these broken fools, I don't think it was hard for them to lie in wait. Perhaps they didn't know how big a bite they'd taken," Valla said, gesturing to the absolutely gore-drenched Victor.

Victor grinned, exposing teeth stained pink with the blood that had splashed into his face during his slaughter. He shook his head, though, and said, "Nah, they knew Borrius was in there." He gestured to the coach. "The imperial was screaming at the men to 'kill the old man.'" He looked at Lam and asked, "Did you find who killed the driver?"

"No. They were either very fast or very stealthy. Perhaps that assassin is who informed the Ridonne about Borrius."

Victor hawked up a large wad of coppery tasting bloody saliva and spat it into the grass, then, looking around at the massacre, listening to the groans and wails coming from the tall grass, said, "We've got some prisoners you can question."

"Yes, and we need to get the army ready to march. I'm deploying the airships tonight; we need to find where that Ridonne fled, especially if he has more men or an actual army nearby. We might have our first real test sooner than I'd hoped." As she spoke, Rellia turned to the coach and knocked on it, calling out, "You can open up now."

"Should I chase that fucker down?" Victor squeezed Lifedrinker's haft in his fists, twisting them slightly, enjoying the heat emanating from the weapon.

Lam shook her head. "No. We can't afford to be reckless. You beat him, yes, but if he has brethren nearby, you could walk into an ambush. Do you think you could take two of them? Three? I can tell you he wasn't one of the strongest." Lam dropped down from the top of the carriage. "I've heard of Ridonne twenty feet tall, wielding flames that would be more at home spewing forth from a volcano."

"Tall tales," Valla scoffed.

"We'll see," Lam said, shrugging. "I'm afraid I mean that literally—we'll see."

24

TRAVEL ACCOMMODATIONS

After the skirmish with the Ridonne and his squad of stealthy assassins, everyone, especially Rellia, agreed it would be wise to return to the encampment; her luxurious send-off dinner was canceled. After they'd all reaped their rewards in post-battle Energy, Victor helped the other high-tier members of their party secure the surviving imperials, gagging, binding, and hobbling them with magical rings and chokers that Rellia produced from one of her storage containers. When that was done, some thirty enemy combatants lay or sat helpless before the carriage, stewing in the blood and fluids of their vanquished comrades.

"Edeya, you and Darro will stand watch over these prisoners while we return to camp and send out an escort to bring them in." Rellia mounted the first step into the coach as though the matter was settled.

"Is that wise?" Victor asked, frowning. "What if the Ridonne returns or the sneaky asshole who killed the driver? Nah, I'll wait here with the prisoners, and after your escort picks them up, I'll head into town for some last-minute shopping."

"Shopping?" Lam asked, her wings twitching briefly as she wiped at her face with a damp rag, trying to clean away the remnants of combat.

"Yeah. I need some better accommodations for the trail. You know, a big tent, a bed that fits me, stuff like that. I've got plenty of storage space; I might as well load up."

"I'll stay with him," Valla said, folding her arms and leaning against the carriage.

"And if we're attacked on the way back to camp?" Rellia pressed, moving to stand before Victor, trying to lock eyes with him. "It's clear Borrius was the target . . ."

"The soldiers are dead or captured. The Ridonne ran away, licking his wounds. I think we're fine for the night," Borrius said, enunciating his words in a languorous drawl.

"Are you bored, sir?" Rellia scoffed. "Was this bloodbath too small to garner your attention?"

"Not bored, but this is hardly the first time someone has tried to assassinate me, either. Come, Rellia, let's return to camp. We've much to discuss." With those words, the matter was settled, and soon Victor and Valla were left alone, standing over the broken soldiers, the stench of shit, guts, and blood heavy in the air. Victor jerked his head, indicating he wanted Valla to follow him, then he moved a dozen yards upwind of the battle site. He folded his arms, watching over the huddled survivors.

"I'm surprised they weren't tougher," he said after a while. "There were close to a hundred, all told, and you guys held them off for a long time."

"Most of them are probably Tier Two. Lam is Tier Four, and Rellia and I are Tier Five. They fought bravely, madly even, and I believe that's what the Ridonne was counting on for their success—insane disregard for their own safety. I wouldn't be surprised to learn that a Mind Caster conditioned these troops to fight to the death. It's a testament to your ability to evoke fear that you made them break. If the negative effects of your banner are as potent as the positive, then I pity the poor fools."

"You felt it, huh?"

"When you came close, and that light shone on us, it was as though the battle began anew. My arms didn't ache, the wind returned to my lungs, and I thirsted for the glory of combat. Then, when you began to maul and slaughter their rear ranks, I couldn't help but want to reciprocate. Lam and Rellia responded similarly. Let's not forget to mention those enormous hounds of yours. Ancestors, Victor! They were terrifying!"

"Yeah, things worked out all right. Still, that Ridonne was a lot tougher than I expected to face here on Fanwath. If the Empire is openly moving against us, we might have some trouble ahead."

"I'm not so sure they are. These men aren't marked with any imperial insignia, and the Ridonne was careful to escape. Tell me, do you think he could have kept fighting?"

"I thought he could, yeah." Victor rubbed at a spot of blood he'd missed on the back of his hand. "Surprised me when he bolted."

"So, he might be acting in an unsanctioned manner. We can hope, at least."

Victor stewed on those words for a while, watching the prisoners and occasionally glancing in the direction of the camp. After a while, he got bored and walked over to the nearest of the bound imperials. He reached down and pulled his gag loose, then asked, "What was the name of that Ridonne?" When no answer was forthcoming from the man, a Shadeni with short black horns, he tried again. "I already beat his ass. He's not coming to save you. What was his name?"

"I cannot answer." The man spat a wad of blood from his battered mouth. He'd lost an arm in the melee and looked to be in great pain.

"I'll give you a bit of healing if you do."

"Even if I wanted to, m'lord, I cannot. I've geas upon geas upon my spirit. I'm doomed as it is."

"Leave him, Victor. It will take Rellia's Mind Caster days to unwind the spells binding them—if he can."

"Huh," Victor muttered, stuffing the gag back in the soldier's mouth. He looked up sharply at the sound of approaching riders and, within moments, he and Valla were surrounded by twenty heavily armored legion soldiers, all riding roladii clad in red chainmail barding. The biggest roladii Victor had ever seen was being ridden by none other than Polo Vosh, and when he jumped down, Victor clasped wrists with him, truly glad to see the man's smiling, furry face. "Polo!"

"Victor! I heard you tussled with a Ridonne! It's all over the camp already."

"I did! I think I learned a thing or two during our duel; he was skilled with the sword. Have you been holding back on me? I'm asking 'cause it was a lot more fun than our sparring sessions."

"Fun!" Valla almost choked on the word.

"Ha! Of course you'd think it was fun! Tell you what, Legate. When we make camp tomorrow, let's put what you learned to the test. I'll do my best to keep it interesting."

"It's a deal!" Victor clapped him on the shoulder and then turned, getting ready to summon his mustang.

"Did you bring me my mount?" Valla asked, looking around.

"What? That great cat? Who would dare approach such a thing? Would it even follow a tether without mauling my roladii?"

"Uvu wouldn't do that . . ." Valla frowned, her words trailing off, and then she sighed and shrugged. "Maybe he would."

"Don't worry. You can ride with me, Valla." Victor concentrated momentarily and then called forth his mount using glory-attuned Energy. He used only a fraction of the Energy he'd used to summon his five giant coyotes. Still, somehow, he intuitively knew it was enough to bring forth a mighty horse. His intuition served him well—a golden, shimmering puddle of Energy appeared in the trampled grass nearby, bubbling as it grew to the size of a small pool, and then, in an explosion of brilliant golden sparkles, a deep red mustang burst out of it, bucking wildly as it landed on the flattened grass. It stood on its hind legs and whinnied loudly, golden eyes blazing and hooves sparking as it brought them down before Victor.

"Whoa!" Polo said, backing up and laughing with delight. "What creature is this?"

"This is one of my spirit totems. He's a mustang, a proud creature from my homeworld." Victor reached up, rubbed the horse's snout, and added, "Hey there, *guapo*. What a good boy. Ready to run?"

"Is that his name? Handsome?" Valla stepped up next to him, gently stroking the horse's shoulder and then tousling his thick, dark red mane.

"Well, nah, I just think he's a handsome boy. Don't you? I don't think he cares for a name. My coyotes surely don't." The mustang nuzzled Victor's shoulder, snorting hot breath into his neck, and he laughed, pushing the horse's snout away. "Come on," he said, stepping to the side and easily pulling himself onto the horse's bare back, gripping his mane to steady himself. "He's tough, don't worry." He reached down a hand, and when Valla took it, he swung her up onto the horse behind him. "See you soon, Polo!"

As Polo waved and hollered his farewell, Victor urged the mustang to run, and then they were off, ripping through the tall grass as he'd never done before. Thistle was fast, but it soon became apparent that he couldn't hold a candle to the mustang. Valla whooped with delight and wrapped her arms around his waist, squeezing tightly. Thankfully, both she and Victor had plenty of experience riding on the backs of galloping mounts, and there was definitely something magical about the creature because the ride was remarkably smooth, even without riding tack.

Victor leaned forward, his hands grasping the mustang's mane, his cheek next to the animal's neck as they rhythmically rose and fell with the horse's gallop. Valla, in turn, held tight to his sides, leaning forward against his back, and Victor decided he liked that feeling a lot and began to wish he wasn't wearing his thick wyrm-scale armor. Pushing those thoughts aside, he pressed his face into the wind and couldn't help the joyful howl that escaped his lips while they raced over the plains. The mustang's hooves sparked against the ground with magical Energy, leaving a trail of golden motes in their passage, and he grinned, imagining what anyone seeing them from a distance would think of the display.

The carriage had been attacked roughly halfway between the army encampment and Persi Gables, and, at the speed his mustang raced, the ride to the city only took a dozen minutes or so. When they leapt the berm up to the cobbled road that approached the gates, Victor heard Valla whoop again with excitement. The trees lining the road blurred past, and the gates rapidly grew large before them. He willed the horse to slow, and it did, responding far better than any trained mount might; it was a part of him, after all.

When the guards saw Victor and Valla behind him, they waved them through, but not without boosting Victor's ego a bit with some compliments on his mount and the proud stately manner with which it pranced over the cobbles. Valla laughed as they bounced up and down, and the horse's hooves clattered and sparked against the cobbles. The beast arched its neck, snorting and flashing those bright, golden eyes. Victor beamed, of course, too pleased to even consider attempting to act nonchalantly.

Once through the gates, he turned over his shoulder to look at Valla. They'd both spent some time washing blood from their faces, and, in the process, her hair had come undone from her usual tightly bound style. After the mustang's sprint over the plains, her shoulder-length aqua locks were wild-looking, feathered back, and wavy. Her face was flushed with excitement, darkening the pale blue of her cheeks and giving her an eager, pleasant demeanor. While he looked at her, she rubbed at her left eye with the back of her hand, brushing away some moisture the whipping wind had teased out. "Where to?"

"You're the one who wanted to shop!"

"Well, yeah, but I want to go someplace new. Any recommendations? I mostly want a tent like yours, one that gets larger as you unfold it. I guess I want some furnishings too."

"Head to the fountain square. It's on the way to the noble district. I know just the place."

"You like the horse?" Victor asked, slapping his hand against the bay's muscular shoulder.

"I've never run so fast! Even when Uvu sprints . . ." She shook her head and laughed. "No! I won't denigrate poor Uvu, but let's just say that ride was more than spectacular!"

"Yeah." Victor clicked his tongue, willing the mustang to get moving, and it followed his intent perfectly. "It was, wasn't it?" Ten minutes later, they were in a shop called Chori's Emporium, and Victor was browsing the shelves, looking at all the wonderful, weird things that Chori the Artificer had crafted and put out for sale. While he shopped, he was struck by the fact that he'd intended to shop around stores like this from the first day he'd escaped the dungeon near Greatbone Mine and visited Steampool Vale.

He'd done a little shopping here and there, sure, but always with the goal in mind of getting something he needed. Then he'd move on and say to himself, "I'll come back." He never did, though. One goal, one crisis, and one unplanned trip led to another, and he never really got to enjoy the idea of picking up something he liked. The last time he remembered doing that, really buying something that struck his fancy, was when he'd purchased the wagon with Thayla. "And then I gave it away." He chuckled, shaking his head ruefully.

"What's that?" Valla asked. She'd been browsing on the opposite side of the rack, looking at magical birdfeeders while Victor examined wondrous little brass and copper Energy-driven appliances meant for use on the trail—stoves, teapots, lanterns, water dispensers with tanks enchanted by dimensional magic, and even self-cleaning pots and pans.

"Just thinking about that cool little wagon I gave away to Thayla and Deyni. It was big inside, like a little cabin. I remember thinking about how neat it would be to fix it up, you know, decorate it, fill it with my treasures, books, art, and even trophies. I never even got started."

"You're far richer now than you were back then, Victor. Why not buy a proper travel home? Why do you think I brought you here?"

"Huh? I thought you brought me here to get a tent like yours."

"My tent is lovely, and I appreciate the gesture Rellia made when she gifted it to me, but I was a girl, going off to be in the Legion. You're a legate, arguably one of the most powerful men in this world. Let's get you some accommodations that are worthy of your status." She glanced to the back of the shop where the little Cadwalli woman, Chori, sat atop a tall stool. "Chori?"

"Mm-hmm? Yes, Miss ap'Yensha?"

"She's always seen me as a little girl; Rellia used to bring me here to shop when I was too young to ship off to war," Valla said behind her hand, then raised her voice and replied, "Can you help my friend here with a more significant purchase?"

"Something special? Come closer, then."

"Come on." Valla gestured toward the counter, saw Victor's lingering gaze on the camping appliances, and added, "You can stock up on that stuff afterward."

"Right." Victor nodded and followed her over to the counter; he'd reduced his size significantly before entering the shop, but he still felt too large, squeezing between the crowded sales racks and shelves. "You've a lot of wares," he said by way of greeting.

"Aye, big man. Been crafting goods for decades and decades, and my father before me. Still have many of his wares lying about. Some of the better ones—don't ask me which. So, tell me, something significant, hmm? Seeking a travel lodging?" Even for a Cadwalli, she was small, probably only four feet tall if she weren't on the stool. Her goat-like features were quite pronounced, from her fuzzy snout to the weird red and yellow irises in her over-large eyes. She pronounced some words with a strange warble and moved carefully, each gesture precise.

"Victor is the leader of Rellia ap'Yensha's army, the one she's been forming out on the plains. He needs travel lodgings suitable for a legate and a great adventurer."

"Oh? Well, then, you should have said so sooner! Come with me." Chori slid off the stool and motioned for Valla and Victor to follow her behind the counter and through the rear door. "My travel homes are in the next room; it's something of a showcase."

"We should hurry, Valla," Victor said, suddenly struck by guilt. Should he be shopping around in Persi Gables while the Ridonne conspired against his army? Shouldn't he be there in case the army was attacked? Who else could stand against those weird, powerful imperials?

"We'll ride your mostrang back; it'll hardly take a few minutes."

"Mostrang? He's a mustang, Valla!" Victor laughed, shaking his head.

"Excuse me!" Valla feigned a look of outrage. "How many names have you butchered? I hardly ever corrected you!"

"Yeah, you got me there." Victor gave her a nudge, urging her forward through the swinging wooden door. She went through, and he followed to find they'd entered a room that seemed too large for the structure that housed the shop. The ceiling had to be thirty feet high, and the walls of the square room were twice that in length. The ground crunched as he stepped in, and Victor saw it was covered in loose, pale, cream-colored gravel. Shelves lined the wall to his right, dozens of objects filling them. Some were small, literally resembling matchboxes, and others were bulky, like large, boxy backpacks.

Chori stopped ahead of him, her hooves sinking into the gravel so the hem of her navy blue smock brushed the ground. She turned to Valla and asked, "Does he want something easy to carry or something bulkier? He'll have servants, no? Don't those legates have dozens of underlings to order about?"

"He'll want something easy to carry," Victor answered, done having Valla speak for him. "He's not planning to spend the rest of his life as a legate."

"Oh, clever one, is he?" Chori winked at Valla, then walked over to the shelves, bypassing the backpacks, satchels, larger boxes, and wheeled contraptions that resembled medieval rolling suitcases. She paused before a shelf lined with smaller boxes, some that might fit in the palm of his hand ranging to the size of a shoebox. She looked over her shoulder, narrowed her eyes at Victor, and asked, "Budget?"

Victor thought about the treasure he'd yet to go through in Karnice's ring, the treasure he'd accumulated in Coloss and, even before that, from Boaegh and ap'Horrin. He shrugged and said, "Money's not a concern."

"Well, then," Chori picked up a shallow green stone box about two inches by four and carried it over to him. "I have a lovely leather case for this that will fit comfortably on your belt."

"What is it?"

"It's a travel home. I'm ashamed to say that my father crafted this one. It's been here many a year, waiting for the right buyer. He traveled to Tharcray to learn his craft. Did you know that?" She directed the question at Valla.

"Um, no, I don't think I did."

"Yes. While there, in order to graduate from the Vessi-Ridonne Artificing Academy, he had to prove his skill. This was his performance project, his proof of competency."

"Vessi-Ridonne?" Victor asked, unsettled by the reminder of his recent troubles.

"The Vessi bloodline is extinct. They were the Ardeni equivalent of the Ridonne," Valla said, shrugging.

"Only Shadeni can be Ridonne?"

"That's right," Chori said. "Though I think they're extinct too. I only ever hear rumors. Have you ever met someone who's seen one?"

"I, uh . . ."

"Good question, Chori." Valla laughed, interrupting Victor and saving him the trouble of explaining how he'd just done battle with one.

"Anyway, to graduate, my father crafted this. We haven't sold it because it's made from Whel jade."

"Well jade?" Victor frowned.

"Whel," Chori repeated, enunciating the first part of the word heavily so Victor could hear the *h*. "It comes from the world of Whel, distant from Fanwath, carried here by a rare traveler to Tharcray. My father bought it at auction, nearly bankrupting his family. He says it was worth it because this treasure he crafted won him top honors from the academy, and he made back his fortune a dozen times over the years."

"Okay, so why can't you sell it?"

"Oh, I didn't say we can't sell it. We haven't sold it. It's very dense material and holds more Energy than any ore on Fanwath; I'd only part with it for the right price and for the right person. I've turned away a buyer or two in my day." She set the little box down in the gravel a dozen feet from Victor and Valla, and then she tapped it lightly with her pointer finger. The box began to rattle on the stones, then it hopped, and when it settled, it was twice as big. It rattled again, jumped, and then it was the size of a trunk. This repeated several times, and the box grew each time until, with a final rattling thump that shook the building, it rested before the trio, a jade-green rectangular box the size of a single-wide trailer.

"Whoa . . ." Victor began, but the jade structure flared brightly, limned for a brief moment in luminous green Energy, and steps with a railing sprouted from the side, windows complete with shutters formed in the walls, and a doorway came into being, all crafted from a reddish-brown, satin-smooth wood. Victor saw glass in the windows, but they were opaque, faintly green, and shimmering in a way that reflected any attempts to peer through.

"The space within is four times that of the exterior, and there is a second level below ground just as large," Chori said proudly. "Currently, it's partially furnished, but I can remove the objects within if you'd like to install your own belongings."

"Does that mean you'd sell it to me?" Victor asked, his voice betraying his enthusiasm.

Chori looked at Victor for a long while, then she looked at Valla, and a certain sort of lightness entered her expression, a kind, almost fond expression. She nodded quickly and replied in a soft, faintly tremulous voice, "I would sell to you, aye. Shall we talk about the price?"

25

NO CONSOLATION

In the end, after what felt like an hour of negotiating, Victor didn't pay any beads to Chori for the jade travel home. She'd started by quoting him a price that initially seemed outrageous—five million. When Victor had shaken his head and asked about something a little cheaper, she'd asked him about precious metals, stones, or rare objects from his travels. At which point Victor had remembered Karnice's ring and his enormous trove of weapons, particularly spears.

As he'd pulled out the spears, selecting those that seemed the most resonant and full of Energy, Chori's eyes had widened, and Victor had only laid out five by the time Valla put a hand on his forearm and shook her head; she'd read in Chori's expression that at least one of the spears on the counter had interested her dearly. Even so, Chori was a good negotiator and never let on which of the spears was made of what material that had so intrigued her.

Victor thought about bargaining, about insisting on learning what she knew of the spears. He even contemplated taking them to a different sort of shop, a smith or a jeweler, to find out what the spears were made of and how those merchants might value them. In the end, he'd decided he didn't care that much; the spears were just sitting in his ring, and he'd hardly scratched the surface of the valuables Karnice had stashed away. So, despite his ignorance, he'd made the trade—five of Karnice's spears for a pretty damn cool and unique home that he could carry around on his belt.

After making the deal, Chori had insisted that Victor and Valla explore the home, and as they stood in the foyer, Victor took in the fine craftsmanship and elegant design. Thick, luxurious rugs lay on dark marble floors, and vaulted ceilings allowed diffuse, pleasant light in through windows that were far larger on the inside than out. Victor reached for Lifedrinker before looking around anymore and asked her, "Is it okay for you in here?"

"Is it not comfortable for you? As long as you feel well, I shall also. Do not leave me in this place when you make it small again, however."

"Ah, right. Makes sense." Victor walked out of the foyer and looked straight to the home's rear windows down a long, wide, central hallway. True to her word, Chori's furnishings extended beyond just the fine rugs. The walls separating the various sections of the first level were all crafted from matching hardwood stained in a reddish hue that complemented the trimmings of the home's exterior. On his left, through an open archway, was a parlor filling one corner of the space with plush couches and chairs, coffee tables, lamps, and a squat brass Energy-powered stove that sat in the corner, radiating warmth.

Opposite the parlor was a large room, the walls of which were stacked, floor to ceiling, with built-in bookcases. Victor walked around in it, admiring the hundreds of empty shelves, imagining filling them with books from the many places he might someday visit. A large, square table filled the center of the space with high stools tucked under its eaves, and he imagined it would be perfect for looking at maps or studying reference tomes. He turned to leave but found Valla blocking his way, a contemplative expression on her face.

"Why don't I start your collection with the books Tes gave me?"

"Those aren't meant for me to hoard away."

"No, that's true, I suppose. On that note, we should speak to Chori about magical methods for duplicating books. I could give you a copy."

"Hey! Now you're talking." Victor draped an arm over her shoulders and, careful to keep most of his weight off, guided her out of the room. "Come on, let's see the kitchen." He led the way out of the library through an archway and found himself looking at an enormous rectangular table with more than twenty place settings. Beyond it was the back wall of the home and lining that was a row of countertops and cupboards. A stove sat in the center before a huge window that gave a brilliantly clear view of Chori's showroom. Everything, from the table to the counters to the cupboards to the trim around the windows, was delicately crafted from rich, lustrous woods, all stained in complementary shades of brown and red.

After checking to see that the cupboards were mostly bare, Victor continued to explore the first level, finding a pantry, a bathroom with an adjoining walk-in bath—something he imagined one might find in a fancy spa—and two smallish bedrooms. Near the dining room and kitchen, an ornate brass and jade stairway spiraled downward. On the lower level, Victor found several large, empty rooms and a much larger bedroom with an adjoining bathroom and an enormous walk-in closet. The only furnishing on the second floor was a large bed that matched the craftsmanship of the dining table upstairs.

"Your room," Valla said, clapping him on the shoulder. "It even has a bed that might accommodate your ridiculous frame."

"Yeah. I'm sure not complaining. I'm just glad to see toilets, running water, and plenty of places to stash my stuff. You think the empty rooms down here are for adding more bedrooms?"

"That's one possibility. You could probably design any sort of room you wanted in them—simple storage space, crafting halls, prisoner cages. Only your imagination would limit you."

"Prisoner cages, hmm? But when I make the house small, wouldn't they go insane?"

"That's another good question for Chori," Valla replied, shrugging.

Victor nodded, and after one more look around the spacious master suite, he led the way upstairs and out of the magical house. Chori stood before the front steps, her hands clasped and an enthusiastic grin brightening her eyes. Seeing such a goat-like face wearing that expression was so cute it was almost funny to Victor. "Well?" she asked.

"Yeah, it's amazing. I should have probably done the tour before trading away those spears, but what can I say? I'm impulsive." Victor followed up with the question he had burning in his mind: "What would happen to someone if I made the house small while they were inside?"

"Ah, that would be inadvisable. The effects of the dimensional magic would harm a conscious mind. My father stretched the boundaries of safety by increasing the interior space beyond the exterior limitations already."

"Damn," Victor sighed. He saw Chori's look of confusion and explained himself. "It's not that I'm unhappy with the house. It's just, well, if I can't keep all my things in there, it doesn't feel exactly like a home, you know. Lifedrinker"—he patted the axe—"and any other conscious treasures I might find"—he tapped his bracer where Khul Bach dwelled—"won't be able to stay in there."

"You want them with you, in any case," Valla said.

"Yeah, yeah. I know. It's not a deal breaker. I'm just thinking long term, you know?"

"Of course, Lord Victor," Chori said, far more respectful now that they'd done business together. "My father was the best Artificer I've ever met, but there are likely many others in worlds beyond Fanwath with more know-how. Perhaps the world where you found those spears . . ."

"Eh, maybe. The people of Zaafor didn't strike me as the most creative types."

"Tes . . ." Valla started but trailed off, glancing quickly away from Victor. Not for the first time, he wondered what she was thinking.

"Yeah, anyway, Chori, I want to buy some more stuff for the kitchen. Some of your magical appliances."

"Oh!" Valla added, "Do you have any magical means for copying books?"

"So long as they're mundane in nature, I have just the thing," Chori replied, nodding and motioning toward the jade travel home. "I've removed my bond from the home, so you should bond with it now, Victor. You wouldn't want someone else to gain control over the dwelling!"

"Right." Victor walked up the front steps and rested his hand on the smooth wooden railing, then he touched it with a thread of his Energy. He instantly felt a connection to the home, much as he did the dimensional containers he was bonded with. He intuitively found he could let his mind drift through it, seeing the different rooms and all of the objects within. "Can I access this when it's small?"

"You certainly can." Chori nodded.

"Oh, now that's badass." Victor mentally commanded the house to shrink, and suddenly the handrail he held slipped away from his fingers, absorbing into the smooth green jade along with the window shutters, door, and steps. Then the enormous rectangle of green stone shivered and, with audible *pops*, shrank down in stages until, twenty seconds later, a much smaller hunk of jade sat forlornly in the expanse of gravel. Victor bent to pick it up. As he held it, he decided it almost resembled a green stone deck of cards, but it was heavy and dense and teeming with Energy.

"Here's your belt case," Chori said, holding out a tooled leather box, perfectly crafted to fit the travel home. He slipped the jade box into it and then loosened his belt to slide it through the loops on the case.

"Pretty cool," he said, smoothing his armor down over the small object. "Imagine that! Carrying my house around on my belt."

"Yes. It will come in handy during your travels, no doubt," Valla replied, and Victor frowned at her. Was she being overly formal again?

"You good?" He raised an eyebrow, trying to see some clue in the depths of her bright teal eyes.

"I'm fine, Victor." She smiled, then looked at Chori and said, "The book, um, copier?"

"Yes, yes. Follow me." She led the way back to her shop, and while Valla and Victor perused her goods, she dug around through trunks she had stacked under the counter. After a few minutes, she called them over, saying, "I'm sure there are other ways to copy books, but I worked on this little system as a project one summer, and I'm rather fond of its elegance." Before her, on the counter, was a shallow box made of pale wood. Charred runes had been burnt into the inside walls and bottom of the box, and between them, lines of silvery metal wove a complex spiderweb pattern.

The box was about fifteen inches by thirty and only four or five inches deep. Down the center, it was partitioned, creating two shallow compartments. Chori patted the box and said, "I call this a copybox. You put the original text in the left compartment and the blank text in the right. If they're not a perfect match, the copybox will condense or expand the text to fit the new pages. I mean that quite literally, so be careful. I copied a four-hundred-page history text onto a ten-page pamphlet, but the writing was so tiny that it was illegible. The pages were practically black with ink."

"That's exactly what I was looking for! Thank you, Chori. I'll buy it." Valla gently ran her fingers over the glyphs inside the box.

"Wonderful."

Before they left, Victor spent thousands of beads on enchanted knick-knacks for his house—kitchen appliances, pots and pans, enchanted bedding, and a map of the Ridonne Empire that showed a dot wherever the map was moved. As they left the shop, Victor felt good, and Valla seemed happy. He looked at her and said, "I should put some provisions into my house too. You know, wine, ale, and food that can be cooked—not just travel rations and prepared stuff like I have tucked away in my rings."

"Let's do that now, on the way out of town. I want to buy some blank pages and book bindings, too. I feel like we should hurry, though." Valla looked to the east, down the long, lantern-lit cobbled road and toward the city wall beyond which the army encampment waited in the darkness of the plains.

"Yeah, I guess we should get back." Victor sighed.

"Not eager any longer? You surely charged into battle with that Ridonne eagerly."

"Yeah, yeah. Come on, let's go." Victor didn't bite; he didn't really want to talk about whether he was eager to be responsible for thousands of soldiers' lives. Feeling that stress, he began to think about the other things that had been bothering him lately. His issues with ap'Gravin and Olivia, his *abuela*, and all the expectations people had of him, from Khul Bach to Rellia to every single soldier out in that army. Perhaps feeling that stress, perhaps remembering how she'd comforted him before, he reflexively reached down for Valla's hand.

At first, she took his fingers in her grasp, but she gave them a squeeze and let go, looking away to the right. He looked down at her and stopped, waiting for her to turn and make eye contact. There were plenty of people out and about on the streets, but at that moment, the two of them were mostly alone, with only a few cloaked evening shoppers walking on the other side of that particular street. They were still several blocks from the busy market square Valla had been guiding them toward.

"What?" she finally asked, looking up at him with a weird expression that seemed partly angry, partly pained, and embarrassed.

"I'm sorry I grabbed your hand. I guess I'm getting too familiar with you." As usual, Victor wasn't sure why he chose those words. Was he sorry? He decided he wasn't sorry that he wanted to hold her hand, but he supposed seeing her uncomfortable had made him regret the impulse.

"It's not your fault. I've encouraged you before. Ancestors, I welcome the affection!"

"Then why have you been acting so weird? It's like, well, ever since we got on that airship, you've been more distant. Is it the military thing? Is it, like, inappropriate for me to be affectionate with you?"

"No. Well, yes. Truly, I use that as an excuse." She sighed heavily, looked up at the clear sky and bright moons, then turned back to him. "I want to be candid with you, Victor. I want to tell you my heart." Valla's eyes started to fill with moisture. She glanced around, and it was easy to see she was embarrassed.

"Then do!"

"Will you mock me?"

"What? God no, Valla!"

She frowned, staring into his eyes for several moments, then started speaking, and her words came out like a flood, "Well, I'm 'weird' with you because I want more than simple affection. I want to be the object of your dreams, the woman you obsess about. I'm not a fool, though! I've met her, Victor. The woman who holds that position in here." She gently rapped her knuckles on his wyrm-scale vest right over his heart. "I've seen the spell she has on you, and I don't blame you!"

"Huh?" Victor's eyes narrowed, and genuine puzzlement clouded his expression.

"I love Tes, too! How could I ever be with you when I know, in here"—this time she thumped her hand over her own heart—"that you've settled for me? I won't do it! I won't be a consolation. I won't be someone you pass the time with while you wait for the real thing. I'm sorry, but that's that."

"What? Tes?" Victor's mind raced, and he fumbled for words, wondering how he'd stumbled into a conversation about this.

"Oh, please, spare me the protestations. You've seen her. You've felt her. You know she cares about you, and feeling that affection, that attention from someone like her . . . you'll never forget it. I truly don't think you will. We might be happy for a while. You might pretend to have everything you want. You might even believe it for a time, but now and then, when you're looking out over the lights of a city or tasting a certain food, you'll remember Tes, and your heart will grow distant, and you'll start to wonder. You'll think to yourself, 'What if?' and then . . ."

"Valla! Valla, take it easy." Victor couldn't help the nervous chuckle that escaped him as he reached out and grasped her shoulders. She flashed him a furious scowl, and he clamped his mouth shut. "I'm not laughing at you! I'm not mocking you. I'm just, well, I'm nervous 'cause I didn't mean to open this can of worms! I just wanted to hold your hand!"

"I told you I'm not a fool!" Valla tried to turn away, but Victor gently grasped her arm. She had tears flowing freely down her cheeks; her words had been confusing at first, but now the picture was becoming clear. The whole thing about Tes, about Valla not wanting to be compared to her—it made sense, but it wasn't what he'd been expecting.

"Take a breath. It's all right. Listen, I'm sorry that everything's always so fucking complicated. I don't want it to be. All I know is that you're very damn important to me, and I'm not going to fuck that up. If you're worried about how I feel about Tes, then, well, shit, I don't know what to do about it. How do I fix a problem like that?"

"I don't know. You can't." Valla sniffed noisily, looking left and right. Suddenly, she produced a pale blue cloak from one of her storage rings and pulled it around her shoulders, lifting the voluminous hood.

"Are you . . . hiding?"

Valla didn't reply, but she reached up and tugged the hood farther down, hiding her eyes, leaving only her mouth and chin exposed to the moonlight.

"Sheesh," Victor tried, chuckling, "I wasn't even sure you liked me like that. I can see why you wouldn't want anyone else to know . . ."

"You idiot."

"Doesn't that feel better? Come on! Hold my hand, and you can call me an idiot all you want. Who cares what people think? Who cares if there's some mythical woman out in the universe I'm smitten with? I'm just a dumb guy, and there's hardly any chance I'll see her in the next hundred years, right? I'm not trying to marry you! I just want to hold your hand."

"A hundred years is a long time." Valla still tugged at the edge of her hood, hiding her eyes from him. He saw one corner of her mouth quirking up in a smile, though, as she said, "I'll hold your hand, Victor, but that's all! I won't waste a century of my life on something that isn't real."

"Is it a waste, though?" He grinned and snatched her hand, gently folding it in his palm. "I'd say a nice stroll in the moonlight holding hands with someone you care about is plenty worthwhile, all by itself."

26

ON THE MARCH

Victor sat atop his horse, looking out over the long column of marching soldiers. He patted the mustang's shoulder and turned to where Rellia, Valla, and Lam had stopped, their mounts unable to reach the crest of the scree-covered slope. They also observed the army, Rellia pointing and saying something, her voice lost in the wind. They'd been on the march for nearly two weeks, making steady progress eastward. They couldn't have asked for better weather or easier ground; the grasslands had fallen away beneath their feet, and now, after they crossed this ravine, they'd be only a day or two at the most from Tellen's clan.

Borrius traveled in Rellia's scout airship, keeping an eye on things from above, and he and the other hired airship had confirmed that no imperial army lay in ambush, at least not for a hundred miles in any direction. The evening before approaching this ravine, they'd met to pore over maps, ensuring that there was no way they could be ambushed during the crossing. It was a likely spot—a narrow bridge, only wide enough for a single wagon to pass at once. It would slow them, forcing the army to split. Borrius felt sure that if an ambush were imminent, it would be here.

Victor nudged the mustang, willing it to descend to the others, and it nimbly hopped down, hardly disturbing a loose rock. Something about the mount's spirit nature allowed it to traverse nearly any terrain, barely affected by the ground, be it grass, scree, or mud. "They reached the bridge," he said, coming to a halt next to Rellia's vidanii—a lovely white creature, smaller but far prettier than Thistle.

Valla scratched at Uvu's ear, eliciting a chuffing groan from the big cat. "Let's hope Borrius was right. If I were going to attack us, I'd wait until half the army had crossed. Are you sure you shouldn't be over there, Victor?"

"Nah. If the Ridonne attacks, I'll cast Berserk and jump that ravine."

"Roots!" Lam scoffed, shaking her head.

"Is that considered a bad word among the Ghelli?"

"No. Not really a 'bad' word, but certainly an exclamation."

"I don't know what you're exclaiming about. You could just fly over that ravine." Victor shrugged, winking at Lam as they bantered.

"Enough, enough," Rellia sighed. "If Borrius isn't right, then this was a foolish choice, using this route. We could have traveled northward to skirt this ravine."

"Which would have brought us farther into the Empire and added weeks to our journey," Valla replied, holding up a finger for each point.

"Yeah. We've been over it. What's the point of airships if we don't trust their scouting? Besides, your imperial contacts in Persi Gables insist the Empire didn't attack us. If they'd lie about that, I think it's probably wise to avoid other cities." Victor had just finished speaking when Lam's mount, a large bull roladii, snorted and hopped, suddenly skittish of Uvu, even though the cat had hardly moved, simply lifting a paw to lick at it.

"Rotten roots!" Lam jerked the animal's reins, pulling it away and closer to Victor; none of the other animals seemed to mind his mustang.

"Now, that was a curse, right?"

"Yes, Victor." Lam chuckled.

"Nothing to do but watch and wait at this point." Rellia ignored the interruption.

"Yep." Victor did just that. Watching the foot soldiers progress over the plains was easily his least favorite part of the whole affair so far. He often found himself daydreaming about what the army would be like if he could summon thousands of mustangs. He figured they'd already be assaulting the Untamed Marches if that were possible. The best part of the journey had to be the evenings after the legion set camp. He and Polo would spar, and afterward, he'd host the expedition's leaders for dinner. He wasn't the only one with a travel home, but even Rellia acknowledged that his was the nicest.

He wasn't an expert cook and often enlisted one of the real cooks that had joined the legion in that capacity, and though he enjoyed watching and eating what they prepared, he'd decided that he probably wasn't the type to spend time trying to improve the skill beyond basic. Even so, it was a nice routine. They'd sip drinks and study the map in his little library, making plans and contingencies, then sit around at his big dining table, eating and becoming more than just co-leaders of an army; they were fast becoming friends.

Despite her fear of rumors, Valla had taken up residence in one of the spare bedrooms in his home. He wished something was going on that might be worthy of rumors; after their little stroll through Persi Gables, there'd been little in the way of affection between them. He'd hoped her words had largely been bluster, her espoused desire not to be a "consolation" for him. The truth was, Victor didn't know how to respond to that. Should he have said his feelings for Tes were just a crush, that they didn't matter and weren't real? He felt that she would have read the lie in those words.

As the others kept talking about the road ahead, commenting on the army's progress as it slowly snaked over the bridge, Victor stole sideways looks at Valla, wishing he were smarter when it came to women. Was he doomed to be alone until he someday proved worthy of Tes's attention? He shook his head and almost called himself a dummy out loud. Only Valla knew about Tes. Only Valla would realize she was being compared to the dragon-woman. He could meet someone else. Spend time with someone else. He sighed and rubbed at his head—he didn't want someone else. He wanted Valla, but she was right; he wanted Tes too.

"Something wrong?" Lam asked him, looking up from the back of her stocky roladii.

Valla and Rellia were talking about cavalry drills they planned to implement when they finished crossing and pitched camp, so Victor spoke to Lam in a low voice, "Nah, just thinking about all the stuff I don't know."

"No matter how much you learn, you'll always find more you don't know."

Victor looked more closely at Lam, recognizing the experience behind her words. Her glittering wings were folded behind her, and she sat with her hands, one atop the other, on her saddle horn. Her eyes were distant, and he asked, "Remembering something in particular?"

"Mistakes made, Victor. Many, many mistakes. For what it's worth, I think you're doing a good job so far. You're listening to the advice of more experienced people, you're present and attentive to the captains, and you've been building camaraderie among the commanders. The soldiers have heard of your victory over the Ridonne, and while many quake in fear that the Empire is against us, most of them are buoyed by your strength. It's good that you spar with Polo on the practice green each night—your bouts are the premier entertainment for the troops; they barter for free shifts so they can observe."

"Ha! Thanks, Lam. Yeah, I noticed our audience seems to grow a bit each day. It's fun." While Lam was speaking, Rellia and Valla had moved farther along the hillside. Judging by their gestures, they were looking at and discussing something about the sixth cohort, one of the two fully mounted ones. Victor looked back at Lam, considered whether he should open his mouth about the subject on his mind, and finally said, "Hey, can I ask you something? Just between us."

"Of course." Lam matched his conspiratorial tone, shifting her roladii a little closer.

"Well, I want to joke right now and ask if you can tell me the secret to understanding women, but seriously . . . Oh, shit, it's too complicated. Forget I said anything." Victor sighed, desperately resisting the urge to look at Valla lest Lam figure out what he was thinking.

"You're closer to Valla than she lets on?" Lam asked, glancing toward the mother and daughter, ensuring they weren't listening.

"No. She's very honest about how close we are."

"You want to be closer?"

"Yeah, I do, but she has a very damn valid reason for not wanting that."

"And it's too complicated to explain?" Lam frowned, one of her emerald eyes narrowing as she said, "Ah, let me guess. There's another woman."

"*Chingado*," Victor hissed. "Not exactly, Lam, but yeah, pretty close. It's just . . . " Victor struggled to pick the right words and finally just blurted, "Well, she was a hell of a lot higher level than us—a hell of a lot older. We met in Coloss, and let's just say she's not in our league. I probably won't see her for a very, very long time. Nothing happened, but Valla's not blind—she saw I fell for her; I mean the other woman. Is that a good reason not to be with me?"

"I don't know. I'm not Valla, but I can relate. I'd hate to think the one I gave my heart to was holding something back, waiting, hoping for something more. If you really think it's unlikely you'll meet this other woman again soon, perhaps the feeling will fade. For both of you, I mean. Perhaps you'll come to realize that the woman you're so enchanted by is different in here"—she tapped her forehead—"than out here." She gestured around, indicating the world. "Maybe Valla will come to realize you're serious about her. Maybe she'll see and understand you'd do just about anything for her and decide that's enough." Lam shrugged. "You've got time."

"Thanks, Lam." Victor offered her a rather pathetic smile, and she chuckled. They sat in silence for a long while, watching the army progress, and despite Rellia's concerns, they were soon watching the last of the cohorts cross the bridge, with only the wagons, noncombat personnel, and the rear guard left on the close side.

"That went well," Rellia said as she and Valla rode close again.

"Yep." Victor offered her and Valla a thumbs-up and felt like an idiot.

Rellia, to his surprise, mimicked the gesture and then asked, "Your friend's clan is a day's march from here, yes?"

"Right. I think so. Valla showed you on the map, yeah?"

"Correct. I was just confirming. So, have you had any word? Do you think they'll join our cause? We could use another couple hundred skilled scouts."

"No. Thayla won't be in the spirit realm for a couple more weeks. We'll have to wait and see."

"Well, let's go and oversee the fortifications." Lam urged her roladii down the hill toward the line of big wagons waiting to cross the bridge. By the time they caught up to the tail end of the train, almost all of the wagons had crossed, and it was only a matter of minutes until it was their turn. As they rode over the wooden bridge with its great spans of lumber, clearly crafted with prodigious use of Energy, some Ghelli scouts fluttered up from underneath, their job done. Borrius had insisted on Ghelli being stationed under the bridge during the crossing to guard against sabotage.

"All's clear?" Valla called to the lead scout, a sergeant named Feya.

"All clear, Primus."

Once over the bridge, they rode down from the hillside, rejoining the enormous expanse of tall blue-green grass. Victor knew the plains would extend all the way to the Starfall Mountains, around which the army would have to pass, and after that, they'd follow roads through foothills and forests, and if all went well, in a couple more weeks they'd pass through the Granite Gates and descend into the Untamed Marches. He and the other commanders stopped at the bottom of the slope and watched the sergeants break their cohorts into squads and begin fortifying their evening camp.

The legion was immensely efficient at the procedure of making camp. Every squad knew their role, and they all had the advantage of magic, dimensional containers, and stamina beyond anything a base human could match. Latrines were dug and solid outhouses summoned from dimensional wagons to place over the holes. Trenches were scooped from the earth by squads with members adept in the use of their earth affinity. Walls were thrown up in great sections, once again pulled from magical wagons that circled the camp in opposite directions. Tents were erected, leaving a central area for the commanders to call forth their dwellings. Finally, the wagons were circled, and a mess hall of sorts was set up between them.

After the main camp was done, the mounted cohorts built a corral for their animals, and squads broke up into their shift work, drilling, cleaning, assisting the cooks, standing watch in a staggered perimeter, and, if they were lucky—or unlucky depending on whom you asked—resting, eating, and enjoying leisure time before a later shift. Victor rode through the gates before the soldiers closed them, then made his way to the center of the camp, where he took his usual position to set down his travel home and activate it.

He and Polo typically drilled a couple of hours after the camp was made, and he liked to use this time to hang out in the library with Valla; they'd been slowly working on copying the books Tes had given her, and Victor was finding a new, strange enjoyment in reading through the spellcrafting tomes. Reading through was probably a poor description; he was only about a fourth of the way through the first book in the series. That evening, Valla hadn't accompanied him to the center of camp, so when he went into the jade house, he sat by himself in the library, thumbing through the sections of the book he'd already read.

The minutes ticked by, becoming an hour, and he lost himself studying spell patterns meant to improve the variability of a spell, allowing for multiple contingencies in the target's status that would change the outcome of the casting. He was so deeply engrossed that Valla startled him when she cleared her throat, leaning an elbow on the map table. "Hey," he said, looking up from the chair in the corner where he liked to sit.

"I was meeting with the livestock master. He's concerned about Thistle."

"What? Why?"

"He says he's not eating as much. When was the last time you visited him?"

"Yesterday!"

"Okay, okay. Don't get upset." Valla made a placating gesture with her hand. "He's probably tired of being tethered with a bunch of stupid roladii."

"Yeah, well, he'll be rejoining his sister tomorrow, so that should help a lot."

"Yes, that's good. Are you nervous?"

"About?"

"To see Thayla and Tellen. To hear their decision about joining us."

"Well, I wasn't." Victor closed his book and sat up straighter. "Now I'm feeling like I should be."

"Don't!" Valla laughed. "I wasn't trying to hint at anything. Either way, it's fine, Victor. If they don't join us for the campaign, you can try to get them to relocate closer to the Marches after we've won some land."

"Yeah." Victor nodded. He stretched his neck, frowned, then said, "What time is it? I should probably find Polo."

"Oh, he asked me to let you know he can't spar tonight. He lost a bet with Captain Gaks; his cohort is standing two watches."

"What? No, that's bullshit." Victor scooted to the edge of his seat. "I'm missing out on training, and we're going to have tired soldiers on watch. I'm not cool with it."

"I told him you wouldn't like it." Valla eyed him coolly, perhaps waiting to see how he'd solve the problem.

"What were they betting on?"

"Polo thought we'd get ambushed at the bridge, and Gak said there was no way you'd walk us into a trap so obvious."

"What the fuck? Polo was against me?"

"Not against you, Victor! He simply thought it was too perfect an ambush site. He thought the Ridonne had something up their sleeves."

"Shit. Now I want him to have extra guard duty. At least he's going out with the men. Captains don't usually do that, right?"

"Correct." Valla was smiling, watching him work through the situation.

"You think it's all right?"

"Yes. His men will get four hours of sleep, even standing two watches. They're Energy users, Victor; they'll be fine. As you said, Polo will be out with them."

"Right, well, screw it. I can use a break from the axe. I'm so fucking close to hitting epic! I can taste it! It's driving me crazy. I wish I had that Ridonne around to spar with."

"Gah!" Valla almost choked as she twisted her fingers in a weird gesture. "Don't say things like that!"

"Seriously?" Victor leaned forward, his eyes gleaming with amusement. "I've never seen you make that sign. Are you feeling superstitious?"

"I'm hopeful that the Ridonne you chased away was just testing us, feeling us out, and that he wasn't acting with the blessing of the Empire."

Victor stood up and moved over to the map table to lean against it, standing beside Valla. "Why don't we know yet? Why don't we know that *pendejo*'s name? What's going on with the prisoners?"

"Rellia's Mind Caster has done everything he knows how to do, but he can't crack the geas that clouds their minds. He's killed several of the imperials trying."

"Damn it, Valla. I didn't want to know that." Victor rubbed at his chin, then said, "Well, I can't hide from that kind of stuff, I guess. Is he still trying?"

"Yes."

"All right, well, wanna help me do some cooking? Since Polo screwed me over, I might as well have some fun in the kitchen. I'm going to try my hand at recreating one of my favorites from home—*tamales*."

"Oh?"

"Yeah, come on. Let's see if I can remember what I saw my *abuela* mixing up. I'm sure I need something like corn flour. Shit, do you guys have corn?"

Pazra-dak leaned against the tree bole, looking up at the canopy of massive branches far over his head. He rubbed his shoulder spine, or, more accurately, at the spot on his shoulder where the giant had cut him. He growled at the memory, growled at the feeling of rough, knobby skin where he'd scarred. The first mark a lesser being had ever made upon his flesh. He banished the thought, savoring the night air. It was cool there in the Blue Deep, cool, dim, and quiet. It had better be quiet; he'd ordered his legion to be silent. No sense in letting the fool hunters on the plains have a clue that they lurked nearby.

He folded his arms over his chest, carefully avoiding the spines at his elbows. It had taken him a decade to get used to the things, frustrated by how they complicated his life, from clothing to furniture to lovers. He saw them as the blessing they were now; he'd come to understand that the spines were a mark of his greatness, his strength, his durability, and his right to rule. Not all Ridonne gained them, but those who did were regarded as powerful, the enforcers of the imperial bloodline, not to be trifled with.

He let his golden-tinted vision fall upon his camp and saw his soldiers about their tasks, moving slowly and carefully, never uttering a word as they sharpened weapons, ate cold rations, or maintained the camp. Six thousand soldiers, minus the hundred he'd lost on the plains. Would they be a match for the legion that upstart, ap'Yensha, had gathered? If not for the giant, he would say yes. It didn't matter, in any case—his brother Rosh-dak and his legion would soon be there. With twelve thousand men, they'd crush the fools between them.

He motioned for his witch, Senena, to approach. She straightened up, unfolding from the shadow of a nearby tree, and hurried to him, her skin more black and gold with tattooed glyphs than the red of their people. She'd come close to joining the ranks of the Ridonne, but her father had insisted she embrace the Wanact bloodline. As a result, her spirit was adrift, constantly glimpsing more than the here and now. "Tell me, witch. Will my brother arrive in time?"

"I see him," she said, her voice a husky whisper. "He dives between trees and leaps brambles. I see great trees with mighty trunks, bigger than these. Hope lives in his heart, not despair."

"Good. He runs to us from Twilight Home. If he carries hope, he'll make it. And the giant?"

"I've told you, lord. I cannot look at him. He burns my eye."

"Then burn your eye! Tell me where he is!"

"I see only white fire when my gaze drifts his way. His spirit is stronger than mine, lord."

"Begone. We'll speak later." As she slunk away, Pazra turned to where his scout captain lurked, hunkered down on a stone, chewing the meat from a bird carcass he'd roasted. Ancestors only knew when. "Come here, Gildyn."

"Aye, lord?" the scout replied, leaping up, allowing his meal to fall to the leafy loam.

"What word from your scouts?"

"The giant and his army are close. They crossed the ravine this day."

"So, as we'd suspected, they'll be with the hunters tomorrow." Pazra waved the man away, then pressed his fist against the tree behind him, grinding it into the bark until his knuckles cracked. "Come, brother. Hurry. We've a feast before us."

27

REUNION

The next day, in the late afternoon, the legion set up camp a few miles west of the Shadeni hunter clan's winter and spring campground, and Victor, Polo, Rellia, and Valla rode forth with the hopes of meeting with Thayla, Tellen, and all the other people Victor had been missing rather dearly. Rellia had wanted to bring Borrius, but the one-time legate insisted they'd have a warmer reception without him—his reputation among the Shadeni hunter clans wasn't born of friendship. As for Lam, she had insisted on staying with the army; too many leaders away might encourage a lapse in discipline.

They'd only cleared the army's encampment by half a mile when figures emerged from the grass, and Victor laughed, spurring his mustang toward them. The others followed, though slowly, likely to give him a chance to ensure they weren't hostile. "Hi!" he shouted as he rode up, for lack of a better greeting.

"Is that you, Victor? Where'd you get that fiery-eyed steed?"

"Forget that one, Victor. How'd you grow so much?"

Victor laughed, slowing his mount near the two scouts—hunters from Tellen's band, ones he'd rescued from a monster high in the hills to the east. "Visha! Kolo! It's great to see you again!" Victor dropped from his horse's back and approached them as they shifted the tips of their spears upright. He spread his arms as if to embrace them, but Kolo, wary as always, backed up a step.

"You look like Victor. You sound like Victor . . . You're different, though. You know my name . . ."

"I sure do, Kolo. I remember finding you in a cursed keep in a blood-soaked ravine. I remember killing a real asshole to get you and the others in Tellen's party to safety . . ."

"It's him, Kolo," Visha said, stepping forward to reach up, trying to clap Victor on the shoulder. "Who else would call that devil an asshole?"

"Will you tell us about the changes in you?" Kolo asked, also reaching out to grasp Victor's other arm in his wiry fingers. "You're enormous. Ah! Look at his axe, Visha!"

"She's pretty, no?" Victor winked, then added, "I'll tell you many stories, but first, we should get to the clan. I need to speak with Thayla and Tellen."

"Yes, you should!" Kolo whistled shrilly, and out of the tall grass to the south, a small, sturdy roladii trotted forward. "I'll ride with them, Visha."

"Of course you will," Visha sighed.

"It's my turn!" Kolo cried in mock outrage.

Victor motioned for Polo and the ladies to ride closer and said, "These are my companions."

"Aye." Kolo eyed Valla's mount. "I remember the great cat."

Rellia, riding her beautiful white vidanii, laughed. "Only around my daughter would my poor Tigala escape notice and praise." She gently stroked the animal's neck, and it bleated, making a high-pitched sound almost like a honk—Victor had never heard Thistle make such a noise. When she looked up, she eyed Victor and Guapo. "I suppose she's a bit outshone by that great beast of yours, too."

"How do you think Hob feels?" Polo asked, slapping his big hand on the thick neck of his stocky bull roladii.

Victor laughed, slung himself onto his mustang's back, and said, "Who wants to race?" Everyone ignored the question; they'd all seen him tearing across the plains over the last couple of weeks and knew full well he was being facetious. Shrugging, he started forward, waving to Visha as he rode past.

Kolo rode up beside him. "What news? We saw your great army. Been watching since you crossed the old bridge."

"Should have said hello." Victor chuckled. "I have much to share, but I need to speak to Tellen first. Sorry, Kolo."

"I understand—Ban-tok business."

"Right. At least for now."

"Is that mount as fast as he looks? What beautiful eyes! Why do his hooves spark with magic when he walks? Is he a creature from this world?"

"He's a spirit animal." Victor patted the mustang's muscular shoulder. "Aren't you, Guapo?"

"Is that his name? Handsome? Fitting . . ."

"Yes, it is," Valla answered before Victor could respond.

"Well, I guess so." Victor whooped as the mustang started prancing, lifting his feet high and arching his neck, turning sideways so his eye could flash at everyone, especially Valla. Victor continued to laugh, saying, "He likes you, Valla! I think he might be in love."

"Oh, Ancestors!" Valla cried, urging Uvu to turn and put a bit of distance between herself and Victor.

"Chandri's going to love him," Kolo said, chuckling along with Victor, admiring the huge, prancing mount.

"Is she well?"

"Oh, aye. Busy, busy with the young hunters. Since your little one, Deyni, came, she's taken on a teacher role. A dozen youngsters hunt with her."

"My little one . . ." Victor started to protest but decided it wasn't worth it. He kind of liked the idea that he shared some responsibility for Deyni. When he saw the questioning look on Polo's face, Victor spent some time describing Deyni and talking about how he'd left Starlight for her, filling him in on a bit of his backstory with the clan, and by the time he paused to take a breath and scan the horizon, he saw the low, earthen longhouses arranged in a circle—the clan's campground. More tents were standing in the center of the clearing near the well, and the paddock for the roladii seemed more extensive, but other than that, it was much the way Victor remembered it.

They didn't have to wonder where Tellen and Thayla might be; a crowd of Shadeni had gathered near the campground's perimeter, and Victor saw Chandri, Chala, Tellen, and Thayla all standing together near the front. Deyni sat atop Tellen's shoulders, and Victor felt a foolish pang of jealousy before he wrestled it away and let his joy at seeing them all color his expression.

He didn't ask him to, but Guapo broke into a gallop, leaving the others behind, racing over the distance. He came to a sliding stop before the crowd, whinnying proudly and prancing before them. Victor saw the delight in Chandri's eyes, and once again, his stupid heart ached, remembering holding her hand and kissing her under the starlight. He tore his gaze away from her magenta irises and the sly smile on her black-painted lips, instead focusing on Deyni. He held out a hand and said, "Hand me up that little huntress, Tellen!"

"Are you sure?" Tellen asked, laughing as Deyni began to kick her feet, urging him to hurry.

"Come on, little dragon." Victor laughed, grabbing her wrist. She weighed almost nothing, and he swung her up before himself. "Are you ready to fly like the wind?"

"Victor! Yes!" Her little hands were like clamps on the forearm he held in front of her, keeping her close as Guapo began to trot around in a big circle.

"Don't steal my daughter!" Thayla called out, but there was laughter in her voice.

"Not to worry," Victor replied, making eye contact with her and Tellen when Guapo finished his circle. "We'll be right back!" Then, answering an unspoken command, Guapo reared up on his hind legs, whinnying again. When his front hooves fell, they sparked with glorious Energy, and then he was off, galloping over the plains, his back rolling with his gait but smoother than any truly physical animal could run. Victor ripped past the rest of his party, and all the while, Deyni screamed her pleasure, digging her fingers into his wrist, her dark, braided hair whipping in the wind, tickling Victor's neck and chin.

They ran for several minutes, and then Victor urged Guapo to turn. The horse seemed to challenge himself not to let Valla and the others reach the campground ahead of him, kicking into a gear Victor had yet to experience—the grass became a blue-green blur, and the wind drowned out Deyni's yips and cries of excitement. Seconds later, they slid to a stop, once again before the gathered Shadeni, and Guapo pranced some more before Victor slapped his shoulder and calmed him down with his will. "You big goofy show-off!" He laughed, turning to see that the rest of his party had ridden up behind the wild mustang.

Deyni was dumbstruck, unable to speak, but giggles wouldn't stop welling out of her as she leaned forward on Guapo's neck, hugging her arms around him and rubbing her cheek in his thick, rich mane. "Do you like him?" Victor asked.

"I love him, Victor! I've never seen such an animal!"

"Come on, young one." Chandri stepped forward and reached up toward Victor, her hands barely coming to the top of Guapo's shoulder. Victor lifted Deyni and handed her down, then hopped off the great steed, a little wobbly on his feet after moving so fast.

"He's even faster than I thought," Valla said, giving Uvu a slap on the rump, sending him off to hunt in the plains. "No roladii!" she called after him. The big cat grumbled, not quite a growl, but definitely not a happy sound, then he was gone, slipping into the grass. After that, Victor couldn't have recounted precisely what happened, because he was overwhelmed with hugs, questions, comments about his size, his mount, his armor, his axe, and question after question about where he'd been and why he'd returned with an army.

Victor savored the attention, despite knowing that Rellia, Valla, and Polo were standing off to the side, somewhat awkwardly, probably waiting for him to wrap things up so they could get down to business. It was Thayla, though, who brought an end to the impromptu gathering. She stood off to the side, still flushed with mussed hair after having been engulfed in a Victor-sized bear hug, and yelled, "That's enough for now! We'll feast tonight, but now we must meet with these esteemed guests. Leave your Ban-tok and me to do business!"

Victor was impressed by how quickly the crowd dispersed. It seemed Thayla was more than Tellen's new mate; the clan respected her. When everyone had left—Chandri, Chala, and Deyni last, quite reluctantly, and not without securing a promise for some one-on-one time with Victor—Tellen turned to him. "You never fail to impress. Will you introduce your companions?"

"Yeah, of course." Victor cleared his throat, unable to banish the smile that had already made his cheeks ache. "This is Rellia ap'Yensha, a great woman from Gelica and the chief sponsor of our campaign into the Untamed Marches. Beside her is my dear friend, companion, and one of the leaders of our army, Rellia's daughter, Valla ap'Yensha. And this big man, this big fuzzy man with the friendly face, is Polo Vosh. He's a great warrior and an even better instructor in the ways of the axe." Victor slapped Polo on the back and draped his arm over his shoulders, making his use of the word "big" to describe the Vodkin something of a joke; Victor was a solid foot taller.

"You're going to regret those words next time we spar, pup," Polo grumbled.

"Heh, I'm sure I will." Victor squeezed his shoulder, then he turned to Thayla and Tellen and said, "This is Tellen, the Ban-tok of this clan, and Thayla." Victor released Polo and, reaching into his Core, cast Shape Self, reducing his size to something closer to what he'd been the last time he'd seen Thayla. He stepped toward her, and by the time he grabbed her into a side hug, the spell had finished its magic. "She's also ruling this clan alongside Tellen, but I don't know her proper title."

"She's our Clan Mother, Victor. She's working terribly hard to fill the hole Oynalla left behind."

"I'm honored," Rellia said, stepping forward and ducking her head, reaching for Thayla's hand with hers.

Thayla, to Victor's surprise, didn't reach for Rellia's in return. She stared at her coolly. Her dark magenta eyes narrowed, and she said, "I've met you in passing. I was at the estate of that magistrate . . . His name eludes me. The estate where you tried to kill Victor."

"Ah." Rellia managed to maintain her smile, but she pulled back her hand and looked imploringly at Victor. "We've put that behind us, though, haven't we, Victor?"

"Yes. Come on, Thayla. We've been over this . . ."

"Well . . ." Thayla's stony countenance crumbled as she looked into his eyes. "If Victor can forgive you, then I will try to put the memory behind me. Shall we go inside? If my brief discussion with Victor earlier in the month was any indication, I'd say we've much to discuss."

"Yes. We've cleared the dining hall of our lodge. Come, refreshments await. I'm sure your throats are dry from the ride." Tellen paused and looked at Polo's roladii and Rellia's beautiful vidanii. "Would you like your mounts seen to?"

"No, no," Rellia said, checking to make sure Polo nodded along with her, "They'll be fine here; plenty of grass. Perhaps some water . . ."

"I've got that." Suddenly Polo was holding a short barrel, staggering under its weight as he squatted to set it on the grass.

"Why not just pull it from your container directly onto the grass?" Valla shook her head, a crooked smile aimed at the big Vodkin.

"I . . ." Polo shrugged and made a funny sound through his fuzzy lips.

"All right, let's go." Victor spread his arms as if corralling everyone and walked behind them as they made their way between two long grass-covered buildings to the entrance of Tellen's lodge. True to his words, the big hall at the entrance of the first level was abandoned, though the first of the five long tables was set with a pale yellow cloth and platters of fruit, meats, and cheeses. Clustered in the center were pitchers of fruit juice, wine, and water.

"Sit, please," Tellen said, and then he led by example, pulling out the bench and sitting down near the center. Thayla sat next to him and watched as Victor, Rellia, and Valla sat across from them. Polo, ever his own creature, sat next to Thayla. "So," Tellen began, producing six carved bone cups that Victor recognized well. "I know what you told Thayla, Victor. Your words caused many a sleepless night for her and me."

"That wasn't what . . ."

"No, no. I wasn't insinuating anything." He'd lined up the bone cups, and a dark glass bottle, bulbous and round with a long slender neck, appeared in his hands, and Victor's mouth began to water.

"The good stuff," he breathed softly.

"Aye, my best cheb-cheb. Let us toast."

"It's been too long," Polo said, grunting as he scooted a little closer, watching as Tellen unstoppered the bottle. Tellen grinned, looking from Polo to Valla, then to Rellia and Victor. After he poured the rich, vaporous liquid into the cups, he slid them over the table until everyone had one in front of them.

He picked his up and held it out, and everyone else followed suit. "To old friends and new."

"To crushing our enemies!" Polo said, hot on the heels of Tellen's words.

"To those who warm our hearts," Thayla said, turning to gaze upon Polo with narrowed eyes.

"To hope," Valla said, her voice small and her eyes downcast.

"To a just society." Rellia held her cup high as she spoke.

Victor grinned as everyone's eyes turned to him, and he said, "To glory."

"Yes!" Polo growled, and everyone drank, slamming their empty cups on the tablecloth. "Bearded Turtle, that was good!" Polo moaned, rocking back and holding a hand to his heart.

"Truly, it was." Rellia smiled unctuously at Tellen.

"Well?" Victor prompted, tired of everyone being coy. "What did you two decide? Are you bringing the clan with us?"

"We have a few questions." Thayla reached over the table to wrap her long, slender fingers around his wrist.

"Such as?" Rellia pressed.

"Are the rumors true? Is the Empire against you?"

"Fah!" Rellia growled. "Word has traveled this way already?"

"I heard a whisper on the wind . . ." Thayla winked at Victor.

"Oh, God," he groaned. "You're already talking like her."

"But truthfully"—Thayla turned back to Rellia—"tell me."

"We don't know. We've been attacked by . . . representatives of the Empire, but there hasn't been an official condemnation of our campaign. We've not been declared outlaws, and when I sought answers in Persi Gables, the magisters professed ignorance. People we've captured all have geasa silencing them, cast by a Mind Caster stronger than mine it seems." She shrugged. "Soon, we'll be quit of the Empire's lands, and it won't matter."

"It matters to us if the Legion decides to descend on your army before then. If we're dragging our homes, children, and livestock along in your train, we'll be massacred."

"No fucking way," Victor growled. "I won't let that happen."

"You have what? Six thousand soldiers?" Tellen asked. "The Empire can muster more than forty. Am I mistaken?"

"It's true the Empire has seven full legions." Valla's voice almost startled Victor; she'd been quiet for so long. "However, it would take a monumental effort to bring them all together. Two are needed for peacekeeping near the Vinduv Confederation, the Free Cities. Two patrol the northern and western frontiers. One sits idle in Tharcray. That leaves the legion garrisoned at Twilight Home, but that's a month's journey away through the Blue Deep. If we're swift, I believe the chances are good that we'll reach the Granite Gates unmolested by any imperial armies."

Thayla looked at Valla as though gauging the veracity of her words; then she turned to Tellen. "That makes me feel better."

"That's wonderful . . ." Rellia started to say, but Tellen cut her off.

"What terms do you offer for our aid? What will we gain in this new country?"

"Everyone, from me and Victor down to the lowest foot soldier in our army, will be rewarded with land. The bigger the part you play, the more land you will earn. Victor, Lam—you know her, yes, Thayla?" At Thayla's nod, she continued, "Victor, Lam, and I will divide the conquered lands among us, and then we each will award plots to the soldiers, officers, and"—she nodded to Tellen and Thayla—"contributors to the effort. We're not talking about small parcels—the Untamed Marches stretch far beyond the Granite Gates, millions of acres of forest, grassland, rolling hills, mountains rich in resources, crystalline lakes, and a coastline that rivals that along the Great Western Sea."

"Humor me and explain this like I'm a child: why hasn't the Empire moved into those pristine lands?" Tellen asked.

"Because they're fat and complacent, and the nobility fights too much, too scared to commit the resources. I've bankrupted my family for this venture. Failure will lead to my death and our ruination. More than that, it's fear. Fear of what the System will throw against them when they descend through the Granite Gates."

"The System will challenge us?" Thayla frowned, perhaps remembering the System-controlled dungeon she'd traversed with Victor.

"Yes, but we're up to the challenge." Polo sounded confident as he forlornly spun his empty cup on the table.

"We have Victor," Valla said softly, and everyone's eyes turned toward him.

"Ah." He smiled sardonically. "There's that old familiar pressure." He chuckled and started to speak, aiming to reassure everyone, but the door to the longhouse opened, and a tall Shadeni scout dressed in damp, dark leather stepped into the light.

"Tellen!"

"What is it, Lefen? We discuss important matters."

"I was scouting near the forest. Dark clouds came in unnaturally fast, rolling over the Deep. Hail began to fall, Tellen, and, as I turned toward home, I saw many figures moving among the trees."

"How many?" Victor asked, scooting back, sliding the bench despite Valla and Rellia sitting upon it.

"Hundreds. Thousands. Darkness comes with the clouds, Ban-tok. What is it?"

"Ridonne," Rellia hissed.

28

❧

TWO

Didn't you just say an imperial legion was stationed in Twilight Home? Could that be the source of the trouble we've had? Who commands them?" Rellia asked, turning to her daughter.

"Like all legions, a Ridonne. No one ever sees them, at least no one outside the imperial households. They move in carriages or fly on ships, always observing and commanding from afar. Does anyone know their names? How many there are? No—it's part of their power. The fact that one of them confronted us directly was unheard of. Is he among his troops? Is this another force altogether and not a sanctioned army? Questions we'll struggle to find answers to out here. Perhaps Chokodo-dak could shed some light on it."

"He and his wife are . . . indisposed." Rellia frowned, and everyone was quiet for a moment, contemplating questions they couldn't answer.

Victor's mind raced, his impatience driven to new heights as he began to connect the dots and realize that most of the people he cared about were now in mortal danger. Valla's long-winded response to her mother became background noise as he stood up and started for the door, then stopped, unsure exactly what to do but wanting to do something. He looked at Thayla, and everyone stared at him. "You need to get Deyni, Chandri, Chala—anyone else you want—and put 'em in the wagon and get the fuck out of here."

"We have bolt-holes in the longhouses, tunnels on the lowest levels that lead to hidden caverns. We'll evacuate." Tellen stood up, his face losing some of its color, and began to walk toward the wooden steps that led down to the next level of his longhouse. "I'll get some scouts to spread the word."

"We need to prepare the army. I need to inform Borrius." Rellia stood, and everyone else followed suit.

Victor watched her, frowning, thinking about Tellen's words—hidden tunnels and bolt-holes. He shook his head, thoughts coming together, and said, "No."

"What?" Rellia asked.

"No, Tellen. Get everyone, all your people, and hurry to our encampment. The asshole was waiting here. He was hiding in the Blue Deep. He knew we were coming this way. He probably knows I have a connection here. He's going to kill you all to draw us out, to make us do something stupid. Bolt-holes won't stop him."

"He's right," Valla said. "We're strong in our encampment. We can stand against an equal force there and put the burden of attack on him. If they're on the move, we must hurry before we're cut off."

"Do it, Tellen," Thayla said, locking eyes with Victor. "Let's hurry." She didn't wait for a response, charging for the door and rushing outside, calling out to the hunters nearby. The next twenty minutes felt like pure madness and chaos to Victor as the clan evacuated their longhouses. The hunters were trained for this; Victor knew well that they had often been chased off their hunting grounds by imperial forces or overzealous nobles with their personal armies. It was part of the reason they rotated camps throughout the year, moving on before they were noticed by too many and garnered unwanted attention.

All of that considered, it still took a while for the roladii to be brought into order, fitted with tack, and then mounted up. Everyone in the clan was either riding a mount or a wagon pulled by bigger roladii as they moved out, hurrying as quietly as possible through the darkness of the grasslands.

Darkness was an understatement. Thick black clouds had rolled in, blotting out the moons and the stars and testing the resolve of the children and craft folk of the clan. Victor wanted to summon his banner, wanted to cast Inspiration of the Quinametzin, but he didn't—they were hurrying quietly through the grass, the forest some miles to the south. He didn't want to bring attention to their shadowy procession.

Instead, he rode up and down the column, softly encouraging everyone, trusting in Guapo to inspire them with his flashing eyes and sparking hooves. All the while, he hoped the tall grass sufficiently masked the mustang's showy behavior. He used the vantage of his height to look toward the line of blackness in the distance, just a shade darker than the sky, knowing it was the forest on the horizon. He willed himself to see the Ridonne's forces approaching them, but he couldn't. He had to trust the scouts that Tellen had sent out. Hopefully, the Shadeni, at home on these plains, could outmaneuver any imperials sent to guard against the clan's escape.

The army encampment wasn't far, and after a tense half hour of hurrying silently through the blackness, the lights of the fortifications came into view, and Victor could feel the mood change among the fleeing clan folk. They saw those glowing Energy lamps and murmured with excitement and hope—Victor could no longer contain himself. He reached into his Core and, with a massive torrent of Energy, summoned his Banner of the Champion. Golden light blazed from the prominent sun on his standard, bathing the clan in its light, and Guapo whinnied wildly, rearing up on his hind hooves.

The Shadeni gasped and cried out, and Victor was sure he heard Deyni whoop from the bench of his wagon up the line. He raced his horse along the row of clan folk all the way to the front, waving to Deyni and Chandri as he passed them, then looped the front of the column and raced down the other side, trying to share his banner's positive effect with all the dozens of families. It had been a while since he'd seen the whole clan out like this, and he'd almost forgotten how big a group it was—more than a thousand people, many of them children. What would he do if they were killed because of his need to try to convince Thayla to join him?

That thought driving his words, he began to exhort them to hurry, to urge them to run. "Go! Go; hurry to the palisade! Get inside the camp!" Tellen and the other high-ranking hunters in the clan took up his cry, urging their mounts to gallop, racing along the column with him, trying to get the wagons to move faster. At first, Victor didn't know if he was being smart or foolish; what if one of the wagons broke down or someone fell off? Some of the roladii were overburdened, with several children sharing a seat. His doubts were soon banished when horns began to blow from the direction of the forest, and fiery missiles by the hundreds filled the sky, screaming through the black toward the fleeing clan.

"Run!" Victor screamed, no longer worried about keeping order. What good would it be if they were calm while riddled with flaming arrows? The Shadeni responded to his bellow, whipping their roladii into a gallop. The wagons bounced and jostled their occupants, but the plains were largely smooth, the slope leading up to the camp gentle. He saw Tellen yelling and gesturing to his scouts, saw Rellia charging ahead on her white vidanii, yelling for the sentries to open the gate. When he turned, he found Valla and Polo rushing toward him as the first arrows began to fall, whistling through the air, stinking of pitch and magical sulfur.

"Get down!" Polo bellowed, stepping in where Victor had frozen, his eyes wide, tracking the falling, fiery arcs of the missiles and watching as they *thunked* into wagons or punctured thick roladii hides, dropping them or pulling forth agonized screams—a sound Victor had never heard from the throat of one of the funny, feathered, docile mounts. It wasn't the falling or screaming roladii that had stalled him, though—he'd seen a little girl, probably younger than Deyni, fall from a wagon, a flaming arrow igniting her with its magical flames.

There was no helping it after that; his rage Core began to flow, and he cast Iron Berserk. He vaguely heard Valla and Polo speaking, yelling, and gesturing, but he didn't listen. He did spare them a glance and grunted, "Go to Borrius. Defend the camp." Then he urged his suddenly much larger mustang to charge the distant row of archers just as they launched another volley of flaming arrows at the panicking, surging column of refugees. The only peace in the back of his roiling, rage-filled mind came from the sight of his magical wagon, pulled by the sturdy, quick vidanii, Starlight, slipping through the gap in the camp's fortifications.

With his banner high over his massive shoulders, and his fiery hooved steed tearing over the grass, Victor raced through the darkness, galloping straight through fires that had begun to spread, the grass ignited by the magical flames of the imperial archers. So fast was the mustang that he sucked the wind in behind him, and fires died as Victor charged through. He was among the archers in only a few heartbeats, and Lifedrinker began to reap a bloody harvest as he trampled through them, swinging the axe left and right.

He cut through flimsy gold and black helmets and armor, shattered bows like kindling, and doused the tall grass with the red blood of the imperials. Perhaps they hadn't anticipated him charging. Perhaps they'd rushed ahead to get some volleys off, surprised by the sudden flight of the clan. Whatever the cause, the archers were exposed with no heavy soldiers to guard them and no Ridonne to challenge Victor. He couldn't have counted them, and it didn't matter to him if there were ten or a million of the bastards—Victor was determined to kill every last one of them. Every time his rage began to cool, he remembered that little girl, ignited by a random arrow fired by one of the men or women he was currently butchering.

The archers weren't straw dummies; they tried to flee, to fire upon him, to hide. It didn't matter. Victor's banner was brilliant, and he rode through the grass like death incarnate, trampling and slashing them. If he'd been cognizant, if he hadn't allowed his rage to overtake him, he might have realized he'd killed dozens, maybe hundreds of the archers and that he was slowly being drawn farther away from the army encampment. The archers, perpetrators in his mind, had become bait, and he gobbled it up, a lone light in the blackness of a magical night, blazing as he raced from one fleeing imperial to another.

"What's the mad fool doing?" Borrius asked, standing atop the army's fortifications, watching the blazing standard of their leader as it raced back and forth in the distant darkness. Everywhere was blackness, from the sky to the grasslands to the distant horizon where he knew the enemy lurked in their numbers—the Blue Deep.

"He saw the arrows come down, saw some of the clan folk fall. He's mad with rage," Valla replied. "I should go to him."

She, Rellia, and Lam stood nearby. Everyone else had gone to command their cohorts, readying for a direct attack. Borrius felt good about their chances against an imperial legion. Their army was strong, stronger than the last he'd commanded, and more than that, they had the advantage of fortification. "He should come back. Look how distant he is. They could have a trap prepared for him; what if that Ridonne is out there? What if he's devised a warded cage or worse?"

Rellia removed the looking glass from her eye and said, "He's slaughtering them. I think he's killed half the archers. Don't go out there, Valla; his mount is far faster than Uvu."

"And if this is a trap?" Valla hissed, tugging the hilt of her sword to expose several inches of cobalt metal.

"If it is, it won't be just for him," Borrius said, his mind made up. "They'll want to draw us out, to get us to rush to our leader's aid. The attack on the hunters was likely meant to do just that. Ancestors be praised that you had a chance to evacuate them."

"So, we should just let him die?" Lam asked, her luminous wings twitching with impatience.

"He's not easy to kill," Valla said, and Borrius nodded to her, grateful that, though she was close to the gigantic legate, she had a good head on her shoulders.

"We must prepare. Gather the strongest Fire Casters among us. Let's get some orbs in the sky. No point sitting in the darkness like this."

"Sending the word." Edeya scribbled in the command book. Not half a minute later, all around the palisade, orbs of fiery light surged into the air, bathing the grasslands around them in their warm, yellow-red glow.

"Why fire?" Rellia asked. "Why not pure Energy? The light is brighter."

"Come, you must remember from your studies. Why would we use fire orbs for light?" If Borrius enjoyed anything as much as commanding an army, it was teaching.

"Because they can be made into weapons," Valla replied, her eyes still trained on the distant blazing standard.

"Why this darkness? Is he hiding his numbers?" Lam turned in a slow circle, trying to pierce the blackness with her sharp gaze.

"Likely, or concealing his approach. We could be surrounded. Rellia, I'd like you to send the airships up and get eyes on the ravine we crossed yesterday. If we're wrong about his numbers, we might be wise to stage a fighting retreat to the canyon, cross, and utilize the choke point."

"In this blackness?"

"Do they not fly in storms? In the night?"

"Fine." She nodded to Edeya, and the lieutenant began to scribble out orders.

"We'll lose many lives if we must retreat. Too many noncombat personnel. Too many wagons." Valla sounded grim, and once again, Borrius found himself reassessing her. "Damn it, Victor, get back here." Almost as though she'd summoned them into being with her words, two blazing orbs of light erupted in the darkness beyond their Legate Primus, one red and one yellow, illuminating enormous golden-armored figures on nightmarish steeds.

After a time, when he struggled to find more archers to cut down, Victor's anger began to cool, and he started to consider his actions. It felt good to mete out justice, punishing the callous fools who'd launched deadly missiles into the fleeing Shadeni hunters, heedless of the repercussions of those actions, uncaring that children and peaceful craftsfolk would be killed. Regardless of the pleasure his vengeance gave him, Victor knew he was being foolish. He was never truly without autonomy anymore; his rage and berserk state made it easy to let go, easy to excuse brash behavior, but part of him knew the whole time that he was making himself vulnerable.

The problem with that knowledge was that Victor didn't care. He hoped that the Ridonne would come out and try to take him. He wished the fool would bring a friend or two. Why shouldn't he try to settle things out here on the plains while Tellen, Thayla, Deyni, and all the others, Valla and Rellia included, were safe behind the palisade? So it was with no great surprise, and, certainly, very little fear, when he saw the two Ridonne show themselves. They illuminated the darkness around them, one with a golden yellow orb—Victor recognized the spine-covered bastard he'd already fought—and another with a fat, baleful red light.

They sat atop mounts that looked straight out of a prehistoric movie back on Earth—some kind of raptors with black, leathery skin painted with wild red and yellow patterns and stripes. They were roughly a football field away from Victor, one slightly to his left and the other off to the right, just outside his banner's bright circle of illumination. "A football field." He chuckled; he hadn't thought about football in a long time. As much as he wanted to fight them, as much as he wanted to charge forward and rip them limb from limb, he had to consider the possibility that they might kill him. What would happen to his friends then?

He might be angry, might be willing to fight to the death, but was he willing to let his friends die? No, he decided, staring at those two Ridonne; he shouldn't play their game. He'd let them stew for a while. In response to his desire, his will, the mustang reared up and whinnied loudly, then leapt into motion, ripping over the grass in a wide arc as it turned back toward the camp. Victor heard the stomping feet of the Ridonne's raptor mounts. He heard the creatures, much larger than roladii, shrieking and gnashing their teeth, but they didn't stand a chance in a race with Guapo. The horse literally streaked over the plains, and when Victor looked over his shoulder, tears ripping out of his eyes in the stiff wind of his passage, he saw that they'd pulled off, unwilling to pursue him into the lights around the fortifications.

In seconds, he was sliding to a halt before the gates, having arrived faster than the men could pull them open. Victor's only regret about his actions was that it probably looked like he'd run away. How would that affect the troops' morale? He needn't have worried much—they cheered him and howled at the bloody state of his armor and axe, pleased to have some vengeance for the Shadeni who'd been shot down as they raced for the safety of the camp.

The clan wasn't near the gate; Victor figured Rellia would have ordered them escorted to the center of the encampment with the other wagons and noncombat personnel. He wanted to go to them, to hug Thayla and Deyni, to grasp Tellen's shoulder and apologize for the people he'd lost. He couldn't, though; Rellia and Borrius were standing on the palisade nearby, and the noblewoman met his eye as he rode through, clearly wanting a word with him. Victor hopped down from Guapo, sending him away to frolic on the spirit plane until he needed him again, and then stomped up the sturdy steps to the wooden rampart where the other commanders stood.

Victor was still gigantic and still channeling his Iron Berserk, and when he felt the rampart shudder with his steps, he let the spell drop. Borrius was speaking when he arrived, and Victor caught the tail end: " . . . foolish, but at least he didn't accept their further baiting."

"Yes, yes," Victor grumbled, striding forward. "I'm foolish. I'm impulsive. I'm all that shit. What have you got for me? There are two Ridonne out there, and I killed something like fifty or a hundred archers. How many of Tellen's people did we lose?"

"Twenty-six," Valla said. "Mostly children and noncombat personnel. The arrows hit some hunters, but they proved more resilient; our healers are seeing to them."

"We have scouts and the airships out. When we know more, we can make a better plan," Borrius said, unconcerned that Victor had overheard him.

"What can I do? Should I try to bait the leaders closer? I can't imagine their army will be as effective if we kill those two." Victor leaned against the thick wooden rampart, willing his eyes to see farther into the darkness, wishing he knew exactly what to do.

"They won't take such bait." Borrius chuckled. "Those men are sly; they'll have something—"

"Legate," Edeya said suddenly, interrupting the older man. "I'm sorry, but I have just received a message from *Balestar*." Victor knew the name; it was Rellia's personal airship.

"Well? Out with it." Borrius didn't wait for one of the two people there with the legate title to acknowledge her.

"The bridge is gone, sir." She gulped, looking around the group. "Sirs. The bridge is gone, and they're under fire. *The Petal* attacked them."

"Treachery!" Rellia cried. Victor couldn't blame her; *The Petal* was the name of the airship she'd hired to supplement *Balestar*'s scouting.

Victor's mind raced with the implications as Borrius swore, and Valla reflexively jerked her sword loose from her sheath. Rellia frowned, her eyes going very dark even in the light of Victor's banner. "Ancestors damn them. Despite the bad news, it means he's split his Legion. Should we sally forth? Charge the fools near the forest or perhaps the ones back toward the ravine?"

"No." Borrius sighed and looked back over the field where, minutes ago, Victor had been fighting. "I fear things are worse than that. Two Ridonne. They wouldn't be so foolish as to split their army if we matched them evenly. If I'm not wrong, there are two armies out there in the black. Two legions. We may be in trouble."

29

MORALE

Victor watched as Borrius barked orders, doing everything he knew to prepare the temporary fortification of the legion's encampment for the assault of a much larger force. He commanded the Earth Casters to increase the width, depth, and number of trenches outside the walls, row upon row of them. Water and Fire Casters followed in their footsteps, filling the trenches with deadly traps. Archers lined the palisades, Air Casters enchanting their arrows with magic that would bolster their range and damage so long as they used them before the enchantments faded.

Meanwhile, one of the magical storage wagons was emptied of its cargo—thousands of tons of stone blocks were arranged in a sturdy outer ring of fortifications, meant to slow or stop any charging soldiers who made it through the trenches and pitfalls in the field. Ranged casters stood at the ready, prepared to make traversing the uneven, difficult terrain a costly affair. "Will it be enough?" he asked, staring into the blackness.

"No," Borrius sighed. "It will cost them dearly to take us, but we don't have what we need to defend against two legions properly. If we had a true keep or a mountaintop, some sort of choke point . . . but we don't. We're in the plains, with no significant landmarks for leagues, and the only hope of retreat cut off."

"What if I kill the Ridonne?"

"That would certainly help. Morale is a powerful weapon."

"Mm-hmm," Victor grunted, starting to regret not engaging with the two imperials when he'd had the chance. He supposed they wouldn't have baited him if they hadn't had a plan. "So, you're saying you can't win this?" He gestured out over the battlements where the soldiers were hard at work.

Only Edeya, Rellia, and Valla were within earshot, but Borrius still looked around, frowning, before he answered, "I'm not saying that. If they are too eager or too bold, we might punish them enough in their first assault to make a clean victory impossible for them."

"So," Rellia cut in, "our fate may depend on the pride or foolishness of the Ridonne."

"We'll see. How long can they keep up this darkness?" Victor asked, "When's sunrise supposed to be?"

"We're an hour from dawn, but we won't see it," Borrius replied. "Not unless we turn our Wind Casters to the task. Personally, I'd rather fight in the dark, using their Energy to aid the archers and drop lightning strikes on the enemy; if the imperials are using their casters to bring these black clouds, it will reduce their offensive capabilities."

"Not great for morale, though," Valla sighed.

"That's what I'm for." Victor turned and started for the steps leading down from the ramparts. Valla was close on his heels.

"Where are you going?" Rellia called,

"First, I'm going to apologize to Thayla and Tellen. Then I'm going to do something to help bolster the troops." He didn't hear any response, so he kept walking. Soldiers saw him and saluted, and Victor felt a mixture of emotions—guilt warred with pride, pride warred with sympathy. The soldiers were frightened. They'd heard rumors, seen the Ridonne out on the plains, and seen their leader ride away from them. The darkness was oppressive, despite the orbs of flame hovering over the palisade.

He reached into his Core and cast Inspiration of the Quinametzin, powering it with more Energy than he ever had. To him, the shadows retreated, the lights in the camp and hanging in the sky grew brighter, shed a purer light, and doubts began to flee his mind. The effect must have been similar for his troops because the dozens nearby began to cheer, dropping what they were doing to look at him. Victor stood tall—not a titan, but a giant of a man. He wrapped his fist around Lifedrinker's haft, and he lifted her high, shouting, "They've picked the wrong army to mess with! We're going to water these fields with the blood of the Ridonne if that's what they want!"

The soldiers cheered, though some of them blanched and looked around as though the shadows out there might manifest into something physical, might punish them for even thinking ill of the Empire. Victor kept walking, spreading his inspiration as he made his way to the center of the camp, dread in his heart, but duty pushing him forward—he had to face Tellen. He had to tell him how sorry he was that some of his people had died.

"I've another thought," Valla said, causing him to slow his steps and turn to regard her.

"About?"

"About this darkness and how you should respond. I didn't want to say anything in front of Borrius in case you disagreed."

"Go on." Victor fully turned to face her, glad she'd spoken up before they'd come too close to the circled wagons.

"The Empire wants to break us, to weaken our morale. They're circling us, waiting out in the darkness. They know we won't assault them for two reasons: we have fewer numbers, and we don't know how they're arranged. They sit out there, comfortable in this blackness. Perhaps you should give them a reason to fear the dark."

"Are you suggesting . . ."

"Your terror spell, the one you killed Karnice with. Victor, I've felt it. If you were set loose out there, among their troops . . . Even if they could catch you, would the Ridonne be able to kill you? Perhaps, but, well . . . Maybe my opinion of you is inflated, but I think you'd make them regret trying."

"You think so?" Was Valla honestly asking him to unleash his Aspect of Terror? She'd either managed to block the experience from her mind, or she was a lot more worried about their situation than she let on.

"I do. I think haste is key, too. You have to get out there and sow chaos, fear, and discord before they attack. Let me pass your condolences on to Tellen and Thayla."

"Uh-uh, Valla. I'll think about your idea, but I won't act impulsively. Let me speak with the hunters. I'll be quick. Then I'll run your idea past Borrius and Rellia. If they don't convince me otherwise, I'll do as you ask."

"Oh." Valla pressed her lips together, visibly clenching her jaw, then she blew out a pent-up breath. "Very well. Let's hurry, though." She started walking, and Victor followed suit. "Rellia and Borrius don't know what you can do. They'll try to dissuade you. Keep in mind their ignorance before you let them convince you to hold back."

"Rellia knows what I can do . . ."

"She knows you barely beat her in a duel. She doesn't know you could swat her like a fly now."

Victor wanted to respond, to argue that Rellia had seen him in action since then, but they were walking quickly, and he saw a familiar wagon ahead. His heart lifted to see Thistle and Starlight together, tethered just outside the perimeter of the inner ring. Chandri was setting down a bucket near Thistle, and when she looked up and met his eyes, she ran to him. "Oh, man," Victor had time to say before she crashed into him, squeezing his waist and pressing her face into his stomach, despite the hard armor between them.

"They killed Bassa. They killed *children*, Victor. We didn't even attack them or offer them any resistance! Why would they do that?" She looked up at him, tears streaking her cheeks, and he saw from the state of her face paints that they weren't the first.

"Because they wanted to hurt me. I'm sorry."

"The Empire are the wrongdoers here, Victor." Valla frowned at Chandri.

"She's right. It's not your fault. Tellen and Thayla are with the wounded. Should I get them?"

"Go ahead. I'm going to speak to the people." Victor squeezed Chandri briefly, then stepped up to his one-time wagon and grabbed the top, hoisting himself up. He stood there for a moment, contemplating, looking out over the tents and wagons clustered in the center of the encampment—crowds were milling about or gathered around fires—and decided some more light might help. He reached into his pathways and built the pattern for Dauntless Radiance—some courage might do these people some good. He pushed a massive torrent of Energy into it and then unleashed the spell high overhead, in the dark sky over the milling refugees.

Like a rip appearing in the fabric of existence, a break appeared in the evil clouds, and a wide fan of reddish golden light arced downward, illuminating a hundred feet in every direction with its warm, encouraging glow. Conversations died down, and people looked up, shielding their eyes against the bright glare, and if a smile didn't touch their lips, at least some frowns fell away and tears dried up. For the second time in his life, Victor tried his hand at public speaking. He cleared his throat and shouted, "Proud Shadeni!"

If any of them hadn't noticed him yet, that got their attention, and the hundreds of figures began to gravitate toward him, quieting, waiting to hear what else he'd say. As they approached, they felt the Inspiration of the Quinametzin, and their mood improved markedly. At first, Victor was glad to see it, but then he remembered the dead girl and the dozens he hadn't witnessed dying. He frowned and bellowed, "You've been wronged, and it's my fault. The scum out there wanted to punish me by hurting those I care for. I'm sorry!"

Cries of "No!" or even "We love you, Victor!" came from the plains folk, and when he heard not a single outcry or word of hate-filled blame, tears began to pool in Victor's eyes.

"I want you to know something! If the Ridonne are against us, it's because they're corrupt and evil. We're on the right side of things here. That should be clear by the way they attack children and peaceful hunters. I promise you: justice will find those that ordered the attack. I will find them. If you hear screams in the blackness out there, know it is me, wreaking our vengeance."

The Shadeni were hurt, they were down, but they were strong, proud people, and when they heard Victor's words, his promise of retribution, they started to cheer. They stomped their feet and chanted rhythmic hunting songs, and Victor felt his heart begin to swell. Good as it felt to have their continued support, seeing them gathered like that and hearing their cries of love and gratitude broke something in Victor. He no longer wanted to speak to Thayla and Tellen. He didn't want to ask Borrius for permission. He had Valla's blessing, and he wanted to do as she'd suggested.

He raised his voice, bellowing one last time, "Listen to the night! Listen and know that these imperial bastards chose the wrong people to attack!" With that, he dropped from the wagon and started walking toward the gates. Valla hurried to match his stride, having to jog lightly. "You need to whip the troops up. My . . . shrieks might scare them. Let them know it's me. Let them know I'm out there among the enemy, making them regret this bullshit."

"Victor . . ." Her voice was shaky, breathy. "What if I'm wrong?"

"What?" Despite his anger, the urgency in his gut, and the guilt he felt about the Shadeni clan, he couldn't help it—he grinned at her and said, "Are you worried?"

"I am! This was my idea! I'll never forgive . . ." She stopped, shaking her head, almost jerking it side to side, and added, "I have to be strong. You're the one taking the risk."

"You're not going to make me promise to return safely?"

"Are you . . . are you teasing me at a time like this?" Her bright eyes, different, redder and more luminescent than usual in the weird lights cast by all the magical orbs in the sky, flashed at him beneath scowling brows.

"I'm sorry." Victor sighed and gestured around. "I think I'm just trying to focus on anything to make this all seem less real. We're surrounded by magical darkness with an unknown number of soldiers waiting to attack us.

People I knew, people I'd spoken to, helped, and eaten meals with, were killed just a little while ago! I think the chance to flirt with you let me push some of that away."

"Well. I hope you'll remember me when you're out there. I hope the thought of me praying that you're safe and that you don't go too far will keep you from losing yourself to the beast you become. Ancestors! Are we sure you must do this?"

"I have to do something. Borrius is spinning a lot of bullshit to act like we still have a chance."

"It's true," Valla huffed. "No matter how you frame it, we're likely outnumbered two to one. We aren't alone with our abilities, our preparations." She gestured to the walls and the fiery orbs. "Our fortifications will help, but they aren't castle walls enhanced by glyphs and magic . . ."

"Yeah. I'll try to come back before I run out of juice. Tell Borrius to get hunters out in the grass to try to gauge my success. This might be the moment. If I can break them or cause enough chaos, maybe we should attack."

"He won't like that. I'll pass it on, though!" she added hastily when Victor looked back at her with a frown. "Victor, it doesn't matter. Do enough damage and the imperials will dread attacking. It will make a difference." She reached out to grasp his wrist. Her fingers were cold, and they made him take note of the fact that the air had chilled quite a lot with the thick layer of clouds the Ridonne's casters had called in. His breath plumed as he paused to look down at her again. He let her pull his arm back, pull his hand toward her, and she held it there, against her chest, staring into his eyes. "Promise me you'll come back."

"I will," he said, serious for once. Then he turned and shouted, "Open!" He stomped toward the gates, and Valla let his hand fall away. The soldiers moved to respond, bolstered by Victor's inspiration spell, still coursing through him. Rellia and Borrius, on the rampart above, heard him, and he saw them look over the side.

Rellia called out, "What are you doing?"

"Valla will explain." Victor strode through the gates. He let his Inspiration of the Quinametzin drop, heard the responding groans from the soldiers behind him, and cast Iron Berserk.

"Victor!" Rellia called again, this time from the outward-facing edge of the parapet. He ignored her as he doubled in size and let go of his aura, sighing as the weight was taken off his mind. He took several steps away from the gates, down the shallow slope, and past a pit with boiling water somehow sloshing about in its depths. The Ridonne had tasted his axe, had felt his might, but he didn't know everything about Victor. He didn't know about the fear that lived in his heart, didn't know that Victor could share it with him and his troops.

Victor slowed the flow of rage from his Core, cutting it to just the minimum he'd need to maintain his Iron Berserk, and then he let his fear-attuned Energy course into his pathways, summoning the pattern for Aspect of Terror. With a savage cry of fury and frustration, he let the dark power roll through his body, working its magic on his flesh.

"What's the fool doing?" Borrius asked, leaning next to Rellia to see better what the giant legate had gotten up to. He'd cried out a horrible sound and then hunkered down. Now a cloud of shadows surrounded him, and a terrible weight had fallen on Borrius and all the people nearby. Was the madman going to attack them?

"I've never seen this magic from him . . ." Rellia's voice was a whisper, and no small amount of fear tinged her words.

"He's going to break their morale," Valla said, breathless from her run up the steps as she joined them.

Borrius whirled on her. "You're in on this? What is it? You should have spoken to us about any plan you two dreamed up!"

"I take full responsibility. This was my idea. I also told Victor not to speak to you. I knew you both would try to dissuade him because you don't know what he's capable of. You know nothing of"—she gestured to the man, wholly wreathed in shadows outside the ramparts—"this."

"What is it?" Rellia asked, her face pale, and Borrius couldn't blame her; the weight on his spirit was almost unbearable. Was that the madman's aura? His spell? Some combination of the two?

"He has more types of Energy than rage and inspiration. You saw his banner, the glory. Well, his strongest affinity is darker; it scares him; he's worried it will consume him, so he uses it infrequently." Valla's voice was hushed, her eyes wide, something in them that Borrius didn't recognize. As he and Rellia continued to stare at her, she said, "Fear."

Borrius started to scoff, started to ask her to explain herself, but then a shriek broke the night. It was a sound so awful, so primally terrifying, that Borrius fell to his knees, hunkering behind the parapet. "What the devil?"

"It's him," Rellia said, staring with Valla over the rampart, looking out into the night. "It's Victor. Oh, Ancestors, Valla, he's looking at us."

"Stand still. Ancestors damn it! Tell the guards to lower their weapons!" Valla spoke in a hushed voice, staring past Borrius, and Rellia didn't respond, certainly didn't carry out her request.

He almost straightened, almost turned to look out at what had transfixed them so, but then he worried that he'd be similarly affected. Instead, Borrius cleared his throat and screamed, "Stand down! Lower your weapons. Do not antagonize him!" He glared at the guards on the rampart and saw them lower their bows, faces wan, eyes wide. "What in the world is going on out there?" he grumbled, turning and laboriously pulling himself to his feet.

As soon as his eyes cleared the rampart, he wished he'd stayed down. A creature stood out there, not two dozen strides from the gates. It was enormous, easily the size of Victor in his giant form. Was that him? Borrius couldn't believe it. The creature was hulking, more wolf than man, but, Ancestors, were those black feathers? Was that a hooked beak at the end of its snout? Were those shadows part of it? They seemed to cling to the creature, moving with it as it paced and sniffed at the night sky. "What the rotting grandfathers . . ."

The monster whirled at the sound of his voice. It stomped toward him, and Borrius felt a terror ignite in his chest like he'd never experienced. He felt his bowels loosen, felt adrenaline explode into frozen muscles, and, unable to put together a coherent thought, he stood there and trembled, transfixed by the baleful orange lantern-like eyes of the monster as it lifted its gleaming black beak and sniffed. Borrius would have fainted if he could have. He would have fallen off the wall to escape that glare, especially when the fur- and feather-covered snout peeled back to reveal a maw full of razor-edged, needle-sharp teeth.

The only thought he managed to form was a babbling, hardly intelligible question about how the creature could have a beak, teeth, fur, and feathers. Then, moving calmly and purposefully, Valla stepped between him and the monster. As Borrius took cover behind her and his gaze was interrupted, he found himself able to think again, able to act. He drew a deep breath, ready to call the soldiers to the attack, but then Valla spoke. "Go. Go, Victor. Punish those that threaten us. Break them!"

Borrius heard gravel scraping and loud footfalls fading away down the gentle slope past the trenches and pitfalls his men had dug. Then another wild, terrible shriek split the night, and his bladder joined his bowels in their dereliction of duty.

30

PACT

Victor felt the difference his Born of Terror feat made immediately; though the fear pervaded his body, altering it, changing him from a man of muscle and sinew into a creature of shadow and talon, he still knew himself. This was a massive change from his previous experience with the Aspect of Terror—he knew, deep inside, that he was Victor, that he had a goal in mind, and that feeding upon the fear of all the bright spirits around him was secondary to that. Still, when he stretched his form, free of his temporary chrysalis of shadow, he sniffed at the air, savoring the rich scent of despair.

The world was no longer dark, the shadows fell away, and though he didn't see the bright colors a simple flesh-bound beast might, he could see clearly in the night. The blackness was gone, replaced by a grayscale landscape punctuated by bright lights—spirits ripe for the reaping. He looked down the slope into the wavy grasslands, admiring the rime of frost that was forming despite the late spring date. His breath plumed and huffed as he sniffed, looking out into those fields, seeing the spirits out there gathering near the tall boughs of the great deep forest. They teemed there, thronging and milling about, congregating, waiting for something—him?

He knew more of the bright spirits waited behind him, lurking in the wooden fortress, hiding behind their flimsy walls. He also knew they weren't for him. He was meant to feast upon those in the fields and the forest. He was meant to drive them to madness, to panic. He grinned, spreading the leathery lips behind his beak, exposing rows of fangs. That black, razor-edged beak clicked in a weird, devilish chuckle. Behind him, someone hollered, some throaty human voice bellowing a question. Who would dare?

Victor whirled and stalked toward the palisade, his head nearly high enough to see over it to the other side. Some spirits lingered atop that wall; most shrank back, wilting before him, but one stood tall, the one who'd barked at him. Victor stretched his long neck, extended his double-jointed knees, and pushed his beak-tipped snout toward the spirit, sniffing. Who was this insolent one? Suddenly the ripe scent of opened bowels touched his nose, and Victor growled, offended by the stench. He took another step toward the wall, the hunger in his Core spurred by his anger at that quaking, insolent spirit, pushing him toward violence.

He knew this spirit, did he not? Should it be so disrespectful? Wasn't it one who'd sworn obeisance? Shouldn't he give it a taste of his fear? Shouldn't he share it? Before he could decide, another spirit came into view, one that had been behind the crenellation of rough timber. It was bright, beautiful, and very familiar to Victor. He sniffed at it, leaning close, the other foolish, much dimmer spirit forgotten. As his snout tasted the air, it spoke, "Go. Go, Victor. Punish those that threaten us. Break them!"

Valla! The word came to him, strange and foreign tasting in his mouth. He wanted to say it aloud but knew his tongue wasn't meant for such things—not anymore. Instead, he listened, and he remembered. This was a spirit he cared about, one he didn't want to feel the fear pounding through his pathways. It wanted him to visit terror upon the fools in the fields and forest. If that were so, then he would oblige. He would relish it! Victor turned and responded to an urge born in his bones, in his blood; he screeched his madness, his fear-steeped heart, and willed those who heard him to share in it. He bounded down the slope, leaping pits and trenches, crashing through barriers too flimsy to slow him.

Soon, Victor was tearing through the tall grass, his long limbs devouring the distance between the bright, wonderful spirit and the ones she wanted him to visit destruction upon. She. "That's right!" he growled in a twisted, guttural voice. "Valla!" he roared, but it came out more like a screech than a name. He tore through the tall grass, aiming for a cluster of bright spirits somewhat closer than the larger congregation, a small group of them squatting, lurking behind the grass, conspiring. Victor didn't give them a chance to react to him. He ran on taloned pads that caressed the grass like feathers on mist, and when he burst into their little clearing, it was like an avalanche of shadowy claws descending on Valla's enemies, *his* enemies.

Victor howled and smashed them about, knocking them down, ripping them with his talons, and one by one, crouched over them, drawing the fear out of them as it compounded on itself. He used the Energy he cultivated to feed his form, to extend his spell, and to propel himself from one stunned target to the next. When he'd taken all the group of scouts could give, when they lay bleeding and gasping their last breaths, he tore through the grass, a whispery shadow on the wind, and launched himself against more of the bright spirit's enemies.

Some of the spirits he feasted upon were stronger than others. Sometimes their sharp, shiny claws bit into his flesh or chipped at his bones and talons. It didn't matter; as he drained them of Energy and his Core churned out rage and fear, he healed. Most of the spirits' attacks were fruitless; they slid off his hard bones, his thick feathers, and the shadows that clung to him. He overwhelmed his victims with ferocious speed and power, gripping them with his talons, pressing them down, draining their Energy, and feeding his Core. Each enemy he overwhelmed restored and sustained him. No, he reconsidered, more than sustained—he thrived. As his rampage went on, as he charged from one quaking enemy or group of enemies to another, he grew more and more powerful, more and more hungry.

Soon, it wasn't only the victims underneath him, pinned by his talons, that fed him. No, he felt the fear coming to him from distant corners of the plains, drifting over the grass from the forest. His Core swelled with it, and his form grew denser, thicker with shadows, as the fuel for his frenzied feasting began to outpace his usage. Mad with the glut of pure fear, he lifted his head and screeched again and again as the night wore on.

"They wear on me, those cries! What's he doing out there?" Borrius asked, his eyes wide with stress, sweat beading on his pale blue forehead despite the chill. He'd taken a moment to clean himself up after his brief encounter with Victor's terror aspect, and, not exactly refreshed but certainly less soiled, he'd tracked Valla down; she'd been patrolling the ramparts.

"He's killing them. He's running them down, driving them to mad fear, and reaping the harvest. It's how his fear aspect cultivates." She turned toward another screech, distant, perhaps all the way at the edge of the Blue Deep. Had he pursued them so far? Were they not in the fields?

"I wish we could get him to report back to us and tell us their numbers and locations."

"He probably won't remember much of what he sees out there when he returns to himself."

Borrius frowned as he saw a cluster of guardsmen below, huddled close, whispering with wide, fearful eyes. "He's breaking not only the enemy's morale but our own."

Valla turned away from the grassland, following his gaze, and nodded. "Where's my mother?"

"Near the gate, last I saw."

"Come, we need to do our part." Valla started around the rampart toward the palisade gate, and Borrius, feeling as though control was slipping through his fingers, followed after her.

Ten minutes later, he stood next to Rellia and Lam's aide, Edeya, watching as Valla addressed the cohort captains. "Captains!" she said, her voice sharp and demanding, drawing their eyes away from the darkness outside the walls. "I've called you here for a reason. Your legate primus has left a task for you—we must bolster the troops' morale. We must spread the tale of Victor's rampage outside this palisade. Those screeches ripping the night come from his throat. He's out there tearing apart the imperial forces. He works to make them regret bringing in this night."

"That's him?" Polo asked, straightening up and shifting the great axe slung over his thick shoulder.

"That's Victor." Valla's words were punctuated by another screech distantly echoing over the plains.

"We must join him, in that case!" Sarl said, a rapier materializing in his hand.

"No, Sarl. Victor does his terrible work so we might stand a chance against the Ridonne when they make their offensive. He works to break their morale, to thin their numbers, and to soften the tip of their spear. If we charge now, we'll undermine his efforts."

"What if he's surrounded? What if the Ridonne surprise him?" Yarsha, captain of the fifth cavalry cohort, asked.

"Does it sound like he's in danger? Do you hear any pain in that horrible screech?" Borrius asked, jumping onto Valla's bandwagon. "If those two devils can catch him—which I highly doubt, having seen him move through the night with my own two eyes—then I fear they'll regret doing so."

"Come," Valla said, clapping her hands. "Get out there and encourage the troops. Spread the tale of Victor's work. Let them know the darkness might be against us, but the nightmare stalking through it is one of our own."

* * *

"Desertion is starting to feel like a very real concern, Pazra," the tall, golden-fleshed paragon of the Ridonne said, resting a hand on his shoulder, carefully avoiding the spikes. Pazra pulled away, moving to the other side of his map table. They stood inside his command tent, lushly appointed with thick rugs, opulent furnishings, and ample space for the two huge men and their attendants.

"Brother. Dear Rosh-dak, if you fear your men are deserting, then you must punish them. I can assure you; my men will stand fast."

"Your men are dying," Rosh said, chuckling, looking down his long, straight nose as he was wont to do, always so eager to demonstrate how much taller he was, how much more handsome, how much more loved.

Pazra growled his response. "Small numbers. The beast can slay all night, and it will only be a fraction of us. What is the thing, anyway? Have you set eyes upon it yet? Old bones, but its shriek wears on me!"

"My scouts close in. It seems to hunt at random, never in a straight line. Still, they close the net, and when they do, they'll call to me."

"So sure? When was the last you heard from them? What of the airship your flyers captured?"

"Minutes ago, dear brother. Don't judge my men as harshly as your own. The cries you hear, the gaps in our line—all yours. As for the airship, it will be of no use. The other one brought it down with it; they proved more resilient than my plucky, flying tribune anticipated." Rosh chuckled, reaching up to finger the golden-capped spiral horn that swept back from his temple over his ear. Pazra admired those glorious horns. What must life be like to be so handsome? "In any case, they did their job. We've removed the wench's air support. My men perform their duties with aplomb."

"Your men fare well only because they guard the far side of the encampment. If the beast wends its way toward them, we'll see how well they stand."

"It won't. I'll kill it before then. You should hope I do, at least. My last missive from our dear uncle wasn't very charitable in its language referencing this little military campaign of yours."

"Ours," Pazra corrected. "This is a joint venture, brother."

"So it is, so it is. He sees my involvement somewhat more charitably, however. I came here to help you, after all. He's wondering why two Ridonne and their Legions are needed for a simple uprising orchestrated by a backwater noblewoman. If it weren't for the reports of this champion of hers, this so-called giant, and what the auguries have shown, I fear you'd be in a bit of trouble for allowing things to escalate to this level."

"Brother, is that how you've sold your involvement?" Pazra stood up straight, looking away from the map for the first time, his anger suddenly redirected toward his sibling. "I may not be as handsome as you, as loved, but don't mistake that for a weakness of the mind. I appreciate you being here, and I appreciate your help, but don't try to capitalize on this situation; do not attempt to curry favor among the family. Favor with me? Yes. You have it, but not if it means you will attempt to drag me down. What do you have to gain? I'm already far removed from the succession."

"What is there ever to gain by sibling rivalry? Is not the joy in the contest enough?" Rosh smiled slyly and reached out a long, powerful arm to jostle Pazra's shoulder. "Come, I know you're not being completely honest with me. Do you not attempt to please our mother with your activities? Do you not run to her, squealing the tale of every mistake I've made?"

"I don't, but you do, and she sees through it. You know Far Scribe books can have more than one copy; she's seen all your missives goading me to violence, swearing your assistance. I give you this bit of advice freely: don't try to play our uncle for favor. She'll see through it, and she has his ear. She's well aware of every misstep I've made but also of your involvement."

Rosh chuckled, stroking his chin and narrowing his eyes as he looked down at Pazra. "You did that? Gave her a copy? You little churl!" His chuckle seemed genuine; was he truly so unbothered? "No matter. We'll solve this debacle, and the family will see it was I who came to your aid."

"Excuse me, Lord Pazra-dak," Venet, one of Pazra's tribunes, said, stepping into the light of his lamp and approaching the table.

"Speak," he said, wincing as another horrifying shriek cut through the night.

"It seems the losses are somewhat greater than I first tabulated. There are . . . gaps in the secondary line."

"Gaps?" Rosh asked, his amusement and further words forgotten; their sibling rivalry was old news, and here was something new. His golden lips pulled back from sharp white teeth, exposing bright canines that flashed in the gleam of the light. Pazra hated how his heart grew sick with envy whenever his brother smiled.

"Aye, sir. There are missing reinforcements."

"Not dead?" Pazra asked, a deep frown marring his already scrunched countenance.

"That's unclear. It's possible that some of them rushed the beast to aid the first line, but I'm getting reports of men slipping away deeper into the forest. I was . . . wondering if we should invoke the pact."

"Of course! Desertion isn't something ever to be tolerated," Rosh answered for him, and Pazra growled, feeling the heat of his fiery Energy begin to seep out of his Core.

"Yes!" he barked. "Invoke the pact! Alert the captains—I want an accurate count on our numbers, on how many we lose after the invocation. We'll gain some use from those cowardly fools."

"How entertaining," Rosh said, continuing to gently stroke his golden chin, his long, black nails making a soft susurration as they scraped over his fine stubble. "Yes. This has a lovely symmetry; let us send our own monsters into the night."

Rula ran. Without thought, without a plan, she ran. One thing occupied her mind, and it was an image, a scene, replaying again and again. As she leapt under brush and crashed through low-hanging branches, she saw, in her mind's eye, Tezla-dak being pinned to the ground by an enormous, horrible creature that oozed primal Energies. Energies that brought fear and terror out of Rula. Urges buried in her deepest ancestral memories came to the surface, and she knew one thing: she must run.

She didn't think of her duty, her commander, or the Empire. Only the desire to escape that horrific creature propelled her forward. If she couldn't think of her sergeant, the ever-snarling, ever-angry, ever-present Egrolo-dak, how could she possibly remember the pact? How could she think of a document she'd signed years ago in a time like this? Sadly, it didn't matter if she remembered the pact, for it remembered her.

Rula paused by a thick tree, frozen with fear, hunching against its rough bark as the creature screamed again. As the echoes of that weird, terrible cry began to fade and she felt the muscles in her legs unclench, she looked ahead, choosing a direction in which to sprint. Then her heart exploded. It didn't *actually* explode, but it certainly felt like it. No, she wasn't dead—fire burned in her chest, and she couldn't breathe, but she wasn't dead. She writhed, her hands clawing at the damp, cold mulch of the forest floor. When had she fallen?

As the horrible pain, the hot burning Energy, spread from her chest into her arms and down toward her legs, Rula looked at her hands to see them changing. Her fingers stretched into hard, dark claws, the skin peeling back from black bones. Her wrist cracked, and as she screamed in agony, her bones elongated, and her joints shifted. Her vision changed then, and so did her mind; she no longer felt afraid. All she knew was pain and the unbearable hunger for the Empire's foes.

She lifted her head and, in her red-tinged vision, scanned the sky for the moons, for the stars, for some sign of what she should do. Nothing outside herself held the answer, but something else did. A deep voice, the princeps who'd taken her oath, spoke in her mind. "Seek them. Seek the foes of the Empire. Run to them. Tear them apart. Eat their leaders."

Rula howled, lifting her strange, animalistic snout, long tusks protruding from a lower jaw that her father, a man who'd once doted on her and called her his beautiful princess, wouldn't recognize. Her cry rose into the black night, and others took up the call—dozens, hundreds of voices rose in unison, singing a hungry, desperate, mournful song. Then she turned and began to charge toward the edge of the forest. The grasslands were nearby; she knew that much, remembered that little bit of her old life. The tall grasslands were nearby, and on them, the enemies of the Empire.

31

FEAR-FUELED MELEE

Victor stalked through the night, hunting amid the great, ancient trees, ripping the life and Energy from one foe after another. They were fleeing; he could feel the fear drifting to him through the forest as a bloodhound might catch a scent. While rich, it grew fainter as the spirits took flight, and he hung back, gorging on one downed spirit after another. Something was happening inside him, something in his Core; it grew fat and throbbed, seeking an outlet, and he knew, instinctively, he was supposed to do something with it. That awareness and the pleasure he drew from savoring the Energy kept him from charging wildly into the deep woods.

As the light faded from the spirit he held beneath his massive talons, he arched his back, causing his great shadow-clad spine to creak and pop. He shook his head and shivered at the pleasure of it, feeling the fur and feathers that lined his form vibrate with the movement. Somewhere in his mind, Victor still existed, still fought for dominance over his fear and rage, and that fragment of himself had the wherewithal to wonder why he had fur and feathers. Why not one or the other?

The question felt like a clue. It felt as if it had something to do with the enormous, swelling maelstrom of fear-attuned Energy that sat in his Core. He'd harvested so much Energy and drained so many spirits that night! To what end? He felt the answer to the riddle was right under his thumb—no, his talon—that he was on the verge of making a breakthrough. He could feel the drifting ribbons of fear growing more distant, though he wasn't worried;

hundreds or thousands of prey yet lingered, hiding in the tall grass or among the trees. There would be no going hungry for him.

He continued to stare inward, mind entranced by that throbbing ball of densely packed fear. He'd begun to tease at it, to pull some forth, when a wild, mournful cry echoed through the night and was taken up by hundreds of other throats. What was this? More prey? Victor lifted his beaked snout and tasted the air, tasted the sound, and found it lacking sustenance. No, these sad creatures felt no fear. There was nothing for him in them. Nevertheless, they were intriguing. Where had they come from? Would they compete with him for the spirits? Their wails wound down, but he heard them crashing through the darkness, charging away from the forest toward the tall grass.

Should he give chase? Something in him loved the idea, but what was the point? Why hunt something that had no meat for his hunger? Besides, hadn't he decided to please the bright spirit, the one he recognized? "Valla," he grumbled, sniffing again, seeking a taste of fear. There was a great deal less of it on the wind. What was going on? Had so many spirits escaped? He sniffed again, and though the totality of the fear was lessened, there were some strong scents very nearby.

Victor slowly turned, snout raised, drawing the fear in; one, two, three, four, five spirits slowly approached him, five fear-filled morsels. They came closer despite their terror; this was new! Victor lowered himself, stalking along the frost-rimed, leaf-covered duff. His movements were cloaked in shadow, silent as a whisper as he moved toward the nearest. He was halfway to it, his haunches straining with the urge to spring, when the spirit, and the others converging on him, ceased their movement. He felt a surge of Energy, something clean and bright, no taint of attunement. Rather than wait to see what they were doing, Victor leapt, crashing through a stand of saplings to fall upon the hazy spirit, weak compared to some of the others he'd consumed.

The poor thing wailed as he smashed it to the ground and tore into its shoulder with his beak and fangs, pulling the suddenly ripe, rich flow of fear-attuned Energy into his Core. As he consumed it, he felt the other four fleeing. He chuckled, a dark guttural sound that rumbled in his chest, as blood dripped off his beak. As he feasted, something began to tickle the back of his mind, a feeling of urgency, easy to ignore at first but stronger, more persistent with each passing second. What was this? He had his mission—feast on the fear of these fools, punish them, and please the bright spirit.

He stood taller on his long, shadowy limbs, once again tasting the wind. Something new was coming to him, a taste of fear that hadn't been there before. He stood up further, on his hind legs, stretching his spine, reaching his head into the sky, and stared north toward the grasslands where he'd first rampaged. The other spirits, those not meant for his feasting, were afraid. They were exuding the emotion. It rose like a nebulous cloud over their walled encampment. Again that feeling at the back of his mind scratched at him, less a tickle than a claw now, a sharp reminder of his duty, a pang to wake up his sleeping self—he was Victor, and his men needed him.

The maelstrom of darkly attuned Energy in his Core forgotten, his hunger for fear abandoned, Victor reached to sever the spell that bound him to the Aspect of Terror. Before he could cut it loose, though, a great roaring avalanche of man and metal fell upon him, cracking his bones, ripping his feathers, and sending him tumbling over the frosty ground to smash into the bole of a gigantic tree. His crashing impact was tremendous, cracking the wood, shaking loose old branches and thousands of leaves, and Victor knew nothing but fury. Who had dared to strike him so?

He needn't have asked; a Ridonne, taller than the one he'd met before, stood where moments before Victor had been, a great shield on his left arm and a thick, golden broadsword in his other fist. It wasn't only the sword that was golden; the *man* was golden, from his armor to his shield to his very flesh. Victor felt his bones snap back into place, felt the shadows wrap around his torn limbs, and before a heartbeat might be counted twice, he launched himself at the golden warrior, streaking like a shadowy missile through the night to smash into him. The Ridonne looked surprised, and Victor saw his spirit start to bleed through his physical form. It was brilliant.

Victor's hunger reignited, and he almost forgot about his duty, about his troops, but that pang in the back of his mind returned, ripping into his thoughts, pushing the nightmare away and bringing Victor forward. He couldn't play with this fool. He had somewhere he needed to be. He'd locked his talon-like claws on the Ridonne's shoulders, and as they tumbled through damp, frosty dead leaves, he stared into his eyes, willing him to be afraid. He might have seen a flicker of doubt in those golden orbs, but the man held firm, hacking his sharp, terribly heavy sword into Victor's side.

Victor wanted to fight, wanted to rip that arm off and shove that sword down the imperial's throat, but he felt that godawful pang again, and he knew he must hurry back to the encampment. In those desperate seconds, while they thrashed and struck at each other, he began to imagine Valla in danger,

Deyni being killed, and Thayla being taken. "Enough!" he roared, and, acting on pure instinct, he pushed the massive torrent of fear-attuned Energy out of his Core into his pathways and willed himself to take flight.

A new kind of shriek erupted from Victor's throat—louder, higher-pitched, and loaded with primal memories that stirred the bowels of all those who tarried nearby, turning them to water and pausing the very beats of their hearts. Once again, he felt his limbs stretching and changing. He felt the fur coating his shadowy, skeletal form fall away, replaced by more of the glossy black feathers, and then, with yet another terrible shriek, he raked his talons down the Ridonne's chest, rending his fancy armor and tearing deep, festering grooves through his flesh.

As the imperial cried out and released him, Victor snapped his massive, shadowy wings and launched himself into the black night. The Ridonne sobbed, rolling to his side, writhing in agony. Blood turned black from corruption seeped out of the deep, horrible wounds in his chest. With wide, panicked eyes, he scanned the sky, looking for the monstrosity that had wounded him so, marring his perfect flesh and ruining his peerless armor. Only darkness met his gaze, and that fear, that feeling he'd only felt a hint of before, grew in his chest, darkening his heart and bringing a cold sweat to his flesh.

Victor knew none of that. He didn't bother to look back at the golden warrior. He didn't care. His people needed him, and he could see why. From his new winged vantage, he saw hundreds of dark, twisted shapes leaping over the barriers outside the encampment. He cracked his wings again, shrieking his fury at their audacity, and then he dove, streaking like a nightmare raven as it swooped to snatch a mouse. He crashed into one of the contorted figures. His talons gripped opposite shoulders, and he ripped it in twain, showering the dark grass with blood and entrails.

Another figure charged past him, then another, and soon he saw there were nearly a dozen already fighting on the wall, battering the bright spirits—his allies. Understanding drove the hunger from his mind yet again, and Victor reached into his pathway, severing the spell tying him to the Aspect of Terror. As the magic left him and the shadows obscured his transformation back to his human form, Victor began to cast Banner of the Champion.

When the shadows fell away, Victor stood tall, and a blazing standard erupted behind his back, washing the blood-soaked plains in its glorious light. Victor lifted Lifedrinker, roaring his enthusiasm for battle. Before he joined the fray, before he leapt upon a cluster of the twisted men and women, he called forth his great bear totem, fueling him with a tremendous torrent of inspiration-attuned Energy. As the bear burst into being from a cloud of glimmering white-gold motes, Victor urged his companion to slaughter the twisted men and women assaulting the encampment. Then he used Titanic Leap to send himself flying toward the nearest parapet.

Now that his vision had returned to normal, he noted the red-orange glow all around and realized the soldiers hadn't stood idly by to be slaughtered. Fires burned out on the plains where they'd launched fireballs at the charging, horribly mutated men and women. "What the fuck are these things?" Victor roared as he split one in half with his axe. The being was clearly once a Shadeni, though he'd been twisted beyond easy recognition. He had a long, tooth-filled lower jaw, one eye much larger than the other, and a weird, twisted horn that grew from one side of his head, winding around the back to jut out the other side. His body was similarly disfigured—one limb larger than the others ending in an enormous, clawed paw.

As Victor smashed one and then two of the creatures to bloody fragments, the soldiers nearby cheered and redoubled their efforts. He didn't know what had happened to these people and no longer cared. Victor charged at another group of the monstrosities, hacking them to bits and spreading the bolstering effect of his banner. He felt an urgent need to go farther into the camp, and he jumped from the wooden parapet, landing with a ground-shaking thud near the central pathway. He saw a great cluster of the twisted humanoid figures, hundreds of them, not far away, and ran at them. A glimmering, lightning-wreathed sword flashed among them, and he knew it was Valla.

Victor roared, cast Energy Charge with rage-attuned Energy, and exploded over the ground, erasing the distance between himself and the monstrous figures. He was easily three times the mass of one of the weird, misshapen people, and when he crashed into the crowd of them, he sent several careening into others with such force that the impact split their flesh and pulverized their bones. The chain of collisions was so violent that when Victor recovered from the rapid movement to look for Lifedrinker's next target, he saw that he'd killed several and wounded twice as many.

Valla, Rellia, and Lam fought back-to-back-to-back, Edeya lay broken and bleeding at Lam's feet, and Borrius crouched, shielding his head near Rellia. Victor realized he was lucky he hadn't smashed any of the aggressors into his friends, but he only thought about it for a second; he had work to do. He and Lifedrinker began to dance, then, and what a bloody waltz it was! He worked among the horror-born men and women, cutting limbs, cleaving necks, and smashing through skulls, painting himself, his friends, and the nearby tents red with sprays of hot, misty blood.

The attackers were fearless, unrelenting, and willing to fight with mortal wounds. Victor knew men and women were dying all over the encampment, but he also knew the greatest number of the monsters were there, at that location, trying to kill the leaders of his army. In the clarity of battle, he'd come to realize the pangs he'd felt were from his Battle Awareness feat, urging him to go where he was most needed, and he felt nothing from it now; he was exactly where he should be.

His banner and his arrival greatly bolstered Valla, Rellia, and Lam. When he cleared a swath to them, giving them the freedom to stop guarding their backs, they went on the offensive, and the disfigured one-time soldiers began to dwindle in numbers as the fierce women helped him cut them down. The monsters were tough, mentally and physically—Victor's banner didn't seem to affect them, but it didn't matter; it did its other job perfectly, encouraging and strengthening his friends and, more importantly, all the soldiers in the camp. Even if they were too far from him to get the direct magical benefit, anyone within a mile of him could see that Victor was fighting the monsters, that his banner stood and blazed.

As was his habit, Victor roared and screamed as he crushed, cleaved, battered, and threw the attackers. Echoing him, out on the grasslands, his great, brilliant, inspiration-born bear did the same, and Victor found his love of battle and joy in conquest wouldn't allow him to keep from laughing like a madman during his slaughter. As the creatures mounted the wall, most were killed by the troops atop it. Those that fought their way through, leaping down to charge toward Borrius and Rellia, met their demise on the end of Victor's axe, the edge of Valla's sword, the point of Rellia's rapier, or the terrible smashing Energy of Lam's warhammer.

The stream of mutated men and women became a trickle, and when the last of them died screaming and crying with Lifedrinker draining them of Energy, a break appeared in the black night, and sunlight slipped through. Throughout the encampment, soldiers and civilians began to cheer, and Victor, heaving for breath and grinning wildly, allowed his Iron Berserk to fade. He was nearly out of rage-attuned Energy.

Leaning on Lifedrinker, leaving her buried in the monster's chest, he watched as Lam rushed to Edeya and administered a swirling golden potion to the girl's pale, colorless lips. Victor's joy of battle rapidly faded as he saw the poor injured Ghelli, remembering all he'd done to save her back in the

Greatbone Mine. He began to wonder how many other allies had died or been injured in the attack.

He started toward her, but then, like a secondary sunrise, golden motes gathered on the hundreds of corpses nearby and the hundreds out on the plains and the walls. As the System determined the battle over, the reaping of rewards was nigh and soon those globes of Energy coalesced, streaming over the plains, through the camp, and into the victors. True to his name, Victor was the clear champion when it came to tallying the killing. A torrential river of Energy rushed through the brightening dark, washing him with its current, lifting him into the air, and filling him with its power.

Messages from the System began to fill his vision, and while he hung in the air, helpless to do anything else, he read through them:

Congratulations! You have achieved level 51 Battlemaster and gained 10 strength, 9 vitality, 4 agility, 4 dexterity, 3 will, and 3 intelligence.

Congratulations! You have earned a Class spell: Guard Ally, Basic.

Guard Ally, Basic: You expend some Energy to create a barrier around a nearby ally for a short time, transferring damage they take to yourself. You will suffer double the damage intended for your ally. Energy Cost: 100. Cooldown: Long.

Congratulations! You have learned the spell: Aspect of Terror, Advanced.

Aspect of Terror, Advanced. Prerequisite: Affinity, Fear or related Affinity. You change your appearance to represent something terrifying, an aspect molded from the deep roots of your primogenitors. Using the force of your will, you have refined this form, mastering it and shaping it into something truly terrible that sparks fear in the hearts of those who behold it. While wearing this form, you will passively harvest and cultivate fear-attuned Energy emanating from those who perceive you and cannot resist your will. Energy Cost: Minimum 100, scalable. Cooldown: Long.

Congratulations! You have learned the spell: Impart Nightmare, Basic.

***Impart Nightmare, Basic: While wearing your Aspect of Terror, using gathered fear-attuned Energy, you can corrupt the spirit of another being with a seed of fear, sending it to dwell in their Core where it will grow and fester. This ability will fail upon those whose will can resist your

intention. Energy Cost: Minimum 100, scalable. Cooldown: Dependent on harvested fear.***

When he came down, Victor glanced at Edeya and saw she was standing, leaning on her knees, apparently recovered. Even so, he saw she was missing two of her four wings, and his heart ached for her. Lam was leaning close, speaking softly to her, and he knew there wasn't anything he could say at that moment to make her feel better. In any case, he wouldn't have had the chance—Valla hurried to him and smashed him into a hug.

"You made it back!"

"Of course," he said, pulling her tight, savoring the feel of her, even through their combined wyrm-scale armors. "Come on. We need to see how many we lost. What the fuck are these things?" he asked for the second time, nudging one of the dead monstrosities with his boot.

"They're imperial soldiers," Borrius said, walking over to them, running a hand through his blood-slicked hair.

"What?"

"The pact." Valla's voice was quiet, almost hushed.

"Exactly. Just as we made our soldiers sign a contract, so does the Imperial Legion. Theirs has harsher consequences for desertion than ours."

"They were deserting?" Rellia asked, coming to join the conversation.

"I guess so," Victor said. "I could feel them fleeing, the soldiers out there. I mean, not all of them, but a lot. So, their contract did this to them?"

"The commanders of their army would have to invoke it, but yes." Borrius didn't seem upset; in fact, he wore a savage grin as he continued speaking. "Judging by how many broke through the soldiers on the walls, there must have been a thousand or more. This will profoundly affect their morale, much greater than just the number of losses. A thousand dead imperials is wonderful, but thanks to the fear you invoked, we aren't looking at a thousand dead foot soldiers. We're looking at a mix of soldiers, officers, and even cavalry."

"Roots!" Lam looked up from where she'd been tending to Edeya. "He's right. Look here." She pointed to a nearby corpse. "He's wearing captain's livery."

"We should talk about what's next." Victor eyed Edeya, still leaning against Lam, her cheek on her shoulder, looking away from the group of commanders.

"Can you tell us about their numbers? Their fortifications? Anything?"

"Nothing concrete." Victor shrugged, then tried to elaborate, "It's not that I'm trying to be difficult. It's just that when I'm in that form, when the spell takes hold, I'm different. When I come out of it, the things that happened are like a dream. A nightmare. I'm pretty sure I fought the other Ridonne, but I knew there was trouble here, so I left him." Victor paused, his face puzzled as he tried to remember the details, then he glanced at the sky, at the rapidly diminishing black clouds, and said, "Holy shit, I was fucking flying."

32

A LULL

Pazra-dak looked at Rosh, writhing on his bed, sheets tangled around him, soaked in sweat. His eyes rolled in his sockets, bloodshot and wide. Some living terror wracked his mind, driving him to gibber and froth, his once handsome face nothing but a sick caricature of itself. What had that devil done to him? "Brother. Speak to me. What do you see? What torments you so? Your wounds are healed. The scars, while severe, will fade with time and bloodline advancements."

"It comes! Devil! Wings! Hide! Must hide . . ." He turned and buried his face in the mattress, pulling his wet sheets toward his golden, hairless skull.

Pazra whirled and screamed at Bothelio-dak, the highest-ranking surgeon in their combined armies, "What are you doing to fix this?"

"It's a sickness of the mind, lord! Something has corrupted him, tainted his spirit. Perhaps your aide, the Wanact witch . . ." His words were lost as Pazra struck him with the back of his hand, knocking a tooth loose and sending the fool sprawling.

"Only I will refer to her as such. She is not available, but when she is, rest assured, she will mend this great man's spirit." Pazra looked around his tent at the crestfallen tribunes, the useless legate. He opened his mouth to speak but paused, listening to the distant screams and roars coming from the upstart's encampment. "And why have you not attacked? Why have you not seized this opportunity to follow on the heels of the pact breakers?" His words were spoken to the room, but Legate Ghel-dak knew they were for him.

"Lord," he started, his once haughty voice tremulous. "Our lines are in disarray. Many of the pact breakers were officers. I fear any assault now would be haphazard and lead to massive losses. The, um, upstart's troops seem to be handily crushing the pact breakers. To attempt to capitalize now would lead to . . ."

"Silence!" Pazra waved his hand in disgust, pacing back and forth near the mewling, broken shadow of a man that used to be his glorious brother. His mind worked furiously, wondering where Senena was, why she hadn't come to him, why she didn't know he needed her help. "Damned witch!" he hissed.

"Lord!" a new voice said, interrupting his fuming reverie. He whirled, looking for the one who'd spoken, and saw it was one of the lieutenants, one of the command book scribes.

"What?"

"Captain Chelna reports that the Wind Casters have failed to maintain the clouds. They were exposed to the horror that roamed the ranks. Many were breaking, fleeing, and the pact invocation cost us nearly half their number."

"Ancestors *damn* it!" Pazra roared, smashing a huge, black-clawed fist onto the table where he kept his map. The blow broke the support arm that held up the leaf, and it flopped to the floor, spilling his map and scattering the carefully placed markers. As his aides scurried to clean the mess, he paced, trying to think of a plan. What would he do? His brother would know. Pazra looked at the broken man and almost screamed again, almost struck something. He had to do something before he lost control of the armies. When his brother's legion learned of his condition, would they hold firm? They had better! "Well?" he said, whirling on his command staff.

"Lord?" Ghel-dak asked.

"*Lord?*" Pazra mocked. "You worthless bastards! What would you do if I weren't here? Our lines crumble, we've lost the darkness, and their hellspawn beast has brought low one of the Ridonne, one of our greatest! Do we have an accurate headcount? The creature seems to have retreated or left—do we have any men remaining? What will you do to manage that gigantic mongrel that I fought on the plains? My brother won't be much help at this rate!" He gesticulated madly while he ranted, pointing left and right and finishing with a flourish at his pathetic brother.

"Lord, I believe it would be best to stall for time. We need to regroup, to gather our men, fill in the gaps in command, and, hopefully, find a way to help your brother."

"And how shall I do that? How shall I stall?"

"You must bluff," one of his tribunes said, jumping in to rescue the foolish legate. Pazra motioned for him to continue, and the slight, neatly dressed man said, "Act as though the removal of the clouds was done as a gesture of goodwill, a chance for them to gather their corpses and consider your offer."

"My offer?"

"Yes, lord. We're here because the noblewoman has raised a full legion without imperial sanction. She's been overheard speaking about imperial corruption. Tell her she can turn herself over, disband this illegitimate army, and we'll let those she deluded with false promises walk away, their lives intact."

"What is your name, Tribune?" Pazra stalked menacingly toward the man, looming imposingly over him and the two aides by his side.

"I am Venis-dak, lord."

"Venis-dak, I hereby promote you to legate. Ghel-dak will serve as your second."

"Lord!" Venis said, clapping his fist to his chest in a sharp salute.

Victor watched the dark, ominous clouds drift through the sky, a stiff breeze helping to undo the work of the Ridonne army's casters. He let his gaze fall to the wrecked airship outside the western fortifications—Rellia's ship, *Balestar*. It had finally limped home, smoking and with a much lightened crew, carving a trench in the ground as it slid to a crash landing. The surviving sailors had spun quite a tale about a flying squadron of imperial troops that had attacked *The Petal*, overpowered its crew and then turned their Energy-driven ballistae on the *Balestar*.

Rellia's ship didn't go down easily, though, and ended up winning the engagement, though it had barely made it home. "Two weeks?" he grunted, looking down at Lieutenant Darro.

"That's what the engineers say, sir. Two weeks to get that ship back in the air."

"Assuming the army besieging us doesn't do more damage in their attack." Victor stretched, cracking his back noisily as he scanned the distant horizon. Even here, facing westward into the grasslands, he could see the line of encircling troops, their fortified trench lines, and fires. Smoke lazily drifted into the pale sky. Changing the subject, he asked, "How's Edeya?"

"She puts on a brave face, sir, but Lam has given her light duty. I'm told she almost died."

"Yeah, she looked dead when I joined the fight. I'm glad she was only injured."

"Aye, sir, but to a Ghelli, the injury is rather bleak. I know she couldn't fly yet, but she'd had hopes."

Victor frowned at the words and said, "That's nothing to worry about. When she advances her race sufficiently, she'll grow new wings, right?"

"I believe so, though such advancements are few and far between . . ."

"Bullshit. If we were in town, I'd buy her what she needs right now. Hey, do me a favor. Go find her and send her to my travel home. I've got a job for her while we've got a lull in the action."

"Aye, sir!" Darro turned to hurry away, but Victor grasped his shoulder.

"Hold on. After you do that, find Valla and the other commanders and tell them where I am, but then go to the Shadeni encampment and tell their Ban-tok I'd like a word. Lead him to my travel home."

"Understood," Darro said, and when Victor released his shoulder, he walk-jogged toward the wooden rampart steps and charged down them. Victor turned and started in the same direction at a much more relaxed pace. It wasn't that he was particularly at ease; being surrounded by enemies, knowing they could attack at any time, gave him a certain baseline of stress that would probably have been overwhelming a year ago. These days it felt like just another day.

Borrius was sure the imperials wouldn't attack that day, arguing that they'd need time to reestablish chains of command and formulate an organized strategy. His money had been on an attack coming the following day at dawn. Victor wasn't so sure; the Ridonne seemed to like the dark, and he wondered if they wouldn't wait until Victor's army was lulled into a false sense of ease, expecting a morning assault, and then strike in the middle of the night. In any case, Victor had left that discussion and plans for further fortifications and prep work to other commanders. He'd wanted to walk around the wall, take stock of things, and let the troops feel his presence.

The sky still seemed overcast, but, wrinkling his nose, he knew much of that was due to the pyres the troops had built on each side of the encampment. They were burning huge piles of imperial soldiers with magical flames. Of course, the dead, twisted men and women had been searched first, their magical talismans, weapons, and storage devices collected by the quartermaster and his assistants. Victor reminded himself to ask how such things might be distributed.

When he got to his travel home, set up on a slight rise near the southern central portion of the encampment, he noticed that Rellia's vidanii and Uvu were tethered near her travel home, next door to his. "So, Valla and her mother are having a conference." He shrugged and went into his house. He felt like being alone or at least only seeing certain people. The night's activities had taken a lot out of him, and the thought of listening to people discuss strategy and make demands of him seemed a bit much at that moment. "Time for that in an hour or two."

He walked to his library and leaned over the map, making a liar of himself as he started trying to imagine the layout of the nearby land, the size of the imperial army, and what he could do to make up for the still huge gap in their numbers. He lifted Lifedrinker from her harness and set her on the table before him, gently caressing her dark, star-filled, living wood handle. "We counted eleven hundred corpses around the encampment. If we're optimistic and guess I killed hundreds more, say four hundred, which I have a hard time believing, that still leaves us outnumbered almost two to one."

Lifedrinker trembled under his touch, and he heard her sharp, smoky voice in his head. *"One or ten thousand—the numbers mean nothing. Can a thousand ants slay a great wolf? Kill them; if they begin to overwhelm you, depart. One such as thee cannot be held by such as they."*

"Ah, I know you know me better than that."

"Aye. You will not leave your pack. So, we must slay their alpha and take his pack."

"Shit, *chica*." Victor chuckled. "Were you a wolf in a past life?"

"I have memories from before I was me. The haft you made for me, that wood you caress in your mighty hands, love. It came from a great tree, standing tall and proud in a dreamy place where stars shone like lanterns in the night. I remember wolves, many, many wolves. I watched them—no, the tree watched them. I see dreamy memories of them challenging each other, loving each other, and raising pups to be new leaders and hunters. Love, you are like some of those great wolves. If you desire it, you can take your challenger's pack. If they won't have you, kill them or send them running—they should not tarry in your presence."

"Seriously?" Victor asked, stunned by Lifedrinker's verbose response. "I had no idea you could remember things from before you were . . . you. I remember the name of the place where this wood came from. The woodworker told me." Victor scratched at his jawline, searching for the memory. "Something Vale. Starlight? No, that's just me thinking of the image you painted in my mind. Coruscating." Victor snapped his fingers. "Coruscating Vale."

"It matters not what others call it. The name is the memory in my mind—blue grass, the breeze making the branches of my children dance beneath my boughs. The birds and animals that frolicked in my . . . Victor! Are you tricking me? Those aren't my memories; they're like the memories of a parent. My memories start with thee!" Lifedrinker sounded genuinely peeved, and Victor almost laughed, but he was too worried he'd offend her. Instead, he moved his hand to the Heart Silver of her blade and rubbed his thumb against the warm metal.

"Okay, *chica*. Okay. I didn't mean to confuse you."

If she had an answer for him, it wasn't forthcoming, at least not in time to keep Edeya from interrupting. The lieutenant had entered his home, and he heard her calling, "Victor? Legate, sir?"

"In here, Edeya. I'm alone, so drop the legate shit." He straightened up and watched as the young, diminutive Ghelli stepped into his library. She stood straight, her shoulders back, and he saw a new scar notching the pale brown eyebrow over her left eye. Her two left dragonfly wings stood out proudly from her back, but only jagged stumps were visible on the right side. He was proud of her in that moment, standing tall, putting on a brave face despite the injuries she'd just suffered.

"Hey, Victor." She offered him a half-hearted smile, one that evoked a lot of memories of Greatbone Mine and the times they'd been assigned to the same task, joking about other delvers on their team.

"It's been a long time since we were in the mine together. I mean, not *really* all that long, but it feels like a hundred years, yeah?"

"Yeah." She approached, stopping near the table. "Roots. If I'd known how you'd turn out, I would've treated you differently."

"Well, I'm glad you didn't."

She smiled again, then looked at the map, frowning. "You wanted me for something?"

"Yeah, I have a job for you. Just a sec." Victor ran a hand down his wyrm-scale hauberk, magically parting it, and then he began thumbing through the various pouches and little sacks hanging from his magical belt. "I collected a bunch of jewelry from those imperials back there near Fainhallow, the ones who tried to kill me," he said, untying the heavy, supple leather sack. "I know a bunch of it is magical, and I'm sure there are a few dimensional containers. You know, one of those guys was a princeps, and one was a consort or some shit—a woman meant to be one of the Emperor's wives."

"Yes—Chokodo-dak and Reesha-dak." Edeya nodded, then asked, "You didn't turn those things over when you handed off the prisoners?"

"Huh? Hell no. I killed those guys and captured the other two. These are my spoils. I mean, some belong to Valla, but she trusts me."

"I see." Edeya's eyes said she thought he should have shared the loot with Lam if no one else. Victor turned the sack upside down, spilling out the exquisite jewels, from Reesha's veil to the many rings and necklaces. Edeya gasped, "Roots!"

"Yeah. You can see from the quality of what they wear on the outside that the things inside the dimensional containers are probably pretty good. I want you to go through all this stuff and catalog it."

"Now?"

"You can take it with you. I trust you. If you're worried about being robbed or something, you can keep this stuff in my house and do your work here. Understood?"

"Yes, Victor. I can do that." Edeya nodded, and, with wide eyes and careful fingers, she began to gather up the jewels, putting them back into the sack.

"Now, I want to talk to you about something else."

"Yes?" Her voice was small as she continued to look down, slowly turning a beautiful diamond choker in the light.

"I don't want you to worry about your injuries."

That got her attention. Edeya dropped the choker and looked up at Victor, a startled expression on her face as though he'd said something alarming. She narrowed her eyes, her brows pulling together, and growled, "I . . . Victor, you have a way of saying the worst thing!"

"Ah! There's the old Edeya! Don't get mad, though! Hear me out, okay?" As if he were afraid she'd try to run away, he reached out and grasped her wrist, not hard, not forcefully. He just wrapped his big fingers around the slender, bone-thin appendage. When she didn't pull away and didn't say anything, he continued, "In my adventures, I've come across a lot of things that are probably considered very rare by people you've known—things even Lam would be amazed to see. I bet Lam tried to comfort you by saying she'd work to help you advance your race, yeah?"

"Yeah." Edeya's eyes started to well with moisture.

"Lisen to me. We're going to get all sorts of spoils on this campaign. These"—Victor lifted the sack from her hand and let it thunk down onto the table—"are just the start. I won't be surprised if one of those rich *pendejos* has just what you need in one of their rings—a racial advancement treasure. If you find one, I'll give it to you."

"Victor . . ." she started to protest, but he kept speaking.

"If you don't, we might find one after we defeat this army out there." He waved vaguely toward the wall. It didn't matter which direction; the army was all around them. "If we don't, then we might find one when we get to the Untamed Marches. If we still haven't found what you need, I'll go to a city, buy one or two or three, and get you fixed up better than ever. Do you understand me? You're my friend, Edeya, not just a lieutenant in my army. I take care of my friends." At his words, the tears brimming in her eyes began to stream down her cheeks, and Victor pulled her in, crushing her against his stomach.

"Oof!" She laughed, sniffing noisily. "I'm glad you opened your armor, but your body is hard as wood. At least you're warm." She wormed her arms around his waist and dug her face into his shirt, sniffing and sobbing, and Victor held her there for several minutes, happy he'd said the right thing for a change.

He was thinking about how to push her away without upsetting the perfect moment when he heard Valla call from his foyer, "Victor! Are you here?"

"Yeah," he replied, gently extricating himself from Edeya's grasp. Her face was a mess, red and puffy, and her eyes bloodshot, but she seemed happy.

She smiled at him. "Thank you, Victor. Thank you for looking out for me so many times."

"Bah." He chuckled and jostled her shoulder. "I only saved you once or twice, right? I'm sure you kept me out of trouble just as many times."

"Victor!" Valla said from the doorway, her voice breathy as though she'd been running.

"Yeah?" He looked at her, raising an eyebrow.

"The Ridonne is out in the grasslands. He's flying a parley flag; he wants to talk."

33

PARLEY

Victor sat atop a titan-sized Guapo, dwarfing his companions and their mounts. Rellia rode to his left, Valla and Borrius to his right. Borrius, like Rellia, rode a vidanii, a beautiful creature with dark gray hair and shorter horns than those on Starlight and Thistle. It was barded in glittering brass-colored chain armor, a showy creature, clearly never before used in an actual battle by Borrius, but still impressive looking. "Do you think he knows who I am?" Victor asked, nodding toward the distant figures waiting under a bright blue standard—the Empire's signal for parley.

"He knows much about you, no doubt. He's fought you, for one thing," Rellia said—they'd seen through her spyglass that it was the spiked Ridonne, the burly, tough bastard Victor had tussled with outside of Persi Gables, who'd come to talk. The other two beside him, riding simple armored roladii, were Shadeni, both wearing Legion regalia. "He no doubt has spies among the nobility in Persi Gables and Gelica, and the Ridonne are well known to have powerful augurs in their ranks."

"Despite all that, I'd like you and Borrius to do the speaking. I'll listen and interject when I think it will be effective. I may just lurk behind you and glower the whole time. Don't prompt me to speak. Act like I'm not there."

"A clever ploy." Borrius nodded. "Keep them guessing about his standing among us."

"Don't attack them." Valla's words were soft, clearly meant for only Victor. Of course, the others could hear her, but they held their tongues, and Victor wondered if this had been discussed earlier; were they leaving the dirty work up to Valla?

"I know what parley means, Valla."

"I'm sorry." She reached up fruitlessly; his hands were well out of her reach while he rode the gigantic mustang.

"No worries." He chuckled. "I've done some boneheaded things in my day. You guys don't suppose he's here to surrender, do you?"

"The Empire doesn't surrender," Borrius said, but then he amended himself. "Not mere mortals in the Legion, at least. Perhaps a Ridonne could suffer a loss and not be killed outright."

"Mortals?"

"The Ridonne view themselves as something more than the rest of us. They think their bloodline makes them special and gives them the license to treat us as lesser beings, even though anyone who improves their race enough could extend their lives similarly. I suppose it comes from them having access to more racial advancements than most of the populace. Some say the Emperor has been alive since the forming of Fanwath."

"Ha. What is that, four hundred years?" Victor scoffed. "They should meet the Warlord, eh, Valla?"

"I hope not. I'd hate for them to learn the things he knows."

"Shit. No kidding." Victor scowled, memories of his time in Coloss flashing through his mind.

"If he doesn't wish to surrender, the best we can hope for, Victor, is for you to goad him into an early assault. If the moment seems right, don't hesitate to impugn his honor or to give him an ultimatum that may push him into hasty action."

"Is that wise?" Rellia looked at Borrius, eyebrows arched. Victor could see she was irritated at not being consulted about Borrius's machinations.

"I believe so. The more time they have to recover and prepare, the less we can hope to seize from the boon their losses in the night granted us. We should be quiet, however. We're close enough for good ears to hear us now." Borrius demonstrated his caution by speaking in a harsh whisper.

Victor grunted his agreement, and everyone stopped talking. He watched the Ridonne's raptor-like mount grow larger as the distance closed. It was an impressive creature, but he thought it looked ugly and small compared to Guapo. Its bumpy flesh was dark black, but the orange and yellow stripes on its side and head were kind of neat, he had to admit. It had a broad, flat skull and big, vertically slit eyes that shone amber in the bright sunlight—the black clouds had nearly all drifted away.

As they came to a stop a dozen yards from the Ridonne's delegation, Rellia in the middle, Valla and Borrius flanking her, and Victor looming largely behind, the Ridonne said, his voice booming, "Rellia ap'Yensha, I presume?"

"That's correct. I'd love to hear your name and reason for using an imperial army to attack my troops unlawfully."

"I am Pazra-dak, and nothing I do on these lands is unlawful, for I am Ridonne." His mount fidgeted and snorted through its slit-like nostrils, its thick hide pulling back from a dense row of dagger-like teeth. A low growl rumbled in its chest, but Pazra-dak jerked his reins, and it quieted.

"Ridonne you are, sir, but we're at a loss." Borrius gently stroked the neck of his beautiful vidanii, calming it in the face of the enormous raptor's show of hostility. "Would you be kind enough to explain why your army has been so hostile? Surely the murder of small children can't serve to further the storied history of this great Empire."

"Where a threat to this Empire exists, I cannot afford to be sentimental. Come, ap'Yensha, do your people not know why we are here? Will you feign ignorance?"

"I cannot feign that which is genuine, Lord Pazra-dak." Rellia's brows turned down in a scowl. Her vidanii hadn't budged, standing stock-still, and Victor had to admire her poise in the face of the Ridonne's accusation. He was an intimidating figure, golden armor gleaming, black spikes protruding from his shoulders and legs, but most of all, his great bulk dwarfed the others—all save Victor.

"Your family was granted a Writ of Conquest, yes?"

"More than a century ago, sir."

"And in that Writ, were the restrictions on household army sizes waived?"

"Household army sizes . . ." Rellia genuinely sounded puzzled.

"There is no household in the Ridonne Empire that may raise a levy of more than three thousand soldiers. Nor can any combination of households put together their levies to circumvent that limit."

"Lord Pazra-dak, the citizens were enthusiastic about a push into the Untamed Marches!" Borrius interjected. "How well known is that limitation? Has anyone tested it? I've never heard such a rule in all my days—"

"No one has tested it because it would be madness. Such an openly hostile act against the Empire is tantamount to suicide. Yet here I am, ready to enforce it." Pazra spoke loudly, quickly, cutting Borrius off.

"Sir," Rellia tried again, "if there is such a law, it is not in any book or code that sits in the very extensive libraries of house ap'Yensha!"

"If? Do you call me a liar, woman? Let us set aside that transgression. Will you deny the reports coming out of Gelica that you've openly spoken to members of your family about, and I quote, 'corruption in Tharcray'?"

"I . . ."

"You cannot deny it, can you? Lady, trust me when I say I can smell a lie." He paused and looked at each member of Victor's party, staring at them for long seconds—everyone except Victor; when their eyes met, Pazra smirked and quickly moved his gaze to Valla. "Will you see your daughter die here on these plains, Rellia? Will you see the many thousands of fools who've come to follow you die to appease your ill-formed, sentimental idea that there's been some sort of mishandling of justice? Turn yourself over, and all these people may walk away with their lives. Even this brute who dared to cross blades with me. I'll favor him with my benevolence and presume he knew not whom he faced."

Again, Rellia started to speak, "I . . ." and again, she was interrupted, this time by Valla.

"Absolutely not!" Uvu took two quick lunging steps toward the Ridonne, growling in that deep, throaty rumble that only a great cat can make.

"Tribune Valla, calm yourself and your beast," Borrius barked.

"Yes, young woman," Pazra said, glowering at her. It was good, Victor mused, that he looked at Valla and not at him. Victor felt sure his glowering expression was enough to either send the Ridonne into retreat or spur him into a fight.

"If you think we'll stand idly while my mother sacrifices herself for us, you've very little understanding of the loyalty this army has to her." Valla jerked Uvu's reins while she spoke, wrestling the angry cat back under control and getting him to back up a few paces.

"Is the army so loyal they'll throw down their lives?" Pazra scoffed.

"They are," Borrius said, voice calm and cultured. "They are very loyal, and more than that, they are weary of supping on the dregs of the Empire. We'll claim our lands in the Untamed Marches, or we'll die fighting for that right."

"You sound confident," Pazra said, "but I've known confident men to be wrong. Are your men so eager to die after what they experienced in the dark?"

"Surely you jest." This time it was Borrius who scoffed. "We suffered very light casualties while slaughtering more than a thousand of your troops. No, forgive me, not just troops. We counted more than fifty officers among your dead. Tell us true, Pazra"—the Ridonne bristled at Borrius's omission of an honorific—"are you here to try to coax a surrender because your army is in disarray?"

"Ha!" Pazra forced a laugh, but Victor saw the twisted grimaces on his companions' faces. They weren't so good at bluffing. "I assure you, I could command this army without *any* officers. I am Ridonne. My bloodline is gifted with leadership abilities that will make crushing a much, much smaller army trivial. Now, speak, Rellia! Are you ready to hand yourself—"

"This is bullshit," Victor growled, letting his voice rumble deep in his chest.

"Excuse me? Bull . . . shit?"

"Yeah, Pazra. You're scared shitless right now. I know it because I can taste it coming off you like a stench, like a sick, sticky, rotten fish odor. Where's the other one? The tall, pretty one. The one I fucked up last night?"

"You!" Pazra's eyes widened, and despite Victor's antagonistic, disrespectful tone, rather than shout obscenities or threats, rather than charge forward to confront someone speaking to him in a way he'd probably never experienced, he shrank back, and in that moment, everyone could see the fear behind his eyes, not only Victor.

"That's right," Victor said, flooding his pathways with dark, purple-black fear-attuned Energy and releasing his aura so it fell, heavy as a lead blanket, on everyone around him, causing the mounts to fidget and whine and their riders to groan uncomfortably, even his allies. Victor leaned forward, his entire form limned in black, smoky shadows, and growled, "I'm going to give you one warning and one chance, Pazra. Take your troops, every single one of them, and flee this place. Slink away like the child-killing worms you are, and I won't hunt you down and kill you tonight."

When Victor paused, to gather his thoughts and take a breath, Pazra opened his mouth to speak, but Victor snapped, "Don't speak! Listen! Take your fucking army and leave this place, or I swear, I'll come again each night that you try to lay siege to us, and I will kill you in the darkness. I'll kill you and every officer in your army." He nodded to the two Shadeni flanking Pazra, shrinking back from Victor and his dark aura. "I'll kill them, and I'll drive your men to madness, bleeding your army, drinking the fear that pours out of you until there's nothing left." Victor let Guapo know what he wanted with a thought, and the horse pranced forward, snorting, stopping just in front of Rellia and Borrius.

He reached down and rested a hand on Lifedrinker's haft, then he said, "Borrius, how many days can you hold our fortification against an army, even one twice our size?"

"Days? I can hold our position for weeks." Victor was proud of the firmness in the older man's voice and reassessed his earlier opinion that the man wasn't as strong as he was clever.

"It will be a matter of days before I've destroyed your army, Pazra. If you think I'll hand Rellia over for some bullshit charges, some hearsay from jealous nobles in Gelica, you need to think again. I'll tell you this one time: we're not interested in your Empire. We're not interested in your family. We're heading outside these lands, and if you or anyone from Tharcray or the Imperial Legion come to try to stop us, we'll destroy them, and if any more of my people are harmed, I'll take the fight to the capital. I won't stop until the Ridonne are a memory, forgotten and cursed like the Yovashi. Take this chance, this one chance, to save yourself and the poor, foolish soldiers who follow you." He spun Guapo, the great mustang's hooves sparking, to face the others. "Let's go."

Victor watched as Rellia, face pale and eyes wide, turned her vidanii and started to ride back toward the encampment, Borrius and Valla right behind her, then he spun and faced Pazra again. "You've got until morning tomorrow to break your siege and march north. Not south, not into the forest, and not east or west. You need to get your asses farther into the Empire."

"How *dare* you!" Pazra managed to hiss, his pinched, reddish-gold face darkening as it flushed with blood.

"How dare I? For too long your family has monopolized true power in this world. Think about it. How would you treat Rellia if I weren't here? How would you act right now if I hadn't visited you in the dark and destroyed the morale of your troops and if you hadn't thrown away a huge number of them because they had the audacity to fear me? Imagine what you'd do to Rellia. Now understand that I can do the same to *you*, and I really want to, Pazra. Believe that. When the sun rises in the morning, if your army isn't marching, I will come out of that encampment, I will find you, and I will kill you."

Guapo lifted his front hooves, whinnied loudly, and then charged after the others, leaving Pazra and his lackeys to watch with mouths agape. When he caught up, Rellia looked at him, something like fear in her eyes, and said, "I can't believe you just threatened the entire imperial family."

Victor pulled back his aura and let his Core absorb his fear-attuned Energy. Then he said, "I mean, could I really make things worse?"

"No." Borrius chuckled. "I don't believe he'll take his army away, however. No, I believe he'll muster his troops and attack us with everything he has. Excellent job, Victor; he'd never be able to live down such a disgrace. No, he'll gather his forces, his allies, and he'll try to win a decisive victory tonight."

"I thought maybe he'd be scared enough to bail. I *am* going to kill him if they don't leave."

Borrius nodded to Victor, smiling. "You did us a favor. Rather than wear us down, saving his troops, he'll come at us madly, and his soldiers are, indeed, going to be wary—after his losses in the dark, we'll have a good chance."

"We have more than a chance," Valla said. "If Victor rides forth and kills that giant bastard, they'll break."

Pazra fumed. He rode atop Xinz, the great raptor his father had purchased from the world of Era'neh, and he contemplated murder. He *wanted* to kill that bastard giant who'd dared to speak to him with such insolence, but he wasn't sure he could. That doubt troubled him the most; had the brute been right? Was Pazra afraid? If he didn't think he could win, he must contemplate flight, and if he genuinely took that possibility seriously, he had to consider the men who rode with him. At the very least, he would have to murder them. Better he murder all his commanders and blame the rebel army. He knew the folly of that road, though; his mother would see through his lies.

Pazra looked at his two tribunes. They avoided his gaze, eyes down, no doubt wondering if they were about to die. "Do not speak of this meeting. It will further degrade our morale. I will know, and I swear to you, if you utter one word of that mongrel's ultimatum, I will have your hearts fed to Xinz."

"Yes, lord!" they both said in unison.

He waved their words away and continued, speaking calmly—regally, if he were any judge. "Of course, I'll ignore that buffoon's demands. We'll crush these worms. I don't care how strong he is; he won't stand against my brother and me."

"Is the prognosis good, then, lord?" Venis-dak asked, and Pazra decided to indulge him; after all, the man had shown promise.

"Even now, Senena works with him. She will purge the poison from his mind, have no doubt."

"Wonderful news, lord. We'd feared she'd been lost in the fray . . ."

"Fool," Venis said, distancing himself from Ghel-dak. "Lord, I had no such fear."

Pazra scowled at Ghel-dak and finally settled on sighing with displeasure. Let the man stew on things, wondering how angry Pazra was, how he might find himself punished when the time was right. He turned to Venis and said, "Get me a full accounting of the troops, make certain you've enforced new contracts on the promoted officers, and report to my tent in an hour. I will speak with Senena and my brother." Without awaiting a response, he urged his raptor to run, and soon he'd left the two men behind.

When Pazra entered his command tent, he stepped through the foyer and sitting room into the rear, curtained-off area where his bed, study, and bath lay. Through another curtain, he found Senena burning incense and muttering over the shivering form of his withered brother. "How goes it?"

She didn't answer at first, and he contemplated slapping her. He decided her aid of his brother was too important to interrupt. Perhaps she couldn't speak; she seemed strained, her lips rapidly moving as she feverishly muttered her nonsense. He stared at her for several long moments and was about to ask her again when her eyes shot open. She began to cough, a great racking cough that left her face dark purple and her eyes watering before it calmed. Wheezing, gasping for air, she looked up at him through the dark black hollows of her eyes.

"Well?" he pressed.

"He comes back to us. I fought the poison in him, took much of it, and destroyed it in my Core, but some still lingers and festers. He'll need my betters at the capital to make him well."

"Will he recover enough to fight?" Pazra eagerly stepped toward the bed, reaching down to grasp his brother's long, golden arm. It was clammy and cool. "Sickly." He tsked. "Unseemly."

"Brother," Rosh-dak croaked, cracking open one blood-washed golden eye. "Did we flee?"

"No, brother. We still encircle the upstart and her army."

"The nightmare, the . . . the beast . . ."

"Yes, brother. I know it hurt you."

"It's too strong. We must perform the rite, no matter the cost."

"The rite?" Pazra recoiled, released his brother's arm, and began to pace. He glanced at Senena and jerked his fist toward the curtain. "Get out." She ducked her head, the bones and charms clicking in her braids, and scurried away. Pazra looked at his brother and said, "Will you bear the cost?"

"I'm ruined, brother. I will bear it."

"So be it," Pazra said, and in that moment, he couldn't have been prouder to call Rosh-dak brother. A true champion of the Ridonne, a true, glorious paragon. It was time to make that bastard giant pay the price for his insolence!

34

A LOTTERY

"Well?" Victor stood to one side of his map table, looking around at his commanders. "Let's hear it." The lighting in his little library was comfortable on the eyes; a lamp above the table kept it well illuminated. Borrius, much recovered from his several brushes with death during the night, stood on one side of the map, frowning as he stroked his chin. Valla and Lam stood opposite him, and across from Victor was Rellia. Everyone stared at the map, and Victor wondered who would speak first. He'd been expecting it to be Rellia, but she'd grown quiet and introspective ever since the Ridonne had outed her as the reason for their army's current troubles.

"I have several ideas," Borrius said finally, clearing his throat and gesturing at the map currently on display—a close-up, hand-drawn depiction of their encampment and the surrounding grounds, all the way to the Blue Deep. The big paper had been marked, probably by Darro, with imperial troop locations as observed by the army's scouts.

"Well, let's start with your best one," Victor prompted.

"My best one? It involves a great deal of personal risk to you, Legate."

"Go on." Victor's words were almost instantaneous, heading off any protests from Valla or the others.

"I considered many ploys. However, we're rather limited by the terrain— no passes to take advantage of, no cover to speak of, and entirely surrounded by a larger force. We don't even have true fortifications. You're aware of all this, but I feel I need to explain my reasoning. If I could think of a clever ruse or feint, if I could devise some way to escape this encirclement without massive losses to our noncombatants, I wouldn't suggest what I'm about to say."

"Oh, for the love of . . . Out with it!" Lam growled.

"I suggest that we continue our entrenchment. We fight a massively defensive battle and stall for time while Victor charges forth and slays the Ridonne. I know you can thrash common soldiers, but we should wait for them to attack so that you aren't overwhelmed by sheer numbers. Even you cannot slay indefinitely, or am I wrong?"

"Ha. No, you aren't wrong. As my injuries mount and time drags on, my Energy fades. I could fight free, using my size and abilities, but if I want to fight one, or probably two, Ridonne, it would be hard if I had thousands of Tier Two soldiers on my back."

"They'll surround themselves with just such a force, and not only second tier; they'll pick out their best troops, Tier Threes and a few Fours. If they have ten thousand troops, they'll keep two thousand around the Ridonne." Valla thumped the table with her fingertips as she spoke.

"I had a similar thought." Borrius nodded, gesturing to the drawing of their encampment. "This might be a problem if we weren't so solidly entrenched, and if we didn't have an extra five hundred ranged fighters newly added to our ranks."

"The Shadeni clan." Rellia spoke for the first time in the meeting.

"Yes, so they'll help to bolster the defenses. What's that to do with Victor and his gambit against the Ridonne?" Lam asked.

"It will allow us to send troops with him," Valla said, nodding in understanding.

"Suicide!" Rellia shook her head. "Victor may be able to fight or *jump* free, but what of those troops? They'll be deep behind enemy lines, outnumbered . . ."

"I won't take a bunch of people to die so I can have an easier fight."

"Do you wish us to win this battle? Do you want to keep even greater numbers from dying?" Borrius's voice rose, brittle with disdain, scowling at Victor. "Sacrifices must be made in war! I hate to label them as sacrifices so bluntly, but the soldiers who go with you will risk everything to save the entire army."

"How many?" Rellia asked.

"An elite force of five hundred should do," Borrius immediately answered, clearly having thought his idea through to logical conclusions.

"And if I'm right, and thousands of troops guard the Ridonne?"

"Five hundred strong men and women can create a large enough perimeter around Victor for him to do his work. If they hold until he's won, there's no guarantee the imperials won't break, and many of those heroes will live to fight again."

"I'll lead them," Lam said, looking at Victor, meeting his eyes and nodding solemnly.

"Like hell!" Valla's eyes sparked with outrage. "I will lead them. You can come if you want."

"Valla . . ." Rellia started to say, then she stopped, looking at her daughter, looking *up* at her daughter, taking in her wyrm-scale armor and the determined, fiery look in her bright, green-blue eyes, and she shook her head. "I'll join you."

"Bah!" Borrius scoffed. "We cannot have all our commanders out there! Rellia, you must stay with me."

"Hold on a fucking minute," Victor growled, leaning his prodigious bulk on the table. "I didn't agree to this shit yet. I might go along with the idea, but first, we need to agree that only volunteers are going to join this fight. If we can't come up with five hundred volunteers, I'll go with however many we get. If Lam and Valla want to come, obviously I'd be a horrible hypocrite to try to stop them, but that doesn't mean I like it. Rellia, I agree with Borrius—we need you here."

"This isn't right." For the first time in a while, Victor saw genuine anger in Rellia's eyes. "This entire problem is because of me! Because I trusted the wrong people in my family, let my lips loosen with too much wine, and blathered about my distrust of the Empire, speaking my treason to traitorous boot lickers. I can end this now. Let me go to the Ridonne and accept his parley offer!" When she finished speaking, Rellia was looking at Valla again, staring into her eyes, tears pooling in her own.

"Absolutely not!" Valla growled.

"No." Borrius held up a hand, and to Victor's surprise, he was chuckling. "No, dear Rellia. Firstly, I promised your mother to protect you. Secondly, we"—he gestured around, obviously not meaning only those in the room, but everyone outside it, the entire army—"are not interested in having our conquest cut short. We will see victory here, and then we will see it again in the Untamed Marches. We'll have that, or we'll have death."

"You speak for everyone?" Rellia snapped.

"Indeed, I do! That's what it means to join a legion! Those men and women out there"—again he waved his hand in a big arc—"joined this endeavor for many reasons, but they all agreed to follow our command. We will *not* be stopped by these imperial *conscripts*." When he said "conscripts," he sneered, and Victor had a feeling it was an old insult.

"What do you mean? Conscripts? The Legion isn't voluntary?"

Lam looked at Victor and cleared her throat. "Not for everyone. I joined freely, though many in my station wouldn't have. Nobles, on the other hand"—she nodded at Valla—"usually enlist. Even so, many, many soldiers do not willingly sign up for war. They're recruited, and sometimes they're rather reluctant."

"We would crush Pazra-dak's army if another hadn't come to support him. If you kill the Ridonne, Pazra and the other, then we will crush them still. We'll have them fleeing before an hour passes if you cut the head off the snake." Borrius continued speaking as though the topic hadn't diverged.

"So?" Valla steered the conversation back on course. "How will we get our force through their main lines to defend Victor?"

"With a charge, with Victor as the spearpoint." Borrius pointed at the map, placing his finger near the gate of their encampment, and then drew a straight line over the grasslands to the drawing of a tent labeled "Ridonne."

"Cavalry? All of us?" Lam frowned, and Victor could see she was trying to wrap her head around the logistics.

"Do we have that many mounts?" Valla asked.

"No, closer to two hundred . . ." Rellia said, but then her eyes widened. "The Shadeni."

"Will they let us use their roladii? A few hundred?" Valla looked to Victor with her question.

"Yeah, they will, but it sucks we have to ask it of them."

"Their lives are just as dependent on this action as the rest of ours." Borrius shrugged. "If you could uncast the die that threw their lot in with ours, I'm sure you would, but there's no going back. The hunter clan is with us, for good or ill."

"Well," Victor said as he straightened up, "I've been putting off talking to Tellen and Thayla. I'll go do it now and break this news to them." He looked at Valla and Lam. "Gather the troops, and I'll address them in a few minutes, say half an hour." They nodded to him, and Victor turned to leave.

"Victor," Rellia said, and he turned back, raising an eyebrow. "Thank you. Thank you for not throwing me to the Ridonne, and thank you for risking yourself to try to win this confrontation."

"We'll win, Rellia. We'll win, and don't thank me. Thank the soldiers, though; I think it'll mean a lot coming from you." Victor hurried out of his home, and with purpose and haste, he made his way through the encampment to the Shadeni wagons and tents. He didn't have to announce himself—he was a spectacle going through the camp, receiving shouts of welcome and drawing a small crowd everywhere he moved. The Shadeni saw him coming, and one of them must have alerted Tellen and Thayla, for they were waiting when he walked between two large wagons.

"Victor!" Tellen rushed forward, Thayla behind him, wearing a less enthusiastic expression. "I've been hoping you'd find time to stop by!"

"I should have come sooner, Tellen, but I kept getting interrupted." Victor laughed at the absurdity of his words. "Well, you know what I mean."

"We saw your speech in the darkness. Saw you standing atop your wagon, stealing the hearts of our people." Thayla wore a slight smirk, betraying her real feelings. "Victor, did you punish them? Did you make them pay for what they did to our people?"

"I did, Thayla. I killed more than I can count. I drove them mad with fear until their vile contract twisted them into monsters and sent them here to be slaughtered. I know it wasn't all of them, and no matter how many there were, it will never bring back the people you lost, but I hope you'll feel some justice was done. I'm not finished, either."

"It wasn't your fault, brother." Tellen grasped his shoulder, and Victor smiled. Had Tellen ever called him brother before?

"Not directly, but I can't help feeling if we'd taken another route and if I hadn't been set on trying to recruit you to our cause, they never would have bothered you." He frowned and added, "I have more to ask of you, more pain to cause you."

"Out with it." Thayla stepped closer and dropped the haughty, angry act. "You know we'll help where we can."

"We need your people on the walls, anyone who can shoot a bow or throw ranged magic. Our fortifications won't hold without the number of troops we've designed them for, and I have to take almost a full cohort out on an attack—five hundred troops."

"You'll take five hundred against more than ten thousand? Don't look surprised—we have ears. We know their numbers." Thayla took Tellen's hand while she spoke, and Victor could see the worry in her eyes, the dark circles there. She'd been crying, probably consoling the families who'd lost loved ones in the flight from their winter camp.

"Yeah. I'm going to take five hundred and punch through their lines when they next attack. They're going to fight to give me a chance to kill the leaders, the Ridonne."

"They'll die . . ." Tellen said softly.

"Probably. At least a lot of them will, which makes my next ask a little hard."

"What?" Tellen pulled Thayla close as though using her to brace for Victor's bad news.

"To make a successful charge, we'll want mounts, and we don't have enough cavalry or enough mounts. We need—"

"You'll have them. However many roladii you require! We have nearly eight hundred here." He jerked his thumb back toward the Shadeni section of the encampment.

"Really? I'd thought you'd be more upset . . ."

"If you and your troops will risk your lives, then we can risk some livestock." Thayla sighed. "Don't you know us by now?"

"Yeah, of course I do. It's just that I feel shitty 'cause we've done nothing but bring you trouble so far. I'm going to make it up to you!"

"I know you will, Victor." Tellen held out his hand, and Victor engulfed it with his big fist, squeezing the man's wrist. "Tell me, though, why wait for their attack? Why not rush out now and attack their leaders?"

"The idea is that if they're mid-attack when we charge out, we won't have their whole army trying to stop me from killing the Ridonne—hopefully, just a couple of thousand. My troops will try to keep them off me while I fight." Victor shrugged; it made sense to him, but he didn't know if it was the right move. He was trusting Borrius to know how the imperials operated. "Anyway, if you wouldn't mind choosing three hundred roladii and driving them toward the gates, I have to go figure out which soldiers will go on this . . ." He almost said "suicide mission" but didn't want to be flippant about the lives his soldiers would be putting on the line. "Dangerous mission."

"Victor, be careful. Deyni is hoping to spend some time with you soon. Don't let her down." Thayla stepped forward and grasped his wrist with her two hands, holding on until he met her eyes. "Promise me."

"*Chingado*, Thayla! I can't promise! I promise I'll do everything I can to win and come back, okay?"

"No. Promise me you'll kill those bastards!" She squeezed his wrist, her nails digging into his skin, and Victor saw that she was raw with emotion, feelings she'd been holding down with the force of her will.

"I will fucking kill those bastards," he growled.

"That's more like it." She let him go, and Victor nodded, then turned, hurrying toward the encampment gate. Troops were already starting to gather; some were milling lazily toward the gate—soldiers on their free shift. Most, though, were being driven in perfect marching formation by their sergeants. Their discipline faltered whenever Victor walked by, and many called out greetings or cheered. A few howled, mimicking the horrible cry of his Aspect of Terror, and Victor couldn't help smiling at their boldness. He unslung Lifedrinker and lifted her high, meeting the soldiers' eyes and nodding as he strode past.

When he got to the gate, the other commanders were already standing on the parapet above it, and Victor broke into a jog, heading for some nearby stairs so he could join them. He stomped onto the reinforced wooden walkway, pleased by how sturdy it was—the engineers had been hard at work bolstering things with materials and Energy. When he stood at the center of the gate, looking back into the encampment, the troops were still gathering, and Rellia asked, "Were they receptive?"

"Yeah, we'll have our mounts, and their people will join our troops on the walls."

"That's excellent, Victor." Borrius pushed closer and nudged past Rellia. "Did they have any concrete numbers for you?"

"No, but it will be plenty. More than the five hundred you guessed. Most of the hunters are good with a bow."

"Excellent, excellent." Borrius nodded, pulling back, oblivious to the scowl Rellia had directed at him.

Valla, standing with Lam on Victor's left, asked, "Do you want us to speak?"

"Nah, I know what I'm going to say." He glanced around the platform, then, nodding, said, "You all should back up a pace or two. They hurried to comply, and Victor chuckled, then he cast Titanic Aspect, taking a deep, steadying breath as his perspective changed and the ground grew farther away. He heard a lot more muttering and even some scattered cheers from the troops, and he looked out over them, watching as the last few units marched into position. Nodding, he loosened his hauberk and reached in to pull out the voice amplifier Lam had given him.

After he activated it, he squared his shoulders and yelled, "Troops! Listen up." His voice boomed out and echoed over the encampment, and in its wake, silence reigned, silence so complete a cough to clear a throat stood out like a squalling child in a quiet room. "Thank you," Victor said, speaking normally, trusting the magic to carry his voice far enough. "We made it through the long, dark night! Congratulations on your victory, troops!"

Cheers and shouts answered that proclamation and Victor couldn't help smiling, couldn't help holding Lifedrinker high again, shaking her to more and more cheers. "They can hear you!" he roared. "They can hear you cheering, and they know fear! Trust me—they *know* fear!" When the double meaning of his words registered, the troops' cheering and stomping grew to thunderous levels, and Victor pumped Lifedrinker up and down, loving every minute of it. When he started to glow with a sparkling, golden aura, he realized he'd let glory-attuned Energy seep out of his Core, filling his pathways, and he laughed, shaking his head ruefully; he was a hound for glory. There wasn't any denying it.

"Listen now!" he roared, and the cheering and stomping almost instantly stopped. "Our expert on the Imperial Legion, Tribune Borrius"—Victor pointed to the older man who stood up straight and visibly began to perspire—"is quite certain the imperials will attack us with everything they have tonight or early in the morning. They will try to overwhelm us because they know damn well that we'll win in a drawn-out conflict." He paused for a moment to see his words register on the troops. He waited just long enough for them to start muttering, then he continued.

"We have a plan to break them, however. I'm going to ride forth with the greatest swordswoman in this army, my tribune primus, Valla." Victor reached down his mighty fist and snatched Valla's wrist between his thumb and forefinger, lifting her arm high. The soldiers began to cheer, but Victor held up a gigantic arm silencing them, then continued, "Not just us, though. We'll also ride with the mighty Tribune Lam." Something came over him, steeped in glory as he was, and he roared, "Lam the Empire Breaker! Valla Ridonne Bane!" He stepped to the side, almost stomping on Rellia and Borrius as they scurried back, and held his hands out, showcasing the two women.

His words had the desired effect; the troops went wild with cheers, breaking their formations, howling, waving weapons, and firing spells into the air to burst in every color and element. Valla glared at Victor but knew she couldn't rebuke him. She drew Midnight and held her high, and Lam spread her magnificent wings, lifting herself into the air, spreading her arms wide, apparently enjoying the glory. Victor watched them for a few moments, then, with a huge smile, he turned on the troops and roared, "That's not all!"

It took a moment for everyone to quiet down, but by the time Lam settled beside Victor, most of the muttering had dissipated. "We three will be riding out to kill the Ridonne who lead that army." Victor threw his great arm in a wide circle, indicating the distant troops. Again, the soldiers started to cheer, but he kept speaking, his voice booming over them. "We'll need some soldiers to ride with us, brave soldiers willing to pit themselves against a much larger force. We want volunteers because there's a good chance they'll die out there. I'll be busy fighting the Ridonne, and I need courageous, strong soldiers to keep the bastard imperials off my back." As his words died down, the troops were quiet, but they didn't look crestfallen; they looked as if they were holding their breath, eager to hear his next words.

"Do I have any volunteers?"

As the troops erupted with shouts and frenzied hand waving, and nearly every soldier and many of the noncombat personnel pushed forward, trying to be noticed by Victor, Borrius muttered, perhaps only for Rellia's ears, though Victor heard him, "They're going to kill each other fighting to join him. We'll have to have a lottery—an Ancestors-damned lottery to form a suicide unit."

35

SACRIFICE

Victor and his five hundred cavalry soldiers sat atop their mounts, arranged in a V pattern, outside the battlements of the army's encampment. He'd wondered at the wisdom of getting set outside the walls; wouldn't they make a target for all the Ridonne's troops? Borrius had come up with the plan to give them an obstacle-free charge at the enemy lines, however, and when Victor saw how it worked, he once again realized he needed to start wrapping his head around how things were different in wars that involved magic.

First, Borrius had ordered the engineers to clear a path for Victor's unit to charge through, removing pits, spikes, and barriers. They did their work under the guise of adding more such things, hiding their efforts with piles of grass and fresh dirt, making it look as if the clear runway was, in fact, riddled with traps. Then he'd called in the Air and Water Casters, giving them orders to gather fog around the entire perimeter of the encampment, and they'd done so, somehow forming a dense bank of thick mist that seeped up out of the ground to completely obscure the walls, the defensive traps, and Victor's men when they silently rode out the gate to form up.

Victor thought the fog was a great idea, regardless of how it hid him and his soldiers. When he'd remarked as much to Valla and Lam, they'd agreed but pointed out that the Ridonne had casters, too, and they'd probably conjure a wind to blow it away when they charged. Regardless, it would be too late to stop Victor and his troops. Borrius was sure the imperials would already be committed, spread out in a thin ring to encircle the entire encampment and attacking from all angles in the hopes of finding a weak spot in the defenses, a place to focus their efforts and bring an end to Rellia's "uprising."

Victor looked down at Guapo and grinned with pleasure; he'd summoned the mount with fear-attuned Energy, and though he was still handsome and impressive, he was a mount fit for a nightmare. The mustang was jet black with the fear Energy coursing through him, his mane wild and long, his eyes glowering purple through the flowing shadows that bled off him like heavy smoke. When he ran, rather than sparking hooves, he left a trail of those shadows that clung to the ground and seemed to grasp at people who moved through them. The effect was spooky and gave no small amount of distress to his troops, but when Victor had spoken to the soldiers who'd won the opportunity to run into battle with him, he'd explained that the shadows had no hunger for them; they were for their enemies.

The lottery had been quite a distraction for the troops, and several brawls had broken out when jealous rivals had tried to demand the winning tokens from squad mates. The sergeants and lieutenants had quickly restored order, though, and it wasn't long before the five hundred had been mounted and the order of the charge had been established; the strongest, most hardened troops were in the front lines, ready to break any resistance. As they'd been assigning those positions, the most violent outburst, the loudest objection to being left behind, had come from Polo.

When Victor heard him arguing with Borrius, the older man insisting that all active, troop-commanding captains must be present for the defense, Victor had stepped in. The great warrior was built for this sort of mission; he wore heavy armor, was stronger than any five imperial grunts, and he'd stand a good chance of winning free when Victor finished his work. More than that, Victor knew his presence would inspire the others. Borrius had acquiesced when Victor suggested they give Polo's command to the captain Sarl had replaced, a man named Agus-dak.

"How will we be sure to charge at the Ridonne?" Polo asked, sitting atop his huge, armored roladii at Victor's left. The question broke Victor from his recollections, and he cleared his throat to answer, but then Lam spoke up.

"I had the same question."

Victor looked at Lam and, beyond her, Valla. When his eyes locked on his tribune primus, he said, "I have a plan for that."

"Can we know it?" Lam pressed.

"Sure. I have a spell that will let me feel where they are. I didn't really want to use it because it kind of makes it hard to use my other spells that'll help the troops more, my inspiration and glory-attuned ones. It doesn't matter, though—we have to know we're charging in the right direction, or we'll all get killed for nothing." He spoke in a low voice, his words meant only for the champions by his side.

"When you feel them, can you not drop it and summon your other powers?" Polo asked.

"Maybe. The spell has a weird effect on me. I'll probably be able to cancel it and summon my banner, but I don't want to promise. Be ready to kick ass regardless."

"We'll be ready." Valla moved one of her hands from Uvu's reins to rest on Midnight's pommel.

"That in mind, I think you three should move back." Victor turned to face the first row of soldiers lined up behind him. There were ten rows of troops, each one longer than the one in front of it, with the toughest soldiers, hand-picked by Polo, in the front row and at the outer edges of the formation. "Spread yourselves among the troops. I think you'll each have more impact on morale that way."

"Agreed," Polo said. "I'll take the center of the second line. If the front line caves, I'll bolster things up."

"I'll go to the left outside edge." Lam nodded as if it were settled, then to Valla she added, "Can you take the right?"

"Of course." She shifted that way but lingered while Lam and Polo moved off. "I wanted to be with you. In case the two Ridonne are more dangerous than you think."

"Yeah, I figured you'd feel that way. You'll be able to see and hear me fighting those two assholes, though." Victor looked over his shoulder at the troops again, then leaned close to Valla and whispered, "I won't tell you to stay out of it, but if you see me losing, really think about getting the hell out of there. You can fight free if you try; those guys won't stop Uvu."

"You're just saying that to appease your conscience. You know very well that I won't flee the field if I think you're losing." Victor was his normal size, riding a normal-sized Guapo, but he still loomed over her, much higher on the mustang's back than she was on Uvu's. Even so, she reached up, and he leaned farther toward her so he could take her hand. It was cold, and he wrapped his fingers around the back of it, gently caressing her palm with his thumb.

"It's cold in this fog, huh?"

"Your hand's not cold . . ."

"Nah, I don't really get cold or hot too easily these days."

"I wish I could feel your warmth on more than my hand right now." Her voice was soft, full of layered meanings. Before Victor could respond, she freed her hand. "Come, Uvu; we have imperials to slay." As the cat grumbled his cat noises and started to turn, she locked eyes with him again. "Kill them, Victor. Give the Ridonne in Tharcray a reason to fear us."

Pazra-dak looked at his brother, watching the witch do her work as she tattooed the lines of the rite into his flesh, lines that matched the design of those on the wooden boards upon which he sat. The witch sweated; her hands shook as she mumbled her prayers and painstakingly etched upon his sibling's fine, golden flesh, ruining the perfection, the pride of his family. "Steady yourself, witch!" he growled. "One wrong line and we all may die when the rite is invoked, my brother's sacrifice for naught!"

"I am poisoned!" she hissed, her usual self-control beginning to fray. "I nearly died to save this great man's life, and you bark at me while I bleed my life into this work? Kill me now, then! Kill me, and let's see how this rite fares with my loss!"

"Brother," Rosh-dak wheezed, his voice frail from his ordeal. "Please don't antagonize Senena further. She does good work, work that no one within a thousand leagues could replicate."

Pazra bit back his retort. If his brother wanted peace, he would have it. What else could he do to show his appreciation, his respect? Instead, he paced; he walked in a wide circle around the wooden platform where Senena worked on the rite. They were inside his tent, though everything had been packed away other than the platform. The wood was special, some sort of heartwood from the grove of his ancestors, valuable in its own right but priceless in its ability to hold the Energy of his bloodline and its ability to form the magical connections that would rip open the veil between this world and the plane where his Ridonne ancestors lingered, hungry for conquest.

The rite was taught to all Ridonne children, all who touched the bloodline and began to exhibit a connection to it. Pazra shook his head, correcting himself—the rite wasn't taught to children, only the history of it. No, the rite itself was only known to those who may survive it, those who reached an adequate rank in the bloodline. Senena was an exception, her value as a spiritual guide, teacher, and historian more important than her unclean blood. Rosh was one who'd reached the required status, however. He had been for decades. "Yes," he muttered to himself, "Rosh will hold the ancestor on this plane for a good long while."

"Are you talking about me, brother?"

"I only wish to reassure myself. I only sing your praises, brother. You will make our kind proud tonight. You will crush the giant, then lay waste to the walls of that encampment, slaughtering countless rebels!"

"Aye, I will. With luck, our ancestor will be pleased with me and drag me back to the Vizashath with him." Rosh's voice was hoarse and soft, but his lips turned up in a smile at the thought. Pazra hoped he was right, hoped the tales of the Vizashath weren't lies meant to coerce unwilling Ridonne into accepting the rite. Supposedly the Ridonne, in their heyday, before the System, before the joining of the worlds, learned to open a portal to the plane they called the Vizashath, a place they conquered and claimed as their home. The entity they'd summon would be coming in spirit on a torrent of Energy, and he'd transform Rosh into a true Ridonne for a time—until his body, the vessel, came apart from the strain.

"Ancestors," Pazra prayed almost silently, "let it take him. Let Rosh-dak travel to the Vizashath."

"This is the best place for us?" Rellia asked, looking at Borrius skeptically. He'd positioned his command platform on the northeastern edge of the encampment. It was a tall structure, a tower made of great logs that were kept in one of the storage wagons when not in use. A gangway ran from the tower's center to the wall's ramparts, but ladders led up another thirty feet from there to the wide platform upon which she, Borrius, and Edeya stood. From their vantage, they could see the entire encampment, its walls, and the surrounding plains over the top of the roiling fog banks that hugged their fortifications.

"Yes. Victor rampaged on the southeastern enemy encampment toward the Blue Deep. The troops out here, toward the canyon and destroyed bridge, will be the freshest and least fearful. They'll charge more swiftly and strike this section of our wall first. I want to be close. More than that, I want us to be evident here, hence the use of the tower so close to the wall. It presents a tantalizing bait for them, a distraction for their eyes. Thanks to us dangling ourselves here, Victor's unit will have an easier time with their charge."

"Ah, so nice to be useful," Rellia grumbled, looking out over the walls, proud of the soldiers, hunters, and casters standing ready. They knew an army was coming soon but stood firm and resolute. She was sure Victor's earlier speech helped with that. She still couldn't believe how many of the soldiers had wanted to join his charge. "Their readiness hasn't suffered from the wait. Not yet."

"No, they'll hold that way a good long while." Borrius chuckled, shaking his head in amusement at a memory. "Victor stirred something up in them, and they've all got their heartfast potions ready. Our alchemist has been quite busy."

"Heartfast." Rellia's eyes shifted to the potion hanging on Edeya's belt, a small vial of bubbly blue liquid. "Have you ever taken it?" She asked because she had not; she'd heard of it from Valla and knew it was supposed to make a person eager, alert, and brave. Valla said it was like being a little drunk and excited for your battle the way you might yearn to see a boy you had a crush on. Rellia thought it sounded like mind magic, and she didn't fancy the idea of someone mucking about with her thoughts or emotions.

"No. I've never needed it, not in my command position. I'm eager as it is." The look on his face made a believer out of Rellia; the man's eyes were bright, his posture leaning forward, and he repeatedly drummed his fingers on the railing of their platform as he scanned the horizon.

"You love it, hmm?"

"Of course! This is the greatest game, Rellia. Never mind that nonsense the nobles play on their fancy boards in their parlors! Look at the pieces arrayed before us." He gestured widely with both arms. "Look at the board upon which we play! This game matters, Rellia; this game has real stakes! Our very lives are forfeit should we misstep! I know what you'll say, that politics has just the same thrill. And it may be true, it may be true, but I can't stomach the idea that my moves might take months or years to bear fruit. No, give me a battlefield and I'm a happy man."

Rellia eyed her old mentor, her lips pursing, trying to think of a way to scold him for treating people's lives like a game, but then she thought about his words, that he'd included himself in the accounting. It was true—he and she would be dead should the Ridonne win the night. She saw, over his shoulder, that Edeya looked disturbed, and she frowned at the girl, wishing Darro was with them in the tower instead of down with the captains. "You have something to say, Lieutenant?"

"No, ma'am."

Borrius glanced at Edeya, then waved his hand dismissively. "Until you've risen to command, don't try to judge me, girl. Many, many nights of sleep have I lost thanks to my mistakes, mistakes that cost many lives—more than

I can count. The only way I find peace is to remember my victories and the lives they saved. The Ancestors know my work, and they're keeping an account. I'll see the tally when I'm dead. Until then, I won't listen to criticism from those who can't fathom my decisions." Rellia knew he was speaking for her benefit as well as Edeya's. Ever the teacher, Borrius knew, despite her protestations, that Rellia had much yet to learn.

"I'm sorry if my face betrayed my foolish thoughts, sir." The girl's tone almost made Rellia sorry for her, especially as her eyes drifted to the young Ghelli's wing stubs. Like most people born without wings, she had a hard time thinking of their loss the same way she might have an arm or leg, but she knew Ghelli felt differently. To them, wings were more essential even than fingers.

"Go easy, Borrius. When I was her age . . ." Rellia was cut off by the distant sound of horns, long, brassy-sounding notes that began in the south then rapidly spread, reverberating off each other as more and more metallic throats took up the call. Soon the horns were calling out from every direction, confirming what she already knew—the attack was coming from all sides.

"Imperial war horns," Borrius said, perhaps for her benefit, perhaps for Edeya's—neither of them had served in the Legion. "It's time."

Rellia hurried to the southern edge of their platform, leaning over the railing, looking out over the battlement where Victor and her daughter had arrayed their force. The fog obscured them, for the most part, but she knew they'd charge out of it soon, waiting just long enough to ensure the imperials weren't feinting, that they were truly attacking. "How soon will we know if it's real?"

"Very soon. They'll bring their artillery to bear, try to soften us, and when we resist, when our preparations and casters prove too much, they'll charge." Almost as if he'd called for it, the sky lit up with bright, fiery balls—flaming, alchemical missiles fired by trebuchets. Rellia's mouth fell agape as she tried to count them and lost track after twenty. Weird shadows danced on the grasslands and the fortifications outside the walls as the balls of fire surged through the air.

"Ancestors! We're sitting like feyris for a hawk!" She'd never seen such a sight, so much destructive power hurtling toward a single target; all her fights had been on a much smaller scale.

"We're not helpless. As I said, we're well entrenched. See there." Borrius pointed to the battlement below where several uniformed men and women were raising their hands, frosty Energy gathering around them, thickening the air and raising a rime on their hands and sleeves. Rellia glanced left and right, knowing similar groups of casters stood, spread out along the battlements, ready for such an action. She watched, wondering if they'd launch a counter to the incoming projectiles, but nothing flew forth.

Edeya gasped and said, "They're going out!"

"What?" Rellia jerked her gaze to the sky, and sure enough, the incoming meteoric missiles were winking out, one by one, their fire extinguished. The dark, smoking balls continued to fly toward the encampment, but something had been taken from them, some of their momentum dulled by the countermagic. They fell to thud in the grass, well short of the walls, rolling impotently until they fell into a pit or cracked against a barrier. Not a single soldier was injured.

As the troops below cheered and jeered, Borrius said, "They'll see the futility in bombardment soon. Write this to the captains, Lieutenant: praise your troops and bolster them with encouragement. Remind them that the test is yet to come. Remind them that our legate primus risks his life this night for them, that they have yet to earn the sacrifice he and his soldiers will make."

36

CHARGE

Pazra-dak grasped the Energy crystal at the edge of the spell pattern surrounding his brother, ready to feed him more of their blood-attuned Energy. He wasn't sure he'd have to, but Senena seemed to think it was likely. "How would she know," he growled, frowning at the woman who sat exhausted on the far side of the tent, watching him, watching his brother, through the dark hollows of her eyes.

"I begin," Rosh wheezed, his throat, like the rest of him, raw from the torments the Ancestors-damned, monstrous giant-devil had visited upon him.

"You will teach that fool what happens to those who threaten the Ridonne!" Pazra's words oozed with pride, and as his brother began to mutter his incantation, he looked over his shoulder and called sharply, "Venis!"

The tent flap fluttered as his new legate hurried to his side. "Yes, lord?"

"It is time. Are the soldiers prepared?"

"Aye, lord. We've held a thousand of our best to guard your tent. The others are set, ready to charge. Of course, we'll begin with siege weapons to soften them."

"Any more of their absurd festivities? Wouldn't it be wonderful if the fools drank themselves into a stupor? Did we figure out what they were shouting about? Do they think they've won something, killing the most fearful of our soldiers?"

"No, lord, we speculate they were simply trying to bolster their troops; it can't be good for their morale to see our great force surrounding them.

There have been no more celebrations this evening. The camp grew quiet, and they've encircled themselves with fog, likely to obscure their traps. We'll easily shred their preparations. Shall I move to the field command?"

"Yes. Begin. You know the order of attack. See that you overwhelm that camp, and we'll deal with their little champion. Hurry now, before the Energies in this circle drag your soul from your bones!" Pazra gestured to the platform where Senena had drawn the ritual circle, and Venis blanched when his eyes followed the gesture and took in the sight of Rosh, covered in bloody tattoos, seeping a dense, red fog of bloody Energy as he feverishly muttered the words of the rite. Venis turned on his heel and rushed from the command tent, and Pazra chuckled, pleased to see an appropriate response to the workings of the Ridonne.

"Ready yourself." Senena's voice startled him; somehow, the witch had crept up, walking around the circle. "Already his Core runs low—I feared as much, considering the mental battle we fought just hours ago."

"Truly? So soon?" Pazra frowned, narrowing his eyes, wondering how the witch could see into Rosh's Core.

"Yes. Grasp the crystal, ready yourself, fill your pathways with Energy, and when the time comes—when I tell you—push your blood-attuned Energy into it, and *only* that Energy! The circle will carry it to your brother."

"Must I bleed myself dry?"

Senena, with a mocking, utterly disrespectful note in her voice, replied, "Do you want to summon a weakling from the Vizashath or a great terror of a Ridonne?"

"Witch, watch that insolence. You know what I want."

"Indeed, lord. Here." She produced a dark red vial and handed it to him. "This will restore you should the spell threaten to drain you. I'd give it to Lord Rosh-dak, but he'll be in the throes of the rite and won't be able to think of quaffing it."

Pazra gripped the warm potion, nodding. He should have had some of those himself, but he'd never imagined being tested in this manner. He'd thought to handily crush the upstart's rebellious forces with his brother's aid. Rosh's muttered incantation took on a frenzied note, and his voice rose, cracking with the effort. Pazra gripped the crystal, his palm beginning to sweat, and reached into his Core, pulling forth a thick tendril of the hot red Energy that pulsed within him. He primed it into his pathway, filling it to bursting, ready to send it into the crystal when the moment was right.

His Energy wasn't as pure as Rosh's, but it was potent nonetheless. It would work. He felt as though he was trying to reassure himself, felt something gnawing at the corners of his mind, and he fumed inwardly about it. That damned bastard had given him something he'd never had before—doubt. He'd never doubted the might of the Ridonne, never doubted *his* might. So supremely did they dominate this world that he'd begun to take it for granted. Hadn't his uncle warned him? Hadn't he told both him and Rosh that greater challenges awaited on other worlds? His warnings of complacency rang truer than ever after their encounter with the bastard nightmare-making giant.

"Now!" Senena hissed, interrupting his internal dialogue. Pazra pushed, driving his Energy into the crystal. At first, it resisted him, but as a critical mass of his Energy accumulated in the magical stone, he felt the resistance break. Then it *pulled*, drawing his Energy out of his pathways, emptying them, and then it reached directly into his Core. Pazra gasped at the sensation, groaning as he felt the lethargy of low Energy, and he peeled his eyes open, unsure when he'd even closed them.

The crystal was ablaze with orange-red light, and the same bright Energy traced the pattern carved into the platform on which his brother sat. His brother . . . his brother was transfixed, floating above the circle, limbs spread wide, mouth agape, eyes wide, blazing with Energy, unseeing, as far as Pazra could tell.

"Drink it!" Senena hissed. Pazra jerked his eyes away from his brother and quaffed the coppery potion, sighing with relief as the dense Energy in the liquid surged into his Core, replenishing him. However, the crystal was still hungry, and it pulled at his new stores, drawing the Energy out, flaring brightly as it sent it on through the pattern to his brother. "Old bones," Senena cried, her voice quavering. "He's reached through! One of them has hold—a hungry one!"

Pazra grunted in acknowledgment, looking at his brother, watching as his flesh split, deep orange-red lines marring his body, radiating heat. A bit of motion from the corner of his eye, a sense that someone had moved, made him look over his shoulder just in time to see Senena's back as she fled the tent. "Worm," he growled or tried to growl—it came out more as a wheeze. The spell was pulling too hard, taking too much. With a tremendous effort, he unpeeled his fingers one by one, straining to free his hand from the crystal. He couldn't.

"*Ah-ah-oh!*" Rosh-dak cried, his voice rising in a weird ululation. Pazra looked at him, panic making his movements jerky as he strained against the crystal's pull, against the hunger of the being reaching through the pattern. Rosh was stretching, his flesh continuing to split as his bones elongated. The weird magma glow between his split skin intensified, and his eyes began to blaze with it, literal beams scorching the top of the tent as the man, the once-great, handsome son of the Ridonne, wailed and arched his back.

For his part, Pazra, too, cried out, though his voice was a hoarse whisper as darkness began to creep in around the edges of his vision. He felt the Energy in his Core dwindle to nothing again, and still, the rite didn't leave him be, didn't drop him; it began to pull at his very essence, snatching the blood from his veins, igniting it, taking out the Energy he'd earned through many, many years of cultivation, battle, and triumph. It ripped away the fruits of the many treasures he'd consumed to enhance himself. Though he couldn't scream, couldn't thrash, so weak had he become, Pazra wept. Tears of hot blood ran down his cheeks as he wilted.

Victor and his soldiers watched as the imperial forces launched their many ranged attacks at the encampment. They waited as the defenses held, and the elemental casters in his army dismantled fireballs, tamped down and calmed sudden earthquakes, and shielded the encamped army from icy squalls with great gusts of winds high in the air. All the while, they maintained the layer of fog near the fortifications, and Victor had to admire their skill and tenacity. Surely the imperials had more casters, but they couldn't break those on the ramparts behind him. Victor vowed to award some medals to those tough *cabrones* if he and they survived the night.

After a long while, Victor heard the clarion, staccato horn Borrius had told him to listen for; it meant the charge had begun. "Get ready!" he roared, casting Iron Berserk. As he surged in size, so too did Guapo, and soon his head was up near the top of the fog bank. He couldn't quite see over it, though that didn't stop his troops from cheering when those nearby saw him expand in size. Victor unslung Lifedrinker and held her ready in his right hand. "Good boy," he said, slapping his spirit steed's shoulder. The nightmare mustang whinnied, a fierce, bone-chilling sound that sent a plume of black shadows from his nostrils.

"It's time." Victor mainly spoke to himself, trying to bolster his nerves. He hated the spell he was about to cast. Something about the detachment he felt when he wore the guise of the Inevitable Huntsman made him uncomfortable. Victor was an emotional man, and he liked it. He liked how he loved and hated, lusted and feared—when the world went gray, and all he could think about was finding his quarry, it was as if he wasn't himself, even more so than when he was wearing his Aspect of Terror.

Growling at himself, at his hesitation, Victor built the pattern, and as the spell pulled his various Energies to form justice-attuned Energy and it shared his pathways with his rage, the world inside the fog grew even grayer. He felt the change come over him, and he tried to focus on the images of Pazra-dak and the other Ridonne, the one he'd clashed with while on his nightmare tirade. As other things fell away, love, hate, fear, hope, one thing remained—his need to punish those who'd done wrong, his need to deliver justice. The world grew more and more dim, the people around him more and more meaningless, and then he felt it—a hot pulse ahead and to his left. There. There were those who needed to taste the righteous judgment of his hand.

Without a word, Victor and Guapo started forward, and he felt a deep need to hurry, to bring justice to his quarry, to punish them. He began to urge his steed forward, a great beast, a powerful beast, an animal fit to convey the inevitability of justice. Dimly, in the back of his mind, he was aware of others running with him, spurring their own animals to carry them on his heels. This was fine, he decided, fitting even. Should not the archon of justice have followers? Should others not want to join his crusade?

Still, his nightmare shadow-cloaked mount was far faster than they, and he felt them falling behind. He heard some of them crying out. Were they cheering? Lamenting? Did it matter? At first, his answer was no, but then a tiny voice in his head said, "Slow down," and he pondered that for a heartbeat. Should he? "Do it!" the voice snarled, and suddenly the gray began to fade as some color slipped in. "Time to wake up, *hermano,*" the voice growled, louder now, more robust. "We know where they are. Time to snap out of it!" With the abruptness of a light being turned on, the spell broke, the gray faded from his vision, and Victor laughed, back behind the wheel, so to speak.

Victor urged Guapo to slow. He could see the front line of the Ridonne army ahead of him, maybe half a mile distant, and looking back, he saw he'd surged a hundred yards or more ahead of his troops. While he cantered forward, waiting for his allies to gain on him, Victor summoned his standard, and suddenly the darkness was ablaze with sparkling golden glory. His soldiers, the brave men and women who urged their mounts to catch him, cheered, and Victor lifted his head, roaring his encouragement. He felt them as they drew near, and he willed Guapo forward, setting a breakneck pace, pushing the limits of the roladii most of his troops rode.

When he was close enough to see the individual imperials, Victor laughed to see none were mounted. They were foot soldiers and only five ranks deep; he briefly wondered at the wisdom of trying to attack the encampment from every direction. He continued to charge them, saw them waver in the light of his banner, and then he screamed, "Let's go!" He dug into his Core, pulled out a massive torrent of fear-attuned Energy, and cast Project Spirit, sending forth an enormous cone of dark, twisted tendrils of shadowy Energy that struck the line of spear, sword, and axe wielders ahead of him.

They faltered, eyes going wide, and many of them fled. Some dropped their weapons as they turned. Others fell to their knees, their bodies abandoning them in sheer terror. Victor smashed through them. The great fear-born mustang trampled them like so many children under his hooves. With a tremendous crash, the front of his troops' wedge struck the faltering imperials behind him, and then he was through, continuing straight toward where he'd felt the Ridonne.

He wanted to look back, to witness the glory of his men smashing through the imperial line, but he had to focus and watch for traps and the soldiers no doubt left behind to protect the Ridonne. He'd led the charge, broken through, given his soldiers the bolstering light of his banner, and crushed his enemies' will; it was time to give Guapo his head. Victor leaned forward, and the mustang knew what he wanted. The great steed exploded with speed, driving him over the ground, and leaping a long series of trenches, hardly jostling Victor in his passage.

Victor threw a giant Globe of Insight into the air, leaving behind a brilliant floodlight, exposing the pitfalls for his soldiers as they followed in his wake. Soon, he saw them, a row of soldiers, and his mind, quickened by his many enhancements, calculated their numbers. He could see their front line was maybe a hundred strong, but they were only three rows deep; there were fewer than he'd expected, even if you considered there were probably more around the perimeter of the Ridonne's camp. Victor laughed, and as he sped toward them, he reached out and summoned a monstrous rage-fueled bear totem, setting it loose in the ranks of soldiers ahead of him.

The imperials swarmed around each other, trying to bolster up those suddenly caught amid the rampages of a massive spirit bear. It swiped left and right, sending the soldiers flying, and, in that chaos and disarray, Victor and Guapo crashed into them at great speed. The mustang smashed and stomped through them. He was enormous, his hooves the size of five-gallon buckets made of black, diamond-hard keratin, and he spread shadows of fear all around him, clearing his flanks—none of the soldiers could stand before him or summon the will to try to strike at him as he rode past. In three heartbeats, Victor was through and charging for the tents ahead.

"Good." Victor laughed, taking a moment to realize he'd managed to summon his bear while still riding his mount; had he done that before? He continued to laugh, admiring the beauty of his revised totem spell. Then he was trampling through tents, noting that the camp was empty; had the Ridonne sent the noncombat personnel away? Were they off supporting the attacking lines? It didn't matter; Victor saw an enormous round tent atop a nearby rise near the center of the camp—It was glowing with orange-red light, a beacon to pull at Victor's urge for combat.

He slowed, and as Guapo's thunderous hooves settled and the wind ceased its whistling in his ears, Victor heard the crash as his soldiers slammed into the line of defenders. He listened to his bear roaring and the screams of soldiers dying. A grim smile spread his lips, baring white, clenched teeth. The poor bastards who'd thought they'd drawn an easy duty staying back, protecting their leaders, would have a rough night. Girded for battle, wearing his wyrm-scale vest, his Kethian Juggernaut helm, his dragonsteel belt, and wielding the greatest axe on the planet, Victor urged Guapo forward. "Time to come out of your tent, assholes."

"You were right," Rellia said, her eyes wide as she took in the size of the force coming at them from the northwest. The imperials were like a tide, flowing over the grasslands, thousands of them mounted, riding behind the foot soldiers. Energy globes hung in the air—smoldering orange fire, cool, pale-blue ice, crackling balls of lightning and plasma, and hundreds of bright yellow pure Energy orbs. It was like dawn had come early as the Ridonne soldiers arrayed themselves outside the fortifications, inspecting them, perhaps, before they charged.

"Yes, though I was more right than I'd hoped. I'd hoped they'd spread out more, truly try to test all our fortifications. It seems they're going to concentrate most of their efforts here. Honestly," he said, voice low, "I'm not sure we'll hold for long."

"We have to." Rellia leaned forward on the parapet. "Should we not order more soldiers to this wall?"

"Indeed. Lieutenant"—Borrius turned to Edeya—"alert the captains. We need another full cohort on this wall. Take two hundred soldiers from each of the others."

"Yes, sir!" Edeya said, scribbling in her command book.

"This is going to be a true test. We may die here tonight, ladies. If we do, it's been a pleasure."

"Sir, if I may speak?" Edeya's voice was shaky.

"Out with it; the time for chatter fades," he replied curtly.

"Victor will win. He has to. When he does, he'll come back, and the soldiers out there—they're going to break. We just have to hold them for a while."

"Well, that's the trick, Lieutenant—holding them." He'd just finished speaking when something shook the night, a sound that cut the air like a nail through a board, a scream that echoed over the grasslands from the southeast. It was a sound both foreign and familiar, bringing back memories of the long night when Victor had been out terrorizing the imperials. "Ancestors! Was that him?"

Rellia shook her head, eyes wide with a mixture of confusion and despair. "I don't think so. It sounded different. Wasn't it louder? Deeper?"

"Look!" Edeya said, standing at the platform's edge, pointing toward the southeast where Victor had charged, toward the origin of the weird, terrible shriek. Rellia followed her finger, and there, in the distance—a mile or two— she saw an eerie red light, like a rip in the night. It blazed, putting spots in her vision when she blinked for a few seconds, and then it began to shrink and in just a few moments was gone.

"What in the shit . . . " Borrius started to say but collected himself in time to shake his head and change his words. "It's not our problem. Not yet. We have more immediate things to worry about." At his words, Rellia turned, and sure enough, more horns started to sound, and the imperials began their charge.

37

LIGHTS IN THE NIGHT

Eyes on the glowing tent, Victor dismounted from Guapo and dismissed the sturdy mount. The center of the imperial camp was deserted. No one challenged him, and he could be atop that rise, smashing through the tent in one leap—the mustang wasn't needed. He shifted his Sovereign Will boost from agility and dexterity to strength and vitality. As his muscles swelled with power and he felt the vibrant Energy bolster his already sturdy form, he lifted Lifedrinker and began to stalk forward.

The sounds of battle behind him grew louder as his troops clashed with the Ridonne's guardian forces. He knew if he looked back, he'd see his cavalry breaking through, riding in a loop, and then charging again. They planned to do so over and over until they lost too many mounts, they were surrounded by too many enemies, or one of a myriad of potential circumstances prevented their repeated charges. Victor felt good about their chances; he'd given them a hell of a first charge, and the defenders seemed far fewer than they'd anticipated. Maybe with Polo, Valla, and Lam leading them, they'd actually win.

Victor brushed the thoughts of his troops out of his mind and focused on the task at hand. He began to regulate his breathing, visualizing how he'd crush first one Ridonne and then the other. He figured he'd kill the shorter, spiky Ridonne first; he hadn't seemed as strong as the big golden-skinned one. He ran through his plan of attack, solidifying it in his mind, imagining how he'd charge, feint, and respond to their defensive movements. He was halfway up the rise, passing by empty, smaller tents, perhaps fifty yards from the big glowing one when it exploded.

Exploded was probably the wrong word, he revised, ducking down, shielding his eyes from the bright flare. The orange-red burst of light was so bright, so intense, that he'd thought something had blown up in the tent, his mind drawing ridiculous pictures of cartoon-style TNT barrels. No explosion accompanied the flash, though, and as the bloom faded, he saw a massive rip in the fabric of reality. It wasn't smooth or neatly oval like some of the portals he'd seen; it looked like a jagged tear through which weird red mist flowed, traveling on a current of wind Victor couldn't feel. As the mist passed through and the rip began to shrink, a terrible shrieking cry echoed through the night, loud and multivoiced, like a trio including a bass, a treble, and a warbling, pain-filled soprano.

Something stirred in Victor's chest at the sound, and he began to regress in his berserk state to the way he used to feel before he'd learned his Iron Berserk spell. He felt himself straightening, his shoulders squaring, and a thought, almost foreign in his mind, echoed through his psyche—who was this weakling to scream so in his presence? Victor stoked the rage in his pathways and pushed it into his arms, using Channel Spirit to fill Lifedrinker with it. She shimmered with a red heat, and then the silvery sheen of her axe-head burst into molten orange fury, black smoke drifting into the night as she smoldered and cooked the air. He stalked forward toward the diminishing red cut in the sky.

Distantly he felt his bear fade away as it succumbed to thousands of wounds. He wasn't upset; he'd gotten a sense of conquest from the great beast and knew it had crushed many, many imperials before it fell. He contemplated summoning his coyotes but decided to wait; he wanted to see what lurked in the bright glow of that portal. What creature had dared to utter such a shriek? It had been a challenge, there was no doubt, and Victor felt his blood boiling at the idea. By the time he crested the hill and stood there, looking at the ruins of the great tent under the rapidly fading light of the tear in reality, he was limned with red rage, his chest heaving with fury, his knuckles white on his axe.

The wind blew heavily over the hilltop, and he saw two individuals there at the center of the flapping, torn, smoldering tent. One, a frail-looking Shadeni, scrabbled at the ground, worming his way under the ripped fabric of the tent. The other was large, squatting on its haunches, a shadowy hulk that peered out from hooded brows with lantern-sized glowering red eyes.

Here was his challenger, Victor decided. Here was the one who needed to feel his might.

With a raw, scraping, grating voice, the thing hissed, "A snack to welcome me home? How pleasing!" Then it flew through the air, quick as a thought, toward Victor. Enraged as he was, full of the proud blood of his ancestors, Victor bristled at the thing's words and lifted Lifedrinker, swinging her hatchet-like at the incoming ball of smoky shadows. He might not have been boosting his agility, but Victor wasn't slow, especially when berserk. Lifedrinker, smoldering like a razor-edged coal, smashed into the challenger, pulling forth a wail of agony.

Victor didn't have time to celebrate or gloat; though wounded and stopped short by his cleave, the creature stood tall before him and hacked down with a jagged, blood-red sword at Victor's chest. Victor felt his wyrm-scale vest eat the blow, though the impact was immense, and he had to take a step back to steady himself. He didn't look down at his chest to see the damage done to his armor; he didn't have the time or mental bandwidth for that. He was too engrossed by the appearance of his foe now that it had emerged from its hunched, shadow-clad posture.

The man before him—for it was evident this was a man, not a beast— was nearly as tall as Victor in his Quinametzin form—slighter, perhaps, but impressive in almost every way. More than his height and red-gold flesh that shimmered with Energy and power, the man was handsome in a weird, inhuman sense. His eyes were like golden orbs with red irises, and his hair was a flowing mane of feathery red locks. He'd unfurled two massive wings that spread wide behind him, giving him the impression of a vastly greater bulk. The wings were bedecked with thousands of red feathers that matched his hair, and he wore golden armor similar to what Victor had seen on the Ridonne he'd previously fought.

When his red, shimmering blade didn't split Victor in twain, the weird, handsome man stepped back, twisted his full red lips into a sneer, and said, in that raw, scraping voice, "Succumb. Make this easy. I have slaying to do."

Victor had gathered his wits enough to realize this *was* some kind of Ridonne—a third one. Perhaps he was one of their champions, come to rescue the two others he'd already thrashed. He grinned, thinking of it, likening the pompous, winged buffoon before him to an angry uncle or parent. Rather than speak to the fool, rather than break his rule about shit-talking during a fight, Victor closed the gap between them, only five yards or so, with an Energy Charge fueled by inspiration. He streaked over the ground in a blur

of white light and glittering motes and smashed his enormously dense Kethian Juggernaut helm into the Ridonne's chin.

In the terrible concussion that followed, Victor was shielded by the
Energy of his spell. The Ridonne tried to stand firm and put some Energy
into his pathways, blazing with red-orange light, but it wasn't enough;
as Victor replaced him on the contested soil, the Ridonne tumbled back,
completing a half backflip before his head struck the ground and he slid
through two nearby tents, digging a foot-deep furrow in the grassy loam.
Victor knew better than to stand around and watch what his enemy would
do. He leapt after him, bringing Lifedrinker down in a terrible chop at the
downed giant.

He was soaring downward, Lifedrinker's edge mere feet from the Ridonne's collarbone, when a globe of red Energy expanded from the weird warrior's
chest in a brilliant flash. Like an explosion centered on the tall golden man's
body, the red Energy consumed everything it touched, vaporizing the tent
remains, the grass, and the very soil upon which he lay. Worse, as it expanded
in a point-blank explosion, the outer edge hit Victor as he fell from the sky.

The Energy was hot, angry, and filled with destructive power. Lifedrinker
was the first to feel it, and he heard her scream in tortured agony, a sound that
ripped through his mind. Panicked at the idea that she might be destroyed,
Victor jerked his arm upward, flinging her away. She spun through the air,
smoldering and blackened, to land in the grass fifty yards distant. Before
Victor could feel relief that she wasn't vaporized, he fell into the globe of
destructive Energy and knew nothing but pain.

Victor felt his flesh begin to come apart on his left hand, forearm, and
his knees, as they were the first parts of him to touch that laser-hot sphere.
As he continued downward, and his arm and legs, then his chest and torso,
passed through it, he felt something akin to what he'd experienced when he'd
inhaled the smoke of the firedrake. If whatever Energy was tearing him apart
was fire, he'd feel better, knowing he'd resist much of it, but it didn't burn like
fire. It was something else, some horrible Energy that clawed at him with the
strength of acid and the heat of an inferno.

Many people might have thrashed and tried to roll away or change their
trajectory. Many people might have panicked and folded from the pain. Many
people would have lost the battle in that instant in their desperation to save
themselves, to escape that agony no matter the cost. Victor wasn't an average
man, however. The problem for the Ridonne was that Victor had one thing
in his mind, and it was to rip the heart from his enemy, damage to himself

be damned. Still falling in a red haze of fury and agony, Victor brought both bloody, dissolving hands toward his prone enemy's throat.

As he finished passing through the expanding bubble of terrible Energy, he smashed down on the golden man's chest. Blood showered off him at the impact, leaking from the many breaches in his flesh, but he'd felt worse, seen worse. He was already healing, his powerful flesh absorbing the terrible abuse as his berserk healing and massive vitality worked to undo the damage he'd suffered. Meanwhile, his knees brought forth loud cracks and pops from the Ridonne's big chest, and his hands had found their purchase around his golden throat. Victor squeezed as he leaned forward, eyes red with blood and madness as he leered with bloody teeth at the Ridonne's shock.

As his enemy thrashed and vast torrents of Energy coursed through his golden body, Victor bore down with his enormous fingers, the cable-like muscles in his forearms standing out like the roots of a mighty tree. He squeezed with such fury, such single-minded madness, intent on seeing the eyes pop from the Ridonne's skull, that he almost didn't realize his foe was lifting that long, jagged red blade, aiming its curved edge at the gap between his wyrm-scale armor and the rim of his helm. He meant to decapitate Victor.

Growling, Victor released one hand from the golden man's throat and grasped at his wrist, stopping the sword stroke inches from his flesh. Somehow the reprieve was enough for the Ridonne to recover slightly, to get some blood up to his brain or manage some kind of spell, for, in another burst of hot red Energy, he exploded into a crimson mist that sped over the ground, stopping to gather dozens of yards from the furious titan.

Victor stood up, his death grip foiled, and took stock of himself. He was bloody, but the soreness of his flesh was fading quickly. His pants were shredded to tatters, but his more robust magical gear was intact. His vest was shinier than ever as it glimmered in the weird lights filling the sky from the battles taking place all over the grassy plains. He knew his helmet was fine without looking at it; the damn thing was nigh indestructible. As he stood there stewing in his rage, watching the weird red cloud, wondering if the Ridonne would rematerialize or flee as they all seemed to love doing, he patted at his waist, felt his steaming, ticking belt, and knew it had absorbed much of the spell's potency. What would have happened to him without it?

Watching the mist and wondering what the Ridonne was doing in there, Victor stalked over the ground to his smoking axe. When he picked her up, Lifedrinker hummed, scorched but alive. She radiated fury warring with gratitude, glad he'd been so quick to pull her from her torment but ready to kill the one who'd stung her. Brushing some of the char from her haft, he started toward the cloud, wondering what spell to use to force his foe to show himself. He needn't have wondered; as soon as he closed within ten yards of the cloud, it shimmered, swirled, and condensed into the form of the golden man.

He grinned, whipping his red blade back and forth as he watched Victor. "Well," he hissed, "what a surprise. What have my foolish descendants allowed to walk into their world? Hmm? I can't have this. Come, let us dance; let me see how you use that axe, giant."

"Titan," Victor corrected, and then he cast Energy charge again, this time fueling it with rage, though his Core was running low on the precious commodity.

Borrius watched as his world began to come apart. It started with some irrationally brave imperials who charged on their roladii, got close enough to the ramparts to use wind-attuned spells to mount the wall, and, as they were cut to ribbons, managed to kill a handful of the defensive casters for that side of the fort. What madness would spur men and women, clearly all at or near Tier Four, to throw their lives away so valiantly? They weren't here to defend their families but to stop an army that wanted nothing to do with them! Why would they sacrifice themselves so?

The irrationality of their heroism was the only thing he hadn't accounted for, the only thing that he couldn't have expected; imperial troops were not known for their selfless valor! He'd screamed at Edeya to send for more defensive casters, but they were all busy on their ramparts, and their extrication from duty took too long. Imperial Earth Casters, clearly heavily stacked on this side of the fort, had summoned the soil and teased it forth with rocks and boulders to build an earthen ramp that stretched down from the top of the ramparts some two hundred yards, burying many of the defenses the army's engineers had so painstakingly erected.

Such a working wasn't generally seen on a battle of this scale, Borrius told himself, trying to wrap his mind around how easily he'd been outwitted. Had he been, though? He shook his head. If anyone had outwitted him, it was himself; he'd relied far too heavily on his knowledge of imperial tactics. These soldiers weren't behaving like imperials; the Ridonne must have done something to their minds. It was moot now, he decided, listening to the hysterical clash of magic and steel below him, watching as their rampart was overwhelmed. Rellia was screaming something, orders for Edeya to write down, no doubt. He couldn't focus on her; his eyes were glued to the carnage below.

The imperials were being slaughtered two or more for every man or woman on the wall, but they still came. They fought as if they were possessed even when Borrius had called out orders to use their ramp against them, allowing them to fill it with bodies and then using firebombs and archers to mow them down. Lightning strikes, sleeting gales, pits of magma, all summoned by the remaining defensive casters to great effect, slaying hundreds, even thousands of the charging imperials, but they kept coming. They kept coming, and the greater number of casters out on the field had begun to turn the tide.

As the charging soldiers gained a foothold on the walls and discipline began to fray, the imperial casters brought forth their own miniature hells, unleashing them on the defenders and attackers alike, indiscriminate in their destruction. More lightning strikes rained down, gales of burning, acidic rain washed the ramparts, and tremors shook the earth, crumbling the defensive structure and allowing more and more imperials to pour in. Once again, Rellia's shouts interrupted his thoughts, his observation of the chaos and the end of his world.

" . . . a weapon, now's the time to use it!" she shouted, her rapier in her hand.

"What's that?"

"They're coming up the ladders! Our defenders below are nearly overwhelmed. They'll be on us soon!"

Borrius looked at the opening in the center of the platform, wondering what sort of imperial would show his or her face first. Edeya stood on the other side of the hole, her book stowed away and a large spear in her two hands. Had it come to this, then? Perhaps the army wouldn't lose. Though their platform was nearly overwhelmed, perhaps the other ramparts were moving to bolster this wall. Perhaps their defense was going more easily. It had to be, didn't it? Clearly, the imperials had put their efforts into breaching this wall. Maybe Victor would prevail and return to the encampment in time to rally the troops.

"Well," he said, digging around in his storage ring. "I haven't used it in a number of years, but I used to be fairly good with a mace. I've a shield in here somewhere, too."

"That's the spirit. Let's take some with us." As if summoned by Rellia's words, a soldier wearing an imperial helmet popped his head through the hole, and she drove her wickedly fast rapier through his eye. He screamed and dropped away.

"Commander!" Edeya cried, and Borrius didn't know if she spoke to Rellia or him, but it didn't matter. She continued before either answered, "What's that? In the sky? Are they fireballs? No, some other kind of attack?"

"What?" Borrius asked, turning, still in the midst of strapping on his shield. Sure enough, out in the black night, high above the ground, hundreds of flickering orange lights twinkled in the dark. "Ancestors damn them!" he growled. "They held some mages in reserve to the north?"

"Perhaps, but what a strange-looking attack. What are they?" Rellia grunted as she stabbed at another attacker. She squinted into the black night, watching the weird flickering ochre lights as they slowly drew nearer. "I'll wager it's an alchemical attack. One thing is certain, though; the attackers below will torch this tower soon or knock it down."

"Perhaps. Perhaps they want us alive for . . . questioning." Borrius continued to frown, staring into the darkness, trying to put a name to the mysterious lights. They didn't move like projectiles. Were they some sort of balloon or kite—something meant to explode over the top of the encampment?

"Nothing we can do but hold as long as we can." Edeya's voice was firm. The lieutenant was oddly more resolute and focused in the face of near-certain death than Borrius felt. He looked at her and nodded.

"Yes. Let us extract from them a dear price for our lives." He stepped forward, gripping the familiar handle of his old friend, the cudgel of Blackstar; it was his father's mace, the only weapon he'd ever killed someone with, long before he'd learned that leading men was more rewarding than fighting them.

38

THE HEART TO WIN

Victor smashed into the Ridonne again, and this time the concussion shook the ground, sending up a shower of torn sod, soil, and stones as somehow the golden warrior deflected the impact away from himself. Victor found himself standing face to face with the armored figure, Lifedrinker's edge caught on the blade of that wicked, jagged scimitar. The Ridonne's wings were spread wide, and he brought them forward with a *crack* and thrust with his arms, pushing Victor away and himself back, smirking at the titan's ineffectual charge.

Victor didn't let him gloat, didn't let him taunt him; instead, he dove forward, and, using everything he'd learned from Polo and everything he'd learned fighting on Zaafor, he began to hack at his foe, feinting, slashing, thrusting, even using his free fist and feet to strike out, forcing openings for his axe. This Ridonne was something else, though, something far beyond the two Victor had already fought. It felt almost as if he'd been toying with Victor before; for now he parried, dodged, and blocked his attacks, even using his damnable wings to deflect and rebuff Victor's blows.

Despite his skill, the red-winged giant of a man couldn't do much to harm Victor, either. They danced, and their blows rang through the night, and though the Ridonne snuck a few slashes and thrusts past Victor's guard, his armor ate them, or they left only superficial wounds that closed almost as soon as the blade slipped away. Victor snarled, his fury rising with each moment they fought, and the Ridonne similarly grew frustrated; it was clear he didn't enjoy the delay Victor was causing him. Did he desire to slaughter weaker foes so much? The idea further infuriated Victor.

"So," the Ridonne grunted after minutes of intense battle, stepping back after a fresh parry that had left Victor overextended, "I see why my lesser kin have summoned me. You are a worthy opponent, but in the Vizashath, I've battled worse. Come, flee this world. Leave me to my slaughter. As I grow accustomed to this flesh, my power only grows."

The golden man's words echoed in Victor's head as he circled him and, as his rage ran low and he struggled to keep enough in his pathways to stoke his berserk state, part of his brain puzzled over their meaning. He was growing accustomed to his flesh? Some "lesser kin" had summoned him? The Vizashath? Was this enormous winged Ridonne from somewhere outside of Fanwath? If not for his dwindling Energy, specifically his rage, Victor wouldn't care, wouldn't listen to the mouthy bastard's words; he'd be content to work on him for hours, days if need be—it was excellent axe practice, after all!

As they stood apart, the Ridonne still blathering about Victor leaving him so he could get on with his "bloody work," Victor continued to circle him and glanced inward at his Core. His fear Energy was brimming, his rage nearly empty, his inspiration full, blazing bright, and his glory nearly half gone; his banner, though a great boon, had been slowly eating it away as he continued to energize it past its normal duration. He quickly returned his focus to his foe, though that sickly, dim orb of rage weighed heavily on his mind; if his Berserk spell faded, he'd lose more than half his strength and speed. Worse, he'd also lose his enhanced healing.

He contemplated recasting his Inevitable Huntsman spell, but he didn't think he had enough rage to fuel it—justice required equal parts rage and fear woven with inspiration. Each second he deliberated, his furious red Energy ticked away, and he could see something in the Ridonne's eyes, something like sly cleverness, as he watched Victor circle him. Could he see his Energy dwindling? Victor knew others could do so; Tes could easily see the Energy in his Core. "Enough," Victor growled, and then he poured a massive torrent of fear-attuned Energy into his Wild Totem spell, summoning a pack of huge, nightmarish coyotes.

The golden warrior's eyes widened, and he backed up another step, glancing left to right, seeing the massive, pony-sized hounds coalescing out of pools of steaming, purple-black darkness. Their eyes glowered balefully like violet wisps in the depths of shadow, and they began to yip and whine as they circled Victor's foe. "So, enough testing our metal, then?" the Ridonne quipped, flicking his sword about. "I'd hoped to keep gathering my strength, but . . ." He choked off his words as Victor charged him again, using inspiration-attuned Energy.

He flashed over the ground in a cloud of bright, white mist, and as the Ridonne flooded his body with Energy, the evil-looking hounds leapt at him. They snapped at his legs and wide-flung wrists, and one of them even jumped toward his back, wrapping its razor-filled jaws around the edge of a crimson-feathered wing. The Ridonne made no effort to dodge the totems; he didn't even flinch from Victor's charge. Just as before, he somehow deflected the Energy of Victor's spell, and this time, rather than sending it into the ground, he let it explode outward in a ball of force that rolled away, with him at the epicenter. Victor was flung back by his own power, and his shadowy, nightmarish companions were ripped to shreds, reduced to tatters of shadow that rapidly faded to nothing.

Victor had seen the effects of his Energy charge on his foes, seen how it could ruin a lesser opponent like Chokodo-dak, and seen how it would send even an enemy like this Ridonne flying. For the first time, Victor felt it turned on him, and he didn't enjoy the experience. The concussion wracked his body, ruptured his ears, and burst the tiny vessels in his eyes and nose. As he staggered back, stunned and concussed by the force of his own power, the Ridonne gathered another great burst of his potent red-orange Energy and from the palm of his outstretched left hand fired a beam of it directly into Victor's chest.

Victor's dragonsteel belt was spent, unable to absorb any more for the day, but his wyrm-scale armor, lovingly crafted by a true dragon, took the beam of Energy and mightily reduced it. Still, the lance of Energy bore down, pushing the stunned titan backward, slowly eating through the wyrm scales. As the Energy began to bleed through his armor, the agony of it rending his flesh and bone was like a smelling salt to Victor's concussed mind. He thrashed, trying to roll away from the beam, but the Ridonne tracked him with it, scoring it over his body, looking for a lethal spot to focus it upon.

Screaming with agony every time it bit through his armor or found a gap, digging furrows in his flesh, Victor rolled and dove, trying to somersault away, only to find unarmored parts of himself exposed to the beam. His arms, his legs, and even his neck felt that biting ray as he struggled to get out of it. Finally, in desperation, he bunched his legs and used Titanic Leap to escape the horrible, lancing Energy. He crashed to the earth a hundred yards distant from the devilish Ridonne, rolling and crashing through empty tents, his body smoking, his armor steaming and ticking with the potent Energy it had absorbed.

Victor heard the Ridonne chuckling, and his lack of fury made him aware that his Berserk had faded as he fell. He was his natural size, his natural strength, and he was severely hurt. As he struggled to gather his jumbled thoughts, furiously contemplating the contents of his storage devices, trying to decide on a healing potion to consume, his mind's eye settled on something he'd set aside, something he'd been meaning to use the next time he had a moment's break to concentrate on himself for a while.

Images ran through his mind, memories of racing through a vast wasteland, chasing after Tes, never quite catching her. He remembered how his rage would run low and he'd start to lose his Berserk, and she'd say, "Aren't you hungry, titan-blood?" Victor summoned the wyrm heart from his storage ring, and, lying there, wrapped in the smoldering remnants of enemy tents, he contemplated eating it. It was enormous, even in his half-titan hands. "This will take too long," he grunted, agony surging with the effort; the beam had carved a black welt over his throat and lower jaw.

The pain served to focus his mind, and Victor cast Titanic Aspect, using his most plentiful Energy source, fear. It didn't seem to matter; the Energy didn't affect the spell. He simply surged in size, ripping the fabric of the tents shrouding his body and making the heart look more like a snack than an impossible meal. "Witness my glory, Ancestors," he grunted, then he took a massive bite of the heart. He crushed it between his teeth, savoring the hot, coppery juices as they exploded into his mouth. He swallowed great hunks of it, gulping them down, then bit another third of the morsel away and did the same.

Already he felt the effects—heat was exploding in his gut, coursing through him. Energy poured into his pathways like floodwaters down culverts, draining into his Core, pushing his different attunements to the edges of their ability to contain it. As his Core expanded, the Energy rolled out again, exploding through his pathways and then out of his body, great waves of it. As he choked down the last bite of the wyrm's heart, anyone looking at him would have thought he'd exploded. The fiery, powerful Energy of the heart had fully engulfed him, wrapped around him like a cocoon of smoldering magma.

From the outside, the Ridonne saw a great ball of fiery Energy roiling where Victor had fallen—roiling and pulsing, sending waves of that hot

Energy outward, scorching the tents, grass, and ground beneath, leaving a barren, dead black circle nearly a hundred yards in diameter. The Ridonne had been stalking toward the downed titan, ready to finish his work with that blood-red scimitar, but when the first pulse of that volcanic Energy washed over him, he clapped his wings and, screaming with fury and pain, flew free of the area of destruction.

Victor wasn't aware of the Ridonne or his movements. Though draconic fire boiled in his pathways, flooded his body, and churned around him, he didn't burn. Nothing but pure, unadulterated pleasure coursed through him as his cells absorbed the Energy, his pathways simmered with it, and his mind drifted on currents of flame. He saw gigantic halls beneath the planetary surface, so deep down that only a great creature such as a wyrm or dragon could hope to visit them.

Pillars of basalt a mile high supported arched caverns through which mighty magma flows ran like rivers, and fungi forests stretched farther than the eye could see. Wyrms coiled and writhed together in mating nests, screeching and roaring their enthusiasm. Some of the greater ones, the ancient elders of the hive, coiled around hoards of Energy-rich stones and metals high on the walls, their private nests of tunnels guarded by their very bulk. Here were the greatest of their kind, the most potent wyrms of Zaafor, and no scaleless soft-skin had ever or could ever set foot in these storied halls.

Victor's mind's eye soared through one great cavern after another, where he saw countless wyrms of every age and type. He saw every kind of wyrm Zaafor had to offer in those depths, from mighty rock wyrms to potent magma wyrms. He saw hordes of wealth that would buy a nation on most worlds, wealth buried beneath mountains and mountains of rock, magma, and soil. These places weren't meant for his eyes, but he saw them, and he felt awe; why would any wyrm venture forth from their deep kingdom? The answer came to him as he watched a clutch of eggs hatching, watched the young wyrms fight for space and food, and saw them driven forth by the older wyrms, pushed out to make their future where they might.

As the vision began to fade and Victor came back to himself, he felt invigorated and powerful. He knew something was different about him, something new. He felt more vibrant than ever before; a power deep in his chest roiled and surged. Before he could take the time to investigate himself, though, he remembered the Ridonne and his frustrating battle with the red-winged bastard. Deep in his Core, his rage began to boil, trickling forth into his pathways.

Victor leapt to his feet, his experience with the wyrm heart forgotten; something nagged at the corner of his vision—System messages. He didn't have time to look just then; a pang in his head, a warning from his Battlefield Awareness, told him his troops were in jeopardy in more than one place. He scanned the area for the Ridonne, only to see a great blackened circle of which he was the center.

As the pang wracked his mind again, he turned toward the source, and his eyes lit up with a bright red bloom of foreign Energy. The Ridonne had left him; it had descended on his troops, the brave men and women who'd come to fight beside him to keep the imperials at bay! Rage exploded from his Core, and Victor cast Iron Berserk. In the span of two heartbeats, he was engorged with power, and his vision dimmed to crimson as he used Titanic Leap to close the distance between himself and his embattled soldiers and friends.

As he soared through the air, he resummoned his Banner of the Champion, and bright, golden light lit up the night, throwing back the shadows and revealing the carnage of the battle that had been raging the entire time he'd been busy with the Ridonne and then with his strange vision of the depths of Zaafor. Bodies were strewn in the mud churned up by the five hundred charging cavalry that had accompanied Victor. Bodies of imperials were everywhere, dead roladii were scattered throughout, and his troops were in the center of a long, thin ring of imperial soldiers, pressed into a tight square where they fought, shoulder to shoulder, against their foes.

Victor believed they could win; the imperials, though encircling them, were fewer in number. How devastating his troops' charges must have been! He wanted to scream with pride and praise, but the Ridonne had come upon the scene, and his influence had turned the tide. As he descended toward the conflict, Victor saw dozens of his soldiers' bodies around the enormous golden figure. In a near panic, Victor scanned for Valla and for Lam, and he saw them. They stood with Polo before the Ridonne, backs pressed to their troops, ready to try to fight him off.

Victor squeezed Lifedrinker in his fist, and as he landed on the field twenty yards behind the Ridonne, his banner bathing everyone around in its influential light, he roared. His voice rumbled over the battlefield like never before. It was a palpable thing, that roar; it took hold of the air and shook it, vibrating the hearts and minds of those nearby. It drove courage into his troops and fear into the imperials. The golden warrior spun, eyes wide with surprise. As Victor stalked toward him, he growled, "*Chica,* it's time for you to drink this *pendejo.*"

The Ridonne bloomed with crimson Energy. He channeled it up into his outstretched hand and pointed it at Victor again. Victor changed his Sovereign Will boost from strength to agility, leaving the bonus on his vitality alone. Then, as he charged at the Ridonne, moving like an enraged grizzly, closing the distance in seconds, he cast Project Spirit and bathed the golden-clad warrior in a blanket of pure, potent fear. The Ridonne balked, his beam of red, terrible Energy sputtering as soon as it started, and then Victor was on him, Lifedrinker weaving a web of smoldering destruction.

As his troops backed away, some of them impacted by his brief burst of fear-attuned Energy, they watched the battle with wide eyes. Those on the edges of their formation stood their ground, watching the imperials, but it was clear their will was broken; most of them were fleeing the conflict and had been ever since Victor had roared his challenge and dropped into the corpse-strewn field with his blazing banner. Those who stayed couldn't move; they were transfixed by fear and stunned by the battle between the two giant men.

Victor fought differently than before. His boost to agility was just what he needed, and what was more, the Ridonne looked taxed; whatever limit he suffered from, be it Energy or simply time, he was starting to feel it, and Victor was slipping Lifedrinker past his guard again and again. His first truly damaging blow caught the Ridonne's left wing as the warrior tried to bring it around to knock Victor off guard. Victor was just a touch too fast, though, and he brought Lifedrinker's smoldering edge down on the edge of that great appendage and cut it in half.

"Whoreson!" the golden man screamed, and then he went into a frenzy of hacks, charging his arm and sword with that vile red Energy. However, Victor wasn't one to be battered away with a furious outburst. He ducked his chin and waded into those sword strokes, and as the blade clanged against his helm, he hacked Lifedrinker again and again into the winged warrior's side, from his shoulder to his ribs to his hip to his knee. At the end of the furious exchange of blows, Victor had a few rapidly healing gashes, but the Ridonne lay in the bloody mud, writhing. Victor had nearly severed one of his arms, smashed his armored plate into a concave shape, shattered his ribs, and cut his leg off at the knee.

The Ridonne lifted his scimitar in his one good hand and held it in front of his face as though to shield himself from a death blow, and he gasped, "You've made an enemy here, fool. One who will haunt you through the worlds."

"I'm not scared of ghosts," Victor growled, and then, with all his might, he hacked Lifedrinker into the sword. She drove that crimson blade down until it hit the Ridonne's chest, bit clean through it and the gold-plated armor, and buried herself deep in the golden man's sternum. As the crimson scimitar fell away in two pieces, Lifedrinker bucked and pulsed, pulling herself deeper as thick rivulets of potent red Energy surged into her. The char fell away from her haft, and she seemed to expand, her axe-head growing in mass. "That's it, *chica*; get a good drink." Victor's chest heaved as he gulped in deep breaths.

The Ridonne struggled for a while, blood spraying from his gasping, breathless mouth. He thrashed side to side, clawing at Lifedrinker with his one working arm, but as she drank his Energy and the crimson light faded from his eyes, the once-great winged warrior's thrashing grew listless, and he fell still. Suddenly the battlefield erupted with cheers and bright lights as his surviving soldiers witnessed his victory.

Victor was deaf to it all; the only voice he could hear was Valla's as she ran up to him, drenched in blood. Midnight clutched before her, dripping with gore, she shouted, "When he came, when he fell upon us, we thought you were dead!"

"Not a chance, beautiful, not a chance," Victor grinned, and if he hadn't been fifteen feet tall, he might have tried to kiss her. "Take them." Victor gestured to the cheering troops. "They need us at the encampment." Having resolved this danger to his soldiers, Victor was very aware of another pang, another urge to go and help his embattled army.

"Are the Ridonne gone?" Valla asked as Lam and Polo started shouting orders.

"I think so. I think they brought this *pendejo* here somehow. I'll look for them afterward. Go! I'll catch up, but first, I want to cut something out of this asshole." As Lifedrinker finished her feast, Victor smashed his fist through the hole she'd made and began grasping through the hot insides of the Ridonne's chest, feeling for the warm, stiff organ that was his prize. He grinned, huge, bloody, and red-eyed, at Valla, and she nodded. Then, stumbling in her haste, she joined her voice to those of Lam and Polo, exhorting their troops to action.

Victor wrapped his fingers around the muscular heart of the Ridonne, and with squelching pops, he yanked it free, steaming in the night air. Saliva flooded his mouth, but Victor knew better than to try to savor his prize at that moment. He tucked it away into his storage ring and then turned to the north, where his army's encampment blazed with a thousand magical lights—they needed his help.

39

UNEASY ALLIES

Victor stood and looked around, fury still bleeding into his vision, tinting the night a shade of crimson. He watched his troops charging down the slope, none but Valla mounted. Where had Uvu gone during the battle? Had he been slaying imperials on his own? Victor marveled at the outstanding training the cat must have to come to her now, allowing her to mount for the return to camp. In all the time he'd spent with her, he'd never seen Valla whistle or call the cat; how had it known? "Something to ask her later," he grunted, but then something caught his attention. The corpse at his feet was moving!

"No way . . ." he said, lifting Lifedrinker for some more bloody work, but when he looked down, he realized it wasn't moving; it was shrinking. The corpse was shriveling in on itself, generating a stinky, gray, murky steam. Victor stepped back, waving a hand before his face, not wanting to inhale those gross vapors. When they faded, a smaller figure lay before him—it was the Ridonne he'd fought with during his nightmare rampage, the tall golden one. He didn't look so good anymore. His flesh was split, thin like paper, and covered in weird tattoos; only a shadow of its former golden luster remained. The man's face was frozen in a rictus of pain, and his golden eyes were dim, fogged over in a way that reminded Victor of cataracts.

As he stared at the corpse, he saw beads of shimmering purple Energy begin to pop up all over it, and he knew the System had decided there was enough of a lull in his fighting for him to reap his rewards. He stood tall, watching the tiny beads rapidly expand to fist-sized balls. Then they floated together, shimmering, pulsating, and coalescing into a stream that began to flow around him, *whooshing* in a corkscrew pattern around his gigantic body until it rose to his chest, where it plunged into him, flooding his pathways with raw, potent Energy. Victor arched his back and managed a mighty yawp before the euphoria overcame him. When the moment passed, and he stood there fully renewed, fresh, and ready for battle, he looked at the many System messages vying for his attention.

*****Congratulations! Your absorption of an Elder Wyrm's heart has granted you the seed of a Breath Core.*****

*****Breath Affinity gained: Magma.*****

*****Resistance enhanced: Fire.*****

*****Breath Core: Your Quinametzin bloodline has allowed you to claim the rare and potent power of an Elder Wyrm. The seed of your Breath Core will germinate, growing in potency as you consume appropriate Energy sources. The Breath Core exists within you in conjunction with your Energy Core. It grants you an affinity for the Wyrm's breath (Magma). As your Breath Core grows, so too will your resistance to Fire and related elements. Further boons based on your Breath Core's affinity (Magma) will be granted as it matures.*****

*****Congratulations! You have achieved level 52 Battlemaster and gained 10 strength, 9 vitality, 4 agility, 4 dexterity, 3 will, and 3 intelligence.*****

"What the hell?" Victor grasped at his chest where, even now, he could feel the roiling, hot potential, the power he'd wondered at earlier. Despite his situation, standing in the middle of a battlefield, his troops in need, he couldn't help looking at the first page of his status sheet:

Name:	Victor Sandoval		
Race:	Human (Quinametzin Bloodline): Advanced 7		
Class:	Battlemaster: Epic		
Level:	52		
Breath Core:	Elder Seed: Base 1		
Core:	Spirit Class: Advanced 5		
Breath Core Affinity:	Magma 9.0	Breath Core Energy:	5/100

Energy Affinity:	3.1, Fear 9.4, Rage 9.1, Glory 8.6, Inspiration 7.4		Energy:	12568/ 12568
Strength:	240	Vitality:	353 (378)	
Dexterity:	108	Agility:	131	
Intelligence:	98	Will:	479	
Points Available:	0			
Titles & Feats:	Titanic Rage, Ancestral Bond, Flame-Touched, Titanic Constitution, Titanic Presence, Desperate Grace, Challenger, Elder Magic, Born of Terror, Battlefield Awareness			

"Holy shit," he whispered, "I can fucking breathe fire?" Before he could examine himself further or attempt any mad experimentation, an almost crippling pang of urgency struck him. Victor jerked his head toward the encampment. He was needed in many places, and there wasn't a clear priority.

He started jogging toward the distant camp, explosions of faraway magic blooming in his eyes. As he ran, he summoned Guapo with a torrent of glory-attuned Energy, and as the beast sprang from a glittering, golden pool, he swung himself onto the mustang's back. "Let's go!" He leaned forward, grasped Guapo's mane, and squeezed his knees. The spirit animal knew what he wanted, and, trailing his brilliant banner, he tore over the battlefield, quickly overtaking the surviving troops of his unit.

As his banner's light fell on them, they cheered, their urgency to fight renewed, and Valla briefly paced him with her great cat. She called out, "Is something wrong?"

"Yeah! I think we're losing the siege!" he shouted over his shoulder, and then Guapo really turned it on, and he streaked away from her. He'd cleared half the distance back to camp in something less than a minute, and he could see that the walls facing him weren't exactly overwhelmed. In fact, the enemy troops were all but nonexistent, just a few scattered units here and there, but all of them seemed to be trying to work their way around the walls to the far side of the encampment.

Victor let his gaze lift and instantly saw where he was needed; the far side of the camp was swarming with activity. He couldn't see exactly what was happening, thanks to all the magical attacks exploding in the night. Wild lightning strikes, bursts of flame, explosions of Energy in almost every imaginable color, and, most obscuring of all, clouds, geysers, and sheeting rains of Energy-based liquids all combined to make an obfuscating haze. He contemplated riding around the perimeter to smash into the enemies on the far side but decided to charge straight for the wall; he could leap over it.

As he rode, the pangs in his head urging him onward came more and more frequently, and he began to wonder if he was too late. If he arrived to wade into the enemy troops, broke their spirit, and drove them out of the camp, what good would it do if half his army was dead? What if Rellia and Borrius were already gone? Had he taken too long with the Ridonne? How long had he lain in the cocoon of fire? Had it been very long? His unit had fought the imperials left behind to a standstill while he'd absorbed the wyrm's heart—that couldn't have happened quickly . . . Victor shook his head, banishing the fruitless speculation, and leaned forward, urging Guapo to give it his all.

The tower shook, rocking wildly, and Edeya cried out, dropping her spear and sliding to the railing, grasping the sturdy planks with both arms. Rellia danced nimbly over the boards, displaying her grace and unnatural agility as she grabbed Borrius's wrist in fingers like steel bands. "I've got you," she said, halting his tumble—he'd nearly gone over the top of the railing.

"Are they bringing it down?" he grunted, steadying himself on the wooden rail the same way as the lieutenant.

"I don't know. They've stopped—perhaps it was a warning."

"Perhaps," Borrius sighed. The three of them had killed dozens of imperials trying to mount the tower. Many had come up the ladder, but quite a few had scaled the exterior. A few Ghelli had even flown up. Rellia was a match for them, though; her speed and deadly accuracy with her rapier made defending such a small space child's play, especially when it became clear the imperials were, in fact, trying to take them alive. "Perhaps it's time to hand ourselves over . . ."

"I thought we were fighting to the death," Edeya gasped, wincing in pain as she knelt to recover her spear. At some point, she'd taken an arrow to her hip; the broken shaft still jutted forth, blood drizzling along it like a leaky keg tap.

"What's the point?" Borrius gasped, leaning forward to breathe better. Pinprick stars filled his vision, and he felt woozy. He gestured to the north, where the flickering lights had grown steadily closer over the last fifteen minutes of desperate fighting. "Perhaps we can stop them unleashing whatever that is on the troops. Perhaps we can prevent the slaughter of our entire army."

Rellia had been pacing around the still-shaking tower's perimeter, looking for the next assault, but when Borrius mentioned the lights in the sky, she stopped and stared. He watched her lean forward, watched her mouth fall agape, and then listened as she hissed, "Those are wings!"

"Your eyes are better than mine, but those don't look like Ghelli." He squinted, wishing, not for the first time, that he'd squandered some of his savings on racial advancements instead of buying favor in Tharcray. He supposed there was nothing to be done now, but if he could go back in time, he would certainly do things differently. What had his many years serving the Empire gotten him? It was a cold, hard truth that he hadn't gained any consideration from the troops breaking down this tower.

"No," Edeya said, also squinting into the night. "We'd see the motes falling down; such flight would require very advanced wings."

Her words rang true. Even Lam couldn't fly that far, and her wings gave off sparkling motes that showered the air around her. If she could soar like those supposed flyers to the north, Borrius could only imagine the light show.

A rough voice shouted up from beneath the ladder hole, interrupting their speculation, "Will you come alive? Our leaders wish to question you. Order your troops to surrender, and many may yet live!"

Rellia was still staring into the black night to the north, but Edeya ran her eyes around the camp, perhaps hoping for desperate salvation. Borrius stood up straight and cleared his throat, ready to talk to the man below, if for no other reason than to stall him. A gasp from Rellia halted the half-formed words in his throat, though, and she hoarsely whispered, "Ancestors . . . are we so cursed?"

"What?" Borrius lifted his shield, his arm numb from the exertion, and stared at the ladder hole, wondering what the imperials had planned if he didn't respond.

"They aren't Ghelli. They're Naghelli." Rellia's voice was hushed, full of dread, disbelief, and defeat.

"Impossible!" Borrius couldn't help his scoffing tone. "They're all dead—generations ago."

"I've seen paintings. I've heard stories. I know what I'm seeing. Let me paint you a picture: ochre and red wings, lanky bodies, pale flesh, glittering dark mail. It's like they're flying out of the painting my grandfather had hanging in his reception hall. You know the one, Borrius!"

Scorn and disbelief began to war with dread at Rellia's further description. "What dark deal have the Ridonne wrought? How could the Naghelli be here now? They'll kill us all!" Borrius felt his heart hammering in his chest, nightmare stories running through his mind.

"I said, are you ready to talk? You don't all need to die tonight!" the rough voice called again from the ladder.

"What have you fools done?" Borrius wailed, his mind going from defeat to utter despair. "The Naghelli? Where were you bastards hiding them all these years?"

"Wait," Rellia said. "Wait, Borrius." Her voice carried a note of something different, and she whirled on Edeya. "Did Victor not have an encounter with Naghelli on his way from the mines?"

"Aye, lady. In a pocket realm—a dungeon. Only a handful, though, perhaps two score. They were in league with the Death Caster, Belikot."

"That's more than two score!" Borrius cried as the glowing ochre-stained wings loomed larger, and even he began to see the dark figures suspended between them.

"What if . . ." Rellia started to say, and then the winged figures began to burst into weird blurs, their wings leaving streaks in the air as they fell upon the imperial army where they were pouring through the breached wall into the encampment. Wails of alarm and surprise warred with death screams from the mass of soldiers below. Borrius watched Rellia's face, saw the shock there as she heard those cries—perhaps the imperials, too, had assumed their Ridonne masters had sent the flyers to aid them. It seemed everyone had been wrong.

When Victor leapt upon the southern wall of the encampment, the soldiers still there, stoically holding their positions, cheered for him, the light of hope igniting in their blood and soot-stained faces. Bodies were strewn everywhere, far more wearing the imperial uniform than not. "What's the story?" Victor boomed, towering over the soldiers, his banner blazing with light, bathing the wall and the ground around it in its brilliant glow. His Battlefield Awareness, and his gut, told him he needed to get to the far side of the camp where the light show signaled the wild combat still underway.

A lanky woman with bright yellow eyes staring out of her helmet's visor shouted in a husky voice, "They broke through at the northwest corner! Legate ap'Yensha called almost all the troops to defend there. Sir, flyers arrived a while ago, and everything went mad. Should we go? Should we hold the wall?"

"Flyers?" Victor frowned and bent his legs, readying another leap. "Hold the wall," he grunted, and then he was gone, exploding into the air, lifting Lifedrinker, fully healed, heavier, and with a haft better suited in size for his enormous hand. She vibrated with eagerness, ready for battle, and like a distant echo on the wind, she filled the air with a soprano war cry, her spirit hungry for conquest. Victor landed near the center of the encampment, and then he sprinted toward the battle, his banner throwing crazy shadows on the ground as he tore through the camp, passing tents, wagons, huddled noncombat personnel, animals, and wounded soldiers who'd fought their way free of the furious melee.

When he came upon the chaos of battle, he saw men and women fighting desperately and saw the tower where he knew his commanders were supposed to be standing. Then he saw them, the Naghelli, weaving among the imperial forces like winds of death, cutting them apart with that deadly, unnatural speed of theirs. When the light of his banner fell upon the chaos, ragged cheers rose from the throats of his troops. The imperials surging through the breach in the wall, already faltering from the onslaught of the Naghelli, broke. They turned and, pursued by soldiers with hearts engorged by glory, fled the way they'd come.

Victor screamed his encouragement and bounded through the fighting, smashing Lifedrinker into imperials as he passed them, ending death struggles and eliciting more hoarse cheers from blood-streaked faces. Victor took two bounding steps and then leapt past the tower toward the crumbled fortification, and when he came down, he stood among the fleeing imperials. He roared, hacking Lifedrinker left and right, spraying hot red mist as she ripped through the enemy soldiers, and then, as if his banner, his presence, and his killing weren't enough, he conjured forth a rage-fueled bear totem, letting it loose a hundred paces down the earthen ramp the imperials must have constructed.

The bear came into existence roaring and swinging, and the poor imperials could do nothing but try to speed their already desperate flight. Victor's army, like him, was eager for the glory of combat and saw the fleeing enemies as nothing but encouragement. They charged after them, threw spells, and flung weapons, hacking them down as they ran. Victor's mind was filled with mad battle lust, driven so by rage, glory, and the idea that his army had almost been overwhelmed. He was still cognizant, however, still able to observe his surroundings, and he noted that the Naghelli didn't join him or his troops in the pursuit of the fleeing imperials.

After a time, the slaughter ceased to feed his lust for glory, and Victor slowed. His gigantic figure and blazing standard were a beacon to his troops, and when they saw him give up the pursuit, saw him lower his smoldering axe and watch the scattered, overwhelmed imperial remnants dashing into the darkness of the grasslands, utterly defeated, they gathered around him. They lifted their weapons and cheered, savoring the glory of victory. Victor spun to look back at the camp, saw his bear pacing around the base of the earthen ramp, saw more friendly troops and Naghelli atop the wall, and he lifted his axe and roared. The bear stood up on its hind legs and roared almost simultaneously, and the troops joined in, waving their weapons and screaming their lust for life and their pride in triumph.

At some point, while he'd been pursuing the fleeing imperials, Valla, Lam, and Polo had arrived with their troops, and Victor could see Valla up there, at the top of the earthen ramp, sitting atop Uvu's back, facing a group of Naghelli. He figured it would probably be wise to join her and make sure he introduced Vellia to the commanders. "Oh, brother," he sighed, turning and stomping back toward the wall, gesturing for the soldiers to follow him. "Just what I needed: Vellia, Rellia, and Valla in the same room." Shaking his head, he decided he'd better enunciate his *v*'s and *r*'s very clearly.

He walked quickly, being fifteen feet tall, and soon he'd outpaced his soldiers, though they jogged to keep up as best they could. He strode up the earthen ramp, and as he came up to the level of the battered parapet, he saw that Valla, Rellia, and Borrius were standing across from a dozen Naghelli. He thought he saw Vellia near the center, but most of the attention was on the tall, lanky man at the center. He wore glittering black chainmail and an ornate platinum crown atop his white hair, and he wielded two slender longswords, their blades dancing with silver-blue Energy.

The swordsman had a presence that drew Victor's eye, eclipsing the other Naghelli nearby, and he instantly knew who he was. He couldn't think of his name, but he remembered Vellia saying that her "faction" of the Naghelli had someone on their side, a man who was, according to her, the greatest swordsman in the world. No one was speaking at the moment he walked up, but everyone looked tense. Whatever words he'd missed must not have been overly friendly.

Heads turned and eyes focused on him, and he spotted Vellia standing to the swordsman's left, just a bit behind. She sketched an elegant curtsy when his eyes fell on her, and Victor couldn't help a grin spreading his lips.

"You know these Naghelli, Victor?" Rellia asked, breaking the silence.

"Well . . ." He paused and looked over the Naghelli on the wall, then farther into the encampment where a great crowd of the winged cousins of the Ghelli clustered together. They held naked weapons and looked at the soldiers surrounding them with hostility in their dark, depthless black eyes. He knew they probably hadn't been close to anyone other than themselves in a very long time, and he hoped his army could keep their cool. "I know Vellia." He nodded to the beautiful woman with her black gossamer wings patterned with glowing orange Energy. "I probably fought a few of the others around here, but we should be good now. Thanks for helping with the imperials."

"May I introduce our leader?" Vellia asked, stepping forward.

"Please," Victor said, and he'd cooled down sufficiently to be well aware of the frowns and scowls on the faces of the commanders and troops standing nearby. Inwardly he railed at himself for not taking the time to brief Rellia and the others on the possibility that the Naghelli might try to join them. Why had he not asked about them? Why hadn't he sought answers to his own questions about why they were so hated? He knew the answer was simple if not satisfying; he'd been busy with a lot of shit since the Ridonne showed up back near Persi Gables and hadn't thought about it.

"This is Kethelket," Vellia said, gesturing to the tall swordsman, "Prince of Zerevia, the greatest swordsman in this world and the elected leader of us"—she gestured at the group of Naghelli standing on the wall—"the last of the Naghelli."

40

ANCESTORS OR GODS

Kethelket, this is Victor, the one who freed us from Belikot." Vellia bowed rather than curtsied this time, sweeping one arm low, dragging it over the rough, bloody boards of the battlements, and remained that way, nearly folded over, for several seconds until Victor figured out she was waiting for him, or maybe anyone, to speak.

"Thanks, Vellia." He was too large to properly shake any of their hands, too large even to get close without jostling people around, so he spoke to everyone, allowing his voice to carry, not trying to be quiet, "We just fought a hell of a battle. The Ridonne who led these attackers are dead or have fled. Our soldiers are tired, and no doubt your people are too. Let's take some time to sort things out and see to the injured, and then we can all meet and discuss what's next. Kethelket . . . am I saying that right?" Victor paused, waiting for the tall soldier to lock his deep black eyes on his and nod, then he continued, "Do your people mind setting up camp nearby? Until we've all"—he gestured at the thousands of soldiers standing around the wall on both sides—"had a chance to get comfortable with each other?"

He could see Rellia wanted to speak, that Borrius was champing at the bit, his bruised, sweaty face giving away his every emotion, but Kethelket spoke before they did. He had a deep, smooth voice, and his words rolled off his tongue with something almost like a lilt. "Thank you, Victor. Thank you for the service you did for the world when you crushed that vile man, Belikot. I know seeing my kind is a shock for all the people here. I know the world has grown to revile us, that the history books have not been kind to us. I'm here to assure you, we seek to change our destiny, we seek redemption, and it was to that end that we joined your battle." As his words wound down, he flicked his two long, slender swords, twirling them with a flourish and driving them home into scabbards, one over his shoulder and one at his hip.

"We will set up camp within sight of your walls," Vellia said, stepping forward next to Kethelket. "We're eager to meet with you and the leaders of this great army."

Victor nodded, and then, almost silently, the Naghelli lifted into the air on their gossamer wings, the ones on the battlement and the others down below. Victor tried to count them, but it was hard as they all kept crossing in front of each other as they flew. He thought it had to be more than a hundred, though, perhaps hundreds. Hadn't Vellia told him she and the thirty or so in Belikot's weird dungeon were the last of their kind? The ochre and crimson glow of the Naghelli's wings drifted through the night to the north, and then, maybe a mile from the camp, they settled to the ground.

As their flight came to an end, it was as if a spell had been broken, and Uvu pierced the silence with a grumbling yawn. Without thinking, Victor reached over his titan-sized hand and rubbed the great cat's head. He arched his neck and pressed his head into his palm, and Victor smiled, scratching the surprisingly soft fur.

"I think you have much to explain, Legate." Rellia didn't speak loudly, clearly not wanting to display any conflict in leadership in front of the troops. Victor was about to reply, but suddenly the night began to lighten, and he frowned. Had dawn come so soon? His answer came to him with the cheers of his soldiers. When he looked out over the battlefield, he saw millions of tiny golden motes drifting up from the bodies of the slain imperials. All around the encampment, the motes gathered, casting an eerie golden glow on the walls that steadily brightened as more and more appeared.

In a matter of minutes, the motes began to flow together, pooling into bigger and bigger clumps, and then, as the soldiers cheered, yammered, and celebrated their continued existence, the motes burst into motion, drifting and flowing toward the soldiers. A sizeable portion plunged into Victor, but it was nothing compared to the influx he'd received after his battle with the Ridonne. He didn't level again, but he saw that many soldiers gathered near the broken wall, including Edeya, Rellia, and even Borrius, received substantial Energy torrents. They whooped with excitement, shouting about levels gained and skills improved.

The System's disbursement of post-battle Energy put an end to any chance for calm, quiet talks atop the wall; the soldiers went mad with celebration, healed, recharged, buoyed by victory; their cheers couldn't be contained. "Do we let them just party, or what?" Victor asked, leaning close to Rellia and Borrius.

"No. For a while, maybe half an hour, but discipline is paramount after a battle. We don't know what other threats lurk out there," Borrius replied.

"Exactly. You killed the Ridonne, Victor?" Rellia stepped closer so she could be heard over the din.

"I killed one. He was possessed by something that made him stronger than usual. Much, much stronger. I didn't see the other one. Either he ran away or something else happened to him." Victor shrugged, and then he let his Iron Berserk and his banner fall away, resuming his usual half-titan size. "Are you guys all okay?"

"We are. Thanks to your dangerous friends. We really need to talk about them—" Rellia started to say, but Borrius cut her off.

"We do, but now's not the time. Let us convene a command council in an hour. Victor's home?"

"Very well." Rellia sighed and stretched, and for the first time, Victor saw just how ragged she looked. Despite the Energy she'd just received, she was covered in scabbed-over cuts and blood splatters. Her clothes were torn, and her hair was disheveled. He wondered how long she'd had to fight to keep the imperials from taking her and Borrius.

Valla slid down from Uvu's back and slapped his rump. "Go hunt!" The cat chuffed and pushed his big head into her, almost knocking her over, but then he turned and bounded down the ramp, disappearing into the night. "I'll follow you to your home, Victor."

"We'll join you soon." Borrius looked around, and when his eyes fell on Edeya, he said, "Lieutenant, you come with me. We'll get some messages out to the captains, establish some duty rotations and, hopefully, get a count on our casualties." The young Ghelli immediately straightened; she'd been fidgeting with a tear in her pants, rubbing at a wound that had mostly healed. She rushed to his side as the old commander began making his way around rubble, bodies, and broken, discarded weapons toward the nearest working stairway.

Rellia started following the old commander. "I'll go with him. You know, you can come with us, Victor, but I think it's going to be—"

"No, he and I have things we must discuss. Thank you, Legate." Valla pointedly used her mother's title.

"Very well. Until the command council, then."

Victor looked down at Valla. "Something up?"

"Many somethings. Can we please get out of this noise?" It was true; the troops were still being raucous, so Victor nodded and motioned for her to precede him. To his surprise, she turned, walked to the edge of the battlement, and dropped off, landing lightly on her feet some twenty feet below on a mound of soil that had spilled through a breach in the wall. Victor followed her, amused at himself; the drop for him was nothing, and why should it be much for her? She probably had higher agility than he did and wasn't anywhere close to a base-level Ardeni.

They walked together toward the section of the camp where the command tents and travel homes were arranged. He might have dropped his banner and his titanic size, but he was still a striking, recognizable figure, so it wasn't a surprise that troops and support personnel called out to him all along the way. He had to pause many times to shake hands, clap shoulders, and commiserate with soldiers mourning a fallen comrade. Valla spoke comforting and encouraging words along with him. As they finally neared his travel home, a familiar voice called, "Victor, hold up!"

He turned to see Chandri running toward him and Valla. "Hey." He raised his hand, offering a wave and warm smile. She slid to a halt before him, and her face was a mosaic of emotions. He couldn't read it but thought he saw some relief, some anger, and something else . . .

"Hey?" She scowled as she repeated the word back to him. "That's what you have to say after that nightmare? We thought the night was lost! Our kin fell back from your wall when the imperials broke through. We set up a perimeter around the wagons, ready to fight to our last breath! Victor, we thought it was the end!"

"Shit." Victor sighed, and while Valla watched with arched eyebrows, he tried to pull her into a hug. She resisted, of course, and as she pulled back, he said, "Listen, Chandri, I'm sorry. My fight with the Ridonne took longer than I'd hoped, and I guess the imperials did better against our walls than Borrius expected. I should have come to you right away. I should meet with Tellen and Thayla . . ."

"They're busy dealing with the clan. We lost forty-three hunters and have twice as many wounded."

"Oh, man." Victor felt the pit of his stomach drop out, imagining the loss the Shadeni had suffered. He lowered himself to a knee, still nearly able to look Chandri in the eye. He asked, "Are the army's medics helping?"

"Yes. Of course." She seemed less angry suddenly, and he wondered if it was the thought of all those dead clan folk.

"What about Deyni and Chala?"

"They're fine. We kept them in the wagon with the youngest children throughout the battle. You can't really hear the outside very well from in there." She sniffed, her brow furrowed, and asked, "You killed the imperial bastard who led the army?"

"One of them. I don't know what happened to the other—probably crawling back to Tharcray with his tail between his legs." Victor squeezed Chandri's arms, wishing she'd let him pull her close.

"That's good, then. Let the Empire fear us. Still, I wish you wouldn't let him get away. What about those flying folk? Is it true they're Naghelli? Are they your friends?"

"They're . . . allies, at least. Yeah, they're Naghelli. I think they're the last of their kind. They're going to join us in the conquest of the Marches, and with them along, I don't think any other armies will be able to sneak up on us. Can you pass that along to Tellen and Thayla? Please tell them I want to see them as soon as they can break away."

"I will, Victor." Chandri pulled back, glanced at Valla, who'd been standing nearby quite patiently, and then turned back to Victor and grinned. "I shot many, many arrows into those imperials! I gained a level!"

"Oh, shit! That's what I like to hear, Chandri!" Her fierce grin was a welcome expression on her soot-stained face, and Victor smiled back as she began to jog toward the wagon enclosure.

Before she was gone from sight, she turned. "Speak to you soon, Ridonne Slayer!" Her teeth flashed as she called out the words, then she was gone, ducking between two tents.

"Your legend grows." Valla smirked and turned back toward his jade travel home, and Victor followed, a look of consternation plain on his face. When he stepped into the foyer, she asked, "The library?"

"Uh, sure. What's up?" He was growing increasingly leery about this conversation she wanted to have. Her mood was always difficult for him to read, but she was being even more curt or mysterious—he didn't know how to phrase it—than usual. She didn't reply until they were inside the library, and then she turned to him, leaning against the big map table.

"Tell me what happened to you when you fought the Ridonne. Why did he leave you to come and attack our unit?"

"Oh, is that all? He was a tough bastard." Victor shrugged. "He had me down for a minute there, so I ate my wyrm heart."

"You were 'down' for a minute?" Her eyes opened in alarm. "Yet when you arrived, leaping into battle, you seemed to thrash him rather easily!"

"Well, I was fully recharged, and I think that dude was losing power the longer he stayed here, inside the Ridonne's body. Like, I think it was a different . . . person in there. He kind of threatened me, said I'd made a powerful enemy or some bullshit. He said it while dying, so maybe take it with a grain of salt." Victor shrugged again, trying to lift the mood with a sheepish smile.

Valla didn't bite, though. She narrowed her eyes further. "What did the wyrm heart do to you?"

"Is something different about me?" Victor's impulse was to turn around in a circle as if he wanted her to see every angle, but he held still, just a half smile quirking up a corner of his mouth.

"Let me see." Valla surprised him by stepping forward and taking one of his big hands in both of hers. Her fingers felt cool, and she squeezed his palm, massaging the meat of it between her fingers. "You're hot, not just warm, despite the chill. It feels like I'm holding a cup of tea."

"Well, *ahem*." Victor cleared his throat and looked up at the ceiling for a minute, trying to choose his words. "When I ate the wyrm's heart, I gained something from it. I have a Breath Core now, and it came with a new affinity." He shrugged, looking into Valla's wide eyes. "It's magma. I guess that wyrm we killed could breathe magma, but Lifedrinker never gave it a chance."

"You have a . . . Breath Core? I've never even heard of such a thing. You can . . . breathe *magma*?" She sounded incredulous, stunned even, and she stopped squeezing his hand with her fingers, but she didn't let go.

"I don't know how it works. Also, it's just a 'seed,' whatever that means. The System said something about consuming the appropriate types of Energy to try to grow it."

"You're very surprising, Victor. I have to tell you something, and I want you to know it's not easy for me to say things like this. You remember what I said when we spoke about Tes? I still feel that way, but . . ." She broke off and looked down, almost pulling her hands away, but Victor closed his fist, trapping her fingers within.

"But?" he prompted, voice gentle, coaxing.

"But when the Ridonne arrived to attack our troops, I feared you'd lost. I feared you'd died, and my heart nearly burst with grief. I can't stand the idea of losing you. I was moments from throwing myself at him, from doing everything I could to kill him or die trying. I was intent on following you into the spirit realm!" Her words came out as almost a sob, and Victor's teasing smile fell off his face as he pulled her close, their wyrm-scale armors clicking and sliding against each other.

"Shit, Valla! I'm sorry! You know, I was pretty panic-stricken when I saw that asshole's magic going off near you guys. I never meant to let him get that close to you. Damn, though, I don't want you thinking like that." He lifted her chin so her big teal eyes looked into his and continued softly, "Hey, I'm serious. You know I'm going to risk my life over and over again. It's my nature. You know that by now, right? You have to wrap your head around the idea that I might lose someday. That doesn't mean your life's over!"

"I know," she sighed, leaning into him. "Ancestors, you're warm."

"Do you hate it?"

"No! It feels nice." She wormed her hand in between them and brushed it down the front of her armor, opening the scale hauberk so just her soft shirt pressed against him. "Open your armor."

Victor could only comply, and when he'd opened his vest, Valla pushed her arms inside the seam, spreading the sides apart and working her slender, muscular arms around his ribs. She buried her face in his chest and sighed heavily. "God, that feels good. Did I say that right? I hear you saying it all the time."

"God? Yeah. I mean, no, if you ask my *abuelita*. We're not supposed to take his name in vain, but I think most people just accept that they're being naughty and hope he forgives them. I mean, if they really believe." He felt like he was babbling. It seemed Valla had tuned him out as she pressed herself against him, absorbing his warmth and eliciting all sorts of responses from Victor's body.

He tried to lean down, maybe to kiss the top of her head or sniff her hair, but it was too far with her so close, so he reached inside himself and cast Alter Self, reducing his size by a foot or so. Valla didn't even flinch, but she used the reduction in his bulk to get a better grip on his torso with her arms. Chuckling and enjoying the affection, Victor did what he'd wanted to do earlier and kissed her head through her hair, noting the smell of ash, sweat, and, unsurprisingly, blood.

"Don't sniff me," she mumbled, face still buried in his chest.

"Maybe we should take a bath . . ." he tried, but her laughter cut him off.

"Oh, you'd like that! No, the others will be here soon enough. Let's just be close for a while. Let's just savor our victory and thank the Ancestors or . . . gods and enjoy this small reprieve from the madness to come."

"You think we're in for some madness?" Victor asked, stroking her hair, pleased that she'd let it grow a bit and that it had come loose from her usual tight bindings.

"Undoubtedly. The others will soon be in here, hysterical about those Naghelli you apparently invited to join the campaign." Suddenly she pushed back from him and looked up with narrowed eyes. "Tell me about that woman, Victor. The one who so blatantly flashed her cleavage your way."

"Oh, God," Victor sighed.

41

DEATH TALLIES AND CAMARADERIE

Victor tried to explain the Naghelli to Valla. He found himself going back to when he and Thayla had found the skull containing part of Belikot's spirit, and then, in frustration, he said, "I'm just going to have to explain all this again when the others get there!"

"True." Valla sighed and stretched, then she looked at Victor critically and let her eyes run down his form, stopping somewhere below his waist. Before he could get excited about her gaze, she said, "You should put on some different pants. Those are completely ruined."

He looked down and saw that his legs were mostly exposed, only threads holding together the remnants of the once fine magical garment. "Yeah, I've been kinda busy." He shrugged and summoned a new pair out of his storage ring. While Valla perused the battle map, he pulled off his boots, which had held up significantly better, the magic within them slowly repairing the damage they'd suffered, and changed his pants. He'd just pulled his boots back on when he heard conversation coming from his foyer. "Here they come," he grunted, straightening up and moving to lean on the table near Valla.

"Well, you've some explaining to do," Rellia said by way of greeting, striding up to the table and standing across from Victor, storm clouds in her eyes.

"I . . ."

"What madness!" Borrius marched into the room behind the red-haired, crimson-eyed noblewoman. "What mad fool keeps an army of Naghelli lying secretly in reserve? I might have believed the Ridonne would do something so foolish, but my ally? The leader of my own legion? And now you want to add them to our ranks?"

"Yeah, um . . ."

"Excuse my impertinence, Tribune." Edeya stepped out of the shadows beyond the doorway, holding up a pointer finger toward Borrius. "But we'd be dead if not for those Naghelli. You and I, for certain."

"Remember your place, Lieutenant. Stand there."—he pointed to the far wall, some five yards removed from the table—"and take your notes!"

"Easy, Borrius." Lam stepped up behind the much more diminutive Ghelli, resting a hand on Edeya's shoulder, holding the young woman in place even as she tried to follow Borrius's command. "I know we're all a little stressed. I no less than you; the Naghelli are cousins to my"—she pulled Edeya close—"*our* people, after all."

"Any chance you could all chill out and let me explain?" Victor asked, trying to regulate his breathing. He felt himself almost subconsciously channeling some inspiration-attuned Energy into his pathways and felt quite a lot better as it began to permeate his being. As the others grew quiet, he took a deep, steadying breath. "I'm not from Fanwath, obviously. Maybe that's why I was willing to listen to Vellia. That's the woman who introduced their leader, Kethelket, to us. It seems that you all have a deep fear of the Naghelli."

"For good reason!" Rellia barked.

"It's true." Lam nodded to Rellia, signaling her support.

"This is madness!" Borrius growled again, leaning forward, his pale blue skin darkening, flushing angrily.

"You all won't listen to Victor?" Valla's voice was severe, cutting the air like a knife, and the implication was clear—were they all so willing to dismiss his words, to ignore his desire to speak? How far would they take their disobedience? Would they mutiny? As silence fell and everyone began to come to grips with the fact that Victor was, in fact, their leader, Victor found himself standing with everyone's eyes on him, their mouths closed, demonstrating their willingness to listen, if nothing else.

"Thank you." He released his hold on the edge of the table, straightening up, rolling his neck, and squaring his shoulders. With a deep inhalation through his nose, he began to speak again, "I listened to her after I killed the mage that had been ruling the remnants of her people. He was a leftover from a time when Fanwath was at war. More than it is now," he said, nodding as memories came back to him. "Her people had sworn to serve him. Belikot was his name, and there was a time, not long ago, when speaking it aloud was dangerous."

Victor let his words sink in, looking around, meeting each of the other commander's eyes, and when they all remained respectfully silent, he continued. "Vellia didn't use that as an excuse. I asked her point blank if she was just a victim, and she told me the truth: she and her people had done terrible things. They were vile, their souls darkened by their deeds. They joined Belikot for power, not because he forced them." He saw the disgust twisting Borrius's face and the way Rellia's eyes had turned down, and her lips had begun to frown. He knew they were thinking similarly to how he once had when he'd thought he might have to slay all the Naghelli.

"Thank you for continuing to listen." Victor leaned forward again, placing his hands on the table. "She told me that much changed during their exile, during the decades, centuries maybe—I don't remember—that they spent in the pocket realm with Belikot. Most of them began to regret their crimes and the things they'd done in the name of power. Most of them grew to resent Belikot, and though they felt his control was absolute, they began to loathe everything he wanted, the plans he made. She was stunned when I killed him. Stunned and grateful. She swore that she and the faction led by Kethelket would work to atone for their sins."

Rellia cleared her throat and held up a hand as though asking for permission to speak, but Victor said, "Just a minute. I have a bit more to say. I'm not naive, or at least not as naive as I used to be. I know those guys are dangerous. You saw how they fight. Every single one of them has some magic that makes them incredibly fast, and they've had a long, long time to practice with their weapons. That said, there's no damn way that a hundred or two hundred, whatever it is, can threaten this army, not with me here.

"Finally, I want to say that I agree that we need to get some answers from them. First, we need to find out why there are so many of them. Vellia told me there were something like thirty. Secondly, we need to learn their intentions. What do they want with the Untamed Marches? What do they expect? Will they sign a contract the way our troops did? If so, would that make you all feel better?" Victor paused, looked at their faces again, and saw some lessening of the tension in Rellia's brow and an almost thoughtful expression on Borrius's face. Lam leaned on the table, resting her chin in her palms, and Victor couldn't guess what was going through her head. He turned to Valla and said, "I'm done."

"I will be greatly heartened if they'll sign a contract," Borrius said immediately.

"They could kill us all in our sleep." Lam's voice was soft, and Victor stared at her, willing her to look into his eyes, but she continued to stare, almost dreamily, at the map.

"I will listen to them." Rellia turned to Victor. "Can we bring their leader here? We should settle this as soon as possible. We should be marching again by noon to ensure we don't allow the opportunity for another Ridonne ambush."

"Yeah. Let's meet with Kethelket." Victor turned to Lam. "What's going on, Lam? They're not going to kill us all in our sleep."

"Tell that to the residents of Night Boughs."

"Night Boughs? I haven't heard of it . . ." Valla started to say, but Edeya spoke up from Lam's shadow.

"She's talking about a city from the old world—before we were formed into Fanwath. It's an old Ghelli story about how a hundred Naghelli, moving like shadows of death, slit the throats of an entire city."

"Is it true?" Valla's eyes were wide with horror.

"My grandmother certainly thought so," Edeya replied, resting a hand on Lam's shoulder just beneath one of her glittering wings.

"Well," Victor said, "these Naghelli are not here to kill us all in our sleep! Why the hell would they help fight off the imperials if they wanted us dead? Be honest: is there something about their bloodline that makes them evil? Is it possible there's some prejudice involved here? I'm not saying they never did anything wrong, but don't you think a war between factions might have led to some atrocities and the entire group might have gotten labeled evil? Maybe things written in your histories were . . . slanted."

"I will admit to the possibility," Rellia said, turning to Lam and taking up Victor's cause, "that in times long past, there were Naghelli who weren't reviled. Could not their losing role in a great conflict have driven the remainder of their kind to seek desperate bargains, to join with scoundrels like this Belikot fellow?"

"History from the old world is rather spotty. Tales of the Naghelli are mostly whispered at night from elders to children." Lam sighed and straightened up, taking Edeya's small, delicate hand in hers. "I'll listen to this Kethelket fellow."

"Good. Now, before we move on to that, we should talk about the imperials and the Ridonne. I'm certain one is dead, but the other never showed his face."

"Their army is broken. We slew more than half their number. The survivors are scattered and on the run. If we march with purpose and haste, there's no possible way another of the legions could be moved into a position that will threaten our progress into the Untamed Marches." Borrius sounded sure and confident.

Still, Victor pressed him, "You're certain of that?"

"Yes! These two legions were the closest; one of them must have come all the way from Twilight Home, and the other was meant to be patrolling the frontier. We've destroyed a third of the Empire's standing army! They need their remaining troops to keep the Free Cities in check and to hold back the hordes in the north. The Emperor will never let the legion in Tharcray march forth. If he truly wants to beat us now, he'll have to conscript new troops, taking some cohorts from the existing legions as a backbone, but that would take months. Winter will be upon us before he can hope to march the new army against us. We'll be deep in the Marches by the time spring rolls around. We may even have a base of operations built before they could hope to challenge us."

"Meanwhile, our army will continue to grow in strength." Lam locked eyes with Borrius, nodding in agreement.

"Exactly! So long as we continue to win, volunteers will continue to trickle in, and our troops will gain levels from the conquest. This legion will soon be a very tough nut to crack!" Borrius's eyes lit up with excitement as he spoke, and his fist pounded the table to emphasize his enthusiasm.

"So, we don't need to worry about the Empire anymore?" Victor frowned, not so sure things could be that simple.

"Not in the near term, no. If we establish our own lands in the Marches, though, you can be assured that the Empire will view us as a threat. In a year or five or ten, I'm sure a very large army indeed may come against us."

"Leaving them open to their other enemies." Rellia shook her head. "I've thought about this a great deal, Borrius. If we aren't hostile to them, I think the Ridonne will leave us be, especially if our power continues to grow. When we have a foothold and open some portals . . . you can imagine the influx. People grow weary of the Empire's stagnation."

"I wish that bastard Ridonne hadn't gotten away," Borrius growled. "I'm not sure which one of them ordered the attack on the Shadeni clan, but I hate to think one of the responsible parties has escaped."

"I can catch him." Victor looked down and locked eyes with Valla, nodding. "I should. I think it's important that there be consequences for the leaders of this Empire when they attack us. We need to set a precedent. They need to learn that they're not untouchable anymore."

"I like that idea." Borrius slammed his fist on the table again. Victor was enjoying seeing this side of the old man, fired up and ready for action. "Let's get Kethelket in here, and then you should go, Victor. You should seek out that bastard. We'll get the army sorted and get us ready to march. Do you reckon it will take you long?"

"No, I don't think so, Borrius." Victor chuckled, then looked at Edeya. "Can you message Polo in the book? Have him go escort Kethelket here. I think he's the least likely to be nervous about a job like that."

"Yes, sir," Edeya said, suddenly very deferential. In a way, it made him sad. He felt as though he'd gained her respect but that he'd begun to outgrow their friendship, that she'd forgotten that he was just the dummy from the mines who'd always had his foot in his mouth. He resolved to spend some time with her soon. Maybe they could go over the contents of that bag of jewelry she was supposed to be cataloging for him . . .

"Sirs," Edeya said suddenly, looking up from the command book and interrupting his musings, "there are reports on casualties from the captains."

"Well, let's hear the bad news," Borrius sighed.

"Casualties, including deaths and disabling injuries, are as follows. First cohort: seventy." Edeya read the number clinically and clearly, but Victor could hear a bit of a quaver in her voice as she continued. "Second cohort: eighteen—"

"That's better," Rellia interrupted. "They were on the south wall, right?"

"Correct," Borrius replied. "Continue, Lieutenant."

"Third cohort: one hundred eighty-eight." The table grew quiet at the tally—the third cohort had been stationed on the wall where the imperials had breached. "Fourth cohort: three." Valla let out a pent-up breath, relief evident on her face. "Fifth cohort: thirty-one; sixth cohort: twenty-one; seventh cohort: ninety-four; eighth cohort: sixty-two; ninth cohort: three hundred fifty-seven . . ."

"Old Bones!" Borrius cried.

"They were at the breach as well. They must have taken the brunt." Rellia shook her head, making a *tsk* sound with her tongue.

"Tenth cohort: nine." Edeya closed her book, blinking rapidly.

"Eight hundred fifty," Lam said.

"Aye," Borrius agreed, "Close to a cohort and a half. Do we collapse one of them to bolster the numbers of the other nine? Or do we keep the ten and let those devils who lived serve as the backbone as we add new troops to their numbers?"

"It stands to reason that the survivors in the ninth and the third saw the most action and gained the most experience," Valla said. "If you break them up, it will hurt their morale. I think you should keep the cohorts intact and add to them as we gain new troops. We're due to pass by, what, two towns and half a dozen villages once we skirt Starfall Ridge and turn south?"

"That's right." Borrius nodded. "Don't forget that we probably have a hundred troops with Far Scribe books sharing their exploits with their families back home. Our victories will bring more and more adventurers and fortune seekers. The numbers will swell."

"Did Polo reply to you, Edeya?" Victor interrupted the talk of casualties and troop counts.

"Oh, yes. He did right away."

"Okay." Victor looked around at the filthy, exhausted members of his command council. "I think we could all use a drink, huh? Maybe some refreshments? Let's move the meeting to the big table, and I'll get some stuff together."

"I could kill for a stiff drink." Borrius turned, oblivious to his poor choice of words.

"You did enough of that tonight already," Rellia quipped, and at first, Victor thought she was talking shit about his management of the troops. He opened his mouth to try to forestall a fight, but Edeya beat him to it.

"I was impressed with how you used that mace, Tribune Borrius! You saved me from several arrows, too."

"Well, you were no slouch up there, Lieutenant. I saw you fighting with that arrow in your hip; that couldn't have been easy!"

"Nothing some pliers and a little healing salve couldn't fix, sir." They continued their banter, exiting the library and walking toward the kitchen area. Victor inhaled deeply through his nose and blew it out, trying to send his tension with it.

When he and Valla were alone in the room, he turned to her and said, "I thought Rellia was giving him grief about his command of the troops!"

Valla winked at him. "I think she might have been. Luckily, he's full of himself enough that it went right over his head."

"Did he do badly?" Victor tried to keep his voice hushed.

"I know about as much as you, but I'll try to get the gossip from my mother later." She took hold of his arm above the elbow, and they started after the others. "I wish I could take this armor off, but I want it on when we speak to Kethelket."

"Yeah, I was thinking the same thing. I mean, he already saw me when I was titan-sized, but I still feel a lot more substantial with Tes's armor on."

"It truly is wonderous stuff, isn't it?" Valla let go of him as they entered the dining and kitchen area, but she continued to speak. "I was struck so many times in the melee and when I charged with Uvu. Nothing got through these scales."

Victor nodded, running his palms over the front of his armor, looking at it closely. "That big winged bastard had some spells that got through it, but it stopped a lot of the damage—seems to have repaired itself just fine, too."

"Are you going to cook?" Rellia asked, standing near the kitchen.

"I could, but I have a lot of hot food in my storage containers."

"Probably for the best." Rellia smirked and then moved to the table, sitting next to Lam.

"Was that an insult?" Victor asked the room, letting his eyes dart from one face to the next. Edeya held a hand over her mouth, avoiding his eyes. Lam looked at him directly and nodded, grinning slyly. Borrius grumbled something incomprehensible and started leafing through the command book he'd taken from Edeya. "Hey, I'm trying, you know! I only have basic cooking, but I'll never improve it without practice. I didn't hear any complaints when I made steaks the other day . . ."

"Rather hard to ruin a steak." Borrius didn't even look up as he spoke.

Valla snorted and tugged at Victor's arm. "Come on. Let's pull out some hot dishes and set up some platters. That Naghelli will be here soon."

"Victor," Rellia called over her shoulder, "if you have any of that good cheb-cheb, I'd owe you dearly for a glass."

"Me too, Victor!" Lam echoed.

Victor paused and looked back at the four sitting at the table. "Borrius?"

"Hmm?"

"What do you want to drink?"

"Wine," he grumbled, flipping a page in the book. "Always wine for me, Legate."

"Edeya?"

"Oh, um, am I allowed?"

"Of course!" Rellia laughed, "We fought a battle more difficult than most encounters I've seen in dungeons! We're sisters in blood now, Edeya. If I'm drinking, you're drinking."

"In that case, Victor, do you have any mead? Something sweet like honey . . ."

"I've got a bunch of it." He laughed and nudged Valla. "Come on; I know what you want."

"The pale ale from Fainhallow?"

"Yep. It's cold as ice, too." As they worked to fill some platters with various types of food they'd purchased while in towns and cities, Victor could hear Edeya asking Rellia about her time in dungeons, and every so often, Lam would chime in, remarking about things she'd heard or experiences she'd had. It was nice to see them relaxing, he decided. He was glad none of them had died in the battle.

Of course, those thoughts reminded him of the death toll for the army, and he knew there were people in the camp who were mourning friends or even brothers and sisters. He knew there were people living far away who'd learn about a son or daughter who died in this battle, and his expression turned dark, a glower overtaking his face as he said in a low, raspy growl, "Yeah. I'm going to have to go and find that piece of shit Ridonne who ran away."

Valla set down the hot cheese-and-herb-covered flatbread she was arranging and looked at him. He was afraid she would object, but she just nodded. "Yes. I suppose you are."

42

PAZRA

Pazra-dak suffered. His body ached in a way that he couldn't ever remember happening before. Even when he was young, a child in Tharcray, he'd never been made to hurt so badly. His back ached, his stomach grumbled, his mouth was dry and raw, and his feet bled. Feet! His glorious, shiny black hooves were gone. He'd been running for more than a day now. Running and walking, he silently corrected; his body could no longer sustain the effort of a run for more than a few minutes at a time. How shameful!

The rite, that damnable, mysterious ritual taught to his ancestors by the Ridonne who'd ventured into the Vizashath, had ruined him. Had Rosh known it would do this to him? Had he been aware that his little brother would have to pay some of the toll? Pazra groaned and fell to his knees in the tall grass of the plains. He'd been steadily moving northward, and he thanked his ancestors that it was tall grass he ran through and not forests or mountains. His feet suffered enough.

He fished around in his ring for another drink, pulling forth a bottle of rare wine that he could have traded for a small apartment in Tharcray. He had no water. Why would he, a Ridonne nearing epic advancement, require such a mundane beverage? "What a fool," he chided himself, sipping at the wine, wincing at how it stung his swollen lips. He struggled to stand, but his knees quavered with the effort, his thighs burned, and his feet screamed for reprieve. Time to rest, then, he decided.

He wondered how long his luck would last, how long he could avoid the predators that hunted these plains. Thus far, he hadn't seen anything larger than a feyris scurrying through the grass. Were the big game animals hunted out? Had the Shadeni driven the boyii hounds away? He hoped so, but the farther he traveled, the less likely he'd be able to avoid them. "Shameful," he wheezed, this time saying the word rather than thinking it. Before the rite, he could have smitten a pack of boyii without effort. Now, he feared them. No small surprise, that fear—his Core had become a pitiful thing, his attributes embarrassingly low. Had they ever been so meager? Surely, when he was a child, but not in his memory; his family had fed him fruits and cakes, bolstering his race early on.

With hopeless tears in his eyes, Pazra fell to his side and curled his knees toward his chest. He drifted into an uncomfortable, feverish sleep, with tall, blue-green grass shielding him on every side. His sleep was plagued with nightmares. Most revolved around his mother, confronting him and blaming him for one mistake or another. Occasionally, images of gigantic warriors would march into his mind's eye, shattering any peace he might begin to find. It was after one such dream that his eyes snapped open, and he found himself in the dark.

The sun had set, and why shouldn't it? He had no idea what time he'd fallen asleep. Still, he wasn't used to the darkness. Before the rite stole his advancements, he'd been able to see at night just as easily as in broad daylight. Something tickled his nose, something spicy and comforting. Tea? Pazra jerked upright, ripping a groan of pain from his lips as his abdominal muscles protested. A dark figure sat nearby, a tiny kettle simmering before it on a brass, Energy-powered camp stove. The figure was shrouded in darkness, with black robes obscuring its form and features.

"I'm pleased you live, Pazra," the figure said, and he recognized the voice—the witch, Senena.

"Lord Pazra-dak, witch." His rebuke fell flat; his voice croaked and came out sounding like a pubescent child's.

"No longer, I fear. Your Ridonne bloodline seems to have been stripped from you. Perhaps with the right investment, you might recover it, though I think the Empire might have better uses for such resources, considering your failure."

"You dare!" He struggled to sit further upright and crawl over the flattened grass toward the woman.

"I do, yes. I dare. I could crush you like a bug, Pazra. Don't test my patience. I'm going to keep you alive, after all. I'll help you get to the capital so you can make your report, confess your sins, and suffer the judgment of the Emperor. Should I leave you, I would say it's a safe bet you'll be dead before you leave these grasslands."

Pazra sat there, stunned. He'd never heard such insolence in his life, let alone from this woman's mouth. Senena had *served* him. She was *his* witch! Was he truly so bereft of power? No, no, he shook his head and tried a different approach. "I may have lost my power, but the blood of Ridonne still beats in my veins. With enough investment, I'll soon be able to stand on my own. I have wealth beyond your dreams, Senena! Help me recover, and I'll make it worth your while!"

"Wealth, have you?" Her voice carried amusement as she lifted the kettle and produced two cups, into which she began to pour the luxurious, steamy liquid.

"Yes! In my rings, I have enough beads to buy half of Tharcray! My brother handed me his before he submitted to the rite . . . " Pazra's words trailed off as he held up his hands and beheld his naked fingers. "You!"

"Oh, yes." Senena offered him a cup of tea, and Pazra's traitorous, trembling body wouldn't let him refuse it. He shakily reached out and took the drink. "Yes, dear Pazra. I've liberated you of your rings and the medallion you wore beneath your shirt. I'm sorry, but this is the rule of the land; the weak must bend to the strong, and you are weak now." She leaned forward so the dim orange light of the stove illuminated her hooded face. Pazra looked into those pale magenta eyes set deep within tattooed eye sockets and shivered. "You may rail about the unfairness; you may report my theft to the Imperial Adjudicator who hears your case, but I assure you, nothing will come of your protestations."

Pazra fell back, any glimmer of hope he'd once held deep in his heart flickering and winking out. No, he silently objected, sipping from the rich, potent tea. There was one more hope; he simply needed to see his mother. Surely they'd allow that. Surely they'd let him go to her. He was her last son, after all. She'd help him! She'd take his wealth away from this impertinent witch! "Very well, wit—Senena. You may hold onto my wealth, but when we reach Tharcray, there may be a reckoning for the way you've treated me."

"That's good, Pazra. Hold onto that hope. It will serve you well as we travel."

"You're here, so I'm assuming my inclination to flee was well founded?"

"That's right. The nightmarish warrior from another world has defeated the ancient Ridonne. I watched from afar, and a good thing I did—such destruction was eye-opening. The legion was defeated and sent running, scattered. Most survivors make haste through the Blue Deep, hoping the nightmare won't come to them there."

"Would he do that? Hunt them down?"

"No one, not even our wisest ancestor, knows what he will do. I left when I saw the arrival of the Naghelli."

"What? Naghelli?"

"Yes, Pazra; he has an army of them. They came to his soldiers' aid as our legion swarmed his encampment. You and Rosh-dak were fools. The ap'Yensha woman was never the one to worry about. Legate Borrius was not the head of this snake. The otherworldly champion was the threat. You should have come with ten Ridonne and put him in the ground when you could. It's too late now." Senena sipped her tea, shaking her head and clicking her tongue at him.

"Are you mad? How many times did I ask you for advice on this matter? How many times did I ask you to scry that man and guide me in the destruction of this army? Did you not encourage me to call for my brother's aid? How was I to know what a monster he was?"

"Simply opening your ears might have worked. Your Emperor sought answers and gave you the freedom to choose your own path, and you chose very stupidly! You never had to attack them! Did you seek counsel from those in Gelica who'd dealt with the giant? What of Persi Gables? No, you found a whispered rumor of ap'Yensha's treason and ran with it! You could have confronted her, traveled with her, even. You could have allowed me to get close to the off-worlder, allowed me to see what we were dealing with. How many times did I say I could not view him from afar? How many times did I counsel caution? It was only after you had your fool princeps attack him that I suggested you ask your brother for help."

"That's not—" Pazra began to object, but Senena cut him off.

"I grow weary of this. I don't care what you think, in any case. You're an insignificant mortal. As I said, I'll keep you alive long enough to give your answers to the Imperial Adjudicator. In the meantime, I'll have your silence."

Pazra opened his mouth to reply, but Senena's eyes flared with dangerous silver Energy, and he clamped it shut; he had to play her game—for now. He sipped his tea, allowing the magical brew to run through him, bringing him energy and strength. Senena tossed him a heel of bread, and he ate that, too, satisfying the unfamiliar gnawing at the center of his gut. While he ate, she produced a pair of soft leather slippers and tossed them to him. They were far too small for him, but she let him bond with them, and they expanded to fit him comfortably.

The sun began to turn the eastern horizon shades of yellow and pink, and Senena urged him to stand. In that pleasant light of dawn, they started their long trek through the grasslands. The two imperials traveled that way, Senena setting a pace that Pazra could just barely match for the entire day, pausing only so that Pazra could drink water and occasionally eat a morsel Senena doled out. In the evening, she fixed him more of her magical tea, and he immediately fell into a fitful slumber.

Sometime early in the morning, before the sun brightened the sky or shared its warmth, Pazra was woken by a feeling of dread that clutched his heart like a steel vise. When his eyes sprang open and he searched for a sign of Senena, he found her sitting still as the ice sculpture he'd had commissioned for his nephew's birth. Her eyes were wide, the whites reflecting an unearthly pale glow that seemed to be coming from behind Pazra. Something was there; he could feel it. Something like dread incarnate hung in the air behind him, and Pazra gulped, expecting death to fall upon him.

He closed his eyes, waiting, but when the feeling persisted, and his life didn't end, he opened them again. Senena still sat where he'd seen her, unmoving, barely breathing. With a terrible effort of will, Pazra took a breath and croaked out, "What is it?"

"Justice," a deep, soulless voice said, shivering the hairs on the nape of his neck. Such was the power in that voice, the weight of the aura hanging over him, that Pazra voided his bladder, unable to keep his body from reacting to the fear that coursed through him. He felt adrenaline flood him, and without a thought, he lurched to his feet and started to run. He only made it one step before a mighty grip squeezed his neck, holding him in place. The hand was like steel, hot and full of power. Pazra's knees began to quake, shamefully knocking against each other as he lost control of his body. He hung there, in that terrible grasp, waiting for his judgment, too afraid to try to turn his head to look at the one who held him.

"I will take this one," the horrible voice boomed, and Pazra realized his captor was speaking to Senena. "He will face those he wronged. You will carry word of his fate to the others like him. Ridonne is not welcome where we go." Pazra was still facing Senena, and he saw her shrink back as his captor spoke to her, flinching with each word. Nevertheless, she managed to nod, and then Pazra felt himself being lifted by his neck.

As the man who held him turned, Pazra was brought face to face with a nightmare, a beast of shadow and fear, with eyes of purple Energy glaring at him through drifting smoke-like darkness. It reared, snorting more of that terrible horror smoke, and Pazra's heart began to hammer as his helpless body twitched. "Hush," the emotionless voice rumbled, and then the beast was still. Effortlessly, his captor flung him over the broad shoulders of the nightmare, and then Pazra felt him mount the beast, resting a hand on his back to hold him steady. Pazra still hadn't summoned the courage to look at the one who'd taken him.

In a haze of black shadows and wispy, palpable fear, the beast began to run. Pazra could feel its shoulders working, could see the grasslands, dimly, drifting by outside the cloud of shadows, but the ride was smooth, and the pressure on his back never relented, holding him still as stone on the terrible mount. The tall grass became a blue-green blur as the mount's speed increased, and Pazra had to close his eyes lest his stomach empty itself through his mouth.

After a short time, a terrible pressure of Energy began to form nearby, and Pazra knew it was coming from his captor. The Energy built and built until it seemed the world would implode upon him, and then, with a release that felt like a massive bubble popping, something happened. The world faded, Pazra felt himself becoming transparent, felt his body coming apart, and then, with a snap, he was back to normal; the pressure was gone, and the grasslands were streaming by just as before.

He had no idea what the spell was, but it happened again and again, a dozen minutes or so passing between each weird occurrence. After each one, Pazra felt his sanity slipping further and further away, found himself losing sight of where he was, who he was, and what had brought him to such straits. After some time—he had no idea how long—he felt the massive, horrible steed begin to slow. As it came to a halt, Pazra's captor slid off and pulled him down, dropping him not onto grass but rough dirt.

A moment later, he felt a shift in the Energy around him. The fear began to fade, the weird, cold presence as well, and then, as the shadows fell away, Pazra blinked up into a bright blue sky. He scrambled to his knees and started to stand, but then a different voice addressed him, and that same powerful hand grasped his shoulder, hot and hard as iron. "Hold still," it said, and Pazra knew who it was—Victor, the off-worlder. With the fear Energy faded away, he managed the courage to turn his head, to look up into the giant's angry amber eyes. He only held that gaze for a moment before looking away in shame.

"What do you want—"

"Quiet." Victor jerked his shoulder, forcing him to turn toward another familiar sight, the encampment of his foes. He and the giant were a hundred paces from the wall, standing atop a mound of fresh soil. Why? Why had they built this mound here? The wall was covered with soldiers, and the ground before it as well. Was this their entire army? Had the giant brought him here to gloat? The giant grumbled behind him, "I wish you hadn't fucked yourself up so badly. Not the same image—hanging a puny asshole versus a giant asshole with spikes and hooves. Doesn't matter, I guess. You've got crimes to answer for."

"Hanging?" Pazra had a hard time following the giant's vernacular. He used curses that weren't familiar, and what exactly did he mean by "hanging?"

"Walk." The giant squeezed his shoulder and directed him to turn to his right. A new sight filled his vision, then. A wooden platform, like a stage, with steps upon which the giant propelled him. Pazra stumbled up the steps onto the wooden planks, his footfalls silent next to the resounding thumps of Victor's boots. A device had been constructed at the center of the stage—two poles connected via a beam. They were sturdy posts and tall. Hanging from the thick wooden beam was a rope fashioned into a loop. A short ramp of steps sat in the center of the posts, and Victor pushed Pazra toward it.

"What's happening here?" Pazra managed to ask before the giant squeezed his neck, painfully cutting off his words.

"Stand on the top step." Pazra could only comply, and when he stood there on the step, facing the eerily silent army in the distance, he felt his body begin to tremble, perhaps instinctively knowing what sort of trouble he was in before his sluggish mind could put the pieces together. Victor released his hold and reached up, pulling the rough, thick rope down over Pazra's head. When it had settled around his neck, Victor adjusted the knot until it felt snug.

Absurdly, the whole while Victor fidgeted with the rope, Pazra could only think about how good the man smelled—like spices and smoke. The sky was bright, the blue beautiful, and Pazra tried to remember the last time he'd looked at the sky and appreciated the color. How odd, he thought, to find such a pleasure amid such a resounding defeat. The breeze blowing over the plains was cool but not cold, and he savored it, trying to think of how these sights and smells, these good feelings, were a sign—he might be defeated now, but he would come back from this. He'd find a way to grow in power again . . .

"Soldiers!" Victor roared, interrupting Pazra's reflection. "This is the Ridonne who ordered the attack on our people. Not once, not twice, but at least three different times. Not only did he attack me and the leaders of this army unlawfully and without any sort of trial, but he also ordered his troops to launch arrows into fleeing civilians and children!"

Pazra's eyes bulged as he looked from the grumbling, shouting, stomping army in the distance to the giant beside him. What was this? A trial? Where was the magistrate? Where were his witnesses?

"He might not look like a Ridonne right now, but he is. This is Pazra-dak. Let his name forever be cursed!" Victor roared, and then, without any warning whatsoever, he kicked the stand of steps out from under Pazra.

The onetime-great imperial fell, tightening the noose around his neck and cutting the blood flow to his head. His mind tried to race, tried to grasp the strangeness of his situation, but he was weak, and the lack of oxygen to his brain rapidly affected him. He jerked and thrashed, arching his back as he heaved for breath that wouldn't come. Despite his mind's surrender, his body tried valiantly to hold on to life. But then a heavy hand took hold of his ankle and tugged. With weird, terrible pressure in his neck, the world shrank away, down to a pinprick that burst in a shower of sparks, just like the fancy light shows he'd seen at his mother's last birthday. When they faded, all he knew was black emptiness, and Pazra was no more.

43

ROOM TO BREATHE

Victor watched Pazra's corpse swaying in the breeze, the rope creaking on the gibbet. It was strange to see his dark idea brought to fruition, strange to feel no horror or guilt at what he'd done to the man. He'd thought his justice would be hollow, that he'd probably feel worse after it was over, but that wasn't the case. Instead, he felt good, especially after hearing the cries of vindication from the army in the distance.

The Shadeni hanging from the noose didn't look much like the Ridonne Victor had fought, but he could see the resemblance in the face. Regardless of his recognition, when he'd been in his Inevitable Huntsman guise, he'd felt that this was Pazra—he'd *known*. This was the man who'd needed to taste justice, just as much as the woman he'd found with him was the one who needed to deliver the word of his fate to Tharcray. Victor didn't come to those decisions with logical inner dialogues. He'd simply known that was how it should be. No, he corrected himself, the huntsman had known.

He glanced down the hillock his army's Earth Casters had constructed, then over the grassy plains to the encampment, and saw the sergeants calling their units to order, getting the soldiers into marching positions. It was time for them to get back on the road, to start making progress again to their destination. A small cluster of people was walking through the ranks, heading his way. He studied them for a moment—Valla, Lam, Rellia, Tellen, Thayla, Borrius, and even Kethelket.

Things had gone well with the Naghelli. Kethelket had been smooth with his words and promises, and, more than that, he'd been convincing, believable. It truly seemed that the Naghelli were intent on changing their image, on finding a place of their own where they could peacefully coexist with the settlers of the Untamed Marches. The one-time prince hadn't hesitated in agreeing to sign a contract with the legion and had promised his soldiers would do the same, all 312 of them.

Victor sat down on the edge of the gallows, allowing his Iron Berserk to drop, and as he watched the leaders of his army approach, he thought about Kethelket's words. Victor had asked him where all the Naghelli had come from, reminding the swordsman that Vellia had told him only thirty-something of them lived in the pocket realm with Belikot. His question had brought forth an interesting tale, one in which the Naghelli found Belikot's secret writings. Reading them, they learned that he'd entombed nearly three hundred of their kin in a kind of stasis, waiting for him to wake them. That was where the Naghelli had been in the last months: solving the riddles of Belikot's wards, opening the prison he'd created, and waking the rest of their people.

The rope's creaking distracted him, and Victor looked up at the corpse again. It felt like a dream, his ride to snatch up the Ridonne and bring him back to face justice. "What happened to you?" he asked the body. Something had drained all the power out of the man, reversed whatever bloodline enhancements he'd gone through, and turned him into a mewling weakling. Victor had figured he'd need to subdue the Ridonne before hanging him would work, but the man he'd brought back had succumbed to the rope quite easily. He'd almost hated to see how frail Pazra had become; could such a thing happen to him?

"An interesting spectacle," Kethelket called as the group of leaders trudged up the new-made hill.

"That's a way to describe it . . ." Rellia said, sort of under her breath, her head tilted toward Valla. Victor figured she hadn't meant for him to hear her words, but his ears missed very little these days.

"It was for the troops and for Tellen's clan. I think it's important that our people know we won't tolerate crimes against them. It's important that we frame this man's actions that way, as crimes—attacking children and civilians as they flee isn't something the rulers of any people should be permitted to do, not if they expect to keep their positions of power."

"Yes," Borrius grunted, breathing heavily from the climb. "You explained as much yesterday when you asked us to build this . . . stage." He waved vaguely at the gallows upon which Victor sat.

"Do you disagree?" Victor's dark brows drew together.

"Not at all. This will work mightily in our favor. The Ridonne should know fear when they think of attacking us. Our troops, our people, should know that no one, of any station, is free to assault them."

"As he says, Victor, my people are greatly heartened to see that you are able to stand up to the Empire's strongest." Tellen nodded to Borrius as he stopped before Victor, standing with the others.

"Good." Victor rubbed his hands together as though wiping them after finishing some work. "How long till we march?"

"Less than an hour. Most of the preparations are made." Lam came to a halt next to Kethelket, and it was interesting to see their similarities and differences. To Victor, it was almost like comparing a moth to a butterfly, Lam being the butterfly. Despite the ochre and crimson patterns in the Naghelli's wings, he was like a shadow to her bright light. From her brilliant emerald eyes and hale, rosy cheeks to her dragonfly wings that dusted the air with Energy motes, she simply outshone him.

"Good! Anything I need to do?" Victor slid off the edge of the gallows, a few feet from the gently swaying corpse, and looked at the leaders of his army one by one, making eye contact with each.

"Nothing with regard to the troops." Rellia's voice was tentative, but her eyes drifted to the corpse, and she continued, "We were wondering what happened to this Ridonne. Why is he so frail?"

"No idea. Well, that's not true. After I killed the huge, powerful bastard during the battle, he withered away down to a sickly version of the Ridonne I had fought earlier. I wonder if something similar happened to this guy." Victor jerked his thumb at Pazra's corpse. "Maybe whatever they did to power up the other one took something out of them—something permanent."

"I've never heard of a person losing their racial enhancements. There are those who can give up Energy, even enough to lose a level, with ritual magics. It's something certain Blood and Death Casters can do, though it's always done willingly; to rip someone's power away like that would be to do battle with their will and at a massive disadvantage." Kethelket idly tapped the hilt of one of his swords. Victor again noticed he had one on his belt and one over his shoulder. He wondered at that—was it for a particular fighting style? He also wondered if the man's swords were both conscious. They'd certainly looked impressive the other night on the battlements.

"Shall we ride, Victor?" Valla asked. Victor looked at her, and off to the left, down the hill, he saw Uvu slipping out of the tall grass like a ghost.

"Yeah, I guess we should. We can push eastward, scout ahead a bit."

"I wish you'd stop by the wagon and see Deyni." Thayla stepped toward him hesitantly, finally speaking up, her eyes darting from Victor's face to the hanging corpse, a frown creasing her brow as she spoke.

"I will. Can she ride with us?"

"You'll keep her safe and not stray too far?" Thayla's scowl deepened, and she shook her head. If Victor had to guess, she was annoyed with herself for asking; she knew Victor would do anything to keep Deyni safe.

"Yeah, of course." He held a hand toward her, slightly bridging the gap between them, but let it fall as she wound her fingers together with Tellen's.

"Very well. Thistle can pull the wagon if you want her to ride Starlight . . ."

"I'll ask her, but she might want to ride with me on Guapo." Victor turned his gaze back to Rellia and Borrius. "Let's talk about cohort numbers and placements when we camp tonight. I'd like to discuss ribbons to commemorate the battle—for all the troops, but special medals for the third and ninth. I want you to talk to the sergeants and lieutenants. Get me a list of soldiers who stood out for exemplary bravery or prowess. I'll hand out special awards if we can get some nominations."

"Very good, Legate." Borrius's use of the title and his grave nod told Victor he'd said something the old commander approved of.

Victor started down the hill with Valla beside him, deliberating whether to summon Guapo then or wait until he'd found Deyni when Lam called out, "Victor!"

He looked back at her. "Yeah?"

"Can Edeya ride with you? You should have someone with a command book along, and it will do her some good to—"

"Yeah, of course." Victor waved and smiled, hoping she could see that further explanation wasn't necessary.

"What kind of mount does Edeya have?" Victor asked Valla as she reached up to scratch Uvu's ear. The cat had stalked up to them without a sound.

"I think just a roladii."

"Think she'd like to ride Thistle?"

"Ha!" Valla shook her head. "Of course! Who wouldn't? Come to think of it, her roladii might be dead; we lost something like three hundred during the battle."

"All right. Let's find her; I'll have Deyni ride with me on Guapo and leave Starlight for Thayla's wagon."

"She's there." Valla pointed toward the encampment, and sure enough, Edeya stood on the wall looking down, watching some engineers leading their massive storage wagons around the perimeter, collecting the non-permanent parts of the fortifications. Victor waved his arm, whistling shrilly until she looked down at him, and then he gestured for her to come over. Valla asked, "You like her, hmm?"

"She's an old friend—one of the first I made in this world. She's almost died a few times since I met her, and I'd like to help her stay alive. Besides, she owes me an accounting of some storage rings and other jewels. We can talk about it on the ride."

"Understandable. I like her too, for the record." Valla gave his shoulder a playful shove with her knuckles. "Let's have a nice ride, yeah? It'll be good to put death and battle behind us for a little while—give ourselves a little room to breathe."

"Yep." Victor threw an arm over her shoulders, pulling her into his side. Uvu grumbled but passed it off as a yawn, bounding after something that rustled in the tall grass as Valla leaned into him. "We'll have plenty of killing to deal with in the Untamed Marches. Let's enjoy this little lull, yeah?"

Lesh'ro'zellan gazed through the tall trees at the strange city. It had high whitewashed walls and tall gabled buildings within. The sight was very different from the cities in his homeland, especially the cave-riddled peaks of his home. He sniffed, his nose tickling with all the strange scents carried by the wind. The air was cool, the sky soft and blue, and the weird, lush vegetation made him feel sick for his home. "I'd give much to smell some ash and taste some blood," he growled, contemplating his decision to maintain a peaceful demeanor.

He'd met many soft people in this world, many scaleless ones who'd do just as well roasting over his campfire as sitting beside him. Nevertheless, he'd played his friendly act, unsure of the power structure of this strange place, unsure if the weaklings belonged to stronger foes, perhaps the rulers of this soft land. He had a person he needed to kill, and having armies or champions hunting for him would only impede that aim, would only slow his return to Ashenshoal and Yassa.

His tolerance for the soft ones had paid off, however. His encounters with pleasant red- and blue-skinned people had led him to this city. It seemed the one called Victor had made a name for himself in parts of this world. The villagers and field tenders had heard of him—a great man who fought in arenas and vanquished foes thought stronger than himself. The rumors had led him steadily southward toward this place, this city where the man was supposedly raising an army. Lesh cared not; he'd call the man out, confront him before his troops, and demand single combat. If he lacked the honor or his fear was too intense, Lesh would reap the Energy of any soldiers who stood between them.

"An army or not, I will battle this man." His voice rumbled up from his thick throat as he began trudging over the soft ground, his talons digging into the soft leafy soil as he mounted the berm along the road. The people he'd met had been apprehensive, many exclaiming their lack of experience with "people such as he." He chuckled, imagining how they'd feel if he unleashed his aura or allowed his Breath Core to swell his stature. Regardless, he kept a tight hold on himself and endeavored to match their pleasant expressions.

He stepped onto the road near a wagon filled with bales of agricultural products, some sort of green grass, and red fruit; Lesh had no idea of its use. His people took their meat from the creatures they killed; they didn't harvest it from plants. The funny little animal pulling the wagon shied away from him. It had leathery gray skin and bright feathers around its neck, and it made a timid honking sound as Lesh looked down his snout at the wagon's driver. The little red man looked ready to bolt or do something even stupider, so Lesh tried to forestall any hysterics. "I mean you no harm, small one."

"Great Ancestors! Thank you for saying so, sir. I'm not familiar with your kind; forgive my brief panic."

"Tell me," Lesh said, ignoring the man's words, "is this Persi Gables?" He gestured down the road to the tall gate and the small crowd lining up to get through.

"You've come to the right place if it's Persi Gables you seek, aye."

Lesh snorted and looked from the man's sweating face down to his unkempt, dirty clothing, then over the contents of his cart. Curiosity getting the better of him, he asked, "Why do you carry bound grass in your wagon?"

"Oh, sir, that's not just grass; that's meadow dew. Dairy farmers pay a handsome sum for it—makes holbyis milk rather sweet."

"Holbyis?"

"Aye; we breed 'em for wool, for meat, and for milk."

"Hmm." Lesh's mouth began to water at the thought of some fresh meat, but he decided not to raid his storage ring for a snack. He'd soon be at the gate. "Good luck," Lesh said, stepping away from the little wagon and the rather tasty-looking beast that pulled it. He trudged past the line of other carts, wagons, and basket-burdened people waiting to have their wares examined. Another guard monitored pedestrian traffic, and Lesh stopped before him.

"State your business!" the thinly armored man cried, lowering his pike toward the big dragonkin. Lesh wore a heavy, black-stained leather cloak over the burgundy furs of fire hounds fashioned into leggings and a vest. His cudgel, Belagog, hung from a hook on his thick girdle, but he didn't reach for it. Instead, he turned up his dark, partially scaled lips, exposing long white fangs, attempting to smile like the weaklings he'd met on the road.

"I am here for trade and to seek a friend. Perhaps you know him? His name is Victor Sandoval, and he won a great arena fight in Gelica against some noblewoman or other."

"Oh? A friend of Victor's? Aye, sir, I know of him. Everyone in Persi Gables knows of him. You're a bit late, though; his army marched off weeks ago." The guard, one of the slight, blue-fleshed people, lifted his pike, resting the butt on the cobbles, and shrugged. "You're welcome to come into the city to trade, though."

"His army left?" Lesh grumbled.

"Aye, sir. Um, do you mind me askin' where you're from? Is it the same world as Victor? Are you a different kind of . . ." He looked over at his fellow guardsman, a strange, short, furry individual. "What was it he was called?"

"Hoomin," the hatchling-sized, hooved one replied, waving through a pair of women pulling a handcart filled to the brim with roots and tubers.

"No." Lesh looked around, peering through the gate at the throngs of strange people wandering up and down the cobbled street. He frowned and reached up to run his thick fingers over the smooth surface of one of his three horns, a gesture that always served to calm him. He looked down at the small blue fellow again and said, "Where did his army march?"

"Uh, they're off to try to claim land in the Untamed Marches. I'm not sure exactly where that is, but it's off to the east at the edge of the Empire." He shrugged, looking up at Lesh, and something in the dragonkin's expression must have alarmed him because he took a step back and lowered his pike slightly. "Is everyone from Victor's world gigantic?"

"I'm not from his world, soft one. East, you said?" Lesh turned in the direction from which he'd come, gazing down the tree-shrouded lane. "This road turns north and south beyond these trees. Is there another that leads east?"

"Not nearby; the army was out on the plains. I'm sure you could pick up their tracks. I almost joined them, you know? My wife, though, she wouldn't have it. We've a newborn at home, and she needs my help in the evenings, elsewise she'd never get any sleep. With the rumors going around, I'm feeling a bit relieved that I stayed home."

"Rumors?" Lesh leaned forward, bridging the gap between them slightly; the man only stood as high as his waist.

"Aye. Word around the city is that the Empire is against them—rumors coming in through Far Scribe books tell tales of Ridonne nobles attacking them personally. There are family members of some of the soldiers claiming Victor killed a Ridonne and that they defeated two imperial legions; it can't be true, can it?" The guard shook his head. Lesh couldn't help noticing how he'd lowered his voice to a hush when he discussed the "Empire's" supposed actions. Just as back home, it seemed politics were complicated in this world.

Lesh reached into his dimensional ring and fished out a platinum nugget. He flicked it toward the guard and turned, marching down the cobbled lane toward the rising sun, sparing not a second glance at the stunned man as he stammered his thanks.

ABOUT THE AUTHOR

Plum Parrot is the pen name of author Miles Gallup, who grew up in Southern Arizona and spent much of his youth wandering around the Sonoran Desert, hunting imaginary monsters and building forts. He studied creative writing at the University of Arizona and, for a number of years, attempted to teach middle schoolers to love literature and write their own stories. If he's not spending time with his dog, you can find Gallup writing, reading his favorite authors, or playing *D&D* with friends and family.

www.ingramcontent.com/pod-product-compliance
Lightning Source LLC
Chambersburg PA
CBHW030926120726
47906CB00002B/499